THE WIZARD HALL CHRONICLES

BLACK MARKET

SHERYL STEINES

Rachel Porter Editor
Cover Design by Damonza.com

Black Market
Copyright 2017 Sheryl Steines
All rights reserved.

ISBN: 0-9858652-5-3
EAN – 13:978-0-9858652-5-2

This book is a work of fiction. The names, characters, places, and incidents are products of the writer's imagination or have been used fictitiously and are not to be construed as real. Any resemblance to persons living or dead is entirely coincidental.

All rights are reserved. With the exception of fair use excerpts for reviews and critical articles, no part of this book may be used or reproduced in any manner whatsoever without written permission from the author.

Prologue
1920

HOT, DRY HEAT parched Reuven's body. He took a long swig of water from the crock at his feet as sand and dust blew from the west, coating him in a layer of grime. Setting the jug back in the sand, he wiped his brow, leaving a streak of clean skin across his forehead. At only seven in the morning, the desert thermometer read eighty-nine degrees.

He rested a tired arm on the shovel handle and leaned in, surveying the dig site that covered several acres of desolate desert. Busy men worked in their assigned squares of the cordoned-off grid, charged with removing the earth in hopes that a great treasure lay hidden beneath their feet. Sand and rock flew in the air, landing on growing piles on the outskirts of the dig area. The man-made hills were visible for miles against the flatness of the valley.

Sweat dripped from Reuven's forehead, collecting under his chin. He took another wipe from his dirty rag and bent over for another swig of nearly warm water.

Catching the watchful eye of the foreman, Reuven returned to his digging and plunged the shovel into the earth, eradicating another layer. He loosened the dirt, lifted the heavy pile and tossed it to the ever-growing hill beside him.

Familiar with every inch of his small square, Reuven doubted anything lay beneath the sand other than more sand. Over four weeks into the excavation, nothing had been discovered: no bones, no shards of clay, no baskets or treasures.

It's a desert, after all, thought Reuven as he tossed another shovelful of sand over his shoulder.

Though he knew he was lucky to have work, Reuven hated the job. The living quarters were rough—crowded tents that held in the heat and the stench of body odor. Hard labor left his muscles seized and tired by nightfall; the sun burnt and leathered his skin, leaving him looking older than his twenty-five years. But the money meant that his family could thrive, so Reuven returned every morning to continue the dig.

The shovel scratched into the coarse sand, the metal spade pinged against a hard object, sending vibrations through his hands and up his arms. Cautious, Reuven knelt in the sand, wiping away loose earth.

Over the centuries, wind and little rain had molded a stubborn chunk of earth around an object. Reuven used a hand spade and a pick from his tool kit to carefully chip away the earth. His hands shook as his efforts revealed the straight edge of a hand-carved stone.

Great, now I must get the foreman.

Gingerly, Reuven stood and unfolded his legs, which were numb from hours of kneeling and bending to complete his physically intense labor. He raised his rag above his head and waved wildly, hoping to catch the foreman's attention. It wasn't long to wait; the large man, wide as he was tall, huffed his way toward Reuven's square, passing through the work zones of others and disturbing their work all the way over to the farthest western location of the dig site.

"This better be something," the foreman, a man named Akiva warned through quick breaths as he struggled to take in air. He entered Reuven's work area, hoisting a thick leg over the perimeter rope. With a glower on his fat face, Akiva lowered his rotund body to the ground, sinking into the sand as if the earth shifted beneath him. He pulled off his cap and wiped his strained red face before examining Reuven's find.

Akiva's inspection of the rock and sand caught the attention of those in the spaces surrounding Reuven. Most of the men stopped digging to watch their foreman manipulate the earth.

The stone Reuven had uncovered was smoother than a natural stone, except for the grooves that had clearly been chiseled out by ancient implements. Akiva smiled and concluded out loud that the stone was most certainly carved by man.

"Good, good," he added. "Keep digging. Start over here." Pointing to the location, the foreman dragged himself upward, grunting loudly. Rather than heading back to his tent and his break-fast, Akiva hovered over Reuven, who took up the larger shovel and plunged it into the earth as close to the stone as he could manage without nicking it. After clearing a channel twelve inches long and five inches deep, Reuven got on his hands and knees to chip away the remaining dirt with a smaller spade.

As it grew later in the morning, the sun rose and beat on the back of Reuven's neck. Sweat poured from his skin and evaporated into nothing before it could even hit the warm sand. Reuven glanced up for his water jug, longing for it, licking his dry lips with the little spit he could muster, but Akiva's close observation made him continue chipping away the sand near the flat edge of the stone.

With careful patience, Reuven eventually revealed one inch by thirteen inches of the rectangular stone.

"That is good. Let me see," Akiva ordered and heaved his hefty frame to the stone.

Reuven reached for his jug and swigged the last of his warm water. It slid across his crusty lips but did little to quench his overwhelming thirst. He stood back waiting for the foreman to finish his inspection.

"Ah, that is good," said Akiva as his chubby fingers grazed the stone, feeling for irregularities or hidden symbols. "Good. Very good." He smiled broadly.

"What is it?" Reuven inquired.

"Possibly the top of a column, making this most likely the entrance to a palace of King Solomon."

King Solomon! thought Reuven excitedly.

"Though no one knows for sure. Finish removing the dirt along here." After issuing his orders, Akiva trudged away to find the archaeologist in charge of the excavation.

They hadn't been told the true nature of the dig; the only information given when Reuven was hired was there might be the remains of a trader's market below their feet. As he dropped to his hands and knees, he wondered if the archaeologists had purposely withheld this information from the laborers to control the removal of artifacts from this site.

Knowing something of importance might lie below his feet, Reuven dug with new invigoration, chipping away at the earth until he exposed one full side of the stone.

"Beautiful," the head archaeologist proclaimed in a boom-ing voice as he rushed forward to view the top of the column. He dropped to his knees, his shaky hand trailing the smooth edge that was exposed for the first time in a millennium. The stone gleamed brightly in the summer sun.

"Please dig over there. I'd like to see the top of the pillar before lunch," the archaeologist ordered.

Shrugging, Reuven dug along the second side, creating another channel. The wood handle of his shovel rubbed against his palms, causing blisters to form and burn as he removed more earth. He ignored the pains, looking up only when the archaeologist snapped his fingers and ordered a second laborer to join him by starting on a third side of the square rock.

It's my find! thought Reuven angrily as he plunged the shovel into the sand, cutting close to the top of the pillar.

"Careful!" shouted Akiva. His face crinkled under his wide-brimmed hat; the bright sun strained his eyes.

Reuven cleared the channel until it was large enough and then dropped to the sand to create a path to the column. When he finished, he arched backwards and took a swig from a jug his new partner offered him. The cold, clean water felt good in his dry mouth.

He wiped his forehead, resting against his heels for a moment and watching his counterpart chip away sand.

"Yes, yes. This is most definitely the top of a pillar! Remove the other side," ordered the archaeologist, walking up to them. "Over there."

Sighing, Reuven stood. The ground creaked. It felt spongy underneath his boots. He thrust the shovel into the earth and began digging out the fourth side of the column.

The other laborers had long since returned to their work, and Akiva had moved on to a lesser discovery unearthed on the other side of the large grid. The archaeologist fidgeted before returning to his tent to escape the heat and wait for Reuven to reveal the entire top of the column.

Reuven continued to dig, no longer aware of his shaky hands and dry mouth. His only thoughts were on unearthing the stone that jut out from the bowels of the earth. He concentrated only on the work, on revealing the top that curved downward.

How beautiful! Reuven thought as he brushed away loose dirt and sand.

In the distance, a siren sounded, alerting the crew to the mid-day meal.

"Lunch," said Reuven's digging partner. Covered in sand and dirt, the man wiped his brow and dropped his shovel as he headed in the direction of the mess tent at the other side of the excavation site.

Reuven stood in his newest hole, twelve inches long and five inches wide. He dropped his shovel and pulled his foot from the channel. The ground popped, shifted below him, and vibrated. He fell forward, his hands landing on the top of the pillar.

An explosion? There are none on the schedule today.

He pushed himself up; the ground swayed and creaked. Sand loosened, cascading under his foot. Reuven slipped and reached the top of the column. The unstable structure shook violently.

"Help!" screamed Reuven, but there was silence around him. The men had left their posts, scattering across the dig site and sitting down to lunch. "Help!"

But no one heard his cries as Reuven kicked his legs out, trying to wrap them around the column. His fingers grew tired holding the top of the structure. Sand cascaded into the bowels of the earth.

The column swayed, but Reuven held on as his body swung. Rocks loosened above him and rained down on his head, arms and shoulders. He cried out from the pain and exertion. Tired and hot and lacking energy, he fought gravity as it threatened to drag him inside. Above him, the blue sky blinded him.

Reuven's arms shook, his fingers slipped, and after another minute, he dropped into the hole.

He flayed his arms wildly, desperately reaching for something to grab hold of but finding nothing but loose sand and dirt. The earth swallowed him.

Reuven crashed to the ground. His head bounced against the cool, hard stone beneath him. Dust swirled up, encircling his limp body. The earth groaned beneath him.

Reuven closed his eyes.

❀

Distant voices called from the darkness. *Reuven!*

They're calling me.

Frantic voices, distant and muffled, called him, yanking him out of the fog and urging him to answer. His fellow laborers shouted from the opening above, gradually becoming louder and more frantic.

Reuven's eyes fluttered open. He was unaware of where he was and why he was cold. His head screamed with pain. As the dream-like voices faded, the images around him grew fuzzy and muffled as if he viewed them underwater.

"Reuven!" The dream pushed farther into his memory until only the edges remained.

The silhouette of a human head hovered against a sliver of blue sky and gingerly glanced into the hole. The bright light of the sky pierced the darkness. Once again, Reuven closed his eyes against the glare.

Someone lowered lanterns into the hole, lanterns that hung from thick twine and swung above him. The light flashed against the stone walls and twirled in a frenzy.

"He's here! He's down here!"

They're coming.

As Reuven floated back into consciousness, pain assaulted him. He was now cognizant of his self and of the discomfort that radiated from his head to his neck and down his spine. He smelled fresh iron and felt the sticky wetness of his matted hair where his skull must have fractured in the fall. His stomach lurched and his body shivered. He longed to feel warmth again.

"I'm down here. I've fallen," he called out in a low, small voice, parched and dry. The afternoon wind whipped across the desert, and a wave of sand blocked his view of the sky that was now darkening the cavern. A breeze blew over his already cold skin as it found its way into the cavern, and his clothes rustled as bits of earth rained on him.

"I'm down here." He choked and swallowed sand as panic rose.

They're not coming.

Gingerly, Reuven rolled over and pushed himself up with shaking arms. The room swum around him, and dizziness invaded his brain. He lay back down and took shallow, wheezing breaths that burned his lungs.

Shadows danced on the wall across from the opening as the laborers rushed about to rescue him, unaware that the earth that separated them could barely hold its shape. Sand and stone creaked, threatening to swallow them all.

It's going to bury me alive! Reuven closed his eyes as if that could keep him from shaking or keep away the nausea that overcame him. He soon drifted into another restless sleep.

❋

He blinked rapidly as his location came back to him. His head burned.

The sky was no longer bright blue but rather a shade of orange; the sun had dipped low in the horizon, bringing with it early nightfall.

Voices were distant, yet frantic.

Why haven't they come for me? Where is the ladder to save me?

With no one to save him from his underground tomb, Reuven lifted himself to all fours, ignoring the nausea and the dizziness. Slowly and painfully, he crawled through the near darkness. The only light was a single lantern that still burned above him. As he searched with his outstretched hands for something to burn, his labored breathing caused twinges of dizziness. His back, arms, and legs felt heavy as he bumped into a soft object in the near blackness.

Reuven sat up. Shadows rolled and spun while he fumbled in his pocket for his matchbook and struck the match with a shaky hand. The light bounced rapidly, cutting through the darkness and revealing a small room. The room contained boxes, tables, and several other items that he could only make out as black shadows against the walls. Beside him sat a woven container, round and squat with a lid still intact. He grabbed the handle and peered inside the empty basket.

I could use this to light.

But the match burned to the end, singeing his finger tip. He dropped the stick and placed his finger in his mouth to ease the burn.

The earth squeaked as rock rubbed rock. Reuven looked to the hole above him, which appeared as a shadow in the low light.

It's going to bury me alive.

He lit a second match and held it above his head, widening the ring of light. The pillar stood tall above him, just inches above the hole. Ten feet across from that, a second pillar had once stood. It apparently had long ago crashed into the side of the cavern; a small chunk lay in a dust heap.

Lighting another match, Reuven limped to the pillar. Suddenly, his thick work boot made contact with something hard. The dim light revealed a box. Unfazed, he bent over and peered inside. It was nearly empty. He reached inside and pulled out the only artifact: a ring.

It's heavy, he thought as he palmed the ring. Before examining it, he dropped the match, which had burned down to a stub, and lit yet another.

The ring consisted of a dense band, clearly worn by someone with thick fingers, and a flat top adorned with a raised six-pointed star at the center. Four stones had been set in the metal and formed a square around the star.

What is this?

Reuven remembered Akiva's certainty that this was a temple belonging to King Solomon.

Did he wear this?

Turning the ring in his hands, Reuven discovered an inscription inside, though it was too faded to read in the dark.

He slipped the ring on his finger. It was very loose and very large. He tried in his concussed fog to figure how large a man would have to be to fit this ring.

To keep the ring safe, he cuffed the bottom of his pants, placed the ring inside and rolled the hem tightly.

I should keep it. For my troubles.

A head popped into the hole. "Reuven, we're here to pull you out. Stay awake!" the voice shouted. The earth above creaked, sending sand and stone onto his head. He covered his head and felt the debris in his hair.

Two ladders, nailed end to end, were lowered through the hole and set against the standing pillar. As two of Reuven's co-laborers raced down the rungs, the ladder wobbled against the column, shaking both. Frantic, the men jumped five feet to the floor.

Lantern lights scanned the room; Reuven shielded his eyes from the glare and fell to the floor.

"He fainted!"

When Reuven's eyes fluttered open again, he found himself in the middle of a chaotic rescue. A makeshift stretcher, consisting of two long sticks wrapped in heavy linen, had been lowered inside, and two more rescuers descended the ladder, guiding the stretcher inside. They unfurled it next to Reuven. Three men lifted him on top of the stretcher, strapping him to it. Above them, footsteps pounded the precarious earthen roof, and sand scratched and creaked.

"Get him up." Three men lifted heavy ropes attached to each corner and began their ascension upwards.

It was too much weight. The ladder strained and pushed against the unstable column. Each step upward weakened the ground, which was gradually pulling away from the column.

Above them, fifteen men surrounded the hole, waiting to pull the stretcher through. The earth groaned and grumbled. Dirt and sand, loosened as a result of the extra weight, flooded into the hole. Chunks of rock and sand fell to the ground.

"It's going to crash!"

A split second later, the pillar fell inwards, dumping the ladder, two rescuers and Reuven into a pile of stone. Rock and sand rained on them from above. Men fell through the hole and dropped to earth as an avalanche buried twenty men in the chamber.

1970

Dr. Arden Blakely labeled the most recent body found in the cave-in. Sighing, she signed the toe tag "John Doe #6." Thus far, none of the victims of the recently discovered lost excavation had carried identification on their person. The unidentified bodies would be transferred back to Tel Aviv University for DNA analysis. If any descendants of the men lost in the 1920 avalanche came forward, they could compare the DNA evidence and give the victims back their names and a decent burial. Until then, this was the best the archaeologist could do.

Arden wheeled the recent victim to the side of the tent and zipped the body bag. She sighed at the weight of the all of the deaths before returning to the administrative work sitting in piles on the work table. She scribbled notes on the map of the excavation site noting the location where John Doe #6 was found. Behind her, her assistant from the university, Nicky, swept the sand from the floor. It was an impractical task; the sand was everywhere, though the sound of sand scratching against the canvas was a comforting background noise.

Tired from a long day of examining bodies and attending to the site, Arden bent backwards and stretched her back before continuing to work on the many artifacts found at the site. There were clay shards, a woven basket, a bag full of matches, and more.

Though it was tiring work, Arden was grateful to be doing it. She was proud of her recently awarded doctorate degree that was based on the theory regarding the lost temple of King Solomon. That research had led to a very generous anonymous donation, allowing her to head this excavation. She had eagerly proved this was most definitely the location of the lost dig of 1920, where twenty men had lost their lives in a cave-in.

Days had passed before Arden's team found the fifth body in a void in the ancient cavern. It was there they had also found John Doe #6. The bodies had not been alone. Arden busied herself as she waited for yet another body to be removed from the hard, packed sand.

She examined the pack of matches found in the void. After years of being unexposed to the elements, the paper matchbook was brittle. She carefully turned it in her hands.

Voices grew closer, footsteps crunched against dried sand, and one man grunted.

Nicky smiled and peered outside the tent. "They released the second body from the void," he said, placing his broom against the canvas wall. He picked up the map of the site, ready to take notes on where this victim had been found.

The tent flap opened, and two men carried the body inside. "Hi Dr. Blakely. We have the second body for you," said Ari, one of the many archaeological students working at the excavation site.

"Show Nicky where he was found on the map," Arden reminded them.

"He was found in that void. Right here," said Ari.

Arden glanced at the spot on the chart and down at the victim, whose mummified body now lay on her table.

She examined his legs. Both femur bones were snapped in half and jutted through the legs of his pants, which were stained in blood. The fabric was stiff and unyielding.

"This was dirt that we had to dig him out of here. Buried up to his hips," Ari's partner Shlomo advised.

He was buried alive.

A suffocating, awful way to die—and so much pain. Arden shuddered and ignored the sinking feeling in the pit of her stomach as she began her examination of the body. The skeleton wore a button-down shirt, still stained with his day's work.

She lifted the skull. Once-thick black hair was still, after fifty years, matted to the bone. It crunched when she touched it. Arden turned the hollow skull over and examined its inside. She sighed.

"Anything?" Nicky asked. He was sorting through the location map, making notes; his handwriting scrawled across the page in red ink.

"Nothing yet," she answered and continued to examine the clothing before cutting the shirt off of the skeleton.

Arden considered herself lucky if any letters, diaries, or any form of identification was discovered with the bodies. She had only been fortunate once. Where they had been lucky was the discovery and recovery of shards of clay pots, pieces of fabric, and rotted wood, including the nearly intact woven basket.

"I hear we're having shawarma tonight," Nicky said with a wide smile.

"That sounds wonderful. Why don't you go on over and relax? It's been a long day. I'll be there in about an hour."

"Okay. No problem Dr. Blakely," he said, tossing the map on top of the growing piles of maps, books, and files.

Arden watched him leave the tent and heard his feet shuffle away, back toward the food tent on the other side of the team's compound of tents and living spaces.

When the silence enveloped her, she returned to her examination. As with all the bodies before this one, she surmised the victim was male, first by bone structure and then by the clothing.

His work pants. They were covered in so much blood that the fabric was stiff and wouldn't yield to her touch. She bent the fabric harder, cracking the blood; several pieces fell to the table.

She continued down the pant legs, examining the holes along the worn hems. This victim carried no wallet or other form of identification, and there were no hidden pockets. As she took a second pass down his pant leg, her fingers grazed over a hard lump in the rolled hem.

A bone shard?

She tugged at the fabric, which, after several decades, scrunched together in such a tight knot that it refused to un-bunch. After rubbing it between her hands for several minutes, she managed to loosen the fabric, releasing the hidden item.

What's this?

The laborer had hidden a large iron and copper ring inside the hem of his pants. Arden removed a flashlight and shined it on the decorative ring.

Did you find this down there?

The ring was heavy and ornate, its flat top decorated with a raised six-pointed star with three stones and a set of empty prongs, all positioned in the shape of a square. Arden placed the ring on her finger and noted that it was most likely made for a man, as the very large ring slipped right off.

"What are you?" Arden said aloud to the empty tent.

"Find something?" Nicky asked, entering with a large sandwich and a drink for his boss.

As he lay the food on the table, Arden held up the ring for him to see. If Nicky was impressed, he held it inside.

"Oh, cool. What is it?" Nicky removed a long strand of hair from his eyes for a better look.

"Well, according to all my research on this dig site, the original excavation was looking for a lost temple of King Solomon's. If that's true, this might have belonged to him or someone in his court."

"Nice." Rather than leaving for the evening, Nicky busied himself with straightening the folders and books.

Arden turned the ring over again, looking for distinguishing markings to tell her what the ring was and who it might have belonged to. Inside the band, she saw an engraved verse so faint that she turned on her flashlight to examine the language.

The language of the Canaanites: Syriac and Egyptian! This isn't just a ring.

Arden ran a finger across the words, which were nearly smooth from age and barely readable. Her mind wandered through history, and her thoughts scrambled for ideas until information became clear. Her fingers grazed the six-pointed star, and she ran to her research books on the makeshift bookshelf at the back of the tent.

Her library consisted of ancient atlases and books on Israeli history, ancient languages, and rulers of the ancient world. She chose a tome about the history of King Solomon. If this was his temple, maybe the ring was his as well.

She perused the chapter list, searching for anything about a ring until she found a chapter entitled "The Seal of Solomon."

It's a seal. It can't be.

Arden read the passage, immediately honing in on the description of a six-pointed star used to seal the documents of King Solomon—a star surrounded by four Chintamani Stones. She stared at her ring again and then back to the page, comparing the ring to the illustration inside. Her hands shook.

"You okay Dr. Blakely?" Nicky asked, concerned. He reached for the ring, but Arden tightened her grip on the artifact.

Of all the dumb luck, finding this ring here in the middle of the desert.

The Seal of Solomon.

Her mind wandered through history and through the Bible stories she had studied in college and in graduate school.

The ring, she remembered, was supposedly imbued with the magical powers to control the demons known as *djinn*. She returned to the book.

There!

The djinn: shapeshifting demons also known today as genies.

But demons, they're not real.

Arden could barely contain her excitement. As an archaeologist, a student of science, she didn't believe in magic and demons— and yet this book described the ring she held in her hand.

The Seal of Solomon!

Arden pocketed the ring, gently covered up her victim, labeled the body for further examination, and zipped the plastic body bag.

"I need to leave for a little while," she said to Nicky.

"Where to? Surely nothing's open at this hour," Nicky replied as he continued to straighten the books. "Is it about that ring?"

"Yeah. There's a library in town. The librarian told me to call anytime I needed help. If it's not open, I'll call him. If anyone wants me, I'll be back after the meal."

She couldn't remember ever being this excited. The emotions fluttered in her stomach like a tent full of butterflies, swirling and twirling, rising and sinking. She grabbed the keys to one of the off-road vehicles and hopped inside, driving away from camp. It was the only desert road. Arden was thankful that the town had a library.

I hope it's open.

Her brain churned with wonder and excitement; pictures of ancient cultures flitted inside her head.

Who forged this ring? What was it meant to do? Could it truly be the Seal of Solomon?

As she drove deep in the desert, her car was the only one on the sand-covered road. Arden pushed the speed to the highest she could without skidding and losing control. It was a rough ride in the car, which was meant for driving extremes, and it only got worse as she came around a bend. The speed, too fast, caused the car to fishtail; plumes of sand flew out behind her. Even after she righted the vehicle, sand blew everywhere, blocking her rear view. Determined to make it to town, Arden slammed her foot against the gas pedal and drove along the road.

The sun hung low in the sky and shone brightly in her eyes. Arden lowered the sun shade and drove west, unaware of anything outside the clouds of sand.

BUMP. Her head snapped forward as an unseen vehicle rammed her rear bumper. Surprised, Arden turned the wheel hard and swerved off the road. Using her all-terrain vehicle, she maneuvered the car through the sand, gained control, and jumped back on to the pavement. Again, her foot smashed against the gas pedal until she reached top speed, racing along the road. It did little to deter the other car, which matched her speed and drove alongside of her.

Arden glanced over, unfamiliar with the driver and unable to make out the passenger in the dim light. The driver rammed his car into hers. She held her wheel tightly as the tires spun and her vehicle slid off the road. She pounded against the gas, but even though the wheels churned and smoked in the sand, it was too thick and smooth for her to remove her car.

"Crap! Crap! Crap!" she shouted to herself and glanced at the road. The sand settled and revealed the second car, another like the one she drove herself. It crept backwards until it was even with hers, its engine humming softly. With trembling hands, Arden fumbled with the latch on the canvas door until she finally released it. She jumped from her car and trudged in the sand toward camp.

The car that ran her from the road was her most immediate problem. The engine hummed softly as the tires cracked against the sand. It didn't speed up or come near her, but it followed her, stalked her. Whoever it was inside scared her—terrified her—and it took all her energy to concentrate on taking the next step and the next as she drew closer to camp.

She walked, slogged, and plodded through deep sand, hard sand, and even more kinds of sand. It covered her as the sun finally dipped below the horizon. Fear and anxiety overtook her as the temperatures fell. Arden realized she hadn't eaten and had no supplies. She hoped that camp would somehow spring out of the landscape.

Over the course of an hour, her stride slowed, and her legs began to feel like heavy, rubbery appendages. She longed for a cool glass of water or her creaky old cot; her knee buckled.

Where am I? Camp should be here.

Arden fought back the fear and the tears and determinedly picked up her stride, ignoring the tires against the sand that continued to follow her. Her next step landed in a hole near the road; she stumbled and fell to her knees. She could no longer contain her tears. The car squeaked and moaned behind her, stopping inches from where she sat.

"Help me."

A door creaked open, footsteps crunched against the sand, and two strong hands yanked her up. "Where is it?" The voice was gruff and angry, unfamiliar to her.

"I don't..." she cleared her dry and parched throat. Her head slumped forward as unfamiliar hands patted down her legs, yanking on her pockets and pushing against her breasts. Against the lights of the car, Arden clearly the second man, the passenger, anxiously pacing.

Nicky!

His long, floppy hair fell in his face, and he averted his eyes, unable to meet her gaze.

When the hands found her hiding place, they lifted the ring, and relief filled her chest—until a blinding pain filled the side of her head, and the world turned to black.

CHAPTER 1

FROM THE POINT of view of FBI Special Agent Jack Ramsey, demons and vampires walked the streets, hid at crime scenes, and stared at him wherever he went. Or so he thought. He paid special attention to cases that seemed odd and possibly magical, and he had spent his own time investigating them, until he eventually realized that he knew too much about the magical world and really needed a vacation.

Since the conclusion of the Princess Amelie murder case, ending in the trial of Wolfgange Rathbone, Jack hadn't called Annie Pearce. He still got indigestion when he remembered the special problems that came with magical cases. Instead, he'd decided to move on and work the heavy case load of investigations that came across his own desk—and to hope those other cases worked themselves out.

The farther from the magical case he was, the more he fell back into his normal schedule. He learned how to relax and eventually opened himself up and met someone—a nice lawyer who worked in the building across from his office. It started with coffee, moved to lunch, which became dinner, and finally Jack Ramsey asked Amanda McCoy to join him for a little time away.

The overworked FBI agent booked a trip to Hawaii for the two of them, where he now found himself on a lounge chair in the sand with a beer in one hand and a book in the other, his pasty white skin glowing in the bright sun.

Beside him, Amanda positioned herself lazily across her lounger, crossing her long legs that shimmered with a thick layer of sunscreen. The Type A lawyer had just started on the first of a large pile of magazines—some trashy, some newsworthy—tossed in the sand between them. Pouting her perfect lips, she reached for Jack's beer, drinking half before handing it back to him.

Happily distracted, Jack found it difficult to return to the biography purchased at the airport.

This book seemed like a good idea at the time.

Instead, he watched Amanda, her hand resting comfortably on her leg, her fingers drawing circles against her skin. His eyes trailed from her feet to her hips to the magazine in her hands. His thoughts took a turn to the mundane as he glanced at the pile of papers in the sand, and reached for the Chicago paper at the bottom of the pile.

"No papers," she chided.

"Then why did you buy them?"

"To keep up with the news." Amanda smiled coyly as if tempting him. "You promised. No papers, no phones, no internet." She uncrossed her legs and changed sides.

"Just a peek. That is, unless we're going back to the room," Jack suggested hopefully.

"At dinner." With a grin on her lips, she returned to her magazine.

Throwing his book in the sand Jack exchanged it for the paper. As promised, he refrained from reading the news, opting instead for the sports section where he caught up on the basketball, hockey, and early spring training reports. After reading every line, every score, every opinion piece, and all the sports news that held no interest for him, a bored Jack rifled through the lifestyle section.

Uninterested in the latest fashion or the best sellers list, he tossed the used section on the sand.

Jack grimaced at the editorials, thoughtfully read the food section, and made mental notes on the movie and theater reviews. After reading each section, the FBI agent threw it on the growing pile.

With the final newspaper section left in his lap, he remembered this was vacation and leaned back, breathed in hot, salty air, and stared at the ocean. The waves rolled in, washing away footprints collected during the morning rush of tourists. The water, a clear crystal blue, should have invited him in. Instead, Jack wiped away sweat from his brow with a towel and realized disappointedly that relaxing was hard work and a little boring.

"Go take a dip," Amanda suggested as she reached for her own book, leaving the magazine on the top of the pile.

"No. I'm good. Just finishing the paper."

"News?"

"I promise, I won't do anything with it,"

"You wouldn't be you if you let it sit." She smiled at him, and her white teeth sparkled against the tan she was cultivating. Jack's stomach flipped and flopped in that happy way.

Finally giving in to the tug of the news, Jack opened the front page: murder, a teacher's strike, city hall, gang warfare. Nothing peculiar or odd. Since he was currently in paradise, the news made no difference to his mood. He chose to be happy and worked on relaxing. Accepting his good fortune, Jack thought of taking a nap before lunch and washing his hands of the outside world.

While others played in the warm water and paddled on large boards, Jack returned to the paper, which was nearly finished. He almost escaped thoughts of work, but of course he pushed it and trouble fell in his lap: a story just enough to raise the hairs on the back of his neck.

It wasn't odd to find a murdered John Doe; that wasn't what

caught Jack's attention. It was the picture of the victim. It was his riding cloak.

He reread the article from the very first word. John Doe, found dead in the middle of Busse Woods, a large park just outside Chicago. The police had been unable to identify the victim and requested the help of the community to identify him.

When Jack gleaned nothing more from the story content, he returned his attention to the computer-generated picture beside the article. Long hair tied in a ribbon, a riding cloak loosely draped over the victim's shoulders.

I've seen this before.

Jack remembered well his first and only foray into the world of magic. The cloak on the John Doe pictured in the paper was similar to the one worn by Wolfgange Rathbone the night Jack arrested him for the murder of Princess Amelie of Amborix eight months ago. It was a fashion choice Jack was unfamiliar with, but as he worked with Annie Pearce and her team and had the opportunity to meet several other wizards, he realized that some wizard traditions survived in the modern world. The riding cloak was common in the magical community.

An overwhelming feeling churned in the pit of his stomach. It gnawed at him in a way he couldn't ignore.

A covert meeting gone wrong? A body dump? That damn riding cloak!

Few details were released to the press and Jack hunched over the paper, rereading the article for a third time, gleaning the words for anything that might be relevant.

He noticed the sidebar's short notes related to the main story. At first, Jack didn't notice a connection between the weather service's claim there had been no lightning strikes in the area the day the victim died, until he read the cause of death… *Electrocution?*

"Can a spell do that?" he murmured.

"What, sweetie?" Amanda asked, turning the page of her book.

"Nothing… just normal weirdness," he responded. He

continued to read the sidebar's debate about whether the victim been electrocuted or struck by lightning. After considering the weather at the time of death, authorities had concluded the victim was murdered by electrocution.

After so many months of believing he saw magic all around him, Jack had finally found something. Something weird and worrisome. His left eye twitched.

"Damn," he said under his breath.

"Everything okay?" Amanda rolled over to face him, concern on her drawn lips. Her finger grazed his knee.

Leave it alone! the voice in his head pleaded.

But Jack couldn't leave it alone, not when the feeling overpowered him so strongly. This was the case his mind had thought he was seeing all along. "Yeah. I just need to make a phone call."

"But Jack, you promised." Amanda grimaced.

Jack kissed her, enjoying the taste of pineapple and rum on her lips. A groan of pleasure escaped his lips as he pulled away and stared into her bright green eyes.

"Just one call and then I'm done."

"One." She reached around his neck and held him close, her tongue parting his lips.

Annie who?

A strong sense of duty and his desire to do the right thing bore down on him until the part of his rational brain that saw monsters around every corner made him pull away reluctantly. "Five minutes."

Amanda held up five fingers and frowned at him.

Hopping across the increasingly hot sand, Jack found an empty corner of the beach beside a rock and dialed Annie's number, secretly hoping it would ring to voice mail.

"Hello?"

"It's Jack Ramsey." Apprehension took over his voice. He regretted the phone call immediately.

I'll just tell her I got the wrong number.

"Hey Jack. It's been a while. Four months since the trial, I think. How are you?"

I'm on vacation calling you. How do you think?

It had been a while since he had even talked to Annie. After turning a blind eye to the manufactured evidence and enduring the demanding trial, Jack had avoided Annie. He hadn't seen or heard from her since Rathbone was convicted of Princess Amelie's murder. Both needed time to put the case in the past.

Though Jack regretted this call, it was time to face the facts. Magic existed, and this victim had most likely died due to a spell, jinx, or hex. Jack really didn't know the difference. Unfortunately, hearing Annie's voice caused that old familiar stress to settle in his chest.

"I'm on vacation."

Why didn't I tell her I butt dialed?

Annie chuckled. "Really? And you're calling me. That's not vacation."

"Yeah. Amanda doesn't think so either." Jack glanced at Amanda. Turning in her lounge chair, she met his gaze and smiled as she re-crossed her legs.

"A girlfriend? Nice. Go back to her. Whatever it is can wait."

Silence filled the line. Jack thought maybe Annie had hung up on him, but then he heard a male voice speaking to her in the background, which pulled Jack back to the gnawing feeling in his chest. "I need you to look at one tiny little thing," Jack said. "If it's nothing, great. If it's something... but it's probably nothing."

Jack watched Amanda, who looked incredibly sexy in her string bikini, a golden tan developing on her skin. It didn't surprise him when a lean, muscular, deeply tanned man sat beside her on the lounger and attempted to engage her in conversation. Gracefully, Amanda waved the stranger away. Jack's heart sped up.

"Okay," Annie said on the other end of the line. "If it's something, we'll look into it. If not, you wasted ten minutes of vacation. So what do you have?"

Why did I call again?

Amanda caught Jack's gaze as the man slunk away. She waved him toward her with a wide smile. Jack returned the smile and held up a finger signaling one more minute.

"Okay. It's stupid. But a guy dressed in a riding cloak was found dead in Busse Woods. The cause of death, get this, electrocution. Does that mean anything to you?" The FBI agent had solved hundreds of cases in his career. As he explained this one to Annie, the story sounded just as bizarre as when he had originally read it.

"Are you sure that's where the body was found?"

Annie's request for clarification bothered Jack but at the same time offered him validation. His initial instinct must have been correct. "Yeah. Why?"

"If it was just the riding cloak, I'd think costume, but the portal to the black market is in Busse Woods. It's very possible the victim is a wizard."

"You can check on it?" he asked as Amanda waved to him again, pointing up toward the hotel less than a hundred yards from where they sat. Anxiously, Jack tapped his hand against his thigh, desperate to return to return to his vacation and to Amanda.

"Yeah. We'll look into it. Go vacate."

"Thanks, Annie. I think I owe you again."

"No doubt, Jack. I'll keep you posted."

"Really not necessary," he said before hanging up. Feeling ridiculous for even calling, he sauntered back to Amanda and took Annie's advice to vacate.

CHAPTER 2

KNOCK... KNOCK... KNOCK... *knock.*
Knuckles rapped quickly against the cheap cubicle wall, the hollow pinging breaking Annie's concentration. She pushed away the book she was reading. It was filled with vague theories about elemental spells; she was hoping to learn something useful about fire elemental spells.

She glanced up, grateful for the reprieve. Bucky Hart stood at the entrance, holding the police file Annie had requested.

"Bucky, you rock!"

Bucky, the computer guru of Wizard Hall, sauntered into the office as if he owned it and sat in the chair across from her. "You're such a tease, Ms. Pearce." Bucky plopped his feet on the desk; his left canvas shoe, ripped at the toe, flapped around before settling. He lowered the frayed hem of his Aerosmith T-shirt when he leaned back in the chair, purposely leaving Annie to wait for the manila folder she was so anxious to read.

Cocky, he tossed the folder on her desk. "Open it." Bucky's watery blue eyes twinkled at her.

Annie had seen Bucky break into servers all over the world and find whatever information needed, so she couldn't hide her disappointment when she opened this very sparse file.

"This is it?"

"I can only get you what they have." He crossed his arms against his chest defensively.

Annie felt bad. She hadn't meant to accuse him. "Sorry. It's just so... thin."

Bucky shrugged unapologetically and took out his phone to occupy himself while Annie did a precursory reading of the file just in case she needed more information before he left.

The reading started with the nearly blank evidence list, which was a good indicator as to whether or not the murder was magical. If John Doe had been killed with a jinx, Annie expected a confusing lack of evidence. Her stomach churned as she read the scant list. Either nothing was found on or around the victim or the CSI team had missed all the evidence. She highly doubted the latter option. Those hairs on the back of her neck stood straight up.

Bucky, always thorough, had divided the autopsy photos from the crime scene photos. Annie lay the crime scene shots across her desk. They were eerily familiar; a location she had visited hundreds of times, just outside one of the world's four portals to the black market.

Why leave the body here?

The Busse Woods portal was the most used portal to enter the market. A magical murder just outside the portal couldn't be a coincidence. Annie was becoming more anxious about this murder.

Bucky was listening to music. He drummed his fingers against his thigh, swiped his phone screen, and bobbed his head.

Annie grimaced and returned to the photos. The body had been discovered lying on top of a patch of exposed brown grass. The rest of the clearing outside the portal had been covered in a thick layer of snow before the crime scene unit arrived.

A warm body could have melted that patch. Maybe it was something else.

It was the cloak that had given Jack enough concern to call Annie while on vacation. The cloak was an unmistakable item of clothing still worn amongst traditional wizards and definitely not a common item among nonmagical society. The frayed hem of the cloak was covered in mud splatter, and the victim's expensive leather shoes were caked in mud, leaves, and twigs.

Good call, Jack!

"Who wears a cloak and leather shoes to a forest preserve?" Annie asked out loud.

"Can't think of anyone, 'less they were heading into the market," Bucky said without stopping his swiping and typing.

The market.

The teleportation spot was located behind the evergreen trees, a short distance away from the portal.

Was he running from someone through the muddy trails?

Shuffling through the pictures, Annie recognized a well-worked crime scene. She'd investigated a double homicide with the FBI last year and had spent a lot of time observing their procedures. This crime scene was covered in footsteps that traversed the snow in all directions as separate teams of investigators searched for clues, examined the victim, or interrogated witnesses.

"Do you think we could get an aerial view of the crime scene? I'd like to examine the footprints if I can." Annie said to Bucky.

Bucky glanced up, shrugged, and returned to his phone. "I'll see what I can find."

With a magnifying glass, Annie reviewed the crime scene for signs of spells that hadn't hit the mark. She examined leaves, branches, and tree trunks, searching for broken or singed foliage. Finally, she spotted it: a tiny hint of a wayward spell near the portal. Just a hint of a broken branch and a scorch mark. She circled the picture with a red marker for further investigation when they finally made it to the crime scene.

Behind her, the printer whirled to life, spitting out a complex satellite picture of the crime scene. "Thanks," Annie said.

"You ask, you shall receive." He returned to his phone yet again.

Thanks to the aerial photo, Annie could see that the clearing was marked with footsteps and crossed with long, thin lines. She double-checked the pictures of the John Doe. Sure enough, the heels of the victim's shoes were caked in mud.

He was dragged.

Annie circled the start and end of the drag marks. She sighed.

Was he dragged before or after he died?

"I think he was killed in the clearing," Annie commented to herself. Bucky grunted.

Feeling her time with Bucky growing short, Annie returned to the riding cloak. Her gut told her it was the key. Such a small clue, yet it had set this all in motion. The heavy fabric fell from the victim's shoulders. It had been twisted, either because it had been yanked or because it slipped from his shoulders when he fell to the ground. Annie summoned a magnifying glass to examine the brooch that pinned the cloak together.

What is that design? It's not American or based in witchcraft.

It reminded Annie of several heavy links on a very thick chain. She had never seen the design before and circled it before handing the picture to Bucky.

"Hey, can you find out what this is?"

"Sure. Let's see." Bucky snapped a picture and did whatever it was that he did with his phone, leaving Annie to stare at the photo again.

She drummed her fingers against the desk, impatient as Bucky surfed the internet.

"I'm not finding that exact design," he finally said. "Though from all the symbols I've seen over the years, I would guess we're looking at something Middle Eastern." He held up his phone and showed Annie several designs from the region.

Definitely similar, just not the same.

"So we start with the Middle Eastern databases?" Annie asked, handing him back the phone.

"I'll have Mrs. Cuttlebrink in the library examine the pictures, see if she has any other ideas." Bucky's phone beeped. He glanced at the screen, typed something, and looked at Annie. "Take another look through the file for anything else. I gotta book it," he said and placed the phone on the desk.

Feeling pressured now, Annie glanced through each page quickly for anything that appeared weird or needed additional information. She spotted the witness list. There was one name: Troy Waters. Annie was unfamiliar with this name. He wasn't on any wizard watch list.

Probably nonmagical, she thought.

"Can you search for a Troy Waters?" she asked Bucky. "Find out if he's magical. He found the body."

"On it."

It didn't take Bucky long to put down his phone. "Nothing in the magical databases. And yes, he has an Illinois driver's license."

"For now I'll make the assumption he's not magical. So what do you think?" Annie asked. Over the course of his career, Bucky had pulled scores of police reports and had seen everything. She trusted his first impression.

"First look, like I said, he's wearing a cloak, to a forest preserve. No one dresses like that to hike. He was probably on the way to the market or leaving it. It can't be a coincidence that the victim was found just outside the portal."

His phone buzzed and clicked again. He took a quick glance. "Second thing, there's no nonmagical evidence. I see a few broken twigs and one scorch mark near the portal. I say it's a magical murder," he said definitively.

"I need to get into the morgue and look at the body," she said.

"It's probably time to create some identification for you. This seems to be a recurrence."

Annie chuckled under her breath. This was her second case involving a victim at the Cook County Morgue in Chicago. Under most circumstances, the Vampire Attack Unit removed bodies from the morgue, but since this was an unofficial case sent to her by a vacationing FBI agent, Annie would be verifying the magical murder. She sighed.

"Unfortunately Jack is a really good source," she said, grimacing as she remembered the overwhelming smell of antiseptic used to clean the autopsy room at the morgue.

"The FBI guy?"

She hadn't realized she had said that so loudly. "Yeah. Him. He sent this my way. Unfortunately, his instincts were good." Annie piled the pictures and the notes together and stuck them in the folder. "Let me know if anything else pops up in the file." Annie didn't need to remind him; he did that anyway.

"Who am I?" Spreading his arms wide, Bucky grinned broadly. The gold tooth at the back of his mouth flashed. "All over it. I'll text you if there's any emergency exposure. Anything else?"

"Yeah. I need to know where toxicology was sent."

Bucky tapped away at his phone. "On it. I can lose the file, but you need to lose the samples and remove the body."

"Find anything yet?"

He shook his head. "It's not in the e-file. They're probably still at the morgue. You sending in VAU?"

Graham Lightner, manager of the VAU, would come in after Annie confirmed a magical death. His unit was responsible for switching out the samples, swapping the body, and removing the files. It was imperative that the wizard's extra-two-chromosome secret remained undiscovered.

"As soon as we confirm it's a magical murder, I'll send them in. Thanks for the folder," Annie said.

Bucky pulled his legs from Annie's desk. "When I hear from Mrs. Cuttlebrink, I'll run the victim's picture through the country's database, see if we can come up with a name." He stood and pulled down his shirt, hiding the spare tire around his belly. "Call if you need anything else."

Annie saluted him as he left her cubicle. His feet shuffled against the short-yarned carpet down the hallway.

With two magical missing persons in the Midwest region of the United States, and four others in the Southwest, Central and

Northeast, all Wizard Guard departments were busy. The office this morning was distractingly quiet. Annie sighed as a printer whirled on the other side of the floor.

Jack, you were right!

Annie restrained herself from calling Jack and updating him. Instead, she twirled in her desk chair and stared at the back wall. Pictures lined the shelves: Annie and Cham alone or with their best friends Dave Smith and Janie Parker; Annie with her father; Annie with her sister Samantha and Sam's husband John Chamsky at their recent wedding. Scattered between the pictures were artifacts and books collected from many cases, similar to this. But not like this.

Why outside the portal?

The portal, the entrance to the black market, the place where the nonmagical world collided with the magical one, both fighting to control the space. Here, unstable air prevented nonmagicals from getting close to the portal by creating a sense of dread and danger. It was a high-traffic location, and Annie felt certain that the crime scene investigators experienced the chilled air and the sense of trepidation that blanketed the clearing. Under normal circumstances, nonmagicals instinctively left the area, but the investigators couldn't.

That's probably why there's no evidence.

Her mind wandered through scattered images of a magical electrocution, a brooch of unknown origin, and the body outside the portal. The answers would be found in the morgue cooler.

"Was Jack right?" Cham poked his head into her cubicle, interrupting Annie's mindless wandering. His windblown curly brown hair stuck up and out, and his faded freckles were covered in a rosy red from the biting winter wind. He was cute and sexy all at once, and Annie's stomach fluttered.

She found it funny that he had already heard; they hadn't seen each other all morning. "Yeah. Any news on the missing persons?"

Cham strolled in and flopped down in the chair across from

her before dropping a large pile of folders in the second chair. He summoned her case file.

"Hey!" she complained, but he was already shuffling through the pictures.

"No. We tried scrying for the two missing persons from Chicago, but nothing. There was a strange magical trace in one of the houses. We're trying to determine what spell it was. It's the same thing in the other regions," he said as he continued to view the pictures. His long, thin fingers were nimble as he pulled out another photo and examined the image.

"So what's next?" Annie asked. It was troubling that they couldn't be found via magic.

"Um… we're trying to determine if they knew each other or had anything in common. It's a little weird." He stopped to examine a particular photo, even pulling it closer to his face. "Look at this." He handed her a photo of two evergreens.

Annie knew the significance of this location. The portal hung at the center of the trees that flanked it. It was as if the photographer knew something was there.

"It's the portal—well, the location." Annie looked at him, her brows crinkled in confusion. She was unsure what he was getting at.

"Look again. Just between the trees," he advised.

Staring at the picture again but not yet seeing what he wanted her to see, she closed her eyes and imagined the location. Between the trees where the portal hung, the air chilled her to the bone. Annie shuddered and reopened her eyes.

There!

She finally saw what he wanted her to see: the faint mark that hung in the air. It was the portal—hazy and out of focus.

"Oh crap. That's not good." She held the picture and pointed to the portal.

"Photographic evidence of magic."

Annie circled the portal with a red marker and made a note for Bucky to lose the picture. She stuck it on top of the folder.

Most likely they won't ever notice the anomaly.

But Annie couldn't help think of the reporter Rebekah Stoner, who had been investigating her since Princess Amelie's murder eight months ago. The journalist knew more than even she realized about the existence of magic. It wouldn't do well for her to discover real proof.

"Any thoughts?" Cham asked.

"If I run a scenario, I have to believe this is a wizard coming to the black market, either to purchase something or sell something," she speculated.

There's no other reason for him to be there.

"So if he's there to sell something, the negotiation for price goes badly, and he's killed," Cham surmised.

"That's my assumption. What I can't figure out is, why throw him outside the portal? Why risk exposure? This most certainly would get the attention of the Wizard Guard. Even if Jack didn't lead me to this case.".

He laid the pictures on the desk and sat back in the chair. "Any other scenarios?" he asked.

"He was trying to get to the market to sell something and didn't make it there. Was gunned down, so to speak. He's outside the market, and that's not a coincidence. Buying or selling, those are the options." It was the same either way, though Annie hadn't answered his question. Which led her back to why the murderer had left the body there. No one in the market could have been that stupid.

Annie rummaged through the photos and pulled out one of the victim on the autopsy table. His exposed chest was blackened by a round burn mark that curved, tapered, and thinned at the end. A measuring stick estimated that the burn was six inches long.

"So how does it look?" Cham bent forward.

"Well…" She held out her magnifying glass, examining

the burn. "It's definitely a burn mark. Can you shoot electricity from your hand?" she asked, though she knew the answer to her own question.

He responded with a confused grimace. "Uh, no. You need a spell to control nature. Why?"

"So there're no super-wizards who have that power?"

Cham smiled broadly. "No wizard should be able do that without a spell. Maybe a creature?" he guessed.

Annie handed him the preliminary autopsy report. He held his hand out, his palms facing the ceiling.

"Ignis," he said. A puff of smoke pulsed and swirled above his palm until a small fire ball formed and hovered an inch above his hand. Flames danced and stretched as he added more magic. "What's lightning in Latin?" he asked.

"I… I don't know." Annie summoned the elemental book and perused the contents for a spell to summon lightning.

"Try *fulgur*," she offered.

He released the fire spell and muttered, "Fulgur." A bolt of lightning spit from his palm, singeing his skin. A nauseating scent of burnt flesh hung in the cubicle.

"You okay?"

"That won't kill anyone. Embarrass them, maybe." He shook out his hand. "I've never heard of a creature who can do that. That doesn't mean there isn't any."

He was still shaking his hand, so Annie grabbed his wrist and applied a salve to the charred flesh. The resulting burn was far smaller than the mark on the victim's chest.

"Do you think more than one person sending the same spell could create a bigger burn?" she inquired.

Cham grimaced as Annie wrapped his hand in a bandage. "Maybe. But that's multiple people with exceptionally good aim to hit the same mark."

"Person or demon," Annie muttered. Something had happened outside the market, and she was certain it wasn't a coincidence.

After taping the bandage closed, her fingers grazed Cham's hand. Annie felt lightheaded as her heart beat faster.

"You know; this is the second call from Jack Ramsey leading to a second really weird murder. You should be wary of him." A slight tinge of jealousy was evident in his voice, which surprised Annie.

"Too late."

Annie's essential supplies were stored in the credenza behind her desk. Inside the top drawer was her locked box where she kept all of her false identifications. She bypassed the FBI badge, grabbing the Chicago Police Department identification.

Bucky's right, I could probably use a badge to the Chicago City Morgue. This will have to do for now.

"Hopefully the body will tell us what we need," Annie said.

"You need help?"

"You can't come with me. I'll let Spencer know. Besides, you have your own stack you need to get through." She nodded toward the pile of folders teetering on the chair.

"Yeah. These missing persons. One minute they were there, the next nowhere to be found. All of the families are convinced it was foul play. And the magical trace is just so weird. We're trying to figure out what spells were used."

"When did they all go missing?"

"That's the thing. They all disappeared within the last two weeks. The magic found at each house is the same, but none of us can trace it or know what it does."

"Well, with all the departments working on it, I'm sure you'll find something soon." Supportive and concerned, Annie reached across the desk. Her lips met Cham's halfway. She didn't care that they were at work.

The moment was broken by the ringing of Cham's phone. He glanced at the screen and sighed. "It's Mom," he said and answered. "Hi, Mom."

"Hi, dear. I haven't seen you in weeks. Are you and Annie

free for dinner tonight?" Annie could hear Cham's mother's voice through the phone.

"We can't. I'm up to my neck in missing persons, and Annie's going to the morgue, dealing with a John Doe," Cham said.

"Why isn't the VAU going in? It's their job." Marina Chamsky argued.

"Mom. Not tonight. This weekend. I promise," he said with a sigh.

"You say that all the time. You and Annie and your crazy schedules. All I do is worry about the two of you, running off being unsafe," his mom said, her voice rising to a bellow.

"Mom. These are routine cases. We're fine. I promise." Cham tried to offer her reassuring words.

"I love you and Annie. I just want you safe. Call me this weekend, and we'll work something out."

"Love you too, Mom. I gotta run," he said before hanging up. "Every time," Cham complained to Annie, shaking his head.

"You've been a wizard guard for five years. Why does she still harp on you about that choice? It's kinda getting old." Annie rolled her eyes.

"She still blames you—or, well, your dad for thinking I was blindly influenced by you."

"Because you don't have a brain in your head." Annie reached over the desk and kissed him, her hands roaming to the curls on his neck. "And she still wants to see me?" Annie asked as she pulled away.

"Her head spun 360 degrees. She was so happy when we started dating. I think she worries, is all," Cham reassured Annie.

"Go to dinner. I'll see you when I get back," Annie offered.

He kissed her instead. "Not a chance," Cham replied.

CHAPTER 3

GLADDEN WORCHESTER PACED his black market tent with long, hurried strides. While he pondered his options, his thin fingers, roughed with age and life, absently stroked the bald spot on the left side of his head where the long, purple scar still felt tender, even after a decade. Remembering the banshee attack usually excited him; today it irritated him as he recalled his past failures and poor decisions, one of which he needed to tend to immediately.

After crossing the tent in three strides, he swiveled on his left foot and traversed to the other side, but the marching did little to ease his unrest. He did what he did best and punched at the canvas walls of his tent with consecutive strikes. The stiff fabric flapped wildly, kicking up the dirt floor.

While Gladden released pent-up energy, three elves huddled in the corner whimpering, fearful they'd be Gladden's next target. They watched in horror as their compatriot, a messenger elf by the name of Sacha, lay curled into a ball on the floor with a split lip and missing tooth.

Gladden continued to trace the scar along the side of the head; it was a distraction as he searched for an easy solution to the problem at hand. Every thought that passed through his head led in one direction.

"Fetch me the djinn!" Gladden ordered. *It's time to take care of this problem now!*

"Ma—ma—aster Gladden." The squeaky, stuttering voice belonged to Bitherby, an elf of some distinction, at least amongst the other lower creatures that worked in the market. He bowed low, so low that his flat, wide nose nearly touched the dirt floor. Gladden glared at the elf, who was all of four feet high. Bitherby's oversized brown pants and green shirt quivered against his shaking frame.

"Now!" Gladden roared. The elf scurried and slipped in the dirt before pushing through the tent flap, which fluttered wildly after him.

Gladden stepped over Sacha, who was still shuddering on the dirt floor, and yanked a chair out, taking a seat at his makeshift desk to resume his examination of the ugly artifact resting on the battered wood. Though he had no knowledge of such objects or their value, Gladden stared at the amulet: a necklace containing a large red ruby that he knew to be called the Blood of Branwen.

The previous owner, a blind old hag with cracked and spotted skin, had assured him that the stone stopped the aging process of whomever wore the amulet. She swore on the ratty old grimoire on his desk that the necklace had been ripped from her neck, causing her to age rapidly. With Gladden's very limited knowledge, he had over-paid for what he now believed was a worthless piece of junk.

He grimaced and stared at the cracked and dirty rock, which was surrounded by hundreds of grayish diamonds that hung from a thick silver chain. The chain swayed as he examined the intricate setting. Under the intense light from the desk lamp, it sparkled across the tent.

Gladden had heard the jeers and the hushed tones as the black market merchants discussed the useless purchase of the Blood of Branwen. It angered him so much that he had on several occasions felt the desire to inflict harm on them. It took all that he had not to do so. It would be bad business.

How did this keep that bitch from aging?

The hag had claimed it was created for some duchess who wore it for three hundred years before it was ripped from her neck. Once it was removed, she dried up until all that was left was a pile of ash where she stood.

So why was the hag still alive to sell it to me?

"Damn her!"

He regretted the decision to purchase the necklace and decided it was time to deal with the woman who sold him the piece of shit.

Several groans rumbled across the room.

"Shut up!" Gladden barked. He glared at the three elves still huddled in the corner. They refused to assist their friend, afraid of the same fate. Instead, they cried softly as Gladden returned to the necklace.

Every magical wish granted came with a backfire, a price to pay for the wish fulfillment. This necklace, as long as you wore it around your neck, kept you from aging. Your payment: your soul.

If it works!

Gladden was not known for his business acumen, but he knew this latest mistake would cost him. Everything was slipping away. In anger, he hurled the heavy necklace across the tent. It crashed into the canvas and slid to the floor; the large ruby shattered into dust.

The tent flap flew open, and the djinn who not too long ago had introduced himself to Gladden as Ezekiel strode inside.

"You rang," the djinn sneered, pulling his already taut skin farther around his bony face.

Ezekiel's eyes skimmed the room. He scowled at the elves in the corner and clipped Sacha, who was still lying near death on the floor. The elf groaned as Ezekiel's tall, skeletal frame lowered into a metal chair that squeaked and teetered with his size.

Gladden's stomach lurched at the sight of this demon. He thoroughly regretted the day this foul creature had come to him.

"The nonmagical police were here." Gladden's lips pursed as if he had eaten something sour.

"In the market?" Ezekiel winked and smirked, exposing yellow teeth.

He thinks this is funny!

"No, you asshole. Your wizard was killed outside the portal."

The djinn grimaced, leaned back into the metal chair, and crossed long, wiry arms against his chest. "That's unfortunate. I really need that ring." He thought for a moment before his ugly smile returned to his gray, sickly face. "Whoever killed him must have my ring." Ezekiel got up and paced the tent. This time he sidestepped Sacha.

"This is all your fault!" Gladden shouted. The three elves in the corner finally took flight; the tent flaps quivered after them.

The djinn stopped mid stride and changed direction. Towering over Gladden by a foot, he bent over until their faces were an inch apart. Ezekiel's breath was the stench of death and could knock a grown man to the floor.

"My fault? I don't see how that is the case. You summoned me. You chanted the spell. Remember that wish you made to control the black market? You incompetent nitwit. As I see it, you have the market under your control. You have what you wished for," Ezekiel hissed through a wild, unnerving smile.

"You… you sent that… that man after the ring. It's your fault for bringing the nonmagical police here!"

Ezekiel slammed his fist into the wooden desk top, which shook and teetered before sliding to the floor. He flared his nostrils, and his eyes furrowed, pulling on already extended skin. In a hushed, hard whisper, the djinn jeered, "I suggest you do something to keep the police from finding the portal. It will be bad for all of us if you don't."

"You have been nothing but trouble since you arrived. Leave. You have until midnight. Take whatever is yours and find someone else to twist." Gladden huffed and puffed as he sucked in air.

"I think not, Gladden. You summoned me. Asked me for a little favor. Do you remember that?"

Gladden's eyes grew wide. He feared the djinn with every ounce of his being. "Ye—yes," he stammered.

"You can't default on this deal. Handle the police." Ezekiel marched from the tent.

CHAPTER 4

"DAMN NONMAGICALS... MORGUE... cause more problems," Gibbs said when Annie asked him to join her at the Cook County Morgue. Though John Gibbs was an amazing wizard guard, he disliked most things nonmagical, including nonmagicals themselves.

"Nah. Take Spencer," he said after she laid out the plan.

Ignoring his halfhearted attempt to decline the request, Annie said, "I can't. It's Spencer's kid's birthday tonight."

Gibbs shook his head. "Girl, two calls from that FBI man. Ignore him." He grumbled under his breath one more time, then finally said, "Time?"

"Midnight. See, was that so hard?" she asked. He griped yet again and headed back to his cubicle.

Annie had known Gibbs her whole life. He had worked with her father. Whenever she needed him, no matter the impulse, Gibbs wouldn't deny her request.

However, he wasn't her assigned Wizard Guard partner. That was Spencer Ray, whom she'd been working with since her relationship with Cham changed and they became a couple eight months ago. Couples working together was against company policy, so they had sorted through their cases and switched partners.

Annie didn't blame Spencer for turning her down for this

mission; she'd have hated for him to miss his kid's birthday because of a whim sent to her by Jack Ramsey.

Though I know it's our case.

Under normal circumstances, the VAU handled magical deaths that found their way to the morgues, but because Jack had called Annie, the case was still unofficial. It was her responsibility to verify the death before sending in the VAU.

As she packed the case folder into her field pack, Spencer stopped by her cubicle and stuck his head inside. "Keep me posted," he said.

"I will. Wish Riley a happy birthday for me!" She waved as he headed out to the pizza and video game birthday party.

The phone rang as Annie was ready to leave.

Last call and I'm done.

"Hey Bucky," she said, noticing the caller ID. Anxious to leave, she switched her weight from foot to foot.

"Sorry, Annie. No luck on the exact design, though Mrs. Cuttlebrink also believes it's Middle Eastern. I'll send what we have to the Middle East Wizard Guard and see if they recognize it and our victim."

"Yeah. I agree, that's a good place to start," Annie said.

"Okay. Just sent. I'll text when I hear something."

"Thanks, Bucky." As she hung up, Cham entered the cubicle and placed a picnic basket on her desk. "Hey what are you doing here?" she asked him.

"It's dinner. No closer to finding who John Doe is?" Cham emptied the contents: sandwiches, chips, drinks.

"Nope. Bucky's sending it to the Middle Eastern Wizard Guard, thinking that's what the brooch was. What did you bring? I was coming home."

"Yeah, and you'll worry about the morgue until you leave. Sit." Cham placed a small cheese-and-cracker tray, sandwiches, and a bowl of fruit on top of the desk and lit a candle with a wave of his palm across the wick. The warm glow was lost in the bright artificial lights.

"Not as romantic as I intended," he admitted. He waved a palm at the lights above the cubicle, dimming them.

"Nice." Annie reached for a sandwich and took a small bite. It slid down her throat roughly and sat like a rock in her stomach. She was suddenly aware of how not hungry she was at the moment and pushed the sandwich away.

"You okay?" Cham reached across the table for her hand, rubbing her palm with his thumb, a gesture Annie loved.

Why am I so anxious? "Yeah. It's just..." She fumbled with a cracker, twirling it between her fingers. "We're going to the morgue blind. Besides it being creepy, I don't have the FBI to clean out the employees." Last time she worked in the morgue, Jack Ramsey had the morgue empty; they had no worries about being discovered. This time, she had no idea who was working or when they would be there.

"Eat. I'm sure you'll be fine," Cham said.

After gentle encouragement, Annie worked on half the sandwich and a few pieces of fruit. Conversation flew quickly and easily. By the time midnight approached, they had discussed everything from the current broomstick racing season to spring training and the Chicago Cubs. Gradually, conversation descended into less important topics, all with the idea of keeping Annie's mind from wandering to the morgue.

"I need to head out," Annie finally said reluctantly. Without speaking, Cham walked her to the courtyard of Wizard Hall, the center of four connected Wizard Council buildings that housed everything from the legislature to education headquarters, museums, and the hospital.

They passed a security officer named Griff, who waved as they left through the back exit, the one all magicals used when entering and exiting the building.

With little time left, Cham led her to one of the picnic tables at the center of the park. Even in the middle of the city, moonlight bathed them in a warm glow. Though it was only thirty degrees, Annie felt warm.

As she rested her head on Cham's shoulder, he wrapped his arms around her. She closed her eyes, and his fingers grazed her chin, her cheek, and through her hair. As they moved back to her chin, he pulled her face upward and bent in to kiss her. Sitting on his lap and wrapping her arms around him, she forgot they were in the center of the courtyard, that the hospital wing was still open, and that patients, doctors, and other officials were milling about at this late hour. Suddenly, a door swished and closed with a bang.

"Busy night," she said when she pulled away. Over his shoulder, an elderly man, bundled tightly in winter gear, sat in his wheelchair as a woman Annie assumed was his wife wheeled him outside. Once away from the building, the woman wrapped her arms lovingly around the chair and teleported the entire entity away.

That could be us someday. She leaned against the love of her life and smiled, her arms wrapped around him.

"You okay?" he whispered in her ear.

"Better now. I should go." The sky was clear. With barely a breeze, teleporting to the morgue would be quick and easy.

"VAU standing by?" Cham asked.

"Yeah. Hiding somewhere near there."

"I'll wait for you at your place." He touched her cheek with a rough finger, the one she stitched up so many years ago after an accident during survival training. The scar scratched her skin.

His hand cupped her chin, and he kissed her one last time. With her arms around his neck, she jumped into his arms. As always, he caught her with ease.

❄

After midnight, Gibbs and Annie landed on the roof of the Cook County Morgue. The light was dim at best; they crouched and waited for their eyes to acclimate to the low light, scanning the roof for security cameras.

"Two in the corners on the east side," Gibbs whispered.

Annie spotted two on the west side, both pointing toward the street; she responded in kind.

While Gibbs slunk to the east to scout the edge, Annie headed in the opposite direction and peered down over the city.

"We're clear up here," Gibbs said. With nothing to draw attention to their presence, they met back at the center.

"There's a possibility the medical examiner and staff are in there," she warned.

"Most likely." Gibbs grimaced, the same look he'd given her many times before.

He really hates being here, but he's doing it for me.

"Got a plan? You don't have the FBI to clear them out."

"I gave it some thought before I decided to charge into a government building. We either freeze the room or pull the fire alarm," she said. *It's a plan. I never said it was a good one.*

"I'll freeze the room," Gibbs grunted and led them to the building's entrance, a solid yet simple metal door with a standard lock that wobbled when Annie reached for it.

"I think I could kick this open if I wanted to," Annie commented.

"Not likely they needed something stronger. I doubt we'll see any booby traps."

Breaking into buildings, homes, and government facilities was merely a function of being of a wizard guard. As per standard procedures, Gibbs faced the entry to the left with his palms out. Annie held her hand six inches from the handle, cast the spell, and twisted her wrist as she did. The lock popped open.

Apprehensively, Annie pulled the door open and waited for an alarm to blare. None did.

A cold breeze blew off of Lake Michigan, whipping against them and stinging their faces and hands. Another winter storm was about to blow through the area.

"Gotta move before we can't teleport," Gibbs said.

They stared into the semi-darkness. The shadowy light created by soft bulbs at the floor was strong enough to ensure they wouldn't tumble down the steps.

Annie took a breath. For her, the silence was maddening; it revealed nothing about who was working in the building.

"Is it worth it?" Gibbs asked her, though her answer wouldn't change his mind about assisting her.

I really wish Jack was here to clear our way. "You don't think it is?" she answered as they slid into the Cook County Morgue, taking their first steps into the darkened stairwell.

"Does it matter what I think?"

No, it doesn't.

Whether Jack's hunch was correct or not, the crime scene photos led them to conclude that the victim was a wizard, and it needed to be dealt with one way or another.

Stalling, Annie stopped at the first landing and peered through the vertical window in the door that led to an empty hallway. Fluorescent lights were low, offering enough visibility for them to make it to either the elevator or the stairwell. Many doors lined each side of the hallway.

How many hundreds are still occupied?

"You're nuts," Gibbs whispered.

"Ah, you love me so much," Annie said before descending the next two flights of stairs.

Above them, hinges screeched loudly as a door swung open. Footsteps cracked against the cement floor; the door slammed shut, and the sound reverberated in the empty stairwell.

Annie's heart fluttered wildly as Gibbs yanked her into the corner of the landing, his arm protectively holding her against the wall. She held her breath as footsteps descended the stairs.

Click… click… click.

Heavy steps grew closer. Gibbs prepared to teleport.

Click… click… click…

Hinges squeaked as another door opened. The footsteps trailed down the hallway until the door slammed shut, plunging the hall into silence.

"You can let go now," Annie whispered. Gibbs loosened his grip, took a step closer to the stairs, and glanced up.

"Let's go." Grabbing Annie's wrist, he pulled her down the final flight of stairs.

They took turns glancing through the window to view the empty waiting area outside the morgue. It hadn't changed in the eight months since they investigated Princess Amelie's murder. The small space contained six chairs: three on the wall to their left and the three to the right, which sat under a large window overlooking the morgue. The shades were open, the lights off.

Annie breathed a sigh of relief. "We're alone for now," she told Gibbs.

A video camera whirled and rotated from side to side, sweeping the waiting area and the hallway. When it turned away from their position to scan the hallway, Gibbs touched the corner of the window, dissolving the pane. With a wave of his palm the camera shut off, blanketing them in complete silence. They entered the waiting room.

With no one seemingly coming down their side of the basement, Annie opened the door with a gloved hand.

Gibbs positioned himself at the door. Setting a hand on the wall, he cast a spell; white light flashed around the room before it shimmered away.

"You're good," he said and stood beside the door, waiting for any visitors.

The spell was designed to keep the light from Annie's flashlight from being discovered as she examined the room, getting her bearings. It hadn't changed since she was here last. Steel autopsy tables still crowded the middle of the room; they shined in her low light. They clearly had recently been scoured clean with antiseptic. It hung in her nose, and she grimaced.

Five small desktops hung from two of the walls. Papers and

folders were piled high and teetering on several more desks. Another desk stored several plastic containers filled with evidence; yet another held a hand saw.

Annie started with the folders, each of which was labeled clearly with a victim's name. As a new case, John Doe was near the top of the pile. The file here was thin as the one Bucky had printed for her.

There's probably nothing new.

She perused the file quickly, and noticed an unsettling addition. An X-ray had been taken. She held up the film, examining it with her flashlight. Although she was not an expert, Annie could still tell that the object at the center of the torso didn't belong.

"What is it?" Gibbs asked.

"Don't know."

"Mark the file for the VAU. We need to get out of here before anyone comes back," Gibbs commanded He tapped the side of his leg with his flashlight as he glanced out the morgue window.

Annie cast a spell on the folder and replaced it where she found it, just in case someone noticed.

Texting Bucky, she asked him to find and print the X-ray as she continued to peruse the contents of the morgue refrigerator. It stood in the corner, larger than the one she owned at home. Inside, she found bodily fluids and other biologicals, neatly marked. She searched for the John Doe, grateful they hadn't been sent to the lab yet.

Taking out several tubes, she held them in her hand and chanted a spell.

"Essence of the magic, release itself,
Return to its owner so that none can see."

"Hurry, girl," Gibbs grunted. He continued to pace in front of the large window, his eyes darting around the nearly dark waiting room.

"Almost done," she said. The blood bubbled as the magic

released from the liquid, dissipating into the air. When she was sure the magic was removed from the samples, she placed the test tubes back into their positions and slammed the door shut. "I'm heading to the cooler," Annie advised.

"The VAU should be doing this, not you," Gibbs said harshly.

Ignoring him, Annie pulled open the steel doors; cold air rushed out at her.

"We don't have time," Gibbs grumbled.

Annie rolled her eyes and stepped inside the freezer.

"Just check for magic and leave," Gibbs ordered through gritted teeth.

The last time Annie had been in the cooler, the four large shelving units, four levels high had been packed with the dead, and the overflow of bodies had lain on tables shoved against every available wall space. Today, only the shelves were packed. She started with the first row, glancing quickly at each of the toe tags and moving to the next dead body to see whether it was a victim of a crime or natural causes.

The first row left her without her John Doe. She climbed up, keeping her feet wedged under the body bag. Slowly, she inched her way across, examining the tags. Some victims were zipped safely inside body bags while others lay with the bags opened, their skin exposed to the cold and their hands, feet, and hair tangled messes cascading from the plastic.

The second row also held no John Doe. Annie jumped down and started the process again. This time she was fortunate. The first body in this new row was hers.

She unzipped the bag quickly. The tell-tale scorch mark was dark and still smelled of burnt flesh. She ran a crystal over the short, fat body, bloated and gray with death. The rock glowed with a dim light, dark purple, nearly black, it radiated just enough light for Annie to know, John Doe was hit with black magic.

Gibbs's boots clacked against the cement floor.

"Black magic," she called out.

"Not as crazy as I thought you were. Now hurry up!"

Storing the first magical energy in her crystal, Annie moved to the stomach area where the mysterious object appeared on the X-ray. She moved the crystal across his abdomen. This time, the crystal glowed a clean, bright white light.

That's weird.

"Annie, now!" Gibbs shouted.

Fearing someone was coming, she hastily zipped the bag and marked the body for the VAU with magical locators before contacting Graham Lightner.

"Black magic." Annie said when he answered. His pen scratched against paper.

"Anything else?"

"I marked the file and the body. There's an X-ray that we didn't know about earlier. Bucky's pulling it now."

"Okay. I have the copy of the folder; we have a body to exchange it with. Did you find the evidence?" he asked.

"Gibbs is ornery. There's no time," Annie advised. More scratching on the other end of the phone.

"No problem. We'll handle it. Anything else?"

"Nope, do your thing."

"On it."

Finished in the cooler, Annie joined Gibbs in the empty morgue. He was eyeing the medical examiner, whose identification read Dr. Gordon Martz and who was walking from the hallway to the morgue holding a pile of folders.

Gibbs froze the waiting area and anything inside just as the stairwell door popped open. Graham Lightner and his team exited and joined Annie and Gibbs in the waiting room.

"Hey Annie, Gibbs. Good timing." Graham pointed to the medical examiner.

"Too close," Annie said.

They separated quickly. The VAU entered the morgue, leaving the medical examiner frozen in his spot.

Once inside the stairwell, Gibbs replaced the window on the door just as Annie's phone buzzed in her pocket. It was Bucky Hart.

"I printed the X-ray," he said.

"Any thoughts?" Annie asked.

"No clue what it is. I'll keep the alert on until VAU claims the body and does their thing. Anything else I can do for you?"

"VAU is here, so I think we're good for now. If anything else comes up, I'll let you know."

"So much for an easy case." Bucky whistled through the phone.

When Annie finished the call, Gibbs grumbled, reached for her hand and pulled her back up the stairs.

Milo Rawley answered the door in sweatpants that hung from his shrinking frame and were covered with large stains at the knees. His body swam in a large ripped sweatshirt with a hole on the side; he looked as though he were ten and wearing his father's clothes. He grunted and waved Annie into his house. She followed as Milo, her boss, shuffled his way to the small room at the back of his two-story home. He switched on the light and lowered himself into his squeaky desk chair with an irritated grunt.

"Why are you here?"

"You asked me to come."

At the door, a thin, pretty lady named Annette poked her head inside the small office, checking on her husband and his guest. Her bathrobe was pulled tightly around her, her face clean of makeup, her smile cheerful.

"Hi, Annie. Can I get you anything?" Annette asked cheerfully, as if she were unaware of the early hour.

"She's not staying," Milo groaned.

"Ugh. No wonder they dislike you, dear. If you need anything, Annie, please help yourself." Annette ran a hand through her short curly brown hair and pushed her thick glasses closer to her eyes.

"Thanks, Annette. Sorry to wake you."

"It's nothing, dear," she said. Her footsteps treaded down the hallway and up the stairs to bed.

When the door closed shut, Milo spoke. "You sure it's ours?" He regarded Annie, judged her. For a moment Annie doubted what she thought was the truth.

"It's definitely black magic at the site of the scorch mark where the electrocution spell hit. An X-ray was taken, and there's a white magic object in his stomach. I have the VAU already there."

Milo glanced at her. The low light cast shadows across his sallow skin. His recent weight loss had done little to bring him a healthy glow; it only made him appear sickly. "What's in his stomach?"

"We don't know. According to Bucky, the autopsy is scheduled for morning. Graham will have everything cleaned and taken care of long before then."

Milo picked up a pen and twisted it through his fingers, leaving Annie feeling like a teenager having to justify her actions. She took a slow breath, not giving him any satisfaction. She crossed her legs.

"And the blood?" Milo asked.

"I took care of it. Just sign the forms, and VAU will finish up." She summoned the form and floated it toward him.

Milo unrolled the scroll and read the declaration—her reasoning for stealing the magical body from a nonmagical entity, risking exposure. "You're a smart ass." After scratching his name, he handed it back to her. "It's all official."

Annie took it. "Have you ever heard of a wizard that can shoot electricity from their hands?"

"Nah. You need a spell for that. Gotta be a creature to have that kinda magic." It was the last thing Milo said to her before hoisting himself out of his chair and out of his home office, leaving Annie to let herself out.

CHAPTER 5

Wake me up before you go-go
Don't leave me hanging on like a yo-yo
Wake me up before you go-go
I don't want to miss it when you hit that high

THE ALARM PIERCED the darkness; even in her morning haze, Annie slammed the off button with her fist. As her brain stumbled through the fog, becoming aware of the day, the song on the radio wasn't lost on her.

Her body fought between wake and sleep; rolling over, she watched the bright numbers change to 5:31 a.m.

I could use one more hour.

Against all her wishes, Annie threw the covers off and popped up. Cham turned to his back. As much as she wanted to curl against him, she stood on the cold wood floor.

"You really have to leave so early?" Cham groaned. She leaned over, kissed his soft lips, and ran her hands through his already wild morning hair.

"Perkins Abernathy likes to get the autopsies done early. I have to get there," she said.

"I've got a missing person tracking again," Cham said.

Annie nodded. Another text had been sent to all wizard guards last night. Another missing person was reported on the south side of Chicago with the same unknown magical trace found at their residence.

"I wish I could help." But Annie had John Doe to contend with. She reached down and kissed him one more time. "I love you," she whispered and climbed off the bed.

"Love you. See you later." While he rolled over for a last few minutes of sleep, Annie threw on her work clothes, brushed her teeth, managed her unruly hair, and grabbed a breakfast Danish before heading out to the lab in the basement of Wizard Hall, all the while humming like she was hanging on like a yo-yo.

✿

The sun hadn't risen when Annie landed in the courtyard of Wizard Hall. Cold, blustery wind blew through her hair. She ran into the main entrance to the security desk where the day shift officer sat at his desk, reading the morning edition of the wizard newspaper, *The American Sphinx.*

"Annie. How's the dead wizard?" Manny asked with a wide smile. *He must've been here when the John Doe was brought in.* "You're way too chipper this morning," Annie groaned, then chuckled. "I'll let you know after the autopsy. So how're the wife and kids?"

Manny laughed with Annie. "Good. Two broomstick racers at Windmere." He pointed to the pot in the corner. "Coffee's loaded if you want some."

"Congrats. I wish I could, but no food or drink in the lab," Annie said. She waved and passed through the final entrance to the back hallway of the first floor.

Annie swung around to her left, bypassing the elevators for the stairs and nearly running to the basement. The staircase dropped her out by the library, which was still closed this early. She rarely saw the large, hand-carved oak doors closed shut, the way they would be until the librarian, Mrs. Cuttlebrink, opened them at her consistent time of nine in the morning.

As Annie passed the beautifully carved hanging art, she noticed the depictions of ancient wizard folklore, stories all magical children grew up learning. They were interspersed with scenes from wizard history in the United States, history she had learned as a student at Windmere.

Like they always did, her eyes found the carving of the woman who ironically looked just like her, with long flowing hair that blew behind her. The woman stood beside the carcass of a demon, her foot resting on the body, a sword held triumphantly in the air. Still to this day, no one had recognized the demon type that lay beneath her foot.

Strolling past the closed doors of the Records Chambers, Annie peered into the cafeteria, where elves and wizards were well into preparing for the breakfast shift. A few maintenance employees congregated at a clump of tables in the center of the room. Their laughs wafted through the mostly empty basement as they were either coming off the night shift or starting the day shift. Annie saw familiar faces, including Cham's brother, Jimmy Chamsky, who was jovially regaling his coworkers with some story. Heading past the maintenance office, which was open all night, Annie saw the manager was deep in a pile of paperwork.

The laboratory, where the autopsy would be performed, was hidden away at the end of the hallway. Annie opened the metal door and entered the most orderly and clean space in the entire Wizard Hall. The laboratory, which was built on top of the incinerators, rumbled beneath her feet when she stepped through the door.

The lab consisted of two large rooms. The first half was much like any morgue. Two stainless steel tables were set parallel to each other; above them, large tilted mirrors hung from the ceiling for easy viewing of autopsies.

Cabinets lined the perimeter of the room and were filled with beakers, test tubes, cauldrons, herbs, and other potion ingredients.

To Annie's left, a large work table was piled high with containers and folders.

The far right wall of the morgue contained a huge, thick, indestructible pane of glass, the kind used at zoos to keep animals from breaking through. It overlooked a massive yet empty gym. The walls were covered in blue mats, some stained, others ripped or burnt. Extra mats were piled along the far right wall. This half of the laboratory was used to test spells, potions, and black magical objects. The linoleum floor was covered in scorch marks and potions stains; there was one nasty burn running the length of the room and up the wall to the ceiling.

John Doe lay on the table closest to the window. A large mirror was already positioned above the table, angled for a good view of the body.

Who else is coming?

Perkins Abernathy, the lab manager, was starting his examination by reviewing the X-ray on the light box along the back wall.

"Hi, Perkins."

"Annie. Interesting case." Perkins smiled and returned to the X-ray, taking measurements of the object and its location inside the stomach cavity.

"No kidding. Body came okay, I see." Annie donned the required work suit, slipping on the large blue coveralls, shoe covers, and gloves. Lastly, she placed on a hat with a large faceguard protecting her eyes. Hot under the shield, her breath fogged the visor.

"I still can't figure out what this is," Perkins admitted, joining her at the table but leaving the X-ray on the light box.

"We'll find out soon enough."

When Perkins finished with his gloves and lowered his visor, he began the 'Y' incision through the chest, opening up the skin and muscles. The stench of death hit Annie immediately. She held the side of the table to keep from passing out.

"Okay, girl?" Gibbs asked, entering the lab. He had come from his missing person's case and ran over to back up Annie in this murder case. He yanked on his own gear before Annie could answer. "Abernathy," Gibbs greeted the lab manager, then joined them at the table.

Perkins detached the stomach from the rest of the organs and placed it on the table behind him. Annie tentatively followed.

Perkins ran a knife through the stomach; contents spilled over, landing in a plastic storage box. Another distinct smell assaulted Annie's nose. Something hadn't digested before the victim died.

"You hanging in there, Annie? Gibbs?"

"Yeah. Still gross though," she answered, trying to breathe at the same time.

Gibbs looked over her shoulder, neither fascinated nor bored. Though he was far more used to autopsies than Annie was, he was pale and breathing through his mouth.

He's more bothered than he lets on.

Annie grimaced when Perkins stuck a hand inside the organ. Bodily fluids and flesh squished under his fingers, and she blanched. Gibbs grimaced and looked away, even though the splish-splashing of stomach contents continued.

After feeling around in the stomach, Perkins plucked out the mysterious object, holding it in his palm.

"What the hell?" Annie reached forward. The object was a large, thick ring with a dense band.

"Something worth killing for," Gibbs commented.

Annie wiped away stomach biologicals to examine the ring more closely. It consisted of a flat top, with a raised six-pointed star at the center. Three stones made up the corners of a square; the fourth corner was a set of empty prongs.

"It's missing a stone. Can you check inside for it?" Annie pointed, showing Perkins the missing stone.

He widened the incision in the stomach and dumped the contents into the bowl. Annie looked away, exchanging disgusted looks with Gibbs. Perkins sloshed around in the half-digested food and stomach acid. It slopped against the side of the bowl. Gibbs turned green underneath his shield.

Finding nothing, Perkins examined the inside of the stomach, kneading every recess, bump, and centimeter of the stomach lining. "Sorry, Annie, there's nothing in there."

"It probably didn't pass into the intestines yet, right?"

"Doubtful. Let me see the ring."

Annie passed Perkins the artifact. He collected the ring's magic from his crystal. Saving the trace, he passed the crystal over the victim's intestines, which remained dull and lifeless.

"It could have been lost centuries ago," Perkins suggested.

"Probably," Annie agreed. "Thanks for checking. Do you mind if we clean it off now? I'd like to take it with me."

"Have at it. I'll start a full autopsy and let you know if I find something. Do you need anything from the body?"

"Just the normal stuff, DNA samples, and fingerprints for Bucky. We still need to find out who this is."

"Will do. If you need anything else, let me know."

Perkins began his more thorough examination and became singularly focused on that, paying little attention to Annie and Gibbs at the sink. Annie ran cold water over the ring, rinsing away slime and stomach contents.

"Whoever had this ring made was extremely large," Annie noted as she gently massaged the ring clean.

"Yeah. Looks like."

When the water ran clear, she dried the ring off and handed it to Gibbs, a large man on his own. He slipped the ring over his largest finger. It spun and slid off easily.

Annie dumped the ring into a plastic evidence bag.

"I'm heading to the library to see what I can find on this. Tonight the market?" she asked Gibbs.

"Call when you're ready for me," he said, and they stripped off the work gear, dumping it into the incinerator. It sizzled and popped.

She said goodbye to Perkins, who was so wrapped in what he was doing, he didn't seem to notice.

❋

Mrs. Cuttlebrink, the Wizard Hall librarian, flew through the stacks holding thousands of books, scrolls and tablets; some as early as the fifth century. Wisps of her salt-and-pepper hair danced out of her normally tight bun as she skipped happily on her short, thick legs to the table where Annie perused several books the librarian had waiting for her. "Here's some more for you, Annie."

The first pile contained encyclopedias of Middle Eastern designs. Many represented cults, clubs, religions, and other organizations originating in that area. Mrs. Cuttlebrink was most certain that the brooch worn by John Doe was indeed from that region, as per her research; however, they still had no idea what their particular design represented.

Maybe it was meant to just be pretty.

A second pile of tomes, larger than the first, contained both general books about ancient jewelry and some with a distinct focus on the Middle East. Annie pulled down another book from that pile to peruse.

The harsh library light and dry air caused her to blink rapidly. Annie pushed the book aside and rubbed her temple that ached. She slid her chair backwards, arched her tightened back, and stretched her arms above her head.

Drawing a cleansing breath, Annie sniffed a scent of lemon. As she glanced around the library, she finally noticed that the dark, wood-covered walls gleamed brightly. High bookshelves had been repacked; the books were neatly lined, alphabetized, and reorganized. The cobwebs that normally appeared from the ceiling to the top shelves had been swept away. Even the table, which was covered in books, shined after an extreme cleaning.

It must be slow in the library. Annie chuckled at the thought that Mrs. Cuttlebrink was bored.

"Are you okay, Annie?" the librarian asked.

Even after rummaging the stacks all morning, Mrs. Cuttlebrink still felt fresh and overly excited by this project. "I'm fine. Tired, a little hungry, and... well, frustrated with the lack of... anything."

"Oh, sweetie, we have lots more books to look through." Mrs. Cuttlebrink smiled. The kindly woman held up another book before opening it and skimming the page. As the librarian read the passage and turned the page, her eyes lit up and her smile grew wider like an excited child who had opened a birthday present and gotten what she wanted. Mrs. Cuttlebrink turned the page again; her smile couldn't have gotten any wider. She pointed and tapped the book.

What question did she answer?

In a flash, the librarian pulled up another book, laid it open on the table, and cast a spell with her palms above the books. The pages flipped rapidly, succumbing to the magical order to search out whatever it was she requested. As quickly as it started, the pages stopped, and the book flopped open to the designated page. Mrs. Cuttlebrink scanned a passage and returned to the first book. Her eyes volleyed back and forth as she verified her findings.

Anxious for an answer, Annie examined the piles in front of her and pulled down a handwritten scroll that teetered on top of a pile. Unrolling the paper, she separated several pages, scanning the handwritten notes.

These are the adventures of Nicholas Roerich.

Out of the Russian city, with the scent of people, of animals as they meandered through the muddy streets, I find myself in Tibet, to the clean, clear mountain air that revives my abilities and gives me back my clarity as I search for my place in the universe. I'm sure of the answers I seek...

...The tea awakened me to the purpose of the sky, of the stars, of the meaning of all things not of this world, of all of the mysteries that are for me to discover.

...The people of the mountains shared their yak meat, their berries, and substance, and they let me into their world to show me the grandest of artifacts: the ring of great power, the ring that could make the wearer successful, give them insight, enlighten them.

The band is so thick, made of iron and copper. It is old and well used. It was made for a man of great power, of great girth. The craftsman who created this work of art did so with great care, using the powerful, beautiful, ethereal Chintamani Stones. This is where the power of the ring originates from.

If a wearer has magic within, he could live forever.

Annie scratched the words Chintamani stones on the paper; she had never heard of rocks by that name. She reread the description of the ring. There was no mention of the flat top or the raised six-pointed star, though that could have been added at a later date.

She took the ring from the plastic pouch and placed it on her finger, examining each feature. Cool metal vibrated against her skin; she hadn't noticed the vibrations before. Pulling out the magnifying glass, she examined the raised star and compared its metal to that of the base of the ring. It was most definitely the same metal as the rest of the ring.

It's probably not the same ring.

Annie sighed.

"Do you have something Annie?" Mrs. Cuttlebrink asked.

"Not really. Maybe. There's a description in here about a ring with four stones called the Chintamani Stones. Have you heard of them?"

Mrs. Cuttlebrink smiled. "Yes. I have. Stones from heaven. Can I see the ring?" Annie passed her the hefty jewelry. Mrs. Cuttlebrink inspected it up close, her fingers grazing the remaining three stones. "Yes, Annie dear. These look like moldavite stones. Stones from heaven. Do you know what that means?" Mrs. Cuttlebrink asked.

"Stones from heaven? No. I don't." Annie thought. "Unless... it's literal?"

Mrs. Cuttlebrink smiled again.

"Meteorites," they said together.

"I thought I had something in my reading, but this..." Mrs. Cuttlebrink rolled the ring in her thick fingers and stopped again on the flat surface, staring at the raised star and the stones.

"So, these stones from heaven... what power do they hold? According to the scant passage I read, the wearer lives forever?" Annie asked.

Mrs. Cuttlebrink handed the ring back to Annie. "Well. We know from past cases how many artifacts claim to do that. I highly doubt this ring does that. What I do know about the Chintamani Stones is they supposedly bring luck and fulfillment to the wearer. It also allows the user to see into the past and future. And yes, some cultures do believe the Chintamani makes one immortal."

"That's one powerful ring. Which give motive for the murder."

Annie returned the stone to the evidence bag. "The star might tell us who this ring was originally created for." She glanced back at the scroll for additional information until the location Atlantis caught her eye.

"Oh. Here. Chintamani Stones. Four stones were cut from a larger one. Three of the stones were gifted: one to an abbot at a lamasery, one to Emperor Tazlovoo of Atlantis, and another went to King Solomon." Annie looked at Mrs. Cuttlebrink. "*The* King Solomon?"

"Can I see the passage?" Mrs. Cuttlebrink, took her time to read the scroll. Her hands shook, and the paper fluttered while she read. "Okay, yes. The Russian Mystic Roerich. According to this, four stones were cut from one larger stone and were gifted to four different people. One of these men—or possibly all of them—had rings created. Wealthy, powerful. That would make sense. Let's see…" she continued reading the passage. "There's nothing in this description that matches ours. So ours might have been from one of these men. Emperor Tazlovoo. King Solomon." She looked up from the scroll. "A six-pointed star. The ring please?" She stared intently at the flat top of the ring as Annie handed it to her. "That's it. The stones, the six-pointed star. King Solomon!" Mrs. Cuttlebrink was so enthusiastic that she bolted from her chair and headed to the stacks, as spry as a child.

As she levitated and flew, she displaced the air with her body, leading to popping noises throughout the stacks. Several heavy tomes came crashing down; the force of the crash vibrated across the stone floor and against the wood walls. "No, not this one." Air sizzled and popped again as she floated along the aisle to another section.

Through the air, a book flew toward Annie and skipped across the table. Mrs. Cuttlebrink, close behind the book, was winded and sweaty when she returned. "I didn't put it together until you read that scroll, but I think that's the Ring of Solomon."

Really? "That's a fable. A legend." The words flew out before Annie could stop herself.

Mrs. Cuttlebrink pointed to the book that had skipped and slid beside Annie. The title on the leather-bound book was written in Hebrew, but as Annie waved her palm her across the words, they shimmered and transformed as the magic translated the title: *The Book of King Solomon.* Annie glanced at the librarian with raised eyebrows before opening the faded front cover and reading through the list of short stories contained inside. She shuffled through the yellow, cracked pages.

The ring, created for King Solomon, was forged from iron and copper. Its flat top and raised six-pointed star at the center was used to seal official documents of King Solomon.

Over several years, the ring changed considerably with the addition four Chintamani Stones that were gifted to the king by a rock cutter who had found the stone in his quarry. The stones were reported to bring luck and fulfillment to the wearer. In some cultures, the stones gave the wearer the power to see into the past and future. Some cultures think the Chintamani makes one immortal.

The ring metamorphosed again when the king wished to control the djinn, and his mystics imbued the ring with the power to do that.

My ring!
"So you're telling me you believe the mystical Ring of Solomon

existed and still exists today—and this is it?" Annie had never come across a biblical artifact; she had a difficult time wrapping her brain around what she was holding.

"Yes."

"He couldn't have possibly been able to control the djinn. Unless… unless King Solomon was a wizard?" Annie thought back to Wizard Guard training. She remembered lessons about the djinn—a Middle Eastern version of genies, tricksters who granted wishes for unsuspecting victims. The wish always came with a backfire, another name for a payment in exchange for the wish fulfillment.

But King Solomon, a wizard! The ring wouldn't work without magic.

Mrs. Cuttlebrink broke into laughter, high and innocent like a young girl's. "I'm sorry, Annie, but you're being too skeptical. And after all you've seen as a witch. The brooch design is Middle Eastern, and the djinn roamed the Middle Eastern desert. It's possible, and it's staring you right in the face. Though you are technically correct. I have no proof King Solomon was actually a wizard."

The ring vibrated on Annie's finger, tickling her skin. She had just read two ancient ring descriptions, and one matched her ring.

I can't believe I'm holding something so old and so rare.

"Okay. Say this is the Ring of Solomon. Where has it been for almost two thousand years, why did it resurface now, who wanted it, and who died for it?"

"All valid questions dear. I'll be happy to keep digging for information, but you'll have to go to the black market for the rest."

"Yeah. We're going tonight." Annie sighed as her phone buzzed from her back pocket.

She glanced at the caller ID. "What's up, Bucky?"

"Max White in telecommunications picked up a tip to the police department. Possible murder weapon located in Busse Woods," he answered.

Annie grimaced. "Okay," she said with a deep sigh. "They're bringing an investigative unit back to the clearing?"

"Yeah. That's what Max said."

More pictures and more footprints all over my crime scene.

"I wonder if someone is trying to throw off the police," Annie muttered to herself.

"Then why hide it back at the crime scene? That ties the case very clearly to that location."

The pain in Annie's temple spread to her forehead and down her neck. "That's what's been bothering me. Why leave the body there in the first place? I know criminals aren't necessarily smart, but the magical community knows you don't risk exposure, regardless of your criminal leanings."

"Yeah. Doesn't make sense. You can worry about it later. They're on the way now," Bucky advised.

"Thanks for the info. I'll let you know what comes of it."

CHAPTER 6

ANNIE AND GIBBS teleported behind five tall, wide ever-green trees that blocked their landing from the mass of people that had taken over the clearing where John Doe had been murdered. The two wizard guards observed the scene through the thick branches as crime scene investigators combed the area for additional clues. Police officers charged with guarding the perimeter paced along the barrier made of crime scene tape and traffic barricades, keeping the growing crowd from infringing on the evidence. Journalists and other onlookers were forced to refrain from leaving the small corner. Hundreds of them were corralled so tightly that they could barely take notes or photos as they clawed and argued their way to the front of their makeshift paddock.

It was organized chaos.

Annie focused on the crime scene team, observing them immersed in their search for clues as they trudged through the remaining snow and piles of thick mud. The investigators followed after a police officer who was holding the leash of a very large black lab.

The journalist's pool spread along the trees, getting closer to the location where Annie and Gibbs were hiding.

"What the hell?" Gibbs muttered as he and Annie inched their way around the farthest tree, away from the horde.

They returned their gaze to the clearing where the dog,

so intent and focused on a scent, led his handler in large circles around the perimeter tape, slowly tightening the circles and walking dangerously close to the portal five feet from where John Doe had been found.

Camera flashes sparkled against the bare trees.

The well-trained animal sat in the snow, wagged its tail, and swiped away the snow, leaving its tail covered in mud. Far more attuned to the low frequencies around it, the dog turned to the portal, growled, and bared its teeth.

"They found something," Gibbs mumbled.

Voices grew louder and closer to their location as the journalists continued moving through the trees for a better view of the search.

"We may have to leave soon," Annie whispered.

An unlucky crime scene unit member plunged a shovel into the frozen mud. Instead of the difficult dig they must have expected, the ground yielded easily; someone had recently turned over the dirt.

A magical had to have placed this object here.

The man heaved rapidly. Even though the air was a chilly thirty degrees, he sweated profusely and threw off his heavy winter jacket. He dug a little further until finally the shovel pinged against a metal object. Two members of the crime scene unit joined and assisted by removing the dirt, revealing a long, thin rod with two prongs at the end. The discovery drew *ooohs* and *ahhhs*. Pens clicked and scratched, bulbs flashed.

"Oh, you've got to be kidding me," Annie whispered. She and Gibbs exchanged glances. "There was only one burn mark."

"Throwing off the nonmagical police. Smart plan," he grunted.

"I can't believe the nonmagical police is gonna believe that is the murder weapon. They're not stupid," she answered.

Annie's opinion didn't matter; the press was thrilled with the new evidence. Camera flashes burst in rapid succession, like a lightning storm. Annie paced to clear her head.

"Annie?"

"Gibbs, they planted evidence outside the portal. Why do that? Why tie this place that closely to murder? They could've left it as a dump site only. What the hell were they thinking?" Annie's voice was louder than she had anticipated.

Gibbs glared at her as if warning her to calm down and lower her voice. "That's all fine and good, girl. At least there's a weapon they can explain away."

Annie continued to pace. *Sometimes I want to shake you.* She often believed Gibbs's dislike for all things nonmagical made him ignorant to all things nonmagical.

"We have a glamored, fake body in their morgue, with a burn mark that didn't leave burnt skin on the weapon. It might not even be strong enough to cause that damage. They really fucked up." She was nearly whispering, though her voice rose with each word. *Act like you understand!*

"Girl, it's not my first rodeo. Call Graham, let the VAU deal with it." Gibbs observed the crowd of nonmagicals, their reaction to the murder and to the proceedings. "Any ID on the victim?" he asked.

Annie checked her phone, texts, and emails. Rather than waiting, she texted Bucky, though she was sure that if he had found something, he would have let her know. "Nothing yet," she advised.

Helpless and waiting to begin their investigation, the crowd grew thicker. The police, having had enough of the enthusiastic meanderings and noise, pushed them out of the clearing and down the path to the parking lot. A few civilians lingered in the trees.

Gibbs grew impatient waiting for the cops to clear the scene and for the crowd to disperse. He took his turn to pace their small waiting area.

"You can leave if you'd like. I'll wait for the crowd to clear," Annie offered.

Gibbs grumbled under his breath, summoned a thick, heavy blanket, and laid it in the snow, taking a seat.

"How long you think they'll be there?" he asked.

"No clue. It's not like it is with magic."

Beyond the trees, the dog continued to follow a scent. After twenty minutes, a detective in charge finally determined there was nothing left to find, and the dog was led to parking lot. Annie sat beside Gibbs on the blanket. He took a swig from his flask.

"Want?" Gibbs asked.

Annie grabbed the drink and took a large gulp. The alcohol warmed as it slid down her throat. She shifted closer to Gibbs and let him radiate his heat. After one more swig, Annie handed him back his flask.

"Ramsey's a good reference," Gibbs admitted. Annie was taken aback; he normally had nothing nice to say about the nonmagical community.

"Yeah. Two cases, and both are doozies," she agreed.

The voices they'd been hearing all day dissipated, growing softer as the crowd dispersed and headed to the parking lot. "Shouldn't be long now."

Annie's phone vibrated in her pocket. She took it out and read the screen. "No name. Fingerprints and DNA not in any databases. Bucky sent everything to the Middle East Wizard Guard. They're very interested in the brooch design. But he didn't say why."

Gibbs took another swig and offered her more; she drank and let the alcohol warm her.

Car doors slammed shut, engines revved, and tires crunched on ice and snow as cars pulled away. Annie pushed a branch away and watched the last of the reporters, crime scene techs, and police leave the scene. They waited an additional ten minutes just in case.

"I think it's safe," Annie said finally. She and Gibbs ignored the crime scene tape and entered the clearing. "I'm glad we got the aerial view before they completely destroyed the crime scene."

The sun hid behind a thick layer of storm clouds that weren't predicted to disperse any time soon but that covered the clearing in a gray light. Annie used her flashlight to view the footprints against the mud.

"There's nothing left here." Gibbs kicked the upturned dirt with the steel toe of his boot.

"I think the cattle prod was enough for today," Annie groaned sarcastically.

Gibbs grunted.

Am I irritating you today, Gibbs?

He walked the clearing; his flashlight highlighted several spots as he noted footsteps and drag marks that remained after all of the traffic. The clearing had been thoroughly combed through and traversed by too many people.

I doubt the footprints will be of any help now.

The only part of the crime scene that was still visible from the original aerial view was a square spot where the body was found. Annie waved her flashlight across the patch of mud. John Doe's impression was still in the earth.

She summoned the case file and dug through to find two pictures—one of the victim, the other of the aerial view. His shoes were caked in mud from the soles to the heels and even the toes. Possibly the mud came from running through the forest preserve, but possibly it was a result of being dragged, which would explain the thin lines that crisscrossed the clearing.

As Annie examined the pictures, it became clear that the remains of a line from the portal to this square patch of mud were still visible.

"Annie?" Gibbs asked softly and joined her to peer at the images.

"He was dragged away from the portal and killed here, I think. Before he was able to sell the ring. But then, why kill him and not take the ring?"

"Since the ring was too large to swallow, he magically hid it. Someone killed him but couldn't find it on his body," Gibbs said and summoned his crystal.

"Why not take the body then?" she asked but stopped when she saw movement in the trees. Gibbs pocketed the rock.

"Oh crap," Annie groaned as her worst nightmare approached from the trees: Rebekah Stoner. The television journalist had been investigating Annie, convinced Annie was something other than she said she was.

She doesn't realize how much she really knows.

"Anne Pearce? How nice to see you again." Rebekah's voice carried implication. Annie did her best to avoid any look of surprise or worry.

"Rebekah."

"And who is this? I'm Rebekah Stoner." She held out a perfectly manicured hand to Gibbs, who glowered but reluctantly took hold of it. The journalist winced at his grip. "Ah, I see you're investigating this case as well." She shook out her numb hand and stepped away from Gibbs.

"Just curious," Annie said.

Rebekah Stoner always seemed put together, more so than Annie could ever hope to be while on a case. She hiked through the snow in fashion boots with a thin heel that was caked in mud. Annie smirked when the reporter tripped, getting stuck in the thick, wet earth and ruining the fancy leather boots.

"Damn." Rebekah said while pulling free her thin high heel. Stumbling through the underbrush, she positioned herself dangerously close to the portal. It was all Gibbs and Annie could do to not alert her of something fishy or draw her attention to the magic. But the overly curious reporter couldn't help herself. She glanced in its direction, rubbing her arms for additional warmth even through her very thick winter jacket. She took a tentative stop closer to the portal.

"There's something here," she pronounced.

Annie and Gibbs exchanged glances. His eyes crinkled with a strict warning. Annie returned a grimace of her own.

"Uh, Rebekah. Not sure what you're talking about, but there's nothing here besides us."

The reporter's attention now on Gibbs, who glowered at her as she fidgeted with the fingers of her expensive leather gloves. She took another step closer to the chaotic magic. "Can't you hear it? Something's buzzing, like it's breathing." Rebekah reached out to the portal. Her fingers grazed the turbulent air where the magic fought with the nonmagical plane. She pulled her fingers away.

"There's nothing there, Rebekah," Annie cooed, but she couldn't take her eyes from the portal, as if she really knew it was there.

Annie and Gibbs stood shocked as Rebekah shoved her gloved hand through the portal. Icy wind gusted and whipped around the clearing. Annie shivered, and her teeth chattered.

"Weren't you asked to leave the area? Going to jail for obstruction isn't good for your career," Annie said. The wind continued to whistle through bare trees. The shrill noise unnerved Annie.

Frightened, Rebekah yanked her hand from the portal. The submerged glove came out covered with fine ice crystals. She warmed her frozen hand inside her coat pocket and glared at the empty space.

"Yeah, that would be a bad thing," she muttered. Looking afraid of what she couldn't see, Rebekah backed away. "I hope you find what you're looking for," she said to Annie and Gibbs.

Behind Rebekah's forced smile, was an anxious, unfocused nonmagical, a side effect of the magic surrounding the portal and the protection spell. Why she felt the portal more acutely than other nonmagicals made no sense to Annie and Gibbs. As the reporter continued to gain distance between herself and them, her gaze switched to Annie.

When she safely reached the tree line, Gibbs asked, "So, that's the reporter?"

"Yeah." Annie kept a close eye on her, watching as Rebekah

scanned the muddy earth looking for something only Annie and Gibbs could see.

"Be careful. That girl doesn't know it, but she's on to you. Call Lightner to take care of it. Until then, get rid of her so we can look for magic."

"On it."

Hiding behind a tree, Rebekah waited patiently with distrust and fear as she waited for Annie and Gibbs to finish their search. Annie waved to her with an open palm as if that were perfectly normal to do—and cast a spell in her direction. Rebekah turned abruptly, stumbling in the weeds and mud along the path to the parking lot. Annie continued to add magic to the spell, ensuring Rebekah wouldn't break free and sneak back to the clearing.

A metal door slammed shut, an engine hummed, and tires rolled along the road. Annie dropped the spell.

After a quick glance around the clearing, Annie summoned the aerial view. "Look for magic in that empty square. Based on footsteps that were here yesterday, I think he ran in from this direction." Annie pointed from the parking lot to the portal. "These drag marks make me think he was pulled from the portal and killed in this empty square." She walked to what was left of the bare spot. "I think he died here after being dragged."

Based on the height of the victim, Gibbs held his crystal over the location he estimated the spell had landed. He deftly maneuvered the crystal until the rock lit up. "Got it." He examined several shades and brightnesses of the light, which all pinpointed to one location. "There's four different signatures. Odd."

"There was only one on the body," Annie said. Gibbs grunted. Annie dialed Perkins Abernathy in the lab to verify the number of energy signatures that were really on the body.

"You're kidding, right?" Perkins asked.

"No. Gibbs reads four here."

"And they all lead to one pinpoint of magic? That would be nearly impossible for four separate spells to be cast and hit the exact same location, to create one six-inch-long mark across a victim's chest. Like four different archers slinging their arrows and having all the arrows land in the same spot."

"I know," Annie said, "but that's what we see."

"Okay, Annie. I'll check and get back to you." Perkins sighed.

"So do you think the spells mixed and made it appear like one spell so we wouldn't know?" Annie asked Gibbs after she hung up on Perkins.

"Maybe."

Gibbs and Annie held a total of four crystals, one in each hand. Easily they followed and tracked the magical trace toward the parking lot. Each spell was strong, well-cast and impossibly accurate.

They met at a location where four individual spells belonging to four different people had been cast. Wizards had been standing in a neat row. The remnants of their footprints confirmed that.

"This isn't the kill spell," Gibbs said.

Annie examined the spells she had captured in her own crystals. "What kind of spell do you think?"

Her phone buzzed, a call from Perkins Abernathy. "What did you find?" she asked.

"Five spells. Four summoning, one kill shot," he said.

"Thanks, Perkins." She hung up and turned to Gibbs. "You're right. There are four summoning spells and one kill shot."

Gibbs tracked the magical energy back toward the portal and past the kill spot. He stopped at the turbulent air and ran the crystal through the portal.

"Was he entering the portal when he was hit?" Annie asked.

Gibbs continued to follow the trace in and out of the portal. "Summoned from inside the portal and dragged to the kill spot, looks like." He followed the trace back toward the body drop.

"So," Annie queried.

Gibbs was quiet, lost in his thoughts. "Matches what Perkins found. Summoned from the portal, died here." He glanced inside his crystal again, then back to the ground. His eyes darted from the four footsteps to the portal and back to the drop site. "Scenario?" he asked.

"Well, based on the magical trace, the footprints, and the drag marks, I'd say he was coming to the market to sell the ring and was chased here by the four people who cast those spells. My guess, just based on human nature, is that he stole it from them and was caught before he got inside the market." Annie stopped for a minute. "He swallowed or magically hid the ring in his stomach and figured they were angry enough to kill him. They did so, but they couldn't find the ring. Which leads me to my initial question: Why the hell did they leave the body here, outside the portal? Why not take the body with them?"

"Some didn't care—they took care of business and left. Thought the ring was hidden elsewhere," he murmured.

"Either that or they were discovered and had to leave, or…" Annie looked at him, a serious grimace across her lips. "Or they weren't from the U.S. They might have been unaware of our procedures or the traffic flow into this park" Annie sighed.

And that led back to the Middle East.

CHAPTER 7

"DO YOU HAVE to go back to the market tonight? It'll still be there tomorrow," Cham whispered, so close to Annie's ear that his warm breath tickled her skin. His soft lips grazed her neck, her collarbone. Annie's breath sped up. She clenched a fist to keep control.

His kisses rose up the back of her neck until she arched backwards and ran her fingers through the soft curls at his neck. He slipped a warm hand inside her shirt, but she unclenched her fist and pulled his hand away.

"I have to go," she groaned.

Cham's lips caressed hers, and his tongue pried open her mouth. She had no desire to stop him as his tongue met hers. Annie nibbled his bottom lip, and her breasts heaved up and down against his chest. She clung to him, wrapped her arms around his neck as he lifted her into his lap. She sunk into his kiss, deep into the warmth as his tongue continued to play with hers.

Reluctantly, Annie opened an eye after another minute. The light of the streetlamp outside her window drew her away from him and pulled her out of his protective embrace. She sighed.

"I have to go soon," she whispered. Cham groaned slightly and detangled his hands from her hair.

"Later." He kissed her one last time before Annie climbed from his lap and glanced out the window. The silver Prius belonging to none of her neighbors was parked across the street where it had been since she arrived home. She wouldn't have given it much thought until she took a bag of trash outside and saw Rebekah Stoner sitting inside. The reporter was like a pit bull with a tight grip, and Annie suspected she wouldn't let go easily.

"The reporter's still out there," she told Cham.

"She's definitely persistent." Cham glanced though the sheer drapes as the reporter sipped from her thermos. "You really need to have Graham deal with her." Cham put an arm around Annie's waist and pulled her into his lap where he nuzzled her neck.

"Another problem for another day." She leaned into him, accepting his kiss. His left hand fell to her breast. She let it rest there.

He pulled away. "Annie, she's already figured out way too much. You need to have it taken care of."

"I know." She planted her lips on his to keep from discussing it further. His deep, slow kiss made her head spin. She moaned and writhed as his fingers caressed her nipple.

A cell phone vibrated against the coffee table.

"Stop," she whispered.

"Don't go."

"Dead body, outside the portal. I have to go. Gibbs is ready."

Reluctantly, she sat up and straightened out her shirt. Cham stared with a wistful gaze.

"What?" She ran her fingers through her hair, flattening and detangling the bushy mane.

"You're beautiful."

"I wish I could stay." She breathed deeply, taking in his spicy scent before letting him walk her to the back door, away from the reporter.

Snow fell, not heavy enough to distract her teleportation but just fluffy enough to be pretty.

"Be careful. Call me when you get back. I'll come over."

"Always."

Cham's face was a blur as Annie took off and floated away from that warm and lovely space. She landed easily behind the evergreen trees where it was cold and dark. Gibbs was already there and was assessing their safety through the thick, snow-covered evergreen branches.

"Well?" she asked.

Gibbs glanced at her. His sharp eyes examined her, leaving her feeling exposed. He finished his observations with a smirk. "Your shirt's buttoned wrong," he said, then returned to the clearing.

Embarrassed, Annie zipped her jacket to her chin. "There, can we go?"

He grunted, and she followed him onto a seldom-used, narrow path. She wrapped her arms around herself as the snow fell.

I should've worn a heavier coat.

The chilly air blustered and blew the snow like a whirlpool. "The reporter's staking out my house again," Annie said as she pushed a branch out of her way. Snow blew in her face.

Nothing rattled Gibbs, though he stopped momentarily as if gathering his thoughts before continuing down the path. "Call Lightner and have her dealt with."

"Tomorrow."

Gibbs grumbled something unintelligible. Annie knew he was irritated that she hadn't taken care of the reporter.

I'll get yelled at later.

The teleportation spot was a mile from the lesser-used portal they were planning to use tonight. It was a well-hidden, difficult portal to access, and in the dark the snow-covered path was slippery and rough. Annie's heavy work boots had trouble gaining solid footing.

Low-hanging branches caught in her hair and scratched her coat as the path continued to narrow. The sound irritated her like nails on a blackboard bothered others. She twisted sideways to avoid the sound, but her boots got twisted and tangled in the underbrush and a tight tree root. Annie shook her foot out of the frozen tangle of foliage and slipped against the tree. Finally freeing herself, she picked up her speed to catch Gibbs and his long, steady strides.

All portals were hidden either behind trees and boulders or created in difficult-to-access locations. This portal had been generated behind a six-foot-wide evergreen and hung above a small patch of ground covered in needleweed, a magical ivy that attached itself to anything that came in contact with it. The only way to the portal was through a very thin path four inches wide. Tonight, the path was covered in snow.

"Hold a light out," Gibbs ordered in that irritating way he sometimes spoke to her.

Even though Annie was the lead on this case, it wasn't worth an argument. She pulled out her quartz crystal, swiping her palm across the pink rock. It cast a dim light, enough for Gibbs to send a spell across the patch of needleweed to reveal the still-green fauna. When the small trail was visible, they skirted along the path, avoiding the foliage.

All the portals radiated icy air, colder than the thirty degrees of the rest of the forest. Annie shivered and lowered her hat around ears. A gust of wind blew and swirled around the trees, whistling through the branches.

The portals are active.

Rebekah should have sensed danger, depression, or sadness, and that alone would have made her flee the area if not the portal itself. That was the purpose of the portal and the magical protection around the market. But Rebekah had known it was there, had put her hand through the portal, and had felt the power, the magic. Annie grazed this portal with her fingertips—icy. She pulled her hand away and blew on her fingers to warm them.

It was electric, buzzing.

"Annie. What's wrong?" Gibbs noticed her hesitation.

"Hear that? Something's different with the portal. The wind. It's…" She bent closer to the portal and heard what Rebekah must have heard. "The static. It's popping," she said. Static formed when the nonmagical and magical entities mixed and fought for control of this sliver of space. But tonight it was audible, like a radio station out of range. Gibbs listened intently as the air crackled.

"Different," he agreed.

Annie summoned her cursed athame that was stored in a binding around her calf. With a tight grip, she plunged the knife inside the portal, sparking it to life. A swirling tornado hung before her that pulsed and expanded. Lightning flashed violently, brilliantly lighting the area. She stuck her hand inside; lightning struck again quickly.

"Something's going on," Gibbs said as they crossed the enlarged threshold together. As the last foot crossed the entrance, the portal shut behind them, plunging them into the noisy market.

Though it was dark and cold with a layer of snow on the ground outside the market, the inside was a balmy consistent seventy degrees. Anyone inside was unaffected by activity beyond the protective shield. It was how this market had been maintained for many millennia.

Annie scanned the familiar cornucopia of black magical accoutrements: crystal balls, herbs, body parts, and creatures that roamed the aisles. Wizards dressed in traditional clothing or street clothes crisscrossed the market as they went about their business.

A high shrill rang out above her. She examined the thick stone wall that wove around the perimeter of the market. It stretched high above them and met the protection spell. Annie did a double take. In an empty corner of the market, snow fell through the protection spell and cascaded gently to the ground. It must have breached the spell for a lengthy period of time; there was quite a large pile melting in the corner. Annie touched Gibbs's arm and pointed.

He followed her gaze to the wafting snow and summoned a bit of it, examining it before it melted away. "The protection shield is breaking down," he said.

Above them, beyond the haze of smog, dust, dung, and smoke

that blanketed the market, a patch of Chicagoland sky was visible. In that small patch, the market haze was sucked beyond the protection spell, escaping into Busse Woods.

"That reporter did more than sense the portal," Gibbs reflected.

Annie nodded. "I thought the same thing. I haven't been to the market in weeks. I wonder when and what happened to make it break down. Coincidence, or is it related to John Doe and the ring?" she asked.

"Doesn't matter if it is. The protection shield is breaking down. That's a problem for everyone," Gibbs commented, his gaze still in the night sky. A gust of wind from the woods blew in through the protection shield, swirling the hazy mixture and dissipating the fog. The visible sky was clear and beautiful.

"Did you and Mrs. Cuttlebrink discover anything about the ring?" Gibbs asked. They moved to a sparse crowd.

"We think it's the Ring of Solomon." Annie lowered her voice. Gibbs pulled her arm, yanking her from a large contingent of wizards who, based on their thick accents, seemed to be from Germany.

"Is she sure?"

"Pretty sure."

Gibbs held his finger to his lips, and they entered down a busy aisle.

The black market didn't exist in Busse Woods, only the four U.S. portals did. The physical market lived on an alternate plane of existence that was accessed through these portals. There were magical entrances scattered throughout the world, and the protective shield allowed the portals to remain hidden and safe.

With the largest population of witches and wizards currently in the United States, the busiest hours were dusk to dawn, though the market remained open twenty-four hours a day. English was the most common language, spoken in many foreign accents, though oftentimes Annie could hear French, Spanish, and even Latin. The large contingent gathered around a booth was definitely German; Annie could still hear their animated voices bounce off of the stall walls from down the aisle. Annie and Gibbs turned down a perpendicular passage that took them far from the German group and toward the incinerators.

Hidden from the rest of the market were the minor creatures, the elves and trolls that worked behind the scenes. These creatures weren't fond of humans investigating their space, but mostly they didn't like humans at all. But Annie and Gibbs made an assumption that one of these creatures might be willing to talk, to trade information for security and safety away from the market. Annie could offer them that; she hoped it would be enough for one of them.

The busiest merchants, selling the most requested items had booths close to what was known as Market Center, a large square in the direct middle of the market. Aisles farther from the center saw less foot traffic, and fewer animals roamed through the booths, but more illegal or deadly objects and animals were for sale here. It was generally quieter, and their presence was more noticeable.

The black market was tough, filled with evil wizards, demons, vampires, exchanged goods, and creatures. It was dangerous and dirty, and those that came here for whatever reason did so at their own risk. There was always action; even in the perimeter aisle that circled the market, booths were sparse, with several empty, or broken or missing their canvas coverings. That was a normal day. Today, these booths were deserted; the merchants that sold here had left or were chased away. The only items left were scraps of paper, empty boxes, or a miscellaneous item. Annie and Gibbs continued to the incinerators.

"Gibbs?" Annie murmured. "What the hell happened?"

Gibbs glanced through the stalls, his eyes darting across the nearly empty passage. "A lot of 'em are gone." He seemed as confused as Annie was by the empty aisle and the abandoned stalls.

"The Ring of Solomon plus a death outside the market might have sparked this," he said.

Though animals roamed free in the market, they were of the

magical kind—billdads, otter-like creatures with beaver tails, dragons, stoorworms, magical snakes—but in all the time Annie had come here, she had never seen domesticated pets wandering the aisles. A large shaggy dog ate from a garbage can at the end of the aisle while a cat scampered across the top of tents and jumped across the aisle to land on another garbage can, slinking away upon spying Annie and Gibbs. A pack of snakes slithered under a table, and the last of the group swished its tail behind it as the canvas fluttered.

A short-haired black lab sauntered over, stopped, and sniffed Annie's shoes. She held out her hand, expecting the dog to take a whiff, but it sat in the dirt and pawed at her as if trying to get her attention. It started to whine.

She rubbed the dog behind its ear. "Good doggie. I'm sorry. I have no food for you," she said. As if the dog understood her, it stopped pawing her hand and gave her a snarky look before traipsing back to the empty stall. It barked repeatedly as they walked away.

"Okay. Was that weird?" Annie asked.

"Yeah. We'll ponder that later. Come on," Gibbs ordered.

The portal, the snow, the large contingent of domesticated animals overrunning the market.

How does the ring fit into this?

The incinerators doors were wide open, and the unassuming sign beside the entrance read: **No Admittance, Enter at Your Own Risk**.

Elves and trolls, keenly adept at working in the shadows and hiding from the business that took place in the market, were busy at the incinerators, which were large metal tubes four feet high with an elbow bend into which they tossed in biologicals. When the garbage or the dung hit the fire, it sizzled. Rancid smoke puffed from the tubes and rose into the air, adding to the already thick haze over the market.

Four rows of ten incinerators filled the large space. Each

three-foot-wide hole was manned by two creatures. The work was hot and dirty. The stench and heat of it permeated every pore and seeped into Annie and Gibbs's clothes and hair as they entered.

Elves and trolls were short creatures, no taller than four feet five inches, and most wore child-sized clothing. All of them were covered in dirt and soot from the work. Their tiny bodies hoisted heavy bags or shovels full of sludge and tossed them down the chutes.

In comparison to the elves and trolls, Annie stood at five feet two inches and was for the moment taller than them. Gibbs towered above all of them at five feet eleven. The creatures noticed them immediately. Most scattered, hiding in the many recesses behind tubes and garbage cans or clinging to the half-wall separating two sides. Each of them poked a head out from behind their hiding spot, keeping a close eye on the humans.

Gibbs separated from Annie a few rows ahead to observe and listen while she grabbed a bag of garbage and walked to a group of elves working together to shovel a large pile of dung into one of the tubes.

After Annie dumped the sack of garbage into the incinerator, it banged into the metal chute, tumbling with several thuds before landing in the fire. Whatever was in the bag sizzled. The choking black smoke rose and settled in her already frizzed hair. She coughed and wiped away sweat from her forehead as she eavesdropped on the conversation between two elves who continued shoveling up the muck.

"Master... Gladden... magic," was all Annie could make out over the roaring fires.

What does that mean?

Her presence was obvious. The elves glared at her, their eyes crinkled with distrust. They took their conversation down a few incinerators, beginning their work again.

"You can't be back here!" A squeal wafted to her from an elf half her height. "Ma'am," he added with a bow. Loose skin around his neck wobbled when he stood.

"The *ma'am* isn't necessary. You don't work for me," Annie said.

His wary, frightened eyes darted across the space to the door of the incinerators and back to Annie. "Ma'am. You need to leave." The elf spoke in a near whisper. Annie had to bend low to hear him and meet his eyes.

"I will if you tell me who killed the wizard and left his body outside the portal."

The elf shook his head repeatedly. "You need to leave," he whispered.

He quivered; his children's clothing, a sailor top and brown pants, rustled against his body. He backed away from Annie and raced for the large garbage heap. With bare hands, he grabbed a fist full of muck and threw it down the tube. His sideways glance was fearful, his actions angry. Annie was gravely aware they overstepped the boundaries.

"You knew that was coming," Gibbs snorted, walking up to her.

"Eh, you never know. Maybe Perkins has a hit on the magical trace or Bucky has a name."

The elf busied himself in the sludge, glowering when he looked at her.

But he came to me! Taking that as a sign that he had something to say, Annie rushed forward and shoved her card into his pocket. "Whatever you or anyone else knows will be helpful. I promise I can keep you safe."

Since they were clearly not wanted at the incinerators, Gibbs and Annie slipped back through the doors, integrating themselves back into the market. She dropped a scarf into the waste can and walked down the first aisle, grimacing after taking a whiff of the odor radiating from her hair.

The stench was so strong that the stall owner just outside the incinerators scowled, before heading inside his tent.

"So the creatures won't talk. Any of your contacts you want to hit up?" Annie asked Gibbs. After working in the market for years, the Wizard Guard had gained some confidences they tapped when necessary. It had to make sense, and a contact could not be over-used; it could mean trouble for the stall owner if they were known to squeal to the Wizard Guard.

"Got one," Gibbs said.

Annie sighed in relief. She preferred to not use her contact, Joseph—a man she had met eight months ago. He was already an outsider, and she feared another visit from her would put him in danger. The rest of her contacts seemed too low level to be of any use. She followed Gibbs to his.

They inched their way around the perimeter, taking an angled aisle toward the center. The layout of the market resembled a wheel with spokes. The perimeter aisle was dissected by two perpendicu-lar passageways, one heading east to west and the other heading north to south, both meeting at the market center.

Annie and Gibbs cut down a smaller cross-corridor, one of the ones that dissected the market into eight large triangles much like a sliced pizza. With more traffic near the center, a traffic jam of wizards, witches, creatures, and domesticated animals stopped their trek.

Gibbs's contact was named Arrowhead, a man with disdain for both the Wizard Guard and the black market, who only conducted his business here for the general seediness and for the access to oth-ers like him.

Arrowhead calmly negotiated and assisted customers. Though he was shorter than Gibbs, he was in all other ways a replica of the older wizard guard—long, stringy hair, tight leather pants, and a sleeveless black vest. Normally, Annie found the similarities funny. Tonight, the air was filled with tension.

Annie and Gibbs were pushed by the flow of the crowd. Gibbs caught his contact's glance, but the stall keeper shook his head vehemently, his eyes widened in what appeared to be fear. He dropped his conversation mid-negotiation with a customer and entered his tent.

"Something's going on," Gibbs grunted.

A hushed quiet immediately covered the market; owners and patrons had witnessed the nonverbal exchange between Gibbs and Arrowhead. The crowd glanced anxiously as Annie and Gibbs passed. Some retreated to their tents while others pretended to be engrossed in the wares in front of them, all desperate to ignore them.

"They know," Gibbs said.

They knew the Wizard Guard was investigating the murder outside the market and had been in the incinerators asking questions. Under normal circumstances their presence wouldn't upset the balance in any way, even with patrons and owners obstructing the investigation.

This was something else.

This was fear.

A ragged witch, hunched and wrinkled with long white hair spilling from her hooded cloak, stopped haggling over price and observed them. Her blue eyes widened with surprise; there was no fear in her ancient face. She bent closer to the shopkeeper, whispered, and pointed with gnarled hands. A smile spread across her face.

"We've been outed," Gibbs whispered and grabbed Annie by the arm, maneuvering them through the crowd and bypassing Arrowhead's tent.

"Yeah, probably that merchant outside the incinerators," Annie said as they crossed into a perpendicular junction of two aisles.

"Get them!" a disembodied voice shouted from the crowd. The mob froze but after a moment their collective gaze found Annie and Gibbs, who didn't look back or wait for the crowd to honor the request.

Gibbs tugged at Annie's arm, and she flew after him.

The crowd squeezed all available running room from their path, jamming their bodies together so tightly that Gibbs could barely hold onto Annie's wrist. They pushed against the eager crowd. A large hairy arm reached out for Annie. It belonged to a cyclops, who yanked on her.

"Gibbs!" Her shout was drowned out by the cheers and jeers of the crowd, but Gibbs felt the tug on Annie and slammed the cyclops with a jinx. The yellow, hairy arm shook and dropped her arm. Its owner grunted loudly as Gibbs pulled Annie away.

Footsteps stampeded against the hard ground. Voices protested, criticized, and complained as the wizards were manhandled by their pursuers. The squeaky, high-pitched cries belonging to the elves and the deep, low grunts of the trolls wafted toward them. They were being tossed aside without much thought.

Annie pushed her panic away, keeping her eyes just beyond the end of the aisle, thinking of only making it to the portal and teleporting home. Gibbs wrenched her into the thickest part of the crowd, which swallowed them. The thing that hindered their escape now also hid them from those tracking them.

Annie's elbows flew through the horde of wizards and demons as she was jostled by the crowd. Gibbs lost his grasp on her arm as they got sucked into the flow of the crowd. After a split second of chaos, Annie no longer saw Gibbs.

Pushing through the jam, she shoved a demon into the wizard next to him. The wizard sailed across a table into the booth owner, and both men glowered at her. Ignoring them and the dread she felt inside, Annie ran.

The crowd was nothing but a blur of faces, Gibbs was nowhere in sight. Shouts closed in on her and she glanced behind her. Two tall, gangly vampires searched the crowd and spotted her.

Damn it!

She pushed against a demon and ran. After a moment she spotted Gibbs in the junction between two alleyways. The path was tight and unyielding, and Annie couldn't push through the crowd. Dizzy from the heat and stench, from the push and pull of the crowd, she chanced a teleport to Gibbs. Rather than feeling the freedom of floating through space, she felt a tug on her leg. She was dragged back toward the jam-packed aisle and crashed against the vampire who had pulled her down.

An excited din hovered above her. Evil wizards, monsters, and creatures surrounded her. Instinct and adrenaline coursed through her as she pushed herself from the demon. The momentum against the smooth, dry dirt caused her boot to slip, and the vampire grabbed her shoe with icy hands. Annie shivered.

"Gibbs!" she screamed. He couldn't hear her through the suffocating horde's jeers and taunts.

With her free foot, Annie kicked the vampire in the nose until she felt cartilage crack. He grunted, yet still his chilled clutch tightened around her ankle.

Frantically, she twisted her body away from him, waving her arms. She swiped at anything within her reach and toppled a wizard standing above her. Thrown off balance, he flailed his arms and fell on top of the vampire, who growled. Fangs extended, the vampire dropped his grip on Annie's leg to throw the wizard from him.

Annie scurried away. "Gibbs!" Her panicked voice was no match for the ruckus that enveloped her. "Gibbs!" She knew she was lost. Anxiety crept from her stomach to her throat. She teleported, but those cold, long fingers reached her again, wrapped around her left shoulder, and spun her around. She threw a stiff arm, pushing against the vampire. He grabbed her wrist and pulled.

"Ahhhhh!" The pain was immediate, radiating from her shoulder to her wrist; it took her breath away. Annie felt hot and lightheaded. It was all she could do to keep from passing out from the shooting agony in her newly dislocated shoulder. Realizing she was injured, the vampire yanked on her weakened arm and dragged her down the aisle. Too weak to hold him off, she cast a jinx with her good hand. The spell hit the vampire in the kidney. He jerked, she jerked. The vampire sneered and wrenched her arm again.

"Ugghh!" Tears rolled down Annie cheeks. She was ashamed to show weakness in the middle of the market, but her shoulder burned. Afraid she might lose her dinner, she pursed her lips. As she blinked rapidly, she saw faces sneering and staring at the vampire attack. She conjured a vial of holy water and heaved it on the demon. It shattered against his taut body, bursting in a thousand shards of glass. Liquid spattered against him and soaked his shirt. White smoke billowed in the air, and the stench of burnt skin wafted to her.

The vampire let go of Annie's wrist, and she ran, her arm hanging limply at her side. As she passed the crowd, she stumbled into Gibbs, who in one swift motion reached around her waist and teleported them from the crowd. Again, Annie felt the pull on her leg.

The vampire jumped the teleport!

But this tug didn't hinder their escape. Whoever it was, wrapped themselves around her, and they floated through time and space to the portal. Annie nearly passed out as Gibbs opened the entrance, pulled them through, and teleported them home.

CHAPTER 8

GIBBS LANDED ON Annie's back porch, and the extra weight attached to her leg released itself.

"Oooof." A small body rolled from the deck and down three stairs, landing in a patch of grass in the back yard.

"Look what I brought back from market." Annie winced. Taking in a breath, expanding her lungs, and clenching her muscles was agony. As her left side radiated with pain, she slunk against the back wall of her house to hold herself up.

The elf lay face down in the brown grass; his small body rose and fell, and he shuddered with difficult breaths.

He's alive. "Gibbs," she whispered through a wave of nausea. "Is he okay?"

"It's not your friend," Gibbs said and gently lifted the injured creature into the house, setting him on the sofa. "Can you make it inside?" he called out.

"Yeah. I'm good."

Annie stumbled through the hallway and took a seat in the club chair, laying her head against the high back. As she closed her eyes, a rush of heat filled her body, bringing lightheadedness with it.

"You okay, Annie?"

"Just help the elf." She heard leather squeak and fabric rustle.

"He's been hit." Gibbs said as he pulled on the hole in the elf's brown pants. The edges were singed; smoke rose from his leg where a jinx had burned a hole through the fabric and onto a large patch of the creature's skin, leaving it blistered raw. "I'm calling your boy," Gibbs said.

After a short phone conversation between Gibbs and Cham, Annie heard cabinet doors flying open and slamming shut. Her cauldron squeaked as Gibbs dragged it across the countertop. Water sloshed against its heavy iron sides, which banged against the top of the stove as Gibbs set the water to boil to for the pain potion.

Annie adjusted herself in the chair. Her attempt to ease the pain and make herself comfortable was in vain; her fingers still radiated some pain.

The elf's labored breath rattled his small chest, and a groan escaped his swollen bloody lips. He had been beaten; Annie could see the remnants in the bruises that dotted his face. She looked past the bloated face. Gibbs was correct: it wasn't the elf she'd met in the market. The clothes were different and so was the face. This elf had a higher forehead, a smaller nose. His tiny little body shuddered and shook with pain.

Annie thought back to the market from whence he came, to the many changes that had sprung up. She wondered when and why the market had changed. There hadn't been just an exodus of booth owners; there had also been the influx of domesticated animals.

Master, magic, Gladden.

The words whispered by the elves at the market meant nothing to Annie as a set. She wondered if they were related to the pop of static in the changing portal—the portal that Rebekah Stoner sensed and touched—or to the ring or her John Doe or even the destruction of the protection spell.

The two worlds were colliding.

How did that happen?

Her head swam in a sea of haziness. Words and images flashed quickly but seemed disjointed, without meaning.

Annie pulled herself forward in the chair to give her lungs

room to expand. She took a whiff of the market that permeated her hair and clothes.

This will be a long night.

Gibbs returned with a sodden rag, a poultice for the elf, and wrapped up the creature's shin and calf. "That should help," he said. The elf glanced at him through swollen eyes and shut them, off to a fitful sleep.

The back door screeched open and slammed shut. A familiar gait rushed through the house.

"Hey." Cham kissed her roughly, clearly anxious and worried. "Gibbs said it's your shoulder?"

His fingers grazed her tender shoulder joint. Annie winced in pain.

"Sorry," Cham said. His lips gently kissed her forehead. "Brought something home from the market?" He pointed to the elf, who was resting more comfortably now that the potion was healing his leg.

"It appears so."

Cham sat on the edge of the chair and held her hand with a firm, strong grip, warm against Annie's cold hands. She shuddered, remembering the vampire's chill against her skin.

"We need to get you cleaned up." Cham waved a palm down the back of her favorite jacket, ripping it in half and pulling each side off of her shoulders. Gibbs slipped her arm into a sling. The burning pain was sharp and hot.

"Crap. That hurts."

"Sorry, girl." Gibbs's touch was tender and efficient as he rested Annie's arm inside the sling. After fastening the straps, he ran off to monitor the potion. She heard another cabinet swish open and slam shut.

"I should have come with," Cham said.

A metal spoon clanged against the cast-iron cauldron. Annie jumped.

"Wouldn't have made a difference." Annie's shortened quick

breaths told Cham what he needed to know. As she shifted in the seat, as the pain radiated outward, he placed a pillow behind her, supporting her.

Her eyes fluttered closed.

What were those words? I can't remember.

To keep from losing focus, she squeezed her fingernails into the palm of her hand.

The elf.

As if he could hear her thoughts, the elf stirred on the sofa.

"You okay?" Cham's concern was palpable.

"Yeah. Just hurts. I... I need to ask you something." She opened her eyes, and their eyes met, his worried, hers pained.

"Later. We'll talk after you rest." He helped her adjust in the seat.

"No. I need to ask before I forget." She sucked in a deep breath. Sharp pains invaded her lungs, shoulder, and back.

"Annie."

Those words...

She mentally retraced her steps through the incinerators and felt herself toss in a bag of garbage as she moved in closer to them. Though her head was foggy, the creatures' low, soft voices came to her.

"No," she told Cham. "The elves, at the incinerators. They were saying something about Gladden and a master. Do you know a Gladden at the market? Maybe their master?" she asked through gritted teeth.

"No. I've never heard of Gladden. I guess he could be a master to the elves? Did you hear anything else?" Cham asked.

Gibbs entered with a large glass filled with a thick, yellowish liquid. The taste in Annie's mouth soured in anticipation of the bitter, tangy potion that would sting going down.

"Gladden Worchester works at the market. Drink," Gibbs ordered.

The warm glass teased Annie. Though it would ease the pain,

it wouldn't offer any other comfort and would be miserable going down. She took a first swig and grimaced at the bitterness.

"All at once," Gibbs reminded her.

She chugged the rest and shuddered as the unpleasant liquid tingled against her tongue and throat. As the potion hit her stomach, warmth spread outward from her abdomen to her arms, up through her chest and shoulders and back down through her legs. It rolled over her like waves, attaching to the pain and washing it away.

More alert with her senses more heightened, she heard the elf fidgeting against the leather. The little guy slept—or pretended to. She left him alone.

"Why you asking about Gladden?" Gibbs asked.

"All I could get from eavesdropping were the words *master*, *magic*, and *Gladden*."

"Master?" As the word rolled from Gibbs's tongue, the elf twitched and jerked awake, sliding on the leather sofa. Gibbs bent over the elf, his stare intense. "What do you know about the master," he asked.

The elf sat up gingerly, frowned at Gibbs, and turned toward Annie. "Huxley said you'd keep me safe." The elf's thin, high voice unnerved her.

Closing her eyes, Annie focused on her memories of the market and the vampire that had chased her along the passageway.

What was I doing before the chase?

She dug her nails deeper into her palm, remembering all she could before the chase to the door of the incinerators.

The elf. I slipped the card into his brown pants, I promised him protection if he or anyone else knew what happened to the John Doe.

The incinerator smell hung over Annie like a blanket. She grimaced. The elf picked through the hair in ears and wiped something on the sofa.

"I did promise Huxley, didn't I?" Annie said.

"I can't go back there!" the elf squealed.

"You will be safe; you won't go back to the market." She tried to reassure the elf—but he was an elf, one who worked in the incinerators at the market and who was probably not familiar with human kindness or cleanliness.

"And Huxley. He gave me this." His tiny, grayish-green hand held out Annie's card.

"We'll get Huxley out too. You'll both be safe," she promised. The thought struck Annie: if those chasing them already knew about this elf, his friend was most likely already dead.

The elf grunted and glared at Gibbs before eyeing Cham suspiciously. "Who's he?"

"My boyfriend. I promise you're safe with us. What's your name?"

The elf's eyes focused on Annie, ignoring the men in the room. "Bitherby, ma'am." The elf tilted his work cap. Bits of garbage, dirt, and other biologicals Annie refused to think of floated to the floor.

Annie cringed. "Okay. Bitherby. Nice to meet you. How's your leg?"

Gibbs lifted the fabric from the wound, examining the healing injury. "Nearly healed," Gibbs said. He placed the poultice back and squatted beside the elf. Bitherby shook with him so near. "So, who's the master?" Gibbs asked Bitherby.

"What will you do to protect me?" Bitherby addressed Annie. The pain potion, after its initial jolt of energy, was making her sleepy and clouded her head. Her focus wandered through images of the market.

"Annie." Cham's concerned voice yanked her from the images.

I don't think he'll like either option. "Well, you have two choices," she said. "You either work at Windmere School or I can get you in at Wizard Hall."

Bitherby shook his head vehemently. "No, no, no. I'm not working at the hall. They'll kill me."

Gibbs grunted. Annie glared at him through her fog, silently cautioning him to refrain from saying anything. He shrugged and sat across from her in a second club chair.

"Listen, Bitherby. Everyone at market saw us, saw you jump our teleport. They will find out who led you to us, making you and Huxley targets. You have to get out. Those are your two choices." It was still difficult for Annie to speak and breathe at the same time. She coughed, and her shoulder twinged.

Deep in concentration, Bitherby contemplated his options. His lips curled downward in a profound grimace while he made the most important decision of his life.

"I'd rather work with the brats," he finally said. He sat back against the sofa and scratched, picked at himself, and rubbed against the furniture.

Annie sighed. He was under her care for now, at least until she dumped him on her former headmaster. *I hope Headmaster Turtledove isn't too upset...* "Before I take you to Windmere, we need to ask you about what's going on at the market."

The elf picked at a scab on his elbow. "'kay," he answered.

"Can you tell us about the master?"

Bitherby shifted uncomfortably on the sofa and turned to Gibbs with wide, fearful eyes. When he looked back at Annie, he wrung his tiny hands.

"You're safe with us. I made you a promise," she reiterated.

Bitherby's eyes zipped around the room, to Gibbs, to Annie, to Cham, and out the window. "The... the ma—aster, he runned the market with Mr. Gladden." Finishing, he took several rapid breaths. His eyes still darted across the room as though he expected this master to jump out and kill him.

"Gladden is the master?" Annie asked.

Bitherby shook his head quickly. "No, ma'am, Mr. Gladden runned the market."

"Gladden runs the market?" Gibbs asked, confused.

How come I've never heard of this man? "Who's Gladden?" Annie asked.

Gibbs paced across the fireplace and stopped beside the bookshelves. "Gladden Worchester is a low-level grunt. At least, he used to be. Worked the market, did odd jobs, collected money, ran errands. I only came in contact with him twice—two separate jobs. Once I caught him peddling mummy hands for a seller. Another time, he was shaking down a merchant for protection money. The merchant called the Wizard Guard for help."

"So how did he go from a low-level goon to running the black market?" Cham asked.

Gibbs leaned against the fireplace and rubbed the stubble on his chin. "Must have killed someone and used magic to obtain their power. He's got no personality to worm his way in otherwise."

"That could explain the changes at market," Annie said and explained to Cham about the weakened protection shield, the increase of domestic animals, the lack of merchants, and the increased number of abandoned booths. His eyebrows raised in surprise, though he didn't comment.

"What did Gladden do?" Gibbs asked the elf.

Bitherby's short legs dangled over the edge of the sofa. His uninjured one kicked and bounced in a rhythmic motion to no particular sequence. He shrugged. "One day he just runned the market."

"That doesn't make sense. You don't just run the market. What magic did he use?" Bitherby clearly was wearing heavily on what little patience Gibbs had.

Removing the poultice from his leg and tossing it to the floor, the elf slid off the sofa and hobbled to Annie. He placed small, dirty hands on her knees and glanced nervously around the room before looking Annie in the eyes. "He call a demon who comes, and now he run the market," the elf whispered.

"You sure? You were there when he called this demon?" she asked.

"Yes," Bitherby squeaked softly.

Gibbs as gently as he could, squatted beside the elf. "When did he do this?"

Bitherby closed his eyes and counted with his fingers ticking off numbers. His lips moved as he murmured to himself. "Eight weeks ago," he finally said.

Annie's brain jumped around. The dead body outside the portal, the elves talking about magic, master, and Gladden, the ring found on the dead body.

The ring! The ring that controls the djinn! Something went wrong!

"Did Gladden call a djinn and make a wish?" Annie could barely get the sentence out. It seemed too stupid to believe.

Bitherby nodded slowly. Again, he surveyed the room with roaming eyes.

"Bitherby, you're safe. No one will find you. I promise. Just let us know what happened."

His chocolate-brown eyes swept the room, sizing them up. Annie guessed he was planning his escape.

After a moment, Bitherby said, "One day, Gladden call with a spell, and the master comes to market. He orders us, and anybody who don't listen gets killed. We all's scared of him. Do what he say."

Gibbs, Cham, and Annie exchanged anxious glances. There had been a shift in power at the market, a shift so swift, so quick, and so widespread that it had changed the millennia-old market. It was a change that could expose the entire magical race.

"So Gladden calls the genie, gets control of the market, and now he's killing people?" Cham asked.

"No. Master. He kills. Mr. Gladden, he's afraid of master too." Bitherby averted his eyes and stared at his hands.

"In a nutshell, Gladden decides he wants to control the market, calls a genie, and learns the hard way that there's always a backfire to the wishes you make with genies. In this case, the genie is actually in control. So Gladden finds someone who happens to have the Ring of Solomon, a ring that controls the djinn, a ring that's supposed to be a myth?" Cham asked incredulously.

Annie's head hurt. It was too much for one night.

"And the ring never got there." Gibbs said.

"So we're back to who killed John Doe," Cham said. "And why?"

"Well maybe Gladden didn't like the fact he really didn't control the market. He called for the ring to control the master, who's really a genie. That means the genie killed John Doe," Annie said. She glanced at Bitherby, but he shook his head. "The genie didn't kill the victim?"

"No, Miss Annie."

"Why would Gladden kill the man who was bringing him the ring?" she asked.

Bitherby shook his head again.

"Do you know who killed the victim?" Gibbs towered over the elf.

Yet again, Bitherby shook his head.

"So are we going with the original owner of the ring, someone who doesn't care that they left the body outside the market?" Annie asked.

The wizard guards were silent for a moment, each alone with their thoughts.

It doesn't make sense to kill the man who has the ring but not find the ring and leave him there.

"There wasn't time," Annie shouted out. Everyone glanced at her. "We know four wizards killed him. So they searched him for the ring but found nothing. There wasn't time to deal with the body. Someone was coming. Witches and wizards are going to know about the Wizard Guard. They'll assume we have it, at least at the Hall," Annie said.

"You hid it?" Gibbs asked.

"It's safe," Annie said.

Gibbs grimaced. He knew where she had hidden the ring. The ring was worth killing for, so she understood his concern. But for now, whoever wanted the ring back would assume the Wizard Guard had it at Wizard Hall. Gibbs summoned his cell phone and called Wizard Hall security.

Bitherby watched the exchange with great care. The elf was smarter than he let on, Annie decided, and he knew the information could be valuable to him. Both Gibbs and Cham knew her hiding spot, so she didn't need to say anything further. The elf offered a quizzical look.

I hope he's not loyal to his master.

"After the last attack on Wizard Hall, security's been greatly improved. There shouldn't be a problem, though security's been alerted. You ready to be popped back in?" Gibbs asked.

"In a minute. I have a few more questions before I go to sleep." The elf stood beside Annie, watching her with wide, searching eyes as she turned to him. "What do you know about who killed the man in the forest?"

"I work at the school with the brats, yes?" Bitherby clarified. He quivered so much that his child-sized clothing fluttered against his small body.

"Yes. I'll take you there tomorrow. I promise." She put a hand on his bony shoulder. He took a deep breath, and his body slowed its shaking.

"A man come to market. He hired to find this ring." He slid closer to Annie, his voice soft and difficult to hear. "But it's not Mr. Gladden who summon him. Master did. I saw 'em in the tent when I bring food."

"The djinn wanted a ring used to control his personal species of demon? Why would he do that?" she asked. Annie glanced at Gibbs.

All of the animals… the domesticated cats, dogs, and snakes roaming and slithering through the market.

"Crap. Gibbs. The dogs, cats, and snakes! They're shapeshifters in the market. The djinn wants to control other djinn!" she shouted. It was a plan most likely created as a response to something, and in that moment, Annie couldn't comprehend why one species of djinn would want to control another species of djinn with a ring that could do serious harm to both.

What would he want with them?

"Annie that doesn't make sense. Why would he want something that could harm himself? He'd lose everything," Cham said.

Djinn were tricksters who only thought of the present, not the consequences of their actions. This djinn had no concern for the wish makers and the consequences of their wishes.

He didn't think through his plan!

"He wanted a shapeshifter army. Gladden probably realized he had no real control and wanted to do harm to him. To get rid of him," Annie suggested.

"Still that's a weird plan. Owning a ring that will control you too. That's dangerous," Cham reiterated. "Bitherby, when did all the animals come to market?"

Again, the elf counted on his fingers. His tongue popped out between his lips as he thought.

"Two weeks. They started coming in. Take over everything. Eat all our food, make messes."

Two weeks!

"You sure, elf?" Gibbs reached out to Bitherby and held him by the arms, lifting him off the ground.

Annie and Cham exchanged glances.

"Ye—yes." The elf glanced at Annie, his lips downturned in fear.

"The spells at all of the missing person locations. Did the master, this djinn, did he summon the shapeshifters to the market? Were they people when they entered or beast?" Gibbs asked. Annie had never heard his voice so anxious, high pitched, pissed.

"Master, he made spell. He call them. They come as people, locked them as animals. But he can't control them. They do what they want. Make mess all over." Tears welled in Bitherby's eyes. Since he was still held by Gibbs, he couldn't wipe the tears away, so they landed on the floor.

Noticing the elf's tears, Gibbs placed him back on the floor. The elf ran to Annie.

"It's okay, Bitherby. We just didn't see what happened. All the clues were there. We just didn't see it." Annie glared at Gibbs, who dropped down beside the elf.

"Bitherby. Who was the man who died?" he asked.

"Master call him Benaiah." Bitherby offered no additional information about the victim. Instead, he pulled away from Annie. His short legs carried him to the dining room, where his small feet shuffled against the wood floors. He opened the refrigerator door.

Gibbs followed him and said something in a low grumble that Annie couldn't hear. With a squeak from the elf, he pattered back to the living room. Gibbs carried a bowl of fruit that was too large for the elf to handle. When Gibbs set the fruit down on the table, Bitherby's little hands dug into the bowl. Sugary, liquid spilled around the sides and dripped on the table.

Annie sighed.

"A steak would be nice," the elf said dryly. He shoveled a handful of strawberries into his small mouth. When he chewed, his mouth remained open, and bits of fruit fell out. Annie's stomach lurched.

After taking a large swallow, the elf returned to the fruit. Dirt from his hands mixed with the fruit juice, creating a sludgy mess that swirled in the bowl. Annie retched and held a hand over her mouth. Unable to watch any longer, she closed her eyes and sunk back into the chair. It didn't erase the sloshing sound Bitherby made as he munched on his snack.

Opening her eyes again didn't help the queasiness in her stomach. Bitherby was a pig. He wiped his hands on his shirt, staining the already dirty clothing, then shuffled himself back onto the sofa. Gibbs stood beside the elf, who offered a shrug and sheepish grin.

"Okay, elf. What happened to Benaiah? Was it a bad deal? Did he want more money?" Gibbs asked.

"No! No! He never come back to market. Master sent him away, told him to come back with the ring. He never come back. Find him outside the market, dead."

"Fits the magical trace," Gibbs said.

"At least now we know someone wanted him dead before he could get back to market. So I'm definitely going after the original owner of the ring. Though the Wizard Guard can assume the shapeshifters are the missing witches and wizards and go after the djinn and Gladden." Annie yawned, then grimaced from the pressure on her shoulder.

"Annie, this is yours. Are you up for running the scenario?" Gibbs asked.

She sat and pulled her thoughts away from the elf, who had somehow managed to destroy the living room in under thirty minutes.

"Yeah. It's easy enough. Gladden wants to run the market, so he conjures a genie to make it happen. There's that pesky little backfire he wasn't aware of, and he decides to get rid of the genie. But the genie doesn't like that idea and contacts this Benaiah, who either had the ring or knew where it was. With the ring, the djinn thinks creating a shapeshifting army is his key to keeping control of the market. But he never got the ring, Benaiah was murdered before he could get it to him. So, Bitherby, when did the djinn contact Benaiah for the ring?"

The elf, back on the sofa, swung his legs wildly. "Few days ago, ma'am."

"Benaiah had the ring, then. I get the feeling that the brooch he wore was a group symbol. The Middle East Wizard Guard is very interested in that brooch."

"He stole the ring from the group he belongs to? Why?" Cham asked.

"Bad seed, disgruntled employee, money," Gibbs grunted.

Annie sighed. All they had was supposition but no proof, and they were no closer to knowing who killed Benaiah. She closed her eyes, ready for her bed and for sleep.

"Assume none of the three of you are safe," Cham said. "Especially you, Annie. They know you're injured."

Annie cringed when Gibbs handed her a wooden spoon.

She placed it in her mouth and bit down, finding the existing grooves she had created the last time she dislocated her shoulder. Gibbs released her arm from the sling. She grabbed Cham's hand and squeezed.

"You okay?" Gibbs asked.

She nodded quickly and bit harder until her jaw ached.

Gibbs held her elbow steady and rotated the shoulder. She flinched, and he stopped and waited as she took a deep breath.

"Okay?" She closed her eyes and nodded. He supported her elbow, lifted up her arm, and rolled the joint into the socket.

"Ahhh!" The pain took her breath away. Bitherby jumped and fell backwards.

"Ignore the elf," Cham said as he wiped away the tears she couldn't stop from flowing down her cheeks. Gibbs massaged the muscles surrounding the joint. It was swollen, and the discomfort spread to the middle of her back. He placed her arm back in the sling, releasing the pressure on her shoulder.

"You okay?" Gibbs asked again.

"Yeah."

The elf hopped from the sofa, stepped in the fruit juice that dripped to the floor, and padded his way to the kitchen.

"What the hell am I going to do with him?"

"I'll take care of this," Gibbs offered and followed him. Annie heard Gibbs mumbling and grunting from the kitchen. When he returned, the elf was kicking his legs as Gibbs held him by the collar.

"Let go of me!" Bitherby shouted. Gibbs dropped him on the sofa. He waved a hand across the floor, clearing the mess.

"Drink this." Gibbs held the last of the pain potion, which was mixed with an added sleeping draught to help Annie sleep through the night.

Reluctantly, she held the glass in her hand, not eager to drink the bitter potion. "Before I'm knocked out for the night, I just wanted to know. Bitherby. Who planted the cattle prod?"

Gibbs lost patience with her. "Not important. Drink it now!"

"He kill me!" Bitherby squeaked.

"Bitherby. You're safe. I promise. Now, please tell me: Who hid the cattle prod?" She was impatient with the elf, and the pain was excruciating. The glass shook in her hand until she spilled some of the liquid on her dirty pants.

"Annie!"

"Gladden. Mr. Gladden. He put the pokey thing in the ground because Master made him get rid of the police." Bitherby screeched. The sound of his voice vibrated across the room.

Gibbs glared at her, so she chugged the last of the potion. It caught on her tongue. She clamped down on her lips, forcing the liquid down her throat. Bitherby laughed lightly and tapped his foot wildly.

Instantly, warmth spread down her shoulders and through her fingertips. Her head felt heavy with fog.

"Demons aren't so bright. The cattle prod's just a diversion, Annie. Probably to confuse the nonmagicals," Cham said.

"Yeah. It's nuts." Her heavy eyes closed on their own, and voices fell away into a distant background noise. She was trapped by wooziness; it felt as though she were listening to a conversation under the water.

"I'm gonna take her upstairs." Cham lifted her from the chair. She hung loosely in his arms and listened as a low, gruff voice spoke to a high-pitched scared voice—or maybe it was a dream.

CHAPTER 9

S LEEP ELUDED ANNIE. Not because of Gibbs's potion—
he was a potion master and made them well. She should
have been off to a blissful sleep.

She wasn't. It was the rancid smell deep in her curls and on her
clothes and now in her bed. Annie couldn't escape the odor.

More than that, she was uncomfortable; her left arm lay limply
at her side, pulling on her shoulder. Rather than using Cham for
support, she rolled to her back and placed a pillow over her stomach to stabilize her arm. As she shook the numbness from her hand
and fingers, blood rushed back to her extremities and prickled her
skin.

Shadows moved across the room as the moon lowered in the
sky. Realizing she wouldn't get back to sleep, she gingerly sat up
and waited for the bedroom to stop spiraling around her.

When the world stopped spinning, she took a step on the
wood floor, which felt cold under her bare feet.

I really need a rug.

Annie shuffled to the bathroom and switched on the light,
which was blinding in the otherwise darkened room.

The shower heated up quickly once she turned it on. Steam
rose and covered the walls, the mirror, and the sink in her small
bathroom. She swiped her palm across the mirror and stared at her

frizzy hair that had grown in volume with the humidity from the shower. Streams of tears marked her dirty face.

I wonder if Rebekah Stoner ever comes home looking like this.

With a tired sigh, she plunged her foot into the shower. The water began to erase the stench of the market and warm her tired muscles. She shook in the scalding water, remembering the feel of the vampire's ice-cold hand against her skin.

Annie began to wash with her good hand, but it was difficult to reach her right side. *I didn't think this through.*

Too tired to laugh and too tired to control the tears that rolled down her cheek, Annie lowered her head to the tile wall and cried.

Dirt slid off her skin, catching in the current of water and the textured grooves in the bottom of the tub. It swirled and spun until it was sucked into the sewer pipes.

At least the first layer of market grime is gone.

She shivered.

The bathroom door swung on its original 1930s hinges and squeaked open. The shower curtain peeled back.

"Need help?" Cham touched her good shoulder.

"Sorry to wake you." She wiped away tears and dirt as he slipped out of his clothes, joining Annie in the hot water.

Cham soaped up her massive head of curls. Under the heavy spray of water, the soap glided off of her, and bubbles formed at her feet. Cham rubbed her back and neck, which were tender around her swollen shoulder.

"Feel better?" He kissed her neck and ear before squeezing what felt like gallons of water from her thick, curly mane.

Annie stifled a yawn. "A little." She snuggled against his bare chest. The water beat against them.

"I'm turning into a prune. You done?"

Annie nodded peacefully. He helped her from the tub.

Wrapped in a fluffy, warm towel, she sat on the toilet. The world began to spin again. Beyond the bathroom door, Zola, her Aloja fairy, floated around the bed changing the sheets. For millennia, Aloja fairies had been charged with protecting pregnant women and small children, making Zola's species perfect as a nanny for rambunctious magical children. When Zola came to live with the Pearce family, she was magically bound to the family and would be long after a nanny was needed, unless that magical link was destroyed. In all of Annie's haziness, she hadn't wondered why Zola hadn't felt her pain. That link should have alerted her.

Now wrapped in an extra-large button-down shirt belonging to Cham, Annie let Cham lead her to her bed.

Bed.

As her head touched the pillow, she realized how tired she was.

My hair smells like strawberries.

Glass slapped against skin as Cham summoned a pain potion. Annie grimaced but took a swig from the vial. She shivered at the taste; the foul medicine slid down her throat, but the bitterness remained on her tongue.

"You okay?"

She nodded. The strong potion worked quickly; the world fell away, and Annie floated into the nothingness.

The constant barrage of restless kicks from Annie left Cham unable to sleep. Leaving her in bed, he snuck downstairs and headed to the kitchen cabinet where Annie kept items she wanted secured.

The cabinet was locked with a magical blood lock, accessible with a drop of blood to only a small group. Cham, being one of the only people Annie trusted with the magic, pushed his index finger against a pin in the lower left corner, puncturing the skin and sending a drop of blood into the lock. His blood released the spring, and the door popped opened, revealing a most prized possession: her *Book of Shadows*. The tome detailed the magical experiences of the good wizards and witches who had owned it. Jason

Pearce had received this book from his father, who had inherited it from his mother. It now belonged to Annie. Most of the time, the book had sat alone—until now. The Ring of Solomon, protected inside the plastic evidence bag, now lay on top of the book.

Leaving the ring inside the cabinet, Cham heaved the book out and onto the kitchen table. The well-worn, ancient tome, covered in green leather, was four inches thick and filled with passages about everything from vampires and demons to cursed objects and good magical creatures. Some pages had been used so frequently that the edges were ripped and bent; others were not so well used and looked as though the passage had been written yesterday. Since Cham's family had never had a member in the Wizard Guard, he found the Pearce's *Book of Shadows* fascinating. Holding his palm above the book, he cast a spell and the pages flipped quickly.

"I don't think the Pearce family ever came in contact with that ring."

Cham jumped, disconnecting his searching spell, causing the pages to flop open at a random passage. Zola stood in the doorway between the back hall and the kitchen, staring at him with grayish-green eyes.

She's upset.

Normally, Zola's eyes sparkled a bright emerald green, filled with life and love, unless she were upset or angry or simply irritated. It didn't help that her brow was furrowed deeply and her lips were pursed.

She's really upset. "Hi, Zo." Cham said. He rested his hand over his heart as if that could calm the thumping. He should have heard her coming, but the Aloja fairy had floated across the floor. Not even her flapping wings left a sound.

Zola's nasty grimace left a heavy, unsettled feeling in the pit of Cham's stomach. It was unfamiliar, ugly and dark across her face, and completely against her nature.

"I didn't figure as much," Cham said, finally addressing Zola's comment. "There's nothing in here." As Cham closed the book, his gaze matched hers; neither looked away.

"She's still restless." A rough, icy chill hung in each word, laying the responsibility for Annie's injury squarely on Cham, as if he had personally pulled her shoulder out of its socket. "Annie's not safe with that ring here. I want it out of the house."

Zola's protective stance, though understandable, caused Cham to shudder. "No one outside Wizard Hall knows she has it." But as the words came out, Cham didn't believe them either. It was a known fact that Annie was investigating the death of Benaiah outside the black market. Even without the ring, she wouldn't be safe.

"I'll talk to her, and we'll find a new location for the ring. You know I can't get her to do what she doesn't want to do." Cham tried a smile, but Zola refused to warm to him.

"Try harder. I know the market and those people who run it. They chased her out. They'll find her."

"Zola. I will. I will protect her. Please don't worry."

Zola's eyes swirled and changed from green to black. She was no longer irritated—she was angry. Cham had seen her mad before, but he'd never seen anything like this in her.

"I'm not convinced." Zola turned. Her large fairy wings flapped wildly behind her.

Keeping Annie safe meant gaining knowledge about the ring. But they also needed to know who else wanted the ring. Pushing the book aside, Cham opened Annie's field pack and pulled out *The Book of King Solomon* to peruse its pages.

After skimming the passages, he finally found the snippet, one small paragraph pertaining to the ring that once belonged to King Solomon.

Solomon possessed a ring of great power, one that allowed the king to control the djinn, the demons that roamed the land. With the ring, the king spoke to the demons, controlling them and bending them to his will.

The Ring of Solomon was an amulet or talisman that possessed good magic and was engraved with the name of God. It was sent to the king directly from heaven.

The ring was created out of brass and iron during Solomon's reign between 970 and 931 BC and is recognizable by an engraved six-pointed star and four moldavite crystals that were used to seal documented commands.

There's nothing here!

Cham leaned back against the chair and closed his eyes. The silence lured him to sleep.

Bump… scratch… bump. Cham's eyes popped open and darted around the room. He could hear Zola's words echoing in his head.

She's not safe with the ring here.

Bump… scratch… bump. The sound came from outside. Cham hid the *Book of Shadows*, closing the locked cabinet, and opened the back door, peering outside in the dark and searching for movement in the shadows.

Bump… scratch… bump. Opening the screen, he listened again. The sound wafted up from below him. Stomping on the back porch, he knelt down and shone a flashlight between the cracks.

When he saw the cause of the noise, Cham sighed. "Whatcha doing down there, Bitherby?"

"Cold, sir."

"Keep quiet. I'll be right back." After summoning a sleeping bag and an extra blanket, Cham returned and tossed the items through access door beneath the deck. "Don't wake the neighbors."

"Yes, sir." The elf wrapped himself in the heavy blankets and hid in the corner.

Cham gave the backyard one last look before heading inside.

CHAPTER 10

I'm walking on sunshine, whoa
I'm walking on sunshine, whoa
I'm walking on sunshine, whoa
And don't it feel good

ANNIE GRUMBLED UNDER the covers. The chipper song woke her from a restless night of sleep and a hangover from the sleeping potion. Cham hovered over her to shut off the buzzer.

"Ever used magic before?" she groused, angry he had set the alarm, annoyed he didn't use magic to shut it off, and irritated he hovered over her to do so.

"Sorry. Sorry," he whispered and laid back down, curling her into his arms. Little kisses covered the back of her neck. She relaxed, unable to stay angry with him. She nestled closer, pulling the blanket around herself even though sleep was no longer an option.

Gray light streamed in from the window as dawn made its mark. It was that time of day when everything was dull and slow, and Annie wanted to stay in bed just a little while longer. This was the latest she had ever slept in.

"Almost asleep?" Cham asked. Wind rustled against the window; the winter storm was picking up again. "I'm awake," she groaned and shifted under the covers. The pain potion was wearing out.

"Again, I'm sorry. How's your shoulder?"

"Burns."

His fingers grazed her cheek. "I can make you something."

"Not yet. Stay. For a little while."

Their legs intertwined. Cham snuggled into her hair and laced his fingers through hers.

Annie's mood matched the gray light: dull and listless. Visions of the vampire attack bombarded her brain, paralyzing her, if only temporarily.

Cham tensed when she shuddered.

"You okay?" Cham enfolded her in a tight embrace as if to protect her. He was certainly the safest place Annie knew. She felt love, and safety. Here she was perfect.

"I will be."

Cham twirled her hair around his fingers. When he released the newly formed curls, they cascaded down her shoulder, falling in her face.

"Zola wants the ring out of here." Cham kissed Annie's shoulder; the sensation of his lips against her skin remained even after he climbed out of bed. Annie snuggled against his spicy scented pillow as the bathroom light popped on.

"They don't know I have it."

"Annie, think about it. You and Gibbs were asking questions. They'll come after you for that. I think we should hide the ring at the Hall." Annie sensed the control in his voice; he was attempting to hide his anxiety.

"You're right." She sighed. Cham and Zola were right to be worried. The evil wizards and witches who saw her at the market would stop at nothing to get the ring.

Cham pulled a T-shirt over his body. She gazed at his newly formed six pack, forgetting for a moment that her arm hurt like hell and the entire black market knew where she was.

"What?" he asked. Annie smiled.

"Nothing. I just like the view is all."

As a boy, Cham had been plump, a little doughy around the middle, but since they had started dating, he had started working out. Her reaction to his new look sometimes embarrassed him. His cheeks burned red.

"Relax today and heal your shoulder. I'll come home early." Cham bent down to kiss her. Her good hand touched his chin and cheek.

"Yeah, yeah."

She propped herself up. Pain shot from her fingertips to her shoulder, and her arms hung awkwardly. She let out a groan.

"Lie back down," Cham cooed.

"I'm done sleeping. I'm thinking about heading to the Snake Head Letters and seeing what old Archie knows about it."

"Annie. Please don't go. Rest your arm."

"Fine. But I have to drop off Bitherby. I can't protect him and me."

"Annie…" He returned to the bathroom to brush his teeth and run his fingers through his wild curls.

Annie shuffled in and wrapped her arms around his middle. "Yes?" he asked.

"I need help getting dressed."

✻

"The body is gone!" Ezekiel paced furiously around the small tent, stopped to pick up a cursed crystal and threw it at Gladden Worchester's head. The wizard ducked to avoid the flying rock. It missed him by inches, hitting the canvas tent instead. "My ring is gone!"

The messenger elf scampered away from the master, kicking up dirt from the floor. Ezekiel swung out his palm and threw a spell at the elf, who passed through the tent flap as the spell hit. Sparks flew, setting the flap on fire.

Worried he'd be next, Gladden cowered under his desk, waiting for the master to calm down—or, best-case scenario, leave. His partner continued to rage. A chair flew into the corner, knocking a pole to the ground. That corner of the tent caved in.

The creatures and wizards who had been summoned scattered before the angry djinn took his fury out on them. With them left the others who had been in the aisle conducting business, leaving all the booths empty of patrons and vendors. The lack of voices, of familiar din, of the normal commotion in the aisle gripped Gladden with fear. He was now alone in this part of the market. His body quivered uncontrollably.

Ezekiel stood seven feet tall. His strength was camouflaged by his thin, wiry frame. He wasn't to be underestimated, a mistake Gladden promised himself he would never make again, as the djinn ripped the desk top from the sides of the desk and threw it. The heavy piece of wood flew into the air, scattering objects and papers in all directions before landing across the tent. With the sides of the desk no longer holding up the top, they crashed inward, landing on Gladden, who was still cowering in the dirt.

"You screwed this up. You're to blame!" Ezekiel bellowed. Gladden couldn't meet his eyes; they swirled between black pools and raging fire.

"N—no. No. I didn't kill Benaiah! I never saw him come back. Don't hurt me!" Gladden recoiled, covering his head with his hands.

"Who killed him?" Ezekiel's voice boomed across the tent and carried down the aisles. Those still in the market trembled.

"I don't know. I don't know who did it. It wasn't me. I didn't take the ring! I didn't go to the morgue!" Gladden squealed.

Ezekiel strode across the small tent. His heavy footsteps pounded against the ground, vibrating and shaking the items still inside. "I handed you this market, and look what you did. Idiot!

You screwed it up. The police, they're all over. I told you to take care of it. You made it worse. I should kill you!" The djinn stopped and looked through the singed tent flap.

"No! No! Master. It's that girl and the old dude she was with! The elf! They did it. They must have taken the body." Gladden knelt deeper, so close to the dirt he could smell the musty odors. His arms still cradled his head in protection.

Ezekiel knelt down beside the cowering Gladden and grabbed the wizard's arm, yanking him up.

"The girl, that old man. Yes, they're wizard guards. Yes. The Wizard Guard was snooping around. They must have the body and probably my ring." For the first time in days, the djinn smiled, which pulled his taut skin against his skull and revealed protruding yellow teeth. "Forget the man. Go for the girl. She's injured and only got away because of him. Find her!" he hissed.

CHAPTER 11

I T TOOK ALL Annie had to keep herself from working the
case and heading to the Snake Head Letters, the only wizard
book store, to gather information about the ring. She stayed
in bed after Cham left for work and curled under the covers long
past the time she normally rose. Finally, when she was no longer
tired, she climbed out of bed and trudged down the stairs.

If it weren't for the pain, she would have gone for her morning
run. Instead, she took a stroll through the neighborhood, letting
the fresh air wake her. By the time she returned home, her arm no
longer hurt.

Annie entered her house from the back porch, immediately
noticing a trail of food: fruit and crackers headed from the back
door around the deck to the access panel.

Bitherby!

She rushed to the kitchen window, where Zola lifted an over-
saturated towel from the counter and tossed it in the pile of garbage in the corner, where the can had been knocked over and the
contents spilled to floor.

"Oh, crap." Annie yanked the screen door open and rushed
through the back hall. Immediately, she was tripped by shoes, jack-
ets, and clean laundry, leaving a trail across the floor. Tiny little
footprints covered her clean clothes.

What the hell?

Zola grumbled loudly, Annie rushed to the kitchen where a cauldron sat on top of the stove and flames danced wildly under the thick cast iron. Steam rose, and the potion flowed like lava from a volcano, like the substance on the towel.

"What the hell happened?" Annie shouted at Zola, knowing it wasn't her fault.

"That elf troll!" Zola shouted back. Her hands cut through the air as she cleaned the horror that was now Annie's kitchen.

"Where is he?"

"Under the house," Zola growled.

"Zola, just leave it. I'll clean it up after I send Bitherby to Windmere."

"Annie, that elf is a pig. Just… just get rid of him." Though her voice was steady and calm, Zola was angry. Annie always knew that when the fairy's emerald-green eyes turned grayish green, she was in trouble. Today, those eyes were fully black.

"Yeah. I'm sorry. We… I didn't really think through what to do with the elf until I got him a job. I'll go take care of it." Annie left through the back door, sidestepping the mess, and followed red footprints in the snow. Zola grumbled as she moved items, slamming them against the once pristine countertop.

So much for the relaxing, healing day.

An access panel resided on the side of the porch. Annie tugged at the removable lattice, sucked in a breath, and flashed a light inside. Even just the thought of climbing inside hurt her tender, swollen shoulder. Instead, she sat outside the opening, staring at the elf curled in the corner. He was sleeping and dreaming, and his little legs kicked out as if running. A moan escaped his lips. Annie floated the flashlight to him and tapped his shoulder.

The elf jumped, his small hands flying up, and smashed his head on the underside of the porch. "What, miss? What you do that for?"

He held his hands across his face in self-defense as the light blinded him. His green-gray skin hung off of his tiny frame as if several sizes too large for his petite frame; it was covered with dried bits of food and glistened where the potion had spilled on him. Annie blanched.

"You destroyed my house."

"You brought me here, miss," he said as if it was Annie's fault. Still, the elf stood and bowed in respect.

"Clean yourself up. I'm taking you to school."

❄

As with Tartarus Prison, teleportation wasn't permitted inside the perimeter of Windmere School grounds. Annie landed with the elf in a secure approved area, surrounded by a circle of trees, large enough to contain great numbers of people. She couldn't help remembering her first family weekend at Windmere, when her sister Samantha was a freshman here. Annie had been a gangly little kid, clinging to her dad's leg when they teleported. Even though hundreds of other students and their family members had teleported in along with them, the area seemed big enough to accommodate the hordes that visited. Today it felt small and isolated.

She landed with Bitherby clinging to her as if he might fall through the teleport and land back at the black market. His sticky hands left marks on her legs, remnants of the potion he had been trying to create.

So what else is new?

She pried the elf from her.

"Bitherby, no one will hurt you here. I need you to behave, or there won't be much else I can do for you. Can you do that?" He nodded.

I hope that means he understands.

The snow-covered stone path meandered gracefully along the hill from the teleportation area to the school. Short, square bushes, thin with naked branches were planted on both sides of the path; by summer, they would be full and green.

Still angry at the state of her house, Annie hiked to the front entrance in silence. She was sure the elf had told her everything he knew about the ring and the master. All she needed to do was keep him safe until they resolved those issues.

I promised.

Beyond that, Bitherby was more trouble than he was worth. She was relieved to no longer be responsible for his protection—though now that she was here, guilt settled in her gut at the prospect of leaving the elf with her former headmaster without asking permission first.

As they rose along the hill, the roof of the main building of Windmere appeared. Annie's jaw dropped as the school came into full view. As a student she would come home to a large colonial building with white clad siding, a black roof, and pillars that towered over them, standing guard like soldiers.

Today, she was greeted by a large lodge with massive logs for walls. The green metal roof stood out against the white gray sky. It looked so different, and yet she still felt a familiarity with the grounds and the place. Annie was home.

How long since I was here last?

She ticked off the years in her head since she had graduated, just before she turned eighteen. She was surprised to realize it had been five years since she had been back.

Annie remembered clearly the thousands of books in the old library. The memory was so vivid and strong that she could smell the dust and age. Her mouth watered thinking of the food in the dining room, and she smiled thinking of relaxing in the dorm lounge with her friends or exploring hidden and restricted corners of the school. It was then that Annie realized how much she missed being here.

"M'father built this path."

Bitherby's small voice pulled her away from the memories. She glanced at the elf, never having thought about his life prior to working at the market.

She stopped and viewed the mile-long path, built of ancient stone. Until that moment, she had never given it a thought as to where it had come from. Annie knelt, wiped away an inch of snow, and touched the rough, bare rock. It was cracked with age and had dead moss growing in the joints between each of the carefully laid stones. They were bleached from the summer sun—almost white yet not, a little tinge of beige peeking through, probably the original color. She pictured hundreds of tiny hands laying each piece. It must have taken months at least.

"Are your parents still alive?"

"Aye, miss. Not safe for me to go there though. Shall we?" With an open hand forward, Bitherby motioned for her to continue, a complete gentleman as his little legs moved forward. She jogged to catch him, across the uneven stones laid centuries ago; it occurred to her that Bitherby's dad was probably over two hundred years old.

The wind gusted across the valley and traveled up the hills, burning and stinging her cheeks at the same time. They turned one more bend in the stone path, leading to a metal gate that snaked around the school grounds, which were undulating, sinking, and rising across the hills and valleys for over a thousand acres.

Two gates were covered with a large magic knot, four interlocking circles with arrows that pointed north, south, east, and west. At the center of the knot was an electric intercom with direct access to the security team inside the school. Annie pushed the button; a pleasant, disembodied voice answered, "How may I help you?"

"Annie Pearce to see Headmaster Turtledove."

"One moment, please."

While they waited to be let inside, Annie stared at the new building, at the ski lodge that sat high atop the hill overlooking the school grounds. Large timber walls and several chimneys clad in river rock rose up the walls and out of the roof. Smoke billowed out of the chimney and dispersed as it hit the cold winter air.

Their presence was quickly approved. The gates swung open,

and a giant guard met them at the entrance. The giants were the same creatures that guarded Tartarus Prison. They were descendants of the ancient race known as the Hundred Handers, beings that had once protected the gates of Hades. The guard who greeted them was smaller than other giants. Annie estimated he was only seven feet tall, though he was as thick as he was wide.

His large feet scraped across the stone and pounded as they hit the ground. Each step vibrated against the frozen ground; Annie felt the tremors under her feet.

Even in this bitter cold, the giant wore a thin, long-sleeved cotton shirt under a sleeveless tunic. With his thick arms, he opened the tall, dense doors to reveal the new entrance foyer.

Bitherby grabbed hold of Annie's leg. His tiny body quivered against her. "I changed my mind, miss."

"Giants are safe and gentle as long as you don't piss them off. It's fine."

Bitherby was not convinced. Annie peeled him from her leg, but he grabbed and squeezed her hand as they entered the large foyer.

The doors slammed shut behind them, blanketing them in warmth from the massive fireplace in the corner of the foyer. Surrounded by large, colorful river boulders, a fire blazed and danced. Students congregated on ottomans and overstuffed sofas while waiting for the afternoon class bell to ring.

Annie tried to hide her surprise; the entire foyer and fireplace hadn't been here when she was a student. The only thing remotely similar was the large stone staircase winding up to the second floor and the dining hall still to the left of the entrance doors.

The giant turned up the colossal stone stairway. Beneath every footstep, Annie felt the uneven wear created by centuries of students trudging up and down. Her fingers grazed the stone handrail. It was sturdy and unmoving, though covered with cracks and gouges, proof that students lived here.

Several students lounging by the fire spotted Annie with the giant. Their conversations turned to hushed tones, possibly wondering who she was and why she was here.

I feel very old.

Before she reached the top of the staircase, the class bell rang, sending the quiet hallways into a controlled chaos. Students poured from the dining hall, the classrooms, the foyer. They ran up the stairs and around her until she was lost in a sea of children. Bitherby was sucked into the crowd. The giant, unfazed by the throngs, ambled along toward the office Annie knew so well.

While students passed, Annie stopped at the top of the staircase where a large wall was covered in pictures. Students from past years smiled back at her: the best in class, the broomstick racing teams, the potion making teams, the chess teams, the choir. Her past exploits greeted her like an old friend. She even found the picture of Charlie Andrews her ex-boyfriend. After six months with Cham, Annie felt less bitter about Charlie. Being here in this building, she was even a little sentimental.

Caught up in the memories, she didn't notice she was alone in the hallway with just a few stragglers running to beat the final bell. A door slammed shut, bringing her back to the present; she realized Bitherby and the giant weren't with her.

She sprinted down the hallway, holding her limp arm against her shoulder. The two were waiting for her by the arched entrance belonging to the headmaster. She grinned at the waiting giant and pulled on the heavy metal handle. The door's hinges groaned.

"You stay here," she ordered Bitherby. The giant placed a plate-sized hand on the elf's head; Bitherby squeaked. His eyes pleaded with her to not leave him, but Annie knew he was safest with the giant.

I hope.

Annie closed the door behind her, entering a short hallway that led to the headmaster's office. Whether it was to endure punishment for some crazy scheme or to receive attentive caring after her father died, she had seen the inside of this office more than any of her friends or classmates.

While the rest of the school had made incredible changes to décor, Headmaster Turtledove's office was the same as it had been the last time Annie was here. The circular room with the beautiful arched window on the far wall overlooked the expansive school grounds, which were currently blanketed in a thick layer of pristine snow. Beyond the open lands, large evergreen trees stood tall and thick, a natural perimeter for the school grounds.

Fitzgerald Turtledove sat behind a massive carved desk along the side wall, reviewing piles of paperwork. Behind him, bookshelves wound around the curved walls from the window to the door where she stood. The shelves were bloated with books from potion making to magical history. Between the tomes, a grand collection of cursed objects, crystals, crystal balls, athames, amulets, scrying crystals, cauldrons, candles, and wands were stuffed in any nook and cranny, leaving no blank space on any shelf.

A pair of cursed mummy hands caught Annie's eye. She thought back to her education, remembering that if mummy hands were found on your travels, you would be led astray and eventually die.

Headmaster Turtledove had taught her to collect, study, and learn from all of these objects; it was the only way to understand and protect the magical world. Before she could knock, he glanced up, smiled, and invited her in.

I'm not sure how long that smile will last.

"Well, well, Ms. Pearce, look at you. I haven't seen you since you graduated. I can only assume your visit is due to needing something," Headmaster Turtledove teased her before offering a warm hug.

Headmaster Turtledove hadn't changed as much as the school. When not teaching or interacting with students, he wore relaxed jeans and a Hawaiian shirt and kept his long hair held back from his receding hairline in a loose ponytail.

"You know you saw me last summer at the Wizard Council state dinner," Annie said.

He chortled lightly and sat back in his desk chair, folding his hands over a large tome.

"Yes, well, you haven't been back to school since graduation."

Though he wasn't wrong, Annie laughed in a way that said she had no care in the world, like she was a student away from home.

"And how's Mr. Chamsky? I'm assuming you two are still Wizard Guard partners."

Her cheeks burned red. "Not anymore," she said.

His eyes twinkled as if he had expected that to happen. Annie felt warm and flushed.

"When you see him, please give him my regards."

"Yes, sir." She offered a smile but failed to meet his gaze, finding herself slightly embarrassed. She continued to survey the room.

"So how's the job?" he asked politely, pushing aside his book. Just outside the large window, a broomstick flying class was taking place. Young students screamed in delight as they rose their sticks in the air. Annie glanced at the window; a student teetered precariously on the two-inch-wide broom, righted herself, and flew away.

"It's great. A little weird at times, but I love the work," she answered, returning her attention to the headmaster.

"I knew back then that you'd make a great Wizard Guard. Actually, I think you'd be a great teacher."

Her eyes drew up in surprise. She couldn't hide it and burst out laughing. The headmaster didn't join in; his expression was solemn and serious. "How do you figure?" Annie finally asked.

"I hear things." Headmaster Turtledove looked at her with a grin and rested his chin in his hands.

"I don't think I want to know."

"Well, if you ever have the desire to teach the next generation, I'd love to have you here. Black magic protection, potions, whatever you'd like."

This isn't a joke. "Oh. Okay. If I ever get the urge to teach, I'll let you know." She glanced away, which was easy to do with so many items to stare at.

"So, Ms. Pearce. I know you're busy and have a reason for being here. I won't keep you from your business. How can I help you?"

"I have a little time. You don't have to rush me out. Unless, of course, you're busy."

"Anything for you, Ms. Pearce."

❋

"So this elf, he's outside?" The headmaster pointed to his door. Guilt sat in Annie's stomach.

I should have called. "I am so sorry to spring this on you, but he's driving Zola crazy, and it's only been a day. I really need to keep him away from the black market while we investigate this murder."

The headmaster smiled, sat back in his chair, and folded his hands under his chin, thoughtfully looking at her. "You know we find a place for everyone here. I think the stables can handle him, if he's as unhygienic as you say."

"I'm really, really sorry about this." She apologized again, knowing dumping Bitherby on the school wasn't nice of her to do. "He destroyed my kitchen, and Zola's not at all happy."

A hearty laugh escaped the headmaster's lips; his eyes twinkled. After a moment, he said, "I'm not joking when I said you should teach."

Her smile faded. "Okay. Say that this is a serious conversation. What would I teach?"

"A wizard guard and a potion master? I see a lot in your potential."

He handed her a sheet of paper, a class outline written in neat handwriting.

"A special lecture?" she asked.

"Think about it. It's a one-time lecture, seniors only. It's something I've been playing around with. I thought of you immediately."

Just outside the heavy wooden door and stone walls, they could hear the sound of thrashing. "Crap," Annie shouted and lunged from her chair.

That damn elf!

She skidded out of the door with Headmaster Turtledove close behind. The giant knelt beside the elf, his hands firmly on the small creature, holding him to the floor. Up and down the hallway, pictures hung askew or had fallen to the floor, tapestries had been ripped from their hangings, and doors swung open.

"I am so sorry," she said again.

"You always bring me the most unusual things," he said with a smirk on his face, referring to one of the adventures Annie had while still at school.

A silver-tipped love bird, known to reveal hidden treasures to worthy people, had appeared to Annie late one night while studying. Ignoring school rules, she dragged Dave Smith with her and followed the bird to a restricted wing of the school, where a hidden passageway was revealed to them. After escaping and locking the door to the tunnel Annie and Dave had discovered a box of unknown origin that had of course eventually made its way back to the headmaster.

"Have you ever opened that box?" Annie asked as she remembered the entire night and the punishment that followed.

"Nope. It's well hidden, should you ever think of stealing it." He smirked.

"As you say, I'm a wizard guard and potion master. I'm sure I could find it." Annie winked.

"Well, I will hold you to it," he said as they began the work of assimilating the elf to school life.

CHAPTER 12

THE LEMONY-FRESH SCENT invaded Annie's nostrils as she entered the house. Zola must have spent the morning scrubbing every remnant of the elf from the kitchen and living room. It shined, but the cleaner tickled Annie's nose.

Annie's gleaming table top was still covered with files and books about the Ring of Solomon and Middle Eastern design. An ever-growing case file teetered against her right hand.

After an eventful trip to the school to drop off the elf, Annie was exhausted, and her arm hung limply. She pushed aside the pile and laid her head on a bare patch on the citrusy-scented table.

Right as she started dozing off, her phone buzzed against the wood. She glanced at the screen. "Hey, Bucky, any info for me?"

"Hi to you too, Annie," he said.

Even from the other end of the line, Annie could hear his fingers fluttering across a keyboard.

Does he do anything other than type? "Sorry. I just get so excited when you call," she teased.

"Yeah. I know you, Annie Pearce," he responded. "Just to let you know, your victim is much harder to find than I expected." He never stopped typing. It was possibly another project. Annie wouldn't be surprised if he was multitasking.

"Okay. You can find anything, what's the problem?"

The clicking stopped. Bucky sighed deeply, surprising Annie. She couldn't remember a case where he was ever stumped over the data.

"The name Benaiah isn't exactly popular. I thought it might come up easily. I ran it through every wizard database I could, starting with the Middle Eastern databases. When those led to nothing, I ran it through the rest but still came up with nothing. Then I searched with his picture through the nonmagical databases." Bucky stopped for a minute, tapped a key on his keyboard, and the printer whirled to life in the background. "I searched with the fingerprints and did a facial recognition search. Annie, there was nothing. Benaiah doesn't exist in the cyberworld."

While Bucky continued to type, Annie pondered this. It wasn't uncommon for wizards to be off the nonmagical grid. If they were, they most likely kept a low profile in the magical one as well.

"Well, I'm disappointed but not surprised. Did you put out a notice to all Wizard Guard units in that part of the world to see if anyone knows who he is?"

"I sent the picture to the Middle Eastern Wizard Guard and had a hit on the brooch, as you know." More clacking of keys. "Here's something new from within five minutes: the Middle East Wizard Guard asked if we noticed any tattoos on the body. Did you see anything?"

"No. I don't think so. Hold on a sec." Annie shuffled through the crime scene photos and pulled out each of the pictures of Benaiah, expecting that the investigators would have taken pictures of any tattoos for identification purposes. "Nothing on the body except for the burn mark. I didn't see anything at the autopsy, but I could check with Perkins, see if he noticed something. Did they tell you what we should be looking for?"

As Bucky typed again, she stared at the photos of the dead body—his legs, feet, hands, arms, torso, and back—all the skin was clean.

"The name Benaiah. They said it's an ancient name, not very

common today. They think he could be from an ancient order." Bucky stopped speaking, and the keys stopped clicking.

"What?" she asked.

"Check your email."

Annie pulled up the email and read it. Beside the picture of the brooch was a hand-drawn picture sent by their sister Wizard Guards from across the globe. The design was the same. "That's from his brooch! What does the design mean, then?"

The printer hummed as Bucky continued to print off information. "Exactly. I'm copying everything for your file. And…" He stopped for a moment, a long pause. "Okay, the Wizard Guards have no idea who he is, but like I said, they think he's part of this ancient order known as the Fraternitatem of Solomon, a group that procures items supposedly belonging to King Solomon. They are the self-proclaimed protectors of the ancient artifacts. I'm telling you, this brooch has their panties in a bunch."

"Okay, so if the brooch is from their group and if they're charged with protecting the ancient artifacts, why was he planning on selling at the market?"

"Motive for murder," Bucky offered. His pace of rhythmic typing remained consistent, but then he paused for another moment. "The guards say the Fraternitatem is a mysterious group they've only been aware of for the last fifty years and still know virtually nothing about. They have run up against them several times and always note the link because of the brooch design which is called a Solomon's knot. They're sending me what they have on them and apologize for the lightness of the file. I'll have that for you when you come in next. Tomorrow?"

"Yeah. I should be in tomorrow, unless something happens." Annie mulled over the new information for a moment. "The Fraternitatem of Solomon. I'm gonna jump to conclusions and say they are responsible for Benaiah's death, based on their goals and the fact that he had the ring. Though before we go up against this group, I'm curious why one of their own would try to sell what they're supposed to be protecting."

"Vendetta, revenge, bad seed, undercover operation," Bucky volunteered.

Annie chuckled. Even in the magical world, any of those would be a possibility. "All that magic we found at the scene. The four spells. Do we have a match for those by any chance?"

"Nothing in our databases. I've sent those out. The Middle East Guard is running it against their database. In their email, they're insistent that they don't have much and that this magical trace is the most they've ever had before. I'll let you know if we get any hits. If you need anything else, call."

"Thanks Bucky."

After hanging up, Annie opened her locked cabinet, the one she knew Cham had used the night before. She was surprised to find the pin covered in a sticky substance, probably blood. Cham would have cleaned the lock after use. The hairs on the back of her neck stood up.

Who used this?

She thought about what Zola had said to Cham.

I'm not safe.

With a shaky hand, Annie cleaned the lock before pricking her finger with the pin. Her skin snapped, the lock opened, and the cabinet door popped open. She expected the ring to be missing, but it was still sitting in the plastic bag on top of her family's *Book of Shadows*.

Annie held her crystal above the ring, confirming it was still the same magical ring. When she was sure, she placed it back inside the cabinet and pulled out her tome.

She heaved the book on the table. It wasn't always useful because Annie's family hadn't always been Wizard Guards and therefore hadn't had experience with some of the things she and her dad had seen.

And I've seen things that even Dad wasn't exposed to.

Annie didn't expect to find anything helpful at all. The ring had been thought of as a myth until now, and no one really knew about the Fraternitatem of Solomon. The pages flipped underneath her spell and fell open when she found what she was looking for. Surprised she stared at the page. It was a passage about the Cave of Ages.

What the hell? It's not the Fraternitatem, so why did it stop here?

Immediately, she recognized her father's handwriting and swallowed the lump in her throat as she fingered the curve of his *S*, his slant toward the end of sentences. He had hated paperwork and always rushed to finish. Annie touched the ink while reading about the case, one involving a stolen rock—several rocks, in fact—that possessed the ability to see into the future and return to the past.

The Chintamani Stones?

Rocks flooding the market. Either loose rocks or attached to rings, amulets, hilts of athames.

The wearer can view the past and future?

I've been told they're the Chintamani Stones. They really exist.

Being sold in the black market. Rathbone acting as liaison between the market and ????? Still have no name for the group trying to procure these stones.

Group somewhere from the Middle East. Only told me they were after the same stones I'm looking for.

Followed them to their camp location, could only glean they're somewhere from the Cave of Ages?

Cave of Ages–ancient cave supposedly housing the treasure of King Solomon. The cave is a blue-hued, shimmering cave that can be seen from miles away if you're in the desert at night. It wasn't thought to have existed.

Okay, and this has to do with the Fraternitatem how?

Interspersed within Jason Pearce's notes were doodles. He wasn't a doodler, and yet they were scrawled all over the page. Annie was the one who doodled when she was bored or preoccupied. She drew things with meaning about cases and clues.

I wonder...

She reviewed the drawings, the curves, the angles, the squiggles, the mark in the corner that was hidden in another marking. She took out her magnifying glass and found the word *Fraternitatem* with a question mark next to it.

Turning the book, she followed the curves of the lines he had drawn, looking for anything thing else weird or hidden. She summoned a flashlight and used the pinpoint light to examine the paper, looking for changes in ink or in the paper itself.

I see...

Her fingertips grazed the center of this passage, where she felt a tiny rise. It was so small, she couldn't have found it without the flashlight, but now she couldn't not see it. Summoning a straight pin, she poked a hole in the paper and pulled up gently until her fingers grasped what was inside.

It was a miniscule scrap of paper, not worth anything.

But Dad hid this inside the Book of Shadows.

Annie held her crystal across the paper and read an old magical trace that she was sure her father had cast eight years ago. She waved her palm across the paper, and it grew to its full size.

A map of the Cave of Ages!

"What's that?" Cham asked, surprising her. She hadn't heard his familiar gait enter.

"Hey." She explained the map and the cave and the possible connection to the Fraternitatem.

"Okay. And this is related how?" He kissed the top of her head.

"Sorry. I've been busy here. The brooch Benaiah wore is a Solomon's knot, the symbol for the group whose sole purpose is to protect ancient artifacts once belonging to King Solomon."

"Ah. Now I get it. The ring." He smiled and pulled up a chair beside her. "You were supposed to rest today."

"Yeah, yeah. I had planned on it until the elf destroyed the kitchen and pissed off Zola. I had to take him to Windmere." She rolled her eyes.

Cham glanced around the kitchen and took a whiff. "That explains the clean smell in here," he said. "So this is the map of the cave?" He picked up the map and examined it.

"Not sure. Dad came in contact with this group when he was searching for Chintamani Stones that were flooding the black market eight years ago. He only made the smallest mention in the Book of Shadows. Anything I can learn about the Fraternitatem will be helpful. If they're that powerful, we might not be able to touch them for the murder."

"And the Chintamani Stones are the same ones that are in the ring?" Cham asked. He reached for the *Book of Shadows* to verify for himself.

"Yes. Mrs. Cuttlebrink confirmed the stones in the ring were part of these Chintamani Stones."

Cham skimmed through Jason's notes. "Rathbone worked for them," he said.

"Yeah. I can't believe I might have to look into Dad's death again," Annie said. She was sure that wasn't the direction to take the case. Oftentimes artifacts rotated through the market every few years.

But then, Rathbone had admitted to killing Jason Pearce, and this case was at the same time her father died.

Cham's eyes crinkled with worry.

"They killed Benaiah for the ring. We need to get the ring out of here," he said with finality.

Annie had nothing to dissuade him. *He and Zola are right.*

"So what's your next step?" Cham asked.

"Mortimer. I think he might have an idea of who Benaiah is. If not, he might know something about the ring or the Fraternitatem."

"And your arm?"

"It's fine. I'm working tomorrow. And you—did you get into the market to confirm the shapeshifters are our missing wizards and witches?"

Cham frowned. "Our crystals were useless in the market. There is so much magic they couldn't read individual spells. And once we took them out, Emerson and I had to leave. The Wizard Guard is being watched."

"Who's researching the spell found at the missing persons' homes?"

"Emerson and Mrs. Cuttlebrink are on it, though they haven't had much luck. It appears to be an ancient spell, but not a wizard-created one." Cham wrapped his arm around Annie's shoulder and kissed her cheek before he softly whispered in her ear. "Feeling okay tonight?"

She pushed him away, but her hand lingered in the middle of his chest. "Just curious. Did you forget to clean the blood lock yesterday?"

He glanced as the cabinet. "I could have forgotten, but I'm pretty sure I cleaned it. Why?"

"It was dirty when I pulled out the book this afternoon."

"Sorry. I'll be more careful next time. So how do you feel? Hungry, tired, in pain?" He smirked. She knew what he really wanted.

"Not as stiff as you." Annie kissed him as he teleported her upstairs.

CHAPTER 13

THE SNAKE HEAD Letters was built on the outskirts of Chicago, across the street from the border of Evanston, Illinois. To hide the store in plain sight, and ensure nonmagicals weren't tempted to patronize the establishment, the building was imbued with heavy magic that changed the store's façade depending on who walked by. A mother with small children might see a sports bar while a single man might view it as a dollhouse shop.

To Annie, the store was nothing more than an ancient, rundown building with cracked windows that were covered in a thick layer of grime. Before entering, she stood by the window and glanced inside, noting the owner, Archibald Mortimer, in a heated conversation with a witch. Annie's hand rested on the ancient green trim, which peeled off at her touch. She wiped the lead-based paint chips on her pant leg and pulled the rotting wood door open by its loose knob.

The musty, moldy stench of age overwhelmed her as she stepped onto loose, spongy floor boards. With each step, the supports creaked. She treaded lightly, sidestepping a section of linoleum, that had worn through to the subfloor. The tiny hole exposed a dim light from the basement.

While the voices argued, Annie slid inside one of the packed aisles, hiding herself behind the books and junk. She peered between two books and recognized the witch—she was the one who had noticed Annie and Gibbs when they were forced from the market. Not wanting to be seen, Annie grabbed a book and pretended to read.

The witch's gravelly voice was rough as if she had a cold or was a constant smoker; she argued and pointed with gnarled hands, accusing Mortimer of cheating.

"No. You miserable witch. That's the price! You wanna go somewhere else, find it yourself. Go do it. Take it or go!" Mortimer's normally colorless face was flushed. Annie tried to get a glimpse of the item he was selling, but the witch blocked her view.

Mortimer glanced up, away from his client, and caught Annie's eyes through a space in the books. She looked back at the words in the tome she held.

"Screw you, Archibald Mortimer. This place ain't worth the time," the witch grumbled.

"Try and get it at the black market why dontcha, ya crazy old bat! Or did ya already and that's why you come to me?" Mortimer cajoled.

The witch examined the item again. With shaking hands, she tossed a wad of cash on the counter and shoved her item inside the large pocket of her cloak. As she exited the store, her cloak swished behind her, and the rickety door rattled shut.

"You can come out now, little girl," Mortimer grumbled. Still holding the book, Annie joined him at his work counter. The outdated cash register drawer was still open and empty. "Whaddaya want?" Mortimer ran his hand through his gray hair, which stuck up several inches, wiry and wild.

Annie was jittery at the prospect of being alone with the old man. Her arm still hurt, and she wasn't in the mood to spar with him. The short, gruff shopkeeper might actually be able to do her harm in this condition. Anxious, she tapped her good hand against the nicked wood of the counter. Her fingers found a dent as wide as a knife blade but not very deep. Someone must have shoved an athame into the wood, maybe during an argument. "Well?" Mortimer finally asked. He shifted his weight to his other foot and crossed his arms against his chest. She stopped tapping and took out a picture of Benaiah, slapping it against the table.

"Know who this is?" she asked and shoved the picture closer to Mortimer. His watery blue eyes glanced at the face. In less than a second, he shoved it back to her.

"Never seen 'im."

"You sure? Take another look."

Mortimer grabbed the picture examining it. "Nah. Don't know him. He's the dead one outside the portal?"

"Yes. Can you tell me anything about his brooch around his cloak?"

Mortimer held the picture to his face. "Stay away from them." His hand shook when he threw the picture at her.

"Who are they?"

"No, no, girl. You stay away from the Fraternitatem. If they think you're in the way, they will come after you."

"The Ring of Solomon." She watched him carefully. His face turned white, and he looked as though he might pass out. "Mortimer. That ring is in my possession. This man died with it on his body. What is the Fraternitatem?"

"Leave the ring somewhere they can find it, and get out of the way." Mortimer slid from behind the counter and headed for his office in the back of the store. The door squeaked open and slammed shut with a bang and a rattle.

Undeterred by his warning, Annie headed to the aisle that housed books on ancient religions. Her fingers traced the spines of antique tomes, atlases, picture books, Bibles, grimoires and Books of Shadows. Annie, a collector of books of all kinds, would have loved to own several of these, but she was only interested in one. She just didn't know which one yet.

Starting with a general book of ancient mythology—Jewish, Greek, Roman, Sumerian, and Islamic—she perused stories about

King Solomon and his temple. Unfortunately, there was no mention of the ring or the djinn Solomon supposedly controlled.

Engrossed in what she read, she didn't hear the office door swing open or Mortimer's familiar shuffle grow closer.

"You can learn about the ring, or you can get rid of it. I suggest you pretend you've never seen it," Mortimer said.

"I need to know what it does," she argued.

"Your life, girl. Stupid girl. Go off, just like your father. Get yourself killed." He swatted the air beside her and shuffled away.

Through the stacks of books, Mortimer leered at her with the kind of look that warned her to leave. Absently she tapped the book she was holding.

"I'm not like my father!" she said defensively, in that annoying sound she couldn't control when she was stressed or anxious. Mortimer knew which buttons to push, which angered Annie.

"You have the ring. Makes you a target. I hear you were run outta the market. I hear all Wizards Guards are being run outta the market."

News traveled quickly in their small magical world, Annie wasn't surprised that Archibald Mortimer already knew. She caught his gaze. "You have an ear to the ground. What's really going on at the market?"

Mortimer shrugged and pretended to straighten a pile of books beside him. Bony, wrinkled fingers wrapped around a tome and moved it from one pile to another. Everything here was old, and everything smelled like dust and mildew. Even after ignoring her question, he didn't leave. He seemed content to play around with the items in front of him, teasing her.

"We know the master is a djinn. We know he hired this Benaiah, a member of the Fraternitatem, to find the ring and bring it to him. Why would a member of the Fraternitatem be willing to sell the ring, let alone give it to a djinn that's controlled by the ring?"

Fear creeped inside Mortimer's watery blue eyes, which paled further as he grimaced. "Leave it be. Bad enough you're asking about the Fraternitatem."

"What do you know?"

"I know enough to not ask questions." He was no longer flushed from his encounter with the witch. His jaw tightened.

"There are a lot of animals, domestic animals at market. We think this is the master's attempt to secure an army, and we think these people are on the missing persons list. The protection spell is breaking down. Snow was blowing in from outside. What do you know about what's happening at the market?"

"Drop it, girl. Get rid of the ring and move on. Forget you've ever heard of the Fraternitatem."

"Mortimer, you know. I know you know what's going on at the market," she pleaded, but Archibald Mortimer stood his ground and glared at her before shuffling away.

❊

With Archibald Mortimer afraid of the Fraternitatem and warning her away from them, Annie pulled the ring from her field pack. The Wizard Guard had storage containers throughout the department that opened through blood locks. She stood at one of hers, storage unit 6A, and punctured her finger with the pin. The lock clicked open, and the door swung forward. Inside the storage unit was a metal box that was permanently attached to the unit. To open this safe, Annie cast a spell at the lock, which opened for her magical trace. The lid popped open; she placed the ring inside and slammed the door shut.

Even with the ring safe inside Wizard Hall, Annie knew it wasn't over. They were still going to come.

When she returned to her desk, she saw the present Bucky had left for her: a new folder with the current information. His note said it all.

Middle East is aware of five members they've come in contact with at smaller markets throughout the world. Here are pictures of two members.

As promised, the file was sparse. For fifty years, the Middle East Wizard Guard had had very little contact with the Fraternitatem. It occurred to Annie at that moment her father quite possibly had gotten closer to them than the Wizard Guard had. She closed her eyes and thought back eight years.

I was fifteen years old.

When she was fifteen, she was living away from home and not seeing her father daily. Still, Annie tried to think of any cases he might have told her about on their weekly phone calls. But Jason Pearce didn't always share what he was working on.

But then, Dad, no one knew what you were working on when you died.

She thought about Wolfgange Rathbone, the man who had engineered the murder of Princess Amelie and Jordan Wellington. After she had been locked in a basement with him for several hours, he had admitted he killed her dad. Everyone at Wizard Hall knew he was evil and worked both sides for his benefit.

Did he work for the Fraternitatem? Did he kill Dad because Dad knew too much?

Without much information about this secret group, Annie realized she had two choices. She could go to the USP Terre Haute Maximum Security Prison where Rathbone would spend the rest of his life to find out what if anything he knew about the Fraternitatem. But with Jack out of town, she would leave that as her last resort.

Instead she chose option two, something she had never done before.

I'll look into Dad's old cases.

She felt it in her gut; she knew it as if it were truth: Her dad had known more than anyone about this group. With that knowledge on her mind, she cautiously stepped into the stairwell to the basement. She grew more anxious at the thought of a connection and soon found herself jogging down the steps to the Records Chamber.

The chamber was large, seemingly too large to be under the building because every year it grew exponentially as needed—a perk of magic.

Annie entered. Not having a bin number or a case file, she started with the computers. Like any other company in the United States, Wizard Hall was completely automated and reliant on technology. First, she tried typing in Jason Pearce and pulling up his case files.

The search returned a long list. Annie scrolled through the case file descriptions looking for anything about Chintamani Stones, the Fraternitatem, the Cave of Ages.

It's here!

She clicked on the file.

RESTRICTED

Reversing out, she tried a different case; again, it appeared that all of Jason's files were restricted.

That's weird.

She tried one more time, clicking on the file for the Fraternitatem and marking down the case number. She would have to look for the files the old-fashioned way.

F-12-08-18745 #4. Case 18745, December 2008, four files included.

It was six months before Dad had died. Annie became more certain this case was why he had died.

It can't be.

She held her breath and readied herself to head back into the stacks to track down the month and year. Blowing out stale air, she pulled out the records drawer where the files should be located.

Even though the files were restricted, Annie found them easily. She pulled the first three from the drawer.

Missing one.

She read the labels of every file in this drawer. When she couldn't find the fourth, she searched the drawers above and below and on either side. The fourth file appeared to be missing.

Odd... or maybe not so odd.

After an hour of trying to track down the missing file, Annie was still unsuccessful. Grabbing the three she had, she left the records chamber for her desk.

The cubicle beside Annie's belonged to Gibbs. When she knocked on his cubical wall, he was reviewing a large book of spells. She assumed it was to verify the spell found at several locations throughout the city.

He's still looking for the missing persons.

"Hey, you got a minute?" she asked.

He glanced up, grimaced, and waved her in. As Annie sat down across from him, he shoved the book to the side. "What's up, girl?"

She plopped the three heavy files on his desk. "We've discovered that the design on the brooch belonged to a group called the Fraternitatem of Solomon, self-proclaimed protectors of King Solomon's artifacts, and they probably murdered Benaiah. The Middle East Wizard Guard doesn't have much on this group, but I happened upon some information in my Book of Shadows—a case Dad worked on about six months before he died. Dad was chasing several of the same stones that adorn the Ring of Solomon, so I thought I'd look into these to see what dad knew about the Fraternitatem. I get this feeling he knew more than anyone else." She pointed to the files.

Gibbs processed Annie's words. His only reaction for a few moments was a downturned lip. Annie couldn't gauge what that meant until he spoke. "I don't know that case. How'd you find it?"

"The word *Fraternitatem* appeared in the Book of Shadows. He

SHERYL STEINES

took notes about rocks that do the same thing as the ones in the ring. Just a note, Gibbs."

He pulled down the first folder and perused the first page. "Could be a connection. You need to be careful. This order—they killed for the ring and never found it. They won't stop with Benaiah."

"I hid the ring in the Hall. But yeah. That won't stop them."

"Six months before he died? Could be what he was working on. Is there a mention of Rathbone in any of these?"

"Yes. He mentioned that Rathbone was the liaison at the market for this Fraternitatem."

"Annie you need to be careful," Gibbs whispered.

"That's why I want to see what Dad knew about them. They've stymied the Middle East Wizard Guard unit. There appears to be no information about them or their people. It just seems Dad knew about them. He had contact with them." She touched the top of the pile and sighed. "The problem is the record number says there should be four files. I only found three."

Gibbs's blue eyes drew closer together, separated by a deep crease in his forehead. Annie didn't often see worry on his face. He normally hid his emotions well.

"We need to order a team of guards for your house," he said.

"No. That's ridiculous. I'd give up the ring before they could hurt me. I'd teleport out. Besides, Cham basically lives with me." She offered a smile, but she knew he wasn't convinced.

"Annie, this is ridiculous!" Gibbs yelled.

Annie jumped. It was the loudest voice she had ever heard Gibbs use. "Seriously, Gibbs. If I find I'm in trouble, I'll call. No guards. I just came here to find out if you might have the fourth file. Based on your reaction, I'm thinking no. Maybe Ryan knows."

Ryan Connelly, the current Grand Marksman, was the leader of the wizard community in the United States. Before becoming the leader of the wizard free world, he was a Wizard Guard and Annie's father's partner until Jason Pearce died. Unless someone here at Wizard Hall wanted the file removed or "lost," Jason

Pearce might have given it to Ryan. Maybe there was something he wanted protected. Annie couldn't believe it had just gone missing.

"Annie. I'm warning you girl. You be careful. You call before you do anything. Do I make myself clear?"

Annie had learned her lesson last year when she almost got caught alone in Rathbone's warehouse while staking him out. She now never went anywhere without someone knowing where she was. "I will," she promised.

"If your dad saved anything, Ryan would know. Otherwise, he might've hidden it at home," Gibbs suggested

She glanced at Gibbs as if he had just offered a revelation.

Where in the hell would Dad hide something if it wasn't in the blood lock in the kitchen?

"Any thoughts where?"

Gibbs snorted. "That folder might have just gone missing. Ever think of that?"

CHAPTER 14

GLADDEN PACED. ANXIOUS thoughts roamed his mind, jumbled and unclear. Though violence as a means to an end didn't bother him, going after Archibald Mortimer caused him much concern. The man, no matter how odious, was very valuable and always a friend of the market.

While mulling over his options for finding the girl, he grunted and growled to himself; those who passed skirted him the best they could, many crossing the street before reaching him. He was garnering more attention than necessary, so Gladden entered a store directly across from the Snake Head Letters and peered out the plate-glass window.

This establishment sold paper, sachets, and potpourri, and the smell assaulted his nose. Gladden wasn't used to the sweet smell; it was nearly too much as he skulked along the window and glared across the street.

Patrons in the store stared at him as though there was something odd, different, or just plain wrong with him. They had no idea just how correct they were.

The scar and missing hair on his head left some nervous. Gladden didn't care. If he turned and looked at them, he'd glare and bare his teeth. They were sharp and protruding and made him look less than human and totally insane. Within fifteen minutes, the store cleared out, and the owner, uncomfortable with the man in his shop, attempted to ask him to leave. Gladden grunted while keeping a view on the Snake Head Letters.

Gladden didn't care what they thought of him, only what the master would do if he didn't find that girl, the weak one with the injured arm. He could take her easily and be done with it quickly as soon as Mortimer told him who she was and where to find her. He was threatening Mortimer first.

He watched the Snake Head Letters carefully and waited for the witch with the ratted burgundy cloak to exit. Finally, she shuffled out the door, her gait slow yet steady as she turned down the alley, preparing to teleport. Gladden grumbled when Mortimer glanced out the window. Seeing Gladden across the street, the shopkeeper lowered the shades and locked the front door.

He knows something.

Unable to hold off any longer, Gladden exited the sickingly sweet-scented store; the bell on the door jingled, and the door rattled as it slammed shut. Gladden crossed the street in a few large strides. Cars stopped quickly, but the wizard ignored the angry blare of the horns.

At the entrance to the Snake Head Letters, Gladden jiggled the locked handle. Already angry, he cast a spell blowing the window out of the front door. Glass shattered and cascaded to the floor. The door squeaked open, and his boots crunched against the shattered glass as he entered the musty, packed store.

Gladden walked slowly, looking down each aisle, and skirted a pile of boxes in the center of the path. He slid behind the counter and thumbed through several notebooks filled with chicken scratches. It was so illegible that he placed the stacks of papers back in their haphazard piles—where he discovered a discarded a one-hundred-dollar bill. Pocketing the money and finding nothing useful among the piles of paper, the wizard headed to the office door, expecting the room to be empty.

The light was still on, and the small desk was covered in boxes, either broken, bent or stained. It would take days to go through the junk to maybe find who the girl was. Leaving the room, Gladden ascended the stairs to the right of the office, taking two stairs at a time to reach the apartment on the second floor.

Gladden didn't knock. He pushed his palms forward, and a jinx flew from his hands and exploded the wood door. Splinters and chunks of wood sprayed across the apartment. A shard landed with such force that it stuck in the drywall across the room.

Archibald Mortimer, wedged between a large armoire and a cracked wall, shook violently as Gladden strode across the sparsely decorated room. With a gloved hand he lifted the shopkeeper by the neck. "I'm looking for a wizard guard. Short, dark brown hair, female. Injured arm. Who is she?"

Mortimer kicked violently, unable to breathe with the hand of Gladden around his windpipe. "Le—le—g—go."

Gladden dropped him to the ground. The shopkeeper fell hard on his ass, jostling his entire body. Coughing and sputtering, Mortimer clutched his neck and finally said, "Don't know who you're talking about. Don't deal with the Guard."

But Gladden knew about Archibald Mortimer, who played both sides if it suited him. Besides, the owner refused to look him in the eye. The wizard kicked Mortimer in the leg, and the old man yelped.

"Don't lie, Archibald," Gladden hissed. "I know you know who she is. Tell me where I can find her."

"What'd she do to ya?" Mortimer smirked slightly, enraging Gladden.

"What she did is none of your concern." Not waiting for Archibald to answer, Gladden threw a hex at the store owner, burning a large hole in the flesh of his upper arm.

"The fuck you do that for? I didn't do nothing. If you want to find the wizard guard, ask in the warehouse district. The vampires, they know the guards." Tears welled in Mortimer's eyes as blood soaked his sleeve.

"I'm asking you." Gladden punched Mortimer in the head,

knocking him backwards. His head bounced on the splinter-covered floor. A sharp piece of wood cut through the skin on the back of his head. Blood ran into his ear.

The old man, slow to get up but slower to answer, pulled himself into a ball. Gladden reached down, pulled Mortimer up by the shirt, and threw him against the wall. His short, fat body crashed into the drywall and fell to the floor face first. Drywall cracked and fell from the studs, leaving a large gaping hole in the wall. Concussed and unable to move, Mortimer remained motionless as another spell contacted his battered body. He slid across the floor, crashing into the stove and leaving a trail of blood along the floor and against the oven door.

"Who is she?"

Unable to breathe or speak, Archibald Mortimer shook his head.

"Is she worth protecting?" Gladden conjured a baseball bat and slapped it against his hand. Mortimer saw the bat, and his eyes widened in fear as the wood smacked into Gladden's hand. In a small voice he whispered, "Annie Pearce."

Gladden stepped over the limp body of Archibald Mortimer, dropping the bat beside the broken man.

CHAPTER 15

TWO CLOSETS FLANKED either side of Annie's bathroom door. Since she didn't own enough to fill both of them, she started her searching with the empty one.

With her scrying crystal she searched for magic across the empty closet, across the floors, the walls, in the three drawer dresser in the corner. She found no magical energy.

Squatting down, she felt for loose floorboards, ran her hand along the baseboards, searching for hidden latches. Finding nothing, she moved to the one that was packed full of clothes, shoes, and purses. After a cursory check with her crystal, she started patting along the walls and floorboard, reaching in between her clothes and other items.

It didn't seem to be hidden in the bedroom. She guessed her dad would hide something in the basement, far from hers and Samantha's bedrooms. He wouldn't want to chance it being too close to them.

Maybe Ryan knows.

She sat on the top of the stairs and dialed her phone.

"Annie, sweetie, hi." Ryan answered. Since he had been her dad's best friend when they attended Windmere, he always treated her as his own daughter.

"Hey, Ryan."

"So to what do I owe the pleasure of this call?"

Do I really want to delve into this, bring this up again?

It had been hard enough for all of them when Wolfgang Rathbone was arrested and put on trial for the murder of Princess Amelie. They all knew he had killed her father.

Would anyone really want me to pursue Dad's death again?

"Well…" She hesitated, still concerned that this was the wrong direction and had nothing to do with the case.

"Annie?"

"Here's the problem. The victim outside the black market—well, I ran into something in my *Book of Shadows* that might be the mostly likely suspect. It's a group called the Fraternitatem of Solomon. And, well… Dad came across them." She said it in one long breath and blew out stale air until her lungs burned.

Ryan took his time to process what this meant. Annie instantly regretted telling him and even considering this as a line of investigation.

"I'm not familiar with this group," he said.

"I found the case files. Dad was looking into the illegal sales of Chintamani Stones. It seems my group was after those stolen rocks."

"Yeah. That I remember. The files should be in the records chambers."

"Got three of the four. The fourth seems to be missing."

Ryan was silent on the other end of the phone, so quiet that Annie could hear his fingers drum against the desk top.

"I have no answer for that, except maybe someone mismarked the case number and assumed there were four folders," he said after a moment.

It was possible. It was probably nothing. "This Fraternitatem is very dangerous. We think four of them killed our guy," she said, hoping to convince him this was the correct line of investigation. Her stomach churned.

"Is there anything in the three folders?"

"I haven't had time to look. I'll be reading through them

tonight. Do you think Dad labeled the case correctly but kept the fourth file?"

Ryan remained silent. Annie thought he might be remembering how Jason worked, what his procedures were, and where he might have stored files.

"Yes. I'm not sure if he'd have kept them at the house. If he did, maybe the basement or garage," he said.

"Thanks. I'm not sure if this is even anything. It's just so… coincidental." It worried Annie that a case belonging to her father could be tied up in hers.

"Annie, if this group is dangerous, learn what you can about them. Bring in help. Ask Emerson for help if you need it." Ryan's worry was palpable, and Annie felt that anxiety in her chest.

"What should I do?"

"I can't tell you that, Annie. All I can say is that if Jason had information on this group, information that will keep you safe, pursue it. Anything else about that case not related to yours— drop it."

"But do we really want to go through this again?"

"No. Not really. But I always figured at some point in time you would be at this place. You did it with Rathbone and now…"

"Maybe I won't need to," she said before telling him goodbye.

❃

Annie wasn't sure she was ready to deal with the fourth file—the file that, if it existed, she was sure had something big inside. Instead of searching further, she sat at the table to peruse the existing files.

Maybe I won't need it.

It was a painstakingly difficult job reading through her dad's notes, seeing his handwriting scrawled over the pages. It tugged at Annie's heart as she flipped the page and begin a new sheet.

The first two folders contained information about the Chintamani Stone. From what she had already learned about the Ring of

Solomon, the stones on the flat top of the ring were cut from that stone. It was originally divided in four smaller stones and gifted to three people, one of whom was King Solomon.

The last folder she had contained information about people Jason Pearce had met on this case. As Annie read through each file, she began to take hasty notes.

Chintamani Stone–a greenish molda-vite stone

Powers of wish fulfillment

Gifted to King Tavaloo and King Solomon

Kept at an abbey in Tibet

Fourth stone lost to time. Appears whoever owns it has been chipping away at it, selling pieces at the black market

The source of the stones: a man named Nicholas Roerich? He was last seen in Morocco.

The Moroccan market, smaller than the main black market, just as dangerous.

While researching, was forcefully taken by a group of men known as the Frater-nitatem. The names I caught during my confinement were Avi, Benjamin, Akiva, Yosel and Benaiah.

My Benaiah?
During my stay with these men at a cave in the mountains, they advised me of their work. They are the Fraternitatem

of Solomon, the group chosen to protect the artifacts of King Solomon. They
claim these stones I'm searching for
come from the rock gifted to him and it
belongs to them. They strongly advised
me, with a carefully worded hex, that I
leave this alone.

So the fourth stone is still missing?

"Not my problem," Annie said out loud.

The Fraternitatem advised me that they
had agents all throughout the world
and would know if I wasn't following through on my promise to leave the
stones alone. They would take care of
everything.

A member of the Fraternitatem had fetched the ring for the
djinn at the black market.

If he was charged with protecting it, why was he so willing to sell it?
I returned the stones as they forcefully
requested and promised not to look for
anymore outside of the black market. I
promised I'd return to them whatever I
found. They referred to their location as
the Cave of Ages.

The Cave of Ages: beautiful, ethereal.
Shimmering blue walls. You could see
the light from the cave for miles in the
darkness.

Dad was there!

There's not much on the Fraternitatem. With help from Sabrina Cuttlebrink, we were able to determine the group had only been known to the Middle East Wizard Guard for about fifty years. Though stories about them surfacing topside have gone back about two thousand. They claim to be direct descendants of King Solomon's court.

Most definitely magical and quite proficient.

Dr. Arden Blakely at The Field Museum in Chicago seemed to know much about the Chintamani Stone and had even heard of the Ring of Solomon being real. She claimed the ring had been found in an excavation site circa 1970 and lost several years later. She has been searching for the elusive ring since. But she offered no help in finding the rest of the missing stones.

Archibald Mortimer, when asked about the dig, said it was just a rumor in 1920 that said the ring was found in a dig site and lost to a cave-in. Ring's been gone for years, he claimed.

Damn, Mortimer! Could've told me that!

Like most magical objects they came across over the course of a case, whether legal or illegal, evil or white magic, most of the time, the artifact had been around for centuries, or in this case, several millennia. She made a mental note to ask Bucky if he could find the location for this Dr. Blakely to learn what she knew about the ring—how it was used or how to disarm it.

Her arm throbbed now; she stored the folders in the blood lock cabinet before climbing onto the sofa and snuggling in.

She glanced out the window. The snow gently fell as it had been doing all day. As the large, fluffy snowflakes cascaded down, her mind wandered to images of the two dig sites. She pondered how many people had lost their lives over this ring.

With the blanket up to her neck, she felt her muscles relax, and her body gratefully accepted a nap.

❧

Crunch… crunch…

Annie's eyes fluttered open. The sound came from just outside the sliding door of the den, startling her from a blissful nap. She thought of the billdads that rooted through the dead garden in her backyard. She rolled onto her back and stared at the ceiling. As she gradually awoke from the nap and became more alert, the scratches continued.

Bitherby? It couldn't be.

She peered through the window blinds. The light was gray and dull, and the shadows in the backyard were deep and dark. Anything could be hiding inside of them, though she saw no movement or fur flying.

It's probably just an animal.

The clock on the table reminded her Cham would be home soon.

Pain again radiated down her arm from overuse. Annie slipped off the sling to stretch her tight shoulder; the throbbing took her breath away.

She strolled to the kitchen and took a swig of the pain potion Gibbs had left in the fridge. Instantly woozy, she grabbed the counter top and noticed that Zola had left a note.

I'll be back with dinner. Rest and don't leave the house.

Zola's orders were scrawled across the paper in her flowery handwriting. Annie chuckled and dropped the note in the garbage.

But that was hours ago!

The scratching returned, Annie turned to the window, expecting it to be Zola having trouble with groceries and the snow. It was darker than it was mere minutes before, and she still couldn't see movement. The shadows were black, empty holes.

Suddenly warm and tired, Annie inched her way to table and rested her head on the shiny table to wait for her head to stop spinning.

The windows rattled against the storm that raged outside.

I'll just close my eyes.

Gusts battered the space between Annie's house and Mrs. Wexler's next door. Garbage cans stored on the side of the house blew into Annie's yard and bounced against the siding.

As the dizziness settled, Annie opened her eyes to complete darkness. With a flick of her wrist, she threw on warm lights. The wind continued to push and pull, picking up dead leaves, twigs, and garbage in a tornado-like swirl.

She chuckled. Mrs. Welter always left the lid off.

As garbage swirled in the wind, Annie watched, unable to pull away from the window. It wasn't because of the swirling trash or her disheveled, exhausted appearance. Something wasn't right about the reflection. Maybe it was the scratching outside that had her feeling off, like she was being watched. She stared at the reflection of the cabinets, the entrance between the kitchen and the hallway, and the stainless steel refrigerator.

Turning quickly, straining her shoulder and neck, she glanced around the newly cleaned kitchen. Newly cleaned... but there were dark streaks of red on the blood-locked cabinet. Someone without access had tried to get inside. The door surrounding the handle was scratched and marked.

Is it the same person who left blood all over the lock?

Annie grew anxious that the protection spell around her house was waning. She knew someone who shouldn't be here had found a way to enter.

But I was only gone this morning, I've been home all afternoon!

Suddenly she realized: Zola still wasn't home.

"Zola!" Annie cried out. She and Zola were linked together, bound by magic, Annie's voice, her calls for her should have been enough for her to appear.

The house remained silent. Even the wind settled to an uneasy quiet.

"Zola!" Annie frantically repeated.

More footsteps scraped and bumped, but not from the backyard. It could very easily be the wind swaying in the naked branches and scratching the roof top.

Maybe.

Throwing on the outside light, she had a clear view of the deck and stairs. Just beyond the light, the backyard had fallen into a desperately thick darkness where she couldn't distinguish between the different shades of black.

The snow was thick and heavy, covering the deck. Footprints dotted the freshly fallen snow and led from the steps to the door and back again. They were too large to be Annie's, and Zola had no need to walk through the snow. If Cham had come home early, he would have woken her.

Who's out there?

She threw on shoes and reached for her jacket.

"Going somewhere?"

Annie turned; a man she didn't recognize stood in her hallway.

❈

Fuzzy shapes moved through the dim light.

Annie's head rolled forward.

Footsteps clicked against the hard floor.

Where am I?

Voices argued. A chilled hand wrapped around her thick, curly hair and yanked her head backwards. The motion pulled on her shoulder, and pain radiated downward. Annie's hands were numb and cold, immobile and bound behind her.

She opened her eyes.

Where am I?

A dim light from outside offered her the only light in the darkness. She was still unable to place her surroundings, so she closed her eyes again, took a deep breath, and felt the chair beneath her. It was hard, familiar. She squirmed; her arms were tied tightly together, causing the intense pain to return quickly.

Annie looked into the darkness. What few images she could see were dark, fuzzy. She took another breath. The stench of death and burning wood wafted to her.

Where am I?

Her eyes adjusted to the darkness as the fog began to lift. A cold hand grazed her cheek. Annie shuddered, and her swollen shoulder shook.

"Is she awake yet?" The male voice seethed impatiently. His footsteps shook the floor, which creaked beneath him as he paced.

A dark shadow cut across the room.

"She's woozy, I think," a second voice replied.

Annie's head spun. She turned toward the voice and could see two orange eyes gleaming. Over the strange man's shoulder, a window let in low light and reflected on a mirror beside it.

I'm still at home.

She pulled against the smooth wood of the chair—her kitchen chair. In her bound state, it was grossly uncomfortable. Loosening the bindings was nearly impossible; they were magically joined together with her palms facing each other. The rope that held her wouldn't budge.

A tall, thin shadow strode along the hallway to the front door.

The Fraternitatem?

Annie filled her lungs with muggy air, putting pressure on her shoulder as shooting pains coursed through her left side.

Cham where are you?

Footsteps stopped in front of her. She got a strong whiff of the market, of dung and dirt and wet animal fur.

"What do you want?" she said through gritted teeth.

"You have something of mine and I'd like it back," the man sneered.

Annie knew she should feel fear. No one knew where she was or what was happening. She was pissed instead.

"Turn on a light so I can see you," she countered.

The silhouette of an arm whipped around, throwing on the hallway light. A tall man towered over her. He lacked hair on the left side of his head, and his bald patch clearly featured a dark line.

A scar?

Annie's eyes darted from his face to his torso and down his legs. He didn't dress like Benaiah. He wore no cloak or identifying symbols. He reminded Annie more of Gibbs, with the tight pants, T-shirt, and a well-worn leather jacket with a rip at the hem.

"I'd like it back," he jeered. His mouth pulled against his taut skin, revealing protruding teeth.

A vampire.

The cold hand yanked on her hair again, sending her head backwards, a jolt of pain so strong she felt nauseated.

"You have to be more specific," she said as she held in vomit that sat in her throat. "Let go of me!" she shouted at the vampire.

The vampire laughed at her discomfort and wrapped more hair around his hand. Annie's eyes dashed across the room as she planned an escape. Fearful either one of them would jump her teleport, she decided she needed to head outside for the alley behind the house. The shelter of a clump of trees could aid her escape.

The vampire removed the hair from her neck, exposing soft skin. His fangs extended automatically, and he looked at her like a piece of meat. Annie grimaced.

"It's wasn't in your blood lock. Nice touch by the way. Where is my ring?" The scarred man kept control of his voice, though Annie could detect his tension.

Is he the master of the Fraternitatem?

Mortimer's warning rang in her ear, like a beacon.

Give them the ring and run for safety.

Panic stuck in her throat; she could barely speak. She turned her eyes toward the kitchen and saw that the cabinet was blown apart. Wood shards scattered across the floor, and her *Book of Shadows* lay in tattered pieces, scorched and still smoking. She drew in a sharp breath. All of her dad's notes, burned and gone.

"You blew apart my cabinet for nothing. I don't have whatever ring you think I have."

The man stepped forward. Beyond the stench of the market, Annie could smell his own body odor of sweat and garlic. She grimaced.

He's protecting himself from the vampire.

"I know the Wizard Guard has the body, and I'm pretty sure that imbecile hid the ring on himself before he died. So give me back my ring!"

His palms went up as if to strike. It took all Annie had to keep from jumping at the sight of him preparing to hex her. She kept her gaze focused on the six-inch scar that ran across his partially bald head.

Did a human or creature do that to you, dude?

"I know you're with the Fraternitatem. I don't have your ring, but I know where it is and can get it for you," she offered.

His eyes crinkled. "Fraternitatem?" he mumbled and blinked in confusion or maybe fear. He clearly worked for someone, but maybe not the Fraternitatem—maybe the djinn or even Gladden.

They're still trying to clean up their mess.

Annie twisted her wrists; the ties dug deeply into her skin. Seeing her squirm, the vampire pulled on her hair again.

"Knock it off, jackass!" she shouted to the vampire.

"I don't think you're in any position to give the orders. Give us the ring, and I promise we'll kill you quickly." The tall man threatened her as though he was in charge, but he acted nervous as he immediately returned to pacing and wringing his hands.

He's not really in charge.

"I don't have your ring. Who told you I did?"

The man sneered and placed his hands on her knees and put his face inches from hers. Even in the dark, she saw every blemish, every scar. He had lived a rough life—most likely entirely at the black market, which seeped into his skin and hair and emitted his scent to her home. Annie grimaced.

"You are a wizard guard, and you've been poking around my market. I know you have the ring, now tell me where it is!" His hand whipped across her face.

The slap echoed and stung her face, like tiny pins pricking across her skin. He didn't offer time for a comeback or witty retort. Immediately, she felt the cold steel of a cursed athame across her cheek, piercing her skin.

He called it his *market.*

"Killing me won't get the answer you want, Gladden." She guessed that he was very desperate to clean up his mistakes.

Annie worked her wrists, twisting them enough to expose her palms. Aiming at the vampire, she cast a jinx that sent the creature flying into the wall, landing against the very heavy and extremely expensive mirror on the wall. It crashed to the floor and shattered into thousands of little shards that sparkled in the light.

Gladden stopped as his plan unfolded. With her untied legs, Annie kicked him in the crotch; he doubled over, incapacitated, and fell to his knees. Now able to move her wrists, she magically released the binding spell so the rope slid to the floor. Lunging from her seat, she ran through the house, yanked open the heavy back door, and sprung through the thin screen door. It bounced several times as she ran through the snow-covered yard, out past the fence and alley, hiding herself in a clump of trees across the street.

Years ago, a narrow trail had wound through these trees. Annie and Janie Parker, her best friend, would follow the path to a secret hiding place only the two of them knew existed. Annie ducked inside the trees and felt her way for that thin path.

I know it's here somewhere.

The opening was now overgrown with branches and bushes and was covered in snow. Annie slid inside the narrow path and followed the uneven ground, her thin shoes covered in snow and ice.

Gladden and the vampire left her house. She could hear their angry banter through the trees. They followed her footsteps in the snow; she pushed forward, pulling a low branch from her face, and headed deeper into the trees.

Their arguing echoed in the forest; she picked up her pace. Branches rustled, snow fell. She could hear them gaining on her.

The trees, even without leaves, were so thick and dense, that they darkened the forest floor. Annie couldn't find the landmarks she had used as a kid. Ignoring her growing panic, she moved quickly and stretched her hands out in front of her, searching for overflow gate that she should have reached by now.

Maybe I'm way off trail and several feet from where I should be.

"She ran in here; I know she's here!" the vampire argued from behind Annie.

"I don't see her anymore," Gladden grunted.

Annie's heart pounded. She slipped and slid, attempting to gain distance until she crashed into the gate and bent forward.

"I smell her, you dumbass!" the vampire screamed.

Annie's shoulder twinged as she teleported over the metal gate, slipped in the mud, and landed on her knees.

Crouching just below the height of the shortest bushes or fallen tree branches, Annie scooted along the trail. When Gladden's flashlight scanned the area, she crawled behind a dead tree stump three feet high and listened as their footsteps crunched along the path.

The flashlight illuminated the tree just above her. She ducked farther in the mud.

"She's not here! Damn it!" screamed Gladden.

Annie felt a small sting on her cheek where the knife had dug a little too deep. She touched it with frozen fingers.

"The girl came here. She's in here, and I smell her," argued the vampire.

"She teleported, you nimrod," Gladden said, easily giving up the search.

Beams of light illuminated the trees to the north. Annie ran south in the direction of her secret hiding spot, the one that even Samantha had never known about.

The earth sloped downwards. She slid across the snow and mud, stumbling in the underbrush. As she slid, her outstretched arm wrapped around a thin tree and yanked on her shoulder. She bit the side of her mouth to prevent a scream from escaping.

With a deep breath, she let go of the tree and jumped into her spot where she remembered it would be, though now it was covered in thick foliage. She turned sideways and sucked in her stomach, fitting herself inside a hole between the root systems of two trees. When she was nine, the spot fit two children easily, though Janie had never liked it underground. Now, as an adult, Annie found herself squeezed in tightly. She rested against the dirt as the voices faded away. Either the men were lost in the trees or they had given up. Regardless, Annie hunkered down and planned her escape.

CHAPTER 16

SCRYING FOR MAGIC wasn't a difficult skill, though not every witch or wizard had the ability, desire, or need to do it. To be safe, Annie assumed Gladden had this knowledge. Most likely, he and the vampire had stolen something of hers with which to find her.

No matter where she went, they would be able to track her—and if they found her, Bitherby was next.

With that realization, Annie believed her safest option was Tartarus Prison.

Who would break into there?

Regardless of that, she needed to get the elf first.

In the quiet darkness, she left her hiding spot. Snow fell through the naked branches and landed on her head. She ignored her cold, wet feet and hair as she closed her eyes and teleported back to school.

Windmere School of Witchcraft was built along the northern border between Canada and Minnesota. From the classrooms or dorm rooms on the northern side of the building, on a clear day you could see into Canada. Today she couldn't see three feet in front of herself; the storm was thick and blew wildly. She attempted to land near the stables on the south side of the school grounds, but when she landed she slid across the frozen snow, landing on her ass.

Gingerly, she rose and stared at the stables, which were made up of three large, weather-beaten barns. They were covered in a thick layer of snow and rumbled under the weight of it. She traipsed across open flat land and followed the sound of arguing, which was so loud that she could hear voices above the blustery wind.

Annie stumbled against a chunk of wood.

What the hell?

At her feet were shattered pieces of roof. She looked up and saw that a chunk of roof had been blown off. Suddenly her heart sank. She feared they were arguing about something Bitherby had done.

She hesitated to open the doors, but the squeal of the elf forced her to. The heavy wood doors hung from tracks and whined when she slid them open.

This barn was a storage building, housing food and other items that allowed Windmere employees to care for the many magical creatures that lived in or around the school. Bales of hay were stacked against the far wall, though one was knocked over with the hay scattered all over the ground. Snow blew into the building where the roof was torn off, and the pile of snow quickly grew larger.

"Bitherby?" she asked the men standing in the darkness.

"Yes," the headmaster said quietly.

Beside him the stable master stood with his arms crossed, his jaw tight and angry. Annie had never met him; he was hired after she graduated. With a scowl he pointed a thick finger in her direction. "This is your fault."

"I apologize Annie. This is Mr. Jacobi our stable master. Jacobi, this is Annie Pearce, a former student of Windmere." The headmaster offered a wane, tired smile.

"No, he's right, this is my fault. I'm sorry. I promise I will fix this mess. Unfortunately, I don't have time. I need to get Bitherby out of here. He's not safe."

"Annie, what happened?" Headmaster Turtledove's soft kind voice was filled with worry.

She explained her visitors and what they had done to her and her house. The headmaster contemplated her situation.

"Bitherby. Come out. Miss Annie is here to see you." His voice remained calm and gentle, even as the stable master glared at the both of them.

Hay rustled along the back wall, and the pile shook and shuddered with the fearful elf who was hiding inside.

"Bitherby, please come out. I need to talk to you." Annie turned to the headmaster. "I'm really sorry about him."

Headmaster Turtledove smirked. "I'm not crazy about the damage but we'll manage. Bitherby come out now," he commanded.

The hay continued to shake as little hands pulled up. Bitherby climbed above the pile. The tiny elf slipped on the smooth, loose stalks and slid to the dirt floor. Seeing the three humans waiting for him, he looked down at his brown pants and batted away the dust and dirt.

"How did you cause the roof to come off?" Annie asked.

Bitherby looked at his tiny hands, the greenish gray skin that hung from each finger, from his palm, from the back of his hand. "I scared, ma'am. Thought I heard the ma—mast—master outside."

"You're safe Bitherby. Demons can't enter the school grounds," the headmaster assured him. "I'm going to step outside and let you talk," he said and exited the building. Mr. Jacobi not as pleasant, glowered at Annie as he followed.

The elf shook when she sat beside him, nestling herself on an intact bale of hay. Bitherby fidgeted and backed away, falling against the hay and sitting roughly in the scratchy straw.

"Even though demons can't get into the school grounds, I'm worried about damage to the school and the students and teachers. We need to leave."

"You said I be safe." As the elf shook, so did the entire bale.

"We'll be going to the safest place I know. They won't come for us there."

Bitherby shook his head and jumped from the bale. "You already say that. Look." He pointed to the mess. She glanced around the stable and shook her head. There wasn't time to deal with it.

"You created this. Where we go next—trust me, they won't get to you."

The door groaned, she pulled up her hands facing the intruder, but it was only the headmaster. He closed the door and joined them near the hay.

"Where will you go?" Headmaster Turtledove asked. For a moment he had apparently forgotten he stood under the hole in the ceiling. Snow covered his bare head and the shoulders of his Hawaiian shirt. He walked farther into the building and brushed himself off.

"Plausible deniability."

The headmaster chuckled softly. "That's an interesting place. You should be safe there. But you'll be safer here, if you stay."

With all of the protections spells around the property and throughout the building, Annie knew Windmere was safe. But the reason she didn't head to any other safe house was the same reason she was leaving the school with the elf. Gladden or the Fraternitatem wouldn't go to the prison. No one would consider breaking in there.

"I can't stay here. Not in the middle of the school year. With all the students around." Suddenly she was aware how eerily quiet it was, as if even the creatures in the forest had gone into hiding.

"No one can get in. We have procedures for this," the headmaster argued. His anxiety was clear on his face and in his voice.

Annie didn't want to put him or the students in danger. "Really? Where will you go?"

The unnerving quiet was replaced by scratching and knocking.

"Where's the stable master?"

"That's a good question," Headmaster Turtledove said. He glanced around the destroyed barn. Voices squabbled beyond the doors.

"I don't think he left," Annie said.

"It's time to get you out of here." Headmaster Turtledove led them across the barn just as a heavy jinx pounded the side of the structure. Pieces of rotted wood rained down on them.

"What the hell!" Annie pulled Bitherby from the falling debris. The building was hit again, and the precarious roof shook and rumbled.

Headmaster Turtledove motioned them to walk against the far wall. He crouched low and peered outside. "I can't tell how many of them are out there, but sparks are flying from just inside the forest."

Boom!

Like a bomb, a hole was blown through the south wall, tossing Annie across the floor with the elf still in her arms. His small body landed on her as her head hit the winter-hardened dirt.

The front wall was burst apart by the hex. Dust and debris cascaded on them. Headmaster Turtledove crawled to the wall and touched the weathered wood. White light sailed around the perimeter—a protection spell. A white aura hung over them, shimmering in the darkness.

Spells hit the protection cover and bounced away, vibrating and softly shaking the building. Headmaster Turtledove lunged for Annie and assisted her to a seated position. She touched the back of her head where a large bump already grew.

"How's your head?"

"I'm okay. Bitherby, you okay?"

"Yes, Miss Annie." The elf clung to her like a small child. His body trembled as his arms reached around her neck.

"How do we get out of here?" she asked.

Trust the magic.

As successive jinxes hit the building, vibrations rumbled across the frozen ground. The headmaster helped her up and led them to the back wall. Though it felt solid, Annie had some idea of what was to come.

He waved his palm across the wall, and the light shimmered with magic. He pushed against the aged wood; it led to a staircase.

Boom!

Another jinx pounded the building; the wall swayed.

"Go!" he urged. "All the way down. Lock yourself in. I'll block the door. Just go!"

With one last look, Annie saw the headmaster joined by several staff members, all aiming their palms toward the intruders, wizards and witches Annie believed must have been sent by Gladden to fetch her. The jinxes flew in a wild light show before the door was slammed shut on them, plunging them into darkness.

CHAPTER 17

ANNIE HAD PROBABLY arrived home several hours before Cham considered leaving work. He had spent the day away from the office, chasing several leads regarding their missing person's caseload. After speaking with two families for a second time, he had learned that their loved ones were indeed either shapeshifters or had the ability to change into snakes at will—and that they all went missing on the same day. Cham was more convinced they were stuck in the market as their animal forms.

And yet, the Wizard Guard was having difficulty going in after them. He sighed heavily as he ended his very long and unproductive day.

After checking back in at Wizard Hall and writing his daily report, he sat back in his chair to catch his breath until his stomach growled loudly, reminding him it was time to leave. He dialed Annie cell phone. It rang several times before going to voicemail.

Maybe she's asleep.

But Annie had gone rogue in the past, putting herself in danger during the investigation of Princess Amelie's death.

She promised she wouldn't do that again.

Cham desperately tried to ignore that sinking feeling in the pit of his stomach and tried to convince himself that Annie was asleep and away from her phone and not chasing some lead without their knowledge.

Glancing at the clock, he cleaned up his piles and headed to her house.

Leaving the safety of the Wizard Hall courtyard, Cham landed on Annie's back porch and slipped in the thick snow piling on her deck. Balancing himself, he reached for the back door, which hung precariously on its hinges, unlatched. Turning around, he noticed the remaining footsteps almost covered by the heavy snow.

Not Annie's, not Zola's. Who was here?

Based on the footprints, Cham determined that two large men had been at Annie's house. The worry in the pit of his stomach screamed.

The open back door flew inward, and a gust of wind rushed into the house. Zola's words rang in his head. *She's not safe with the ring in the house.*

With the comforting knowledge that Annie had dropped the ring at Wizard Hall this morning, Cham entered her house, his palms out and ready.

Each step took thought. His heart beat rapidly, and his stomach churned. Starting in the kitchen, Cham saw immediately that the floor was covered in debris. The blood lock had been blown to pieces, and wood, metal, and paper were strewn across the floor. Annie's *Book of Shadows* lay in pieces, bits of folders were charred, and the smell of smoke hung in the air.

What are those folders?

Curious, he picked up a pile of paper. The edge of the folder read a case file number from 2008.

What case was this?

He illuminated the countertops and floors and followed the trail of debris until he entered the den. With nothing odd in the back room, he headed through the kitchen. His boots crunched across wood and paper; a kitchen chair was missing.

What the hell?

With calculated steps, Cham entered the living room, where the sixth dining room chair had been placed at the center of the room. A pile of rope lay on the floor. Examining the twine, he noticed several drops of blood. He ran his crystal across the binding; white magic had spliced the rope in two. He followed the magic upwards and noted that whoever was tied to the chair had cast a spell.

Annie!

Dropping the twine, Cham took a long look around the room. The heavy mirror he had helped her hang lay on the floor, shattered into mirror dust.

Did you get away, Annie?

Cham ran two stairs at a time to the second floor. Sick with worry, he entered her bedroom. The bed was still made, and the room was empty. Both front bedrooms were empty and untouched.

"Damn it, Annie, where are you?" Panic gripped Cham as he dialed Gibbs and explained.

"On my way," Gibbs said.

Trying desperately to keep his anxiety in check, Cham methodically collected magic from the deck, back hallway, kitchen, and living room, storing the magic inside his crystal.

"Anything?" Gibbs asked when he arrived and found Cham in the living room, examining the broken mirror.

"Two teleportation spells, one spell that broke her protection at the back door. A spell knocked someone out in the back hallway. A spell blew apart the blood lock. And two spells in here: one spliced the rope and another sent someone flying to the mirror." His voice was quick and anxious.

"Someone broke in and attacked the cabinet. When the ring wasn't found, whoever it was waited for her to come home. Knocked her out and tied her up," Gibbs surmised as he examined the space.

"With her and Zola missing, I'd say yes. One of the teleportation spells was newer than the other. However, the spell that knocked her out was later than all the others probably by hours. Whoever was here waited a while." Cham grimaced.

"Best case scenario, the girl got herself untied and escaped," Gibbs said as Cham summoned a map and his scrying crystal.

Cham used Annie's magic that he stored in his crystal and used it to scry for her. His hands shook violently as he maneuvered it across the map. His heart tightened when the crystal remained dull and cold.

"Your parents' place?" Gibbs asked.

"They'd have left me notice, so I'm guessing no. Maybe Tartarus." With the map of Tartarus Prison in front of him, Cham scried for Annie, though the crystal didn't react.

"Tartarus would cloak her," Gibbs reminded him.

"Yeah, right."

Where are you Annie?

He stared at the map of the United States as he thought of the locations Annie might find as safe.

Wait… the elf!

"She went to Windmere. She'll go to protect the elf!" Cham said.

❋

Unprepared for the strength of the snow storm over Minnesota, Cham and Gibbs landed precariously in two feet of snow.

"Damn," said Cham as he buttoned his lightweight spring jacket.

With their heads down, they trudged down the mile-long path to the school, arriving at the gates in forty-five minutes, which was twice as long as the normal trek took. Snow caked their pants, and their hair was drenched with sweat and melted snow. Anxiously, Cham plunged his fingers against the intercom.

"Yes, how may I help you?" said the pleasant voice.

"Robert Chamsky and John Gibbs for Headmaster Turtledove. And hurry, please!"

As if their presence was expected, the giant guard immediately retrieved them from the gate and motioned for them to enter. Cham and Gibbs followed closely, entering into the warmth of the school.

"School changed," Gibbs grunted. Brushing snow from their hair and coats and stomping out their shoes.

"Nice," Cham grumbled back and followed the giant in a direction neither expected, toward the back of the main entry foyer, into a low lit corridor.

"Where are we going?" Cham asked, though he knew the giants did little more than grunt and nod.

"Patience, boy," Gibbs commanded as the giant removed a tapestry hanging from the stone wall, revealing a door. He rapped on the wood with knuckles the size of small stones.

The door squeaked open, revealing stairs that angled downwards. The giant remained at the top of the stairs and waited for the two men to take their first steps into the bowels of the earth.

"You ever been to the school basement?" Cham asked.

"Never."

Dim light from overhead sconces illuminated their way down several flights of stairs. At the bottom, light streamed from the room to the left, which was located directly under the dining hall. When they reached the bottom and turned in, they saw Bitherby sitting on Annie's lap.

Bitherby climbed down from her lap just in time for Annie to lunge for Cham and jumped into waiting arms and buried herself in his embrace.

CHAPTER 18

ANNIE STROLLED WITH Cham through the maze that made up most of the basement under the school. They turned left and made a quick right; the maze of hallways led them closer to the center of the basement in a slow and winding way.

Annie had never been to the basement. It was a little jarring as they meandered in silence without purpose.

Her shoulder ached, and she rubbed the muscle with her bandaged wrist. Cham stopped the walk and took her hand, staring at the wrap.

"I'm sorry I didn't call," Annie said. Above Cham's head, a large water stain marked the cement wall. The musty stench was strong. She grimaced and breathed through her mouth. "We must be just below the lower level bathrooms. They always flooded," she mentioned for no particular reason. She couldn't figure out if Cham was mad or relieved.

"I'm not mad. I was very worried. Now I'm just relieved," Cham assured her with a warm squeeze of her hand. They continued down the passageway.

His silence allowed Annie time alone with her scattered thoughts and memories of her time at school, of that bathroom just above them. It was a large bathroom, roomy enough to work in; she made potions in there all the time as a student. Annie had gotten in the habit of squirreling away as many ingredients as she could from her class and hiding them in the storage bins.

I wonder if I left any behind.

The thought made her smile.

While they walked the maze of hallways, Bitherby sat under the watchful gaze of Headmaster Turtledove, several giants, and Gibbs, who guarded the bottom of the staircase. No one was getting in or out, even though Bitherby had pleaded for the last hour to leave. His small voice had squeaked and bounced off the walls. Annie was glad for the reprieve.

They turned another corner, finally reaching the center of the basement. She still couldn't figure out the pointless maze.

Cham stopped. His gaze on Annie was intense, worried, anxious.

"What?" she asked. He pinned her against the wall, his mouth on hers. Worry, anger, and fear was in the kiss. She molded herself against his chest, feeling all of him. Her skin hummed at his touch. She greeted his tongue gratefully and let out a longing groan.

His hands found her butt, her breasts; she touched the zipper of his jeans. Thoughts of Gladden popped in her head, and suddenly she was done.

"Sorry. I can't do this now," she whispered into his neck.

"No, I'm sorry." He pulled her into protective arms. Annie melted against him. Through his shirt, his heart pounded in her ear. "I'm just glad you're safe."

To reach around his neck, Annie stood on her tiptoes. Her kiss was gentle, soft and slow.

We fit together.

His hands cupped the small of her back.

"I figured you'd go to Tartarus. Since I couldn't verify, I hoped you came here first to get the elf."

She took a deep breath and inhaled his scent, warm and spicy. Cham knew it was her favorite. She closed her eyes.

"I saw the blood lock," he said. "It was torn to pieces."

"I'm pretty sure it was Gladden Worchester. He demanded

I give him the ring. When I confronted him about the Fraterni-tatem, he seemed confused," Annie said. She stepped away from Cham. He furrowed his brow.

I know that look.

"I want to move in with you," he said.

She pondered his unexpected revelation. They had been dat-ing for the last six months, and he had spent many nights with her at her house, yet the suggestion seemed out of context and for the wrong reason.

"For realsies or because you want to protect me?" she attempted to joke in order to ease the tension. She quickly realized that Cham wasn't joking.

"Annie, they're going to come after you. When they do, I want to be there for you."

I love you, she thought. She sighed. "Only if you move in with because you love me and for no other reason."

"I do love you. It's time," he said.

She stepped into his embrace. Her hands grazed the back of his shirt only as far as she could lift her left arm. He stroked her still damp, frizzy hair and kissed the top of her head. He pulled her chin toward him and kissed her lips, his tongue finding hers.

Pipes clinked and water dripped around them. Cham pulled away, touched her cheek, and pulled a loose strand of hair that had fallen in front of her face, tucking it behind her ear.

"So Gladden wants the ring. You think the djinn's forcing him to find it?"

She chuckled and stroked his back with her fingers, causing him to shudder. "Yeah. I'm sure the djinn's really in charge of the market and Gladden. He's definitely forced to clean up the mess."

The center of this maze was ten feet by ten feet. Scorch marks stained the walls and floor. Annie bent down and touched the flaky wallboard. "They might use this space to practice." She rubbed the dust between her fingers. "If Gladden didn't come back with the ring and Bitherby and I are still alive, I'm guessing he doesn't have much time."

"I'll have someone check in on him just in case." Cham glanced around the open area. "Practice space. Nice." Returning back to her, he said, "I have a question for you."

"Sure, what is it?"

"I saw case files in the pile of rubble. What's up?"

Annie leaned against the wall. "It was all going to be explained tonight. But seeing as that plan was squashed..." She smiled, but his returning smile was tentative, as if he thought she might not have told him had he not asked. Annie sometimes felt he still lacked trust in her, especially after how she lied to him last year. But Cham seemed cautiously optimistic when he took her hand.

"I checked the *Book of Shadows* for the Fraternitatem," she told him. "It was there, one word, buried in some doodles. Dad..." It hit her in quiet moments, how much she missed her father.

Cham wiped away a tear that trickled down her cheek. "Jason met them on a case," he finished for her. His fingers lingered on her cheek.

"The stones set in the ring—they're Chintamani Stones. About six months before he died Dad worked a case where these same stones were being sold in the market and the Fraternitatem warned him off of the case. It's not exactly the same, but he met them. Even the Middle East Wizard Guard doesn't have that much on them."

His face broke into a loose smile. "So, being the wizard guard that you are, you looked up the files."

"Yeah. I only found three of the four of the files, though." She grimaced, thinking of the three that were now in tattered pieces, scorched and destroyed. She hoped the missing file was somewhere safe and held the information she sought.

She leaned against the wall, which felt spongy. A potion might have made it so. The mildew in the basement tickled her nose. She thought she might sneeze and hoped to leave this dank basement soon.

"Rathbone admitted to killing your dad. Do you think he was trading on these stones and somehow your dad got caught in that?"

"Dad mentioned Rathbone in the Book of Shadows. Something about a liaison between the market and the Fraternitatem. I'm trying not to concentrate on that right now. Those files were to help me get a handle on the Fraternitatem. This group really has me concerned."

"Wait, you said three of four folders?"

"I think dad might have taken the file out of Wizard Hall and hid it somewhere in the house. Ryan thought that might be a possibility."

She thought about what Cham said mentioned about her dad and Rathbone. Did Rathbone kill him because Dad was going to take him in, or did the Fraternitatem threaten to kill Rathbone if he didn't kill Dad because Dad was bringing them down? It didn't really matter which way it had happened; she knew in her heart the answer was in that missing file.

"Penny for your thoughts?" Cham asked.

"Just thinking about Dad and the stones. Gotta get it out of my thought process. Unless it's about this case, I can't worry about it. We should get back." She reached for his hand and led him the way they came, taking a right and a quick left.

"So is there anything I can get you while you're stuck here? I think they want to wait until the weather lets up to move you to Tartarus. Grounding all of us, I think," he advised. They took another turn. The walls rearranged themselves so that they were walking through a rounded corridor.

"Is anything salvageable from the cabinet? I'd like to continue reading the files. I didn't get very far."

"I'll pick them up in the morning. We're having difficulty getting into the market. Merchants are twitchier than normal. Anything else I can get you?"

"Yeah. In Dad's notes, he mentioned meeting an archaeologist named Dr. Arden... Arden... Oh, I can't remember. I think the jinx rattled my brain. Anyway, he met her in Morocco while investigating the stones. She mentioned the Chintamani Stones and the ring to him. If we can find her, she might know how to use it. We're going to need that ring to turn the shapeshifters back to normal." *At least, I hope that's how the ring works!*

Annie and the rest of the Wizard Guard had assumed the shapeshifters were somehow stuck in their animal forms and unable to leave the market. She was hoping that since the ring was originally created to control the shapeshifting djinn, it could also turn the trapped missing persons back.

She sighed as the wall straightened out; they were heading back to ninety-degree corners.

We should be back by now.

They walked silently with the sounds of the basement reverberating and surrounding them. There was a leak in one of the pipes that hung above their heads; the water dripped in a rhythmic pattern, matching their footsteps.

"I'll have Bucky find her, and I'll interview her, see what she knows. You're off grid now?"

"Yeah. Protection protocol. And I need someone to find Zola. I've been calling her for hours and she's not answering," Annie said. The thought of Zola still missing weighed heavily on her mind. No matter how much they spoke of other things, it was never far from her thoughts. Annie knew something was wrong.

"When did you see her last?" Concern dripped in Cham's question.

"This morning. Something's wrong. I keep pushing that feeling deep inside. But I know it."

"I'll have Spencer go to your house and check on her and make sure she's okay."

"Thanks."

"I'll feel better once you're at Tartarus."

"Me too. The headmaster insists we're safe here. But I'll leave in the morning. Less likely that anyone will be on the prison island during the day. Not with the risk of exposure so high."

With the last turn, they returned to the elf. Annie hated leaving Bitherby alone with the headmaster. Turtledove should have been handling school issues, not Wizard Guard problems.

Bitherby was still whining as they walked up.

"Yes, Bitherby, but you left the space in worse shape than you came to it. We can't have that, now, can we?" the headmaster asked.

"Everything okay?" Annie asked.

"Miss Pearce, Mr. Chamsky." Headmaster Turtledove nodded briefly. "I was just explaining to our elfin friend how we don't leave our hosts worse off."

Annie motioned for the headmaster to join them They stopped on the farther side of the basement.

"Since you and the other teachers were able to chase away the wizards from the black market, do you think we can move to a warmer part of the castle? Somewhere away from the students. It's a little musty in here."

"Annie, I think we can accommodate you with that request. Whoever those men were, I will tell you, they weren't well trained in the casting of spells and were easily chased away. We set up another protection spell further into the forest. It's a bit stronger than we normally need, but the extra safety won't harm anyone." He grimaced. "I believe you have several guards patrolling the perimeter. I expect everyone here is safe and sound." He turned to Cham. "Will you be staying, Robert?"

"I'm not leaving her alone." Cham crossed his arms. It was a conversation started when he had first arrived, with a call to Milo at Wizard Hall. Cham wouldn't leave Annie, and Milo wanted someone else to protect her. Annie stayed out of it. In the end, it was decided that Cham would stay, and Gibbs would pick up in the morning.

Knowing this, Annie couldn't imagine that Gibbs would enjoy

romping around the school, trapped with her and one thousand wizards in training.

※

True to his word, Headmaster Turtledove gave them free reign in a wing of the school used when the student population swelled during the school year. Annie glanced at Cham, who had easily fallen asleep. His breath was slow and even. Under the circumstances, he was peaceful.

Annie was not. Too exhausted to sleep and lacking work or the ability to leave, she headed to the dormitory lounge and switched on the television in hopes that it would help her fall asleep.

Because they were in a wizard school, they lacked access to many cable stations. Annie settled on the Cable Witch Network and leaned back in the deep, comfortable sofa just in time to hear the broomstick racing scores. It was a busy week for all of the teams, including the Chicago Demons, her hometown team, the one that included her ex-boyfriend and the top racer in the country, Charlie Andrews. For him it had been a miserable season plagued with injuries, the last keeping him out of action for the next two weeks. As a fan, Annie wasn't happy about it, though she wasn't exactly sad either.

Annie yawned when the report turned to the weather. Her eyes closed but fluttered back open during the Wizard Council news. Realizing she might have missed any reports on her John Doe, she switched stations, finding the Chicago news, curious if there was any nonmagical update on the case. Even though the body was switched, the files changed, and the magic removed, Annie guessed the police department was still investigating, and something was bound to come about. She just wanted to know.

"Don't you ever sleep?" Gibbs asked and joined her on the sofa.

Annie sighed. She hated being guarded. "Too keyed up.

Checking on Benaiah updates. Just in case. Why are you here? I wasn't expecting you until morning."

Gibbs grumbled and crossed his arms. They sat in silence, watching the news drone on. It was mostly the same information she just heard on the wizard news. She sighed, dropped the remote in her lap, and rested her head against the sofa, no longer watching. Her eyes roamed the room, which was similar to her own former dorm lounge with a large fireplace and comfortable furniture, though the color scheme in this room was darker and heavier, than the dorm she lived in. The furniture, artwork, and rugs were mostly the same and probably all purchased at the same time.

Nearly asleep, she could barely process what she was seeing through half-closed eye as the reporter finally reviewed the updates on the John Doe case. Annie's eyes popped open, and she finally saw it: The portal was so clear in the shot as if it had grown stronger, or maybe the camera was just that good. Annie sat up and moved to the television for a closer view.

"Girl, what do you see?"

"The portal." She pointed.

Gibbs joined her. "Damn," he said. "Who's that?"

He referred to the hiker, someone out after eleven p.m., walking through the forest preserve that was otherwise closed at this late hour. The sweatshirt and oversized pants did little to keep the hiker inconspicuous as he or she examined the portal. All of Chicagoland could see her.

"It's a woman, I think," Annie said out loud, based on the hiker's size and the fact she had hips. Her stomach lurched.

As the journalist continued with her report, the woman in the distance examined the air, sticking her hand inside. Again, the wind gusted and swirled around the clearing. The reporter shivered as the wind blew into the shot.

I know the hiker is Rebekah.

That uneasy feeling settled in Annie's temples where a migraine typically formed. Though she wasn't surprised, her mouth popped open when the woman turned toward the camera; it was indeed Rebekah Stoner.

"What the hell is she doing?" Annie said, incredulous. "People in the Chicagoland area know who she is. She's been doing morning reports for the last year. Is she bat shit crazy?"

"Told you, you shoulda called Lightner."

It was no longer a problem for another day.

CHAPTER 19

GRAHAM LIGHTNER ARRIVED with Allen Crosby, Sky Starling, and Bucky Hart to Rebekah Stoner's condominium. It was after three in the morning when she left for the television studio to prepare her first report of the morning. The wizard guards watched the reporter as she bounded from her home and entered her silver car. After the tires peeled away from her parking spot, they waited ten minutes before heading up to her apartment.

They easily unlocked the door and slipped inside the main room, making themselves comfortable as they searched for anything pertaining to Annie, Jack, and magic.

"Bucky, all things computers and AV equipment," Graham ordered. "Allen, handle the living area. Sky, the kitchen. Like always, low, minimal light. I want anything that looks like magic, even if it seems innocuous—*anything*, even if it seems like something a nonmagical would own."

The lights remained off so as to not draw attention. Their only light, the low dim glow from their crystals, was strong enough to search and low enough for the outside world not to see.

With the jobs assigned, the group broke and spread throughout a comfortable, country-casual décor with heavy pine furniture and floral fabric everywhere. Allen began his search under the soft seats, inside pillows, and under slipcovers, before overturning the pine coffee table and feeling for hidden items. He moved to the wide assortment of books that took up the shelves lining the back wall.

As Allen examined the main living space, Bucky eagerly opened Rebekah's laptop to scrutinize the files. He ignored the sounds of searching as he clicked on the first window. As he reviewed the reporter's files, his eyes grew wide with surprise. A whistle escaped his lips, but that wasn't enough to pull the attention of the others from what they were working on. The hundreds of websites and files surprised even Bucky Hart, who had hacked and broken into more computers than he could even remember.

Cabinets squeaked open, boxes were shaken, and cardboard opened as Sky, off in the kitchen, began a thorough search of the cabinets and drawers. She left nothing unopened.

"Where would you hide files you want nobody to know you had?" Graham asked himself as he walked into the very feminine bedroom covered in pink and featuring a four-poster bed complete with ruffled bed skirt against the middle of the back wall. Knowing humans weren't original in their hiding spots, Graham dropped to his knees, expecting to find simple storage containers under the bed. After finding only dust balls, he slid farther underneath and released the heating vent cover. Flashing the light inside, he realized Rebekah wasn't as stupid as he hoped.

Graham opened the first of several dresser drawers, feeling under Rebekah's clothing and personal objects. Finding nothing of consequence—no potions, herbs, or USB drives—he moved to the bedside table, again finding nothing but some pens and notepads. He pocketed those for further investigation before moving to the bathroom sink, medicine cabinet, and dirty clothes hamper, all of which contained nothing out of the ordinary or odd.

Back inside the bedroom, he started on the small closet filled with clothes, packed so tightly inside that it took some time to run his fingers through the items, searching for anything that didn't belong to the nonmagical world. Quickly, he ran a crystal over the clothing. After coming up empty once again, he closed the door.

The last item was a large armoire that stood at seven feet. The ornate case was decorated with colorful purple and red flowers, and it took up much of the walking space in the room. Graham yanked on the fake, crystal-inspired plastic handles and quickly thumbed through the piles of clothing. He felt behind the television and patted down the sides. There were no pockets or hiding spots along the sides; the shelves and boxes stored on them contained nothing useful. The bottom was covered with shoes, heels in every color and a row of flats. He stepped back, resting against the bed.

It has to be here.

Graham stared at the armoire.

The floor!

There was something about the bottom of the armoire. It seemed... off. The proportions were wrong.

He tapped on the floor. A gentle, hollow sound bounced back to him.

After removing twenty pair of shoes, he patted down the bottom, searching for a latch. Pulling up on a small piece of ribbon, Graham discovered folders, boxes, flash drives, and a phone inside.

With a swipe of his palm across the screen, he turned the phone on and scrolled through the call log. Arnold Schwartz was the only call Rebekah had made from this phone. Graham checked the photo gallery and saw pictures of Annie with Cham, Gibbs, Spencer, and Jack Ramsey. He swiped through the seemingly endless pictures: the team in a parking garage, Annie and Jack in Millennium Park, Annie and Cham outside an apartment building as she carried a book. The newest pictures were of Annie at the John Doe crime scene with Gibbs, searching the ground—and a picture of the portal location hanging between two evergreen trees.

Seeing something in the picture, Graham increased the size. He knew Rebekah had sensed the portal; he knew why when he noticed the haziness of the entrance hanging there. He dropped the phone inside a paper bag.

The folders included blown up pictures from the phone and

notes on the crime scene as well as notes from a meeting between Jack and Annie at the park.

I ran after Anne Pearce. I followed her to an alley with locked doors and no exit. She was missing. Disappeared in thin air. There's something so weird about this woman. Her relationship to Special Agent Jack Ramsey, her reason for being at the double homicide. Why is she so special to be investigating the murder of Princess Amelie?

So why did she disappear? Where did she go?

Teleportation?

Whoa, Graham thought as he placed the folder inside the bag along with the flash drives she stored in the box. When he had confiscated all that was there, he replaced the floor and shoes and headed to the living room.

Bucky continued to delete files and folders in Rebekah's computer, wiping away her search history and her magical bookmarks.

"This girl really found the stuff," Bucky said, wiping another folder.

"Yeah. I found pictures and notes. What did you find?" Graham's jaw dropped as he viewed the website links stored in the computer that Bucky quickly pulled up. "Are these real sites? Real magic or nonmagical magic?"

"A mix. I'm a little concerned Rebekah found so much." Bucky said, his fingers clacking against the keyboard.

"I wish Annie had said something sooner. I found Rebekah's burner phone, folders with notes about teleportation, pictures, and some flash drives for you to look at." He dropped the paper bag on the desk beside Bucky.

"The reporter's smart. I assume we're wiping her memory too?" Bucky reached for the phone in the bag and turned it on, churning through the information was inside.

"Yeah. She knows more than any nonmagical should know," Graham said. "Listen we'll have to hit the studio. There'll be people there at all hours, I'm sure. Quick in and out, freeze the room. Do what you have to as fast as possible."

"What about her real phone?" Allen asked as he finished a search of the bookshelves. He added another book to his pile.

"With her, probably. When I erase her memory, I'll delete what I can," Graham said.

"Good. Look at these books. Chicago Public Library, occult titles. Teleportation." Allen held the pile out.

Graham threw him the paper bag. "Real books?"

"Some."

"Sounds like she took everything she could find and stumbled on the real magic," Bucky commented. "Oh, and here on the phone. This Arnold Schwartz. I've dealt with him before. He's the computer guy with the Chicago Police Department. You'll need to wipe his memory." Bucky dumped the phone in the bag.

"Yeah. I'll handle that tonight." Graham sighed.

"Found these hidden in a box of cereal." Sky headed in with potion cards and a mixture of herbs.

"She was really good. Persistent, and found more than I would have figured," Allen said, adding the books to the paper bag. "I think we need another sweep before we head out."

"Okay. You handle that. When Bucky finishes, I want the three of you to head out to the studio. I'll stay here and wait for our reporter to return."

When the computer beeped, Bucky inserted a flash drive. After he hit enter, the computer whirled, and the screen scrolled through thousands of lines of code as it attacked everything inside Rebekah's laptop, destroying everything.

An hour after arriving and after summoning anything about Annie, the Wizard Guard and anything pertaining to magic, the VAU and the computer hacker headed out to find the reporter.

❈

Fairy magic was different than wizard magic. While wizards needed access to the outdoors—either through an open window or a door—to teleport from inside a building, fairies could pop in and out of buildings, caves, or even from underwater. It didn't matter. Zola, wherever she was, should have been able to respond to Annie and come to her. It wasn't in the nature of the fairy to ignore her charge when being summoned. This worried Annie, Cham, and now Spencer.

After receiving Cham's phone call, Spencer surmised that the fairy had most likely come home before Annie and had been taken, hopefully stashed away somewhere and not done away with. Had she come home after Annie, Zola would most certainly be with her charge right now. Believing she was hidden, Spencer chose to search the garage first on the off chance it was too much hassle to move her elsewhere.

Annie hadn't done much with the space since Jason died. It was filled with tools, odds and ends, car parts, and her 1966 Mustang under its winter cover. Zola hadn't been chained inside, though; when Spencer lifted the cover, the car was empty. After declaring the garage free and clear, he headed into the house and to the basement.

The larger room contained workout equipment, boxes both empty and filled, and a sofa pushed against the far right wall. A closed door on the back wall opened to a storage area and laundry room. Spencer took a deep breath and tugged on the handle. It was locked.

Odd.

Spencer knocked. "Zola, are you in here?" he shouted through the door. When he received no answer, he twisted his wrist six inches from the handle, cast the spell, and popped the lock.

Inside the small room, Spencer found an empty metal chair, open and resting against the cement wall. He knelt beside two iron shackles laid open on the ground, dotted with spots of blood that congealed around the edge. A unique trait of fairies was they were afraid of iron because it burned their skin. These shackles would have rendered Zola's magic useless.

Spencer's flashlight picked up the smallest of clues: more blood spots on the floor, strands of golden hair caught inside the joints of the chair.

She was here!

Spencer bolted from the back room and up to the kitchen. He had a guess as to why they had taken the fairy. He flipped through the piles of paper, searching for a ransom note. He ran to the back door, which had been recently repaired with magic. Finding nothing, he ran to the front door; a note was stuffed inside the mailbox.

We have the fairy. Want her back? You can have her in exchange for the ring. Wait for further instructions.

Crap!

Dialing his phone, Spencer paced through the kitchen until Lial Peng picked up the phone. Lial, new to the main branch of the Wizard Guard, happened to be the best tracker in the department.

"We have a problem," Spencer said.

News traveled fast amongst the wizard guard, so Lial already knew. "Annie's Aloja is missing isn't she?" he asked.

"Someone took her. I just found the note," Spencer advised.

"I'll be there in five."

✼

Arriving to Annie's house, Lial went to work tracking the fairy and capturing her good magic in order to scry for her.

If she didn't come when Annie called, she's hidden or worse.

"Are we telling Annie?" Lial asked. He traversed the house, following the magic belonging to a wizard who wasn't Annie, and catalogued the spells used to determine which trace he would use to track.

"Cham told Annie I was looking for her. Telling her I brought you in might not be a good idea at the moment. Annie needs to stay hidden," Spencer advised.

"Fair enough." Lial collected all that he could find, including the new teleportation spell he found on the front porch. It was the strongest trace he had. "I'll find him, no problem. But the market is changing. We need to be careful how we approach this." Lial took out the newest incarnation of the black market map.

The map was magically linked to the market; as the aisles changed or moved, the map reflected the modifications. It was an ongoing report of the physical space. Lial stared at the map, and his eyes blinked rapidly as he reviewed the additions and corrections.

"Lial?"

"It used to be a wheel," he said softly.

Spencer stared at the map and agreed. The black market was no longer recognizable. Once the shape of a spoked wheel, the map now resembled a maze with a large square at the center. Several of the passages dead ended, while other aisles were loops. "What the hell did that djinn do?"

Lial didn't answer. He removed his scrying crystal and attached it to the magical trace found outside the front door. After he maneuvered the crystal over the map, it remained lifeless and dull.

"He might not be at the market," Spencer suggested.

Lial tried the map of Chicago. For the second time, the crystal refused to light up. Lial called Bucky for information pertaining to Gladden Worchester anywhere in the state of Illinois.

"Here you go. It must be some case, if you're all in on it," Bucky said, immediately sending over the address.

"You have no idea," Lial sighed. With the information, he tried a third time to scry for the wizard in the South Side of Chicago, where his address was listed.

"Damn," Lial murmured when the search returned nothing.

"He's trying to clean up his mess. There's a possibility the djinn had him killed," Spencer said.

"Where does that leave Zola?" Lial asked and tapped his hand wildly against the map.

In one last effort, he used the map of the entire world—a large, three-foot-by-four-foot piece of paper—and slowly, methodically started in one hemisphere and moved to the next, looking for anything resembling trace or the person of Gladden Worchester.

"It's a shame we can't scry on fairy magic," Spencer said sardonically. Thanks to an evolutionary process, fairy magic was unable to be traced or tracked and therefore couldn't be used to scry. It was what kept the Aloja fairies safe—unless they were kidnapped.

"I think we need to tell Annie," Lial said with a heavy sigh.

"Market first, and then Annie," Spencer said.

❋

Annie and Gibbs had warned them of the changes to the market with a very specific description of the portals and the protection spell disintegrating. It was blurring the line between the magical plane of existence and the nonmagical world. Spencer and Lial knew what was coming, and yet neither could hide their shock when they stepped inside a lesser-used portal and took to the market before them.

"How can it smell even worse?" Lial commented as he covered his mouth with a piece of fabric. The normally foul stench that clung to clothing and hair was more powerful, more rancid, and heavier, than it had ever been.

The market no longer teemed with hordes of patrons, and no longer hummed with the careful work of elves and trolls that toiled in the muck and stalls, cleaning and keeping order to the chaotic marketplace.

Dogs ran through the aisles in search of food, rooting through what little garbage piles they could find. A dog fight started between two overly shaggy dogs. Their teeth bared, they barked rapidly until one crawled off.

Cats slunk at the base of tables, abandoned by their booth owners. They ambled across the littered dirt, stained with liquid—possibly blood and remnants of potions that were tossed. Dung heaps grew in the corners, in the middle of the aisles, and on top of abandoned artifacts and other goods. A group of snakes slithered across these piles, forked tongues moving in and of their small mouths.

"This is far worse than I imagined," Spencer said in awe before the pair headed toward the incinerators, which were no longer in their familiar location at the back of the market along the outer aisle. The market was no longer round and no longer consisted of dissecting aisles. They glanced up and spotted the smoke rising in the air, hanging over the market as a dark, black cloud. Spencer and Lial followed the nearest path headed in the direction, though it undulated and curved through a confused mess, a space that looked more like a zoo in the final stages of decay.

They were followed for a time by cats and dogs, who seemed curious as to why these two humans were still in the market since there were so few humans left. Eventually, the shapeshifters grew bored and trailed off, heading to look for food or entertainment.

"We really should rescue the shapeshifters from the market," Lial said as they followed a curve that led to a dead end—a wall without doors or windows, stained with years of dirt and grime, rotted from neglect.

"There must be hundreds of them. That's a massive undertaking that we probably should have started planning when Annie came to the conclusion that they were shapeshifters," Spencer replied. "Just where do we put them, and how do we change them back?"

"I don't know, but the incinerator's on the other side of this wall," Lial pronounced, jumping up to get a view over the fence. He summoned his map of the market, of the new design. "We need to walk all the way back where we came in order to get right back there," he pointed to the wall.

"You're kidding," Spencer said incredulously.

"Sorry, dude. No one's controlling the magic. It's running itself, I think. And to be honest, the paths have changed since the last I looked. The market's gone." Lial stuffed the map back inside his field pack, shrinking the entire bag.

The two turned left and followed the new path toward the incinerators.

As they passed more abandoned booths than they ever could imagine and a flock of sparrows that had found a picnic table covered in herbs and other potion ingredients, Spencer commented, "Shapeshifters are cats, dogs, and snakes. These birds—they're not human shapeshifters. If they can fly through that hole in the protection spell..." Spencer pointed upwards toward where thick smoke escaped through a crack in the protection spell. "What else is getting out? I think we need a crew in the forest."

Spencer texted a message as they trotted around the market. They turned down the passage to the incinerators, where they were stopped by a thick, choking smoke. It poured from the incinerator tubes, rolling out in thick black puffs. The furnace area was a wall of black, charred smoke that was too thick to enter. Without any more room to hold it, the smoke blew into the market.

Backing away, Lial found an empty booth, and unrolled his map. Trying one more time to pick up Gladden's magical energy he ran the crystal over every centimeter of the map, but to no avail. He pocketed his crystal, and as he started to roll the map, he noticed something. Re-stretching it on the table, he bent closer to the page.

His finger, caked in smoke and dust, trailed the path outward from their location to a wall. A wall that opened into nothing.

"There?" Spencer asked.

"Yeah. It's like there's something here. Maybe a hidden room. I say we go there," Lial suggested.

Passing through the square that was formerly the center of the market was an excruciatingly slow journey; they had stepped through a migration of refugees. A mass exodus of vendors moved forth—some with their wares piled high on small carts, others shrinking their entire life's work into bags and hauling them over their shoulders. They seemed sad, disinterested, angry as they trudged their way to the portals and out of the eyes of the Wizard Guard.

Lial and Spencer took the scene in. Their eyes darted from patron to patron, from the stall owners still working with clients to the vampire that was speaking in hushed whispers to another. Pointing at them.

"We need to go," Spencer said.

They turned down a less used path opposite the mysterious wall. To avoid the crowds, they teleported to the nearest portal, stepped through, and headed home.

CHAPTER 20

JUST AFTER DAWN broke, Cham left Annie at Windmere School and headed to her house to salvage what remained of her father's folders or the Book of Shadows. He hoped Zola found her way back home.

"Anything on Zola?" Cham asked Spencer. His heart fell to the pit of his stomach as soon as he saw his fellow wizard guard.

If Spencer is here, that can't be good.

"We're pretty sure she's at the market. Between the smoke and the folks still there, we were run out."

"You haven't told Annie yet?"

"Not until we know for sure what's happened to her. They had her locked downstairs and moved her. I'm sorry, Cham. We tried."

Since Cham had been there last, Annie's house had been cleared of evidence and cleaned. The rope and chair had been shrunk and placed in evidence bags, and the mirror and cabinet had been cleaned up and disposed of. Spencer was sorting through the papers, laying them in neat piles on the kitchen table.

"What's the plan for finding Zola?" Cham joined Spencer, pulling what could be saved and placing each salvageable sheet where it needed to go.

"We need backup. It's not safe in there for us. Whoever's still inside is all for themselves. It's a mess." Spencer sighed.

They sorted in silence, yet the pile seemed to remain large, and the stench of smoke continued to permeate the room.

"Hey, thanks for taking care of all of this." Cham said.

"No problem. I'm just sorry we couldn't get at Zola." Spencer sighed, resting his hand on a tall stack of paper. "From what I can tell, Gladden used black magic to gain entrance to the house. We'll need to ward off some of that. The Fraternitatem is probably smarter and better prepared." Spencer tossed a pile of notes on top of an open folder.

"Who's on it?" Cham picked up a piece of the *Book of Shadows* and laid it on top of the bindings.

"Southwest unit. Shiff and Brite got here about an hour ago. They're researching the spell used to break in. Then they'll reverse it and strengthen the spell. Annie'll be able to come home again." Spencer offered a smile. The late hours affected him too.

"Annie wants something to do. Is this stuff ready for her?"

Spencer pulled another pile from across the table, opened file number two, and stored the pile there.

"Just a few more pieces. Listen, I've read through what I could in Jason's notes. The only relation between the cases is definitely the Fraternitatem of Solomon. They're dangerous, and they were definitely leaning on Jason about those stones," Spencer said. He pulled the stacks of folders in a neat pile.

"Annie didn't think it was related. Though… she mentioned an archaeologist that Jason met while working the case. I want to talk to the archaeologist and see if she knows how the ring works and possibly anything about the Fraternitatem. Since she mentioned the ring to Jason, that is."

"Her name is Dr. Arden…" Spencer glanced at the notes. "Dr. Arden Blakely. If you need help with that let me know. We've all been pulled from our other cases."

"One sec," Cham said and dialed his phone. "Bucky, can you find an archaeologist named Dr. Arden Blakely? Worked for the Field Museum. Chicago to start."

"Sure, Cham. Is she a suspect?" Bucky tapped the keyboard on the other end of the line, already searching for the archaeologist.

"No. Person of interest. Just a hunch."

"No problem. Just a second." Bucky typed another few strokes and then gave Cham an address for the archaeologist Arden Blakely in the Hyde Park neighborhood of Chicago.

"Thanks Bucky. That was quick."

"You gave me an easy one. And I'm in the middle of something else. Do you need anything else?"

"I'm good, thanks. Get back to what you were doing."

Spencer glanced at Cham. "Gibbs is guarding Annie. What's next?"

"I'll take this stuff to Annie and then head to the archaeologist."

"I think Lial and I will take another look at the market and plan how to get Zola out." Spencer placed the folders and miscellaneous papers in a bag for Cham.

"Thanks. Keep me posted," Cham said and headed out.

❋

Rebekah knew there was something odd about Anne Pearce; it had gnawed at her for the last eight months. Diligently researching and scraping together an unusual amount of material, the journalist quite by chance had learned more than expected about a world once unknown to her. It had started with the occult section at the local public library. Slowly, over time, she pieced together unfathomable facts that seemed unlikely—and yet they fit. They explained Anne Pearce.

The more entrenched in the strange information and places Rebekah found herself, the more anxiety crawled inside and took hold. Since investigating the crime scene in Busse Woods, that chill in the air and general paranoia became her constant companion, along with the feeling she was being stalked. Her only solaces were her apartment and her work. Unless she was out with a group, the reporter rarely left home.

Leaving the studio at ten in the morning after the morning report, Rebekah passed through the doors to the parking lot just as three people she didn't recognize entered, their badges hanging from their necks. She observed them stroll down the hall and disappear into the door leading to the stairs. When the door slammed shut, the metallic *thud* resounded in the empty hallway. The journalist, with a bad feeling at the pit of her stomach, ran to her silver car.

Her heart pounded in her ears, and her hands shook while fumbling with the keys. With a deep breath, Rebekah managed to get the keys in the ignition and turn the car on. The engine hummed softly. She flipped the car into reverse, then into drive, and slammed her foot on the accelerator. The wheels churned, and smoke rose from the tires as she peeled the car out of the lot.

Though it was only mid-morning, traffic moved slowly on her way to her apartment, which was less than ten miles from the studio. It took her an hour to arrive.

Rebekah's heart still raced as she parallel parked in a spot on her street, bumping into the car behind her. Taking a heavy breath, Rebekah hiccupped, shut off the car, and rested her head against the steering wheel to cry.

The neighborhood bustled with people traversing the sidewalk to and from the bus or train stations a block to the west. One block from her apartment to the east were the shopping district, small stores, drug stores, and other outlets.

After taking another cleansing breath, she opened her door and saw a familiar face heading down the sidewalk. The man, his face so recognizable, glanced at her and smiled before picking up his pace toward the bar at the end of the street.

How do I know him?

Across the street, a familiar-looking couple headed in the

opposite direction. They crossed the street at the stop sign, turned once, and smiled at Rebekah before heading on their way.

But I know them too.

Paranoid, Rebekah slammed the car door shut and lunged inside the gate to her apartment building. She flew up the steps, taking them two at a time, until she reached the fourth floor. She entered her apartment and threw the door shut.

"Hello Rebekah," Graham Lightner said, just before he slammed a jinx on her.

❄

Cham landed on the quiet street along with Emerson Donaldson, a Wizard Guard in training. Running with a hunch, he felt their surprise visit to archaeologist Dr. Arden Blakely might be less stressful if he had a female officer with him.

He zipped his coat to his chin as the bitter wind from the lake blew through the street; Emerson held tightly to her hat as the gust descended on them.

Few cars were parked on the city street in the middle of the day, and anyone still home was safely huddled in their houses. Cham and Emerson walked cautiously, verifying each address and scanning the street for wayward folks with an unfortunate need to be outside. Two houses up the street, a woman was bundled in a thick parka so that she resembled a large jelly bean teetering on thin sticks. Only her eyes were exposed. As Cham drew closer, he could see that they watered heavily in the wickedly bitter wind. It didn't stop her from waiting patiently for the small white terrier to sniff the fire hydrant before lifting its leg and peeing on the already iced-over apparatus.

Even when the dog finished, the woman glanced up at the sky, wiped a tear from her cheek, and let her dog meander to another spot of brown grass. Shivering violently, her dog made no move to return inside and seemed rather content to sniff the ground.

Cham and Emerson realized they were at their location. The woman stood in their way on the chipped, cracked sidewalk to the building. They loitered tolerantly as gusts of wind chilled them. The woman didn't seem to notice.

Another squall raged down the street; the woman's hood and scarf flew backwards.

I recognize her.

Arden Blakely stood before them, forty years older than the pictures Cham had found before he arrived. Her crystal-blue eyes were the only feature on her face that hadn't changed. She ran a finger through her short cropped black-and-white hair, trying to smooth it even in the heavy wind before pulling the hood back over her head and wrapping the wayward scarf around her neck.

The white terrier, no longer interested in the scents littering the grass, spotted the wizard guards. The dog hopped up and down and barked a high-pitched squeak like a rubber toy. Cham squatted down and held his hand out, letting the dog come to him. It wagged a short, stubby tail, sniffed his outstretched hand, and licked his extremely cold fingers.

Cham chuckled as the small, rough tongue tickled his fingers. "Your dog is really cute. Does it have a name?" he asked.

Arden Blakely smiled lightly, bent down and touched her dog's head. "Sally," was what Cham thought she said.

"Well, hello, Sally." Cham scratched behind the dog's ear. It jumped on his leg.

"Actually, it's Solly. Short for Solomon."

Cham and Emerson exchanged glances.

Maybe she's nuts, or maybe she'll be interested in speaking with us.

"Named after the Ring of Solomon?" Cham asked casually. Arden grimaced, and her hand holding the leash quivered visibly. Though it could be due to the cold, Cham didn't believe so.

"Come, Solly." She yanked on the leash, and the dog yelped as it was dragged away.

"I'm sorry, Dr. Blakely, but I need to ask you about the ring.

My girlfriend is being stalked by someone who wants it. I need to protect her."

She stopped, and Solly used the break to inhale the odd scents in the grass beside him. Finding a new spot, the dog lifted another leg and peed over the brown patch in the small garden. "I thought it might be here," Arden sighed. "Is it at the black market?"

Cham viewed Arden with surprise and concern. Her knowledge at first glance seemed extensive, and that worried him. But then she had met Jason Pearce and told him of the ring.

"No. It's hidden. Is there someplace we can go in private?"

"Upstairs."

Cham and Emerson followed Arden Blakely inside what was once a turn-of-the-century mansion and was now several condominiums. Industrial-strength soap assaulted Cham. The real wood baseboards and hand rails had just been polished; his boots clicked against the newly cleaned tile. He followed Arden Blakely up the stairs as the treads creaked under his weight.

The animated dog bounded gleefully, leading them up to the third floor, unaware of the danger its owner was in. The owner shook with each step as if the air still chilled her—or maybe the reality of the ring made her nervous. Nonetheless, she remained singularly focused on the dog and followed it up the stairs.

The bright white hallway gave way to a closed-up apartment. Window shades were drawn shut; the only natural light broke in from around the shades that looked like a square halo. Warm, stagnant air greeted them. Emerson grimaced and followed Arden as she shuffled through the large room, cluttered with furniture and covered with artifacts. Every square inch of the apartment was filled with something.

Cham skirted boxes filled with scrolls and rolled-up maps, Emerson nearly tripped on a bust of a man; his gold paint was worn and chipped, and the base was scratched.

The archaeologist led them to a corner of the room to a desk, piled high with folders and notepads scrawled with handwritten notes and additional papers. Some folders were so filled with papers that they couldn't stay closed unless something else was laid on top. Arden offered the two wizard guards seats across from her.

"Dr. Blakely, I'm Robert Chamsky and this is Emerson Donaldson," Cham said. When Arden didn't respond to his introduction, he glanced at Emerson who rolled her eyes and offered a shrug.

"I'm sorry to spring this on you," Cham continued.

Arden unhooked the dog, and Solly ran for the kitchen. His nails clicked against the hardwood floor as he waddled through the doorway. When he was out of sight, Arden switched on a desk lamp, which did little to brighten the small corner. Between the gray light from outside, the drawn shades, and the dark wood that encased the room, the small house felt depressing.

Before sitting, Cham moved a large box with an eclectic array of items, mostly likely from a dig site. He spied clay shards, a knife handle, a swatch of cloth. While he placed the box on the floor, Emerson removed a pile of folders from her chair and left them teetering on the edge of the already filled desk.

Arden Blakely hadn't taken her gaze from the opposite corner of the apartment, leaving Cham and Emerson time to examine their surroundings.

It looked like the Snake Head Letters, Cham thought as he crossed his legs and kicked a tome from a pile at his feet. The thick book with worn edges and a loose, cracked binding was entitled *Magical Portals and Where to Find Them*. A groan escaped his lips, and he showed the book to Emerson.

"Where would a nonmagical find this?" Emerson whispered. What she lacked in Wizard Guard knowledge and ability, she more than made up for in her research skills. If she questioned this, it was a good thought: books like this were hard to come by.

"I was thinking that too," he whispered back. "Arden. Where did you get this?" he asked out loud.

The question brought Arden back to the present, to the

depressing room. Her weary smile accentuated the deep lines around her eyes and mouth, and yet her eyes sparkled as if she were giddy.

Maybe she'll be open, Cham thought.

"Yes. Well. I'm sure you know, there are… sellers. All over the world. Very easy to find them if you know where to look. I can only assume they're smaller versions of the real market." The archaeologist rested against the back of her chair, seemingly more in control than moments ago.

The Wizard Guard was aware of illegal auctions, of markets springing up in desolate and difficult to reach regions throughout the world, locations that remained out of the control of wizard authorities. They took much more manpower than there were bodies to investigate them all. These markets could open up one day and be gone the next, or these merchants could sell at any nonmagical market. All reasons why the Wizard Guard preferred the major black market to remain intact. It was easier than monitoring the other less stable markets.

Curious, Cham skimmed the chapter titles and flipped through the tome for words like *portal* and *Busse Woods*. Staring at the information in disbelief, he tapped the book with his thumbs, pounding it like it was a set of drumsticks.

"You know about the portals in Busse Woods then?" he surmised.

Pointing to the book, Arden said, "It lists the portals there. Offers a map to their locations. I'm aware I'm so close. Alas, I cannot get inside." Arden sighed deeply. If she couldn't get inside, that meant she wasn't magical. Even with a cursed object, only a magical could harness the energy to enter a portal.

The fact that Arden most likely had been tracking the Ring of Solomon and knew about the portal worried Cham and Emerson.

She'll need to be dealt with by the VAC, Cham thought.

Jason Pearce had mentioned meeting Arden in a black market outpost in Morocco, according to his notes. With enough currency, those markets were easy to gain access to.

"Did you ever meet a man named Jason Pearce?" Cham asked nonchalantly.

Arden eyes blinked rapidly. They were unfocused, staring seemingly into nothingness. "I've met so many people. I don't recall that name." The archaeologist rooted through her piles of precariously stacked folders and paper.

It was eight years ago, so Cham wasn't surprised, though Jason had marked it in his notes, maybe as a reference for the future.

As he passed the book of portals on to Emerson, Arden's fingers lovingly grazed tablets and tiles, books and notebooks. She moved folders and books from one pile to another, mixing and matching until finding a particular notebook that she finally slid across the table. It was an average, nondescript spiral notebook that was missing the front cover. The pages, brown and crumpled, featured handwritten notes made illegible with water damage and age.

Arden drew pictures and maps, noted equations, and made hypotheses. She had written on every page, using the margins and back cover. Much of the information had been scratched out, rewritten, added to. It wasn't the only notebook. Cham spied several more on the credenza behind her desk. But she wanted him to have this one.

He scanned and flipped through the pages, finding the picture of the ring, a large, thick band. On the face of the ring, an etched six-pointed star surrounded by four stones that created a square.

That's our ring.

He showed the drawing to Emerson.

"You have many lovely items," Emerson complimented.

"Yes, yes. All mine," Arden replied her eyes unfocused. She absently played with a folder on the desk. It was empty.

"Dr. Blakely. How many archaeological digs have you headed? Finding the Ring of Solomon must have been the highlight." Emerson tried again to bring Arden back to them. She seemed lost in her own thoughts.

"Just one. Just the one."

Emerson and Cham exchanged glances.

She's been looking for the ring for forty years!

"Why?" Emerson asked incredulously. It seemed odd to work so hard for your Ph.D. and throw it all away.

The ring wasn't worth that. What was she doing all that time? Cham thought to himself.

"Too much to do. There was no time to search for anything else."

"Dr. Blakely, we need to know what you know about the Ring of Solomon." Cham held up the drawing, Arden's hand trembled at the request.

"Arden honey, what's going on in—?" A middle-aged woman strode into the room. Her flowing dress billowed out behind her, and her long, plaited hair bounced as she walked.

"They're here about the ring," Arden's face lit up as she announced the purpose of their visit, as if they vindicated her life's work. "Ariana, meet Robert and Emerson."

"Where are you from?" Ariana's terse voice rose an octave.

"Sorry, ma'am. We're with the Chicago Police Department, investigating the death of a man who had this ring on him when he died." Cham held the picture and his police badge for her to review.

Ariana grabbed the identification and scrutinized it as if she would know whether it was real or not. "This is ridiculous. The ring is fiction. I wish you all would leave her alone!"

Taken back by the outburst, Cham believed Ariana thought Arden was out of her mind. Arden's face went blank.

"I understand you don't believe in the ring, but I assure you the ring is real. We have it, and we know Dr. Blakely has extensive knowledge about it."

Ariana's shoulders slumped. She backed away without apology or acknowledgement about Arden's work. She turned and ran for the kitchen, making her displeasure known through loud outbursts. Doors opened and were thrown shut; plates and glasses were slammed against countertops.

While the wizards sat in uncomfortable silence, trying to not look toward the kitchen, Arden relaxed, comfortable behind the desk and ignoring Ariana's fit. She easily found a second book and handed it to Emerson. The wizard guard perused the tome; it was Arden's personal diary.

"You're not really with the Chicago Police Department. Who do you work for?" Arden asked with a grin on her face.

Memory modification, Cham noted to himself.

"The Wizard Guard, ma'am," Cham admitted.

"Ah. I always wondered if Wizard Guards were a rumor told to demons and bad wizards, scaring them into behaving." Arden chuckled as if this was all a joke.

"I need to know how you know about us, about magic."

With the question, her face drew downwards, creating deep lines in her forehead and around her lips; her shoulders fell forward and her hands fell limp against the desk.

When she spoke, it was as though from a place long ago, her tone wistful. "I've been tracking that ring since I first lost it. When you track a supernatural artifact, you ultimately meet others searching for the same thing, and you learn of the places. You become familiar with spells and magic."

Leaving the thoughts in the past, Arden returned to the piles on her desk, sorting through the books and folders—forty years of research—and lining it across the rickety desk that swayed each time she moved something.

Emerson was lost in the pages of the diary, reading the meticulous notes that graced the pages—so neatly written and organized, they almost seemed obsessive.

"Cham." Emerson showed the notes to Cham.

There in the pages, a mention of a man named Benaiah.

Cham reached into his jacket for a picture of the deceased. He would have slid it across the desk, but it was so full of stuff, so he stood and handed Arden the picture. "Is this the Benaiah you mentioned in your notes?"

Arden held the picture close to her face, examining every line, every scar on his large, bloated body.

"Yes. This is him. He's dead. I'm not surprised." She handed the photo back to Cham.

"How do you know him?" Emerson asked.

"It's not important anymore." With a shaky hand, Arden fiddled with a folder. The paper rustled. "It's a small community you live in, and for the right price, things are exchanged: information, goods. People show up in multiple locations." She trailed off, her voice dreamy and distant.

Cham laid the notebook in his lap and stared at the archaeologist who seemed unable to stay focused for any substantial length of time. Her mind easily wandered, and certain questions upset her so that she'd retract into her own world. He cleared his throat. "What do you really know about the ring, Dr. Blakely?" The ring. That seemed to be what kept her from retreating inside her head.

"My diary is only part of the story. Here. This is how the ring works. At least how I think it works." Arden relaxed when she spoke of the ring; her eyes cleared, and a smile crept across her lips. She handed Cham a two-inch-thick folder. As with everything the archaeologist owned, it was old, worn, ripped, and yellowed as if it had been through a lot—much like its owner. "The ring—this lovely, powerful artifact—spent a lot of time in Tibet. I almost had it there, and I lost it. I picked up the trail in Morocco, and a seller there led me to another buyer who in turn sold it to Benaiah."

She grew quiet and thoughtful; her eyes glazed over as she became lost amongst her thoughts and memories that had consumed her life for so long. "... I had him. Found him. Hid with my ring for eight years," she mumbled softly to herself. Her quick changes in demeanor unnerved Cham and Emerson. It was as though she were a different person in these brief moments.

It occurred to Cham in the quiet moment that Jason had dealt with both the Fraternitatem and Arden at the same time.

Are they related? Did she work for them?

"Are you an agent for the Fraternitatem?" Cham asked her.

She grimaced. "I knew of them once." Her soft, warm voice was sleepy, maybe drugged. Cham wondered if Ariana kept the archaeologist high to keep her calm.

That would explain a lot.

Cham perused the notes on the ring, unable to decipher the language.

Older than Latin?

"Is there a translation for this spell?" he asked. Again, his question about the ring pulled Arden's attention back to them.

"I can't find it. That's all I could get my hands on. I would think you could just chant it and *poof,* make the ring work. I was not able to." Her forced smile twisted to a scowl. Arden's hands fell to her lap and shook uncontrollably.

"Emerson." He handed her the supposed spell.

Emerson smiled as she perused the language of unknown origin. "I don't know it, Cham. I'll have to get to the library immediately and look for this. Can I take this with me?"

"They're mine!" she shouted at Emerson as if a whole new personality possessed the archaeologist.

Distant footsteps pounded against hardwood floors, and Ariana rushed into the room. "You need to leave. Arden's not well, and you being here is making it worse," Ariana cried out. She handed Arden a mug with rising steam, then turned back to Cham and Emerson. "Leave!"

"I'm sorry," Cham said. "We didn't mean to—"

"Just go, and don't bother us again!"

The wizard guards rushed from the apartment. By the time they teleported from a little used alleyway and returned to Wizard Hall, they realized they still possessed several of Arden Blakely's things.

CHAPTER 21

HIGH ABOVE THE school grounds, in an empty wing of the school, Annie sat inside the window well as snow fell. Fluffy, white flakes covered the racing pits, the lake, and the mile-long path from the teleportation area, blanketing the earth in white.

A fire burned in the hearth; the wood popped, smoke rolled upwards, and the heat, warmed the room so much that Annie had stripped to a tank top and jeans. Even still, sweat rolled down the back of her neck.

She leaned against the window to cool off as the wind whipped against the glass. When she began to shake from the cold, she returned her attention to Dr. Arden Blakely's diaries, which Cham had brought to her less than an hour ago.

Forty-two years ago

For so long, I tried to put the pieces together. Now I'm convinced that there is a hidden temple out there in the desert, one that belonged to King Solomon. I couldn't believe when I found the file hidden in the archives at the Field Museum—the missing dig site that can prove my theory. They thought they found it. They really believed the top of a column belonged to King Solomon's missing temple. But the site caved in, and twenty men lost their lives. Oh, it was a beautiful day when I found the file. I can finally prove my thesis!

The Field Museum will help some with the funding, but it's just not enough money, not yet. I spend my days in research. I think I know every square centimeter of those early maps from the archaeological dig in 1920. And now, these new maps of the area will help me find where the cave-in is. I think I know where it happened.

I was just told I have funding. A lot of funding! Unlimited funding! The excavation will happen! I don't know anything about my generous donor except that the name of the company is called Fraternitatem. It means "Order" in Latin. All I know is, they are very interested in funding this dig. The names of the men involved are Benaiah, Avi, Akiva, Benjamin, and Yosel. All very nice men. I can't wait. All we need now is the government approval to dig.

She reread the list, and checked the remnants of the folders

Spencer had saved for her. In the second file, her father had listed the names of the agents of the Fraternitatem he had met. Though their descriptions and quirks matched Arden's account, there had only been five members either had dealt with.

Only five members of the Fraternitatem? Probably the ones they sent out to do their dirty work!

Annie scrawled their names in a notebook, a reminder to have Bucky look into the names with the Middle East Wizard Guard.

She anxiously glanced at her phone, waiting on word of Zola. No one had let Annie know Zola was safe and sound. Annie knew that meant she wasn't.

"Where are you, Zola?" Annie whispered and peered out at the storm.

Tapping her hand against her leg, she glanced out the window as if Zola might be returning, walking through the thick, heavy snow. She continued to skim the diary, taking notes on what she felt was the most important, necessary information.

We dug for three weeks before we found the void, a pocket of empty space where the cave-in occurred. I knew it! It was right where I said it would be.

The bodies are everywhere. They have no names. Some bones are mangled from the avalanche of dirt and rock. Others are mummies. I can see their injuries as if they were killed today. I'm heartbroken.

Annie took notes. An entry from four days later...

He was the seventh body that day. I processed the body as I normally had, a preliminary examination searching for

injuries. I remember him well. If I had
to guess, at that moment based on his
location, I think he might have been alive
for a long while after the ground broke.
The thought made me shudder. During a thorough search of his clothing,
I found it. It was there, in a tight knot
in the hem of his pants. A ring. It was
beautiful, and I knew right away what
I had.

Maybe I shouldn't have left camp that
night. The car chase scared me more
than I ever had been before. They bumped
me off the road, they knocked me out. I
thought I was going to die.

I woke up and had no idea where I was
or why I was there. I was scared, cold
and hungry. The rock walls glowed in
a blue haze. At first I was happy to
see Nicky, but why was he here, in this
cave too? As my memory came back, I
remembered the car chase from camp
along the lonely road at night. He was
there when I was hit on the head and
kidnapped.

Nicky isn't the same person he was when
I hired him. He's mean, he sneers, he
hits me. I want to go home, but they
won't let me. Not until I give them all

the information pertaining to this fucking ring.

I can't tell you how long I've been at this. Weeks, maybe months. Time moves slowly in the underground laboratory. I see blue all the time, even when they let me out for a little exercise or to eat in the warm sun. They say it's the Cave of Ages. I thought that was a myth too. I still can't get the ring to work. I've read book after book, I've translated spell after spell, but this is just a ring. There can't be any real powers in this inanimate object. Can there? Magic isn't real.

She skipped ahead to seven months later, ignoring the notes on meals or basic research.

The ring is gone. They blamed me for it, because it had to be an inside job. They don't believe me. As I sit here wait-ing for my punishment, I grow angrier. I found the ring. It was rightfully mine. I would have protected it better than they had.

Most of what Arden recorded had little or nothing to do with Benaiah or the ring, Annie noted. She skimmed the rest of the year, then opened the third notebook of Dr. Arden Blakely's diary.

Benaiah told me the Fraternitatem is

setting me free. I've been told I've been here for a year. A year! Time has stood still for me. What will anyone say when I return home? What will I do now?

Shaking as she realized what had become of the archaeologist, Annie continued through the diary, through her years of searching for the ring. The last diary entry was dated eight years prior, around the time Annie's father died. Her hand shook as she read the passage.

Every time I think I have a location of the ring, it turns out to be false-or I just miss it; it's been sold or stolen. It always seems to be just out of my grasp. As per our procedures, I received notice that the ring was found in Tibet. Tibet? That ring has surely gotten around.

I promised Mom that this 'excavation' would be a quick trip in and out. She doesn't need to know what it is I really do. As for the Fraternitatem, I must find my ring and do what I need to do to protect it.

The ring metaphorically slips by me just as I'm about to reach for it, yet again. Today I find myself in Morocco. I no longer tell my family where I am. They ask too many questions, and I'm far too busy to care. This is one of the smallest black markets I've been in. One street, ten merchants on either side of the road. Though the stuff is real magic, it's all crap. I'm at a loss for how my ring ended up here. Benaiah is here, and per the Fraternitatem I need to reach the ring first. If I don't, the least of my responsibilities will be to steal it back. I'd rather find it and hide it from them. The ring is mine. I don't care what the Fraternitatem says.

That wizard guard, Jason something, was here investigating the influx of Chintamani Stones into the black market. They were stolen from my brethren in the Fraternitatem. How they could be so stupid is beyond me. While they are dealing with this wizard guard, I have my chance to take the ring for myself.

Dad!

Seeing his name in Arden Blakely's diary caused Annie's heart to speed until she was dizzy. He was so entrenched with the Fraternitatem, with the archaeologist. Annie was convinced—even without solid evidence—that this was his last case, the case that got him murdered. She dropped the book in her lap to watch the falling snow; the storm had picked up again.

A sour ache roiled in her stomach as Arden's timeline played out in her head. The missing year, the fear, the confusion, not understanding magic and being thrown into this world—it all was a lot to handle so far from family and friends. She had been betrayed by her assistant and lost everything spending so much time forced to work for this group.

How do you forgive and move on? Or don't you?

Whatever happened, Annie thought it might have caused a significant amount of post-traumatic stress.

Does she still work for them? Even in her state. She obviously still has the desire to find and possess this ring.

The ring—the root of all this death and destruction and ultimately, if they weren't careful, the loss of the black market and the exposure of magic. Annie sighed.

Ryan had suggested she use what was in Jason's case files for what only affected this investigation. She hoped Arden could tell her more about this group.

She scribbled more thoughts on her to-do list.

The Cave of Ages. Lial and Mrs. Cutt-lebrink for an exact location.

Her father excluded the starting location or unmistakable landmarks on his map. She thought he was either protecting them or others from finding them and incurring their wrath.

Metal squeaked as Gibbs parked himself on a metal folding chair beside the doorway. His reading materials consisted of several trashy magazines and magical research books. He shifted uncomfortably in the chair of his choice. Annie thought the hard surface was chosen to keep him awake in the warm and mostly silent room.

Periodically, he glanced up and observed both Annie and the anxious elf who in the end was allowed free reign on this floor. With that freedom, Bitherby paced across the lounge, up the stairs and back down again, picking up his speed across the large, flat hearth. He wrung his hands and squeaked softly before changing direction.

Maybe he was homesick or lonely in this new environment

away from friends and family. No matter how much the elf grated her nerves, in this moment Annie felt badly for him.

Her eyes met Gibbs's. He raised and lowered his eyebrows before returning to his book.

I'm bored.

She returned to the snow storm; large flakes gently fell in a continuous wall of white.

Small footsteps pattered across the stone floor, followed by Bitherby's stench. His breathing was labored and anxious and warm against Annie's leg. She met his droopy glance.

"What's up, Bitherby?" She offered a smile that felt pointless. The elf was clearly shaken; sweat rolled down his bald head and hung along his chin.

"The protection spell around the black market is dying. Magic gets out."

As the strong magic that hid the market on the alternate plane of existence weakened, the market would eventually land in the actual Busse Woods, exposing magic to the nonmagical world.

Annie sighed. "We thought that might be what was happening. Snow was blowing into the market. Do you know why?"

"He's sneaky."

"Who's sneaky? The djinn?"

Bitherby nodded. "Master come one day and did something to Mr. Gladden, and he just took over just like that." He snapped his tiny fingers. "Then master kill people who make him mad. We alls scared. Do our jobs, that's it."

Gibbs lowered his book and nodded silently, pretending to read while observing the elf over the top of the page.

"Quick-like," said Bitherby. "No one say anything. Just do what we told."

A stealthy takeover. Silent and deadly.

Did anyone in the market actually see this coming, or did they only know it happened after the fact?

"Maybe our missing persons aren't shapeshifters. Maybe the

master killed them. We haven't had an increase in magical deaths," Annie said.

"Unless they were from other regions. One or two in a region wouldn't draw suspicion. Not if it was within the normal number of murders in a week, month, or year," Gibbs pondered.

"But we have meetings with all the units—and it never occurred to us to look for a pattern?"

Gibbs crossed his arms against his chest and teetered the chair on the back legs. "Annie, he might be killing people who make him mad, but it wasn't enough to raise the red flags. Granted, we missed a lot of clues."

Bitherby sat on a stool. His short legs swung freely without touching the ground. He reminded Annie of a ten-year-old boy, scared and out of place.

She thought for a moment. "So how did he do it? How did he keep the information from escaping? Someone is always willing to talk," she said to Gibbs.

"Fear. He probably threatened the merchants with death if word got out. A few public killings would be all he needed. And you were there. You saw how fast they were willing to turn us in," Gibbs answered and dropped his book in his lap. "It's still our fault and the fault of other Wizard Guard units. None of us saw what was happening."

"And Gladden's always worked at the market?" she asked.

"For a while. You've never seen him?"

When Annie had seen Gladden in her house, she had known she had never seen him before. His face, his scar would have stayed in her memory. "Just at my house looking for the ring."

"He's in trouble with the djinn. Trying to clean up his mess. Not much of a leader, that one."

Annie left her perch on the window and curled herself onto the sofa. "He came after me because I'm lame, and he finds... me." Her voice trailed off as she became lost in thought.

"Annie? You got something?"

She didn't have to think very hard. In their small world, if you wanted to find someone at the black market or in the magical world, there was only one person you needed to go to; Archibald Mortimer.

Damn him!

"Mortimer," she answered.

"I'll send someone after that fucker. Find out what he told. He might know something about your fairy too." Gibbs jumped from his chair with his phone and paced.

Of all the Wizard Guards, Gibbs was the most able to control his emotions. His actions worried Annie.

After a few minutes, Gibbs set his phone down for a moment. "Spencer and Lial are looking into the market, trying to plot out a location for Zola. Elf, you have any idea where the master would hide an Aloja fairy?"

Bitherby's eyes widened, and he shook his head.

"Where, Bitherby?" Annie asked.

"Dungeons," he replied so softly that they could barely hear his shrill voice.

"There are dungeons in the black market. Of course there are." Annie couldn't help the tears that welled in her eyes.

Zola!

"You received additional instructions for a trade. They'll be here soon," Gibbs said. He had returned to playing on his phone, odd for a man who distrusted all things nonmagical. "And Cham and Emerson will head to the Snake Head Letters. Cham's raring for a beat down. You okay, Annie?" he asked.

He rarely used her given name—she was always 'girl' to him. When he used her name, Annie knew she should worry.

"I need to get out of here."

"Patience, girl." Gibbs returned to his paper.

Annie stood, taking her turn to pace. She couldn't help but notice that the storm had let up. She walked back to the window and took a shaky seat to watch a large snowball fight break out on the school grounds. It did little to help her forget what Mortimer did or where Zola might be.

Bitherby searched her things, found a pen and notebook, and lay beside the fireplace on his belly. His legs swung in the air side to side as he intently drew across the page. Annie closed her eyes, but the peace didn't last long once Gibbs ended his phone conversations.

"What?" she asked.

"It was definitely Mortimer who ratted you out. But Annie, he suffered a lot before he did," Gibbs advised. "He's in the hospital."

Annie's stomach churned.

❋

Annie stayed in the lounge for the better part of the day, anxious and bored. Her food, brought to her by helpful elves, sat untouched.

The snow stopped completely, and the clouds rolled away, leaving behind a purplish blue sky crowded with twinkling stars and a full moon. Its light reflected against the pristine snow, which blinded her when she stared out.

Her heart ached.

Zola, we're coming for you!

"Annie."

"Spencer, anything?" Her wizard guard partner hesitantly sat down by her on the window seat. He hadn't called until now, so Annie knew that Zola was still missing.

"We can't find her." He leaned against the stone wall. Tired, his eyes lined with dark purple. He took a deep breath.

"Bitherby said there's a dungeon under the market," Annie said and closed her eyes, afraid she'd cry again. She couldn't let go, not yet, even surrounded by friends.

"We're close. We think we found the location of the dungeons, but they ran us off before we could get there. The people still left in the market, they're… different. More willing to call us out, come after us. There's no policing. It's…" He was apologetic and almost as sad as Annie was.

"Don't. I know you've tried. You'd do more, but you can't. We'll have to find another way." She could barely speak. "I should call… Samantha, Ryan, and Kathy. Let them know."

Spencer placed a well-trained arm across her shoulders. "I can call if you'd like."

"I should. She's… she's my family." Annie rested her head against his shoulder. This time she let the tears roll down her chin onto her shirt. When she shuddered, Spencer squeezed.

"Gladden disappeared. We couldn't find him at the market or at his apartment."

"He didn't get the ring or kill me, so he's probably dead."

The list of people who have died for this ring has increased once more.

"Not that I'm a fan of Gladden's, but I'm hoping he left and cloaked himself well," Spencer said. He switched positions, re-crossing his legs.

"I doubt it." She pulled away from Spencer and wiped her eyes.

"Zola's smart and fiercely protective of you. That will keep her safe." As much as Spencer tried to comfort Annie, they were only words and did little to help.

Annie tried to smile. "How's the market?" She tried to divert her attention back to the case away from Zola in order to reduce her growing anxiety. The fairy had been in her life since she was a baby; there wasn't a time she could remember Zola not being there, whether she was smoothing out Annie's frizzy hair or fixing ripped clothing or kissing a scraped knee or baking her favorite cookies. It hurt too much to think of her alone in a dungeon or dead.

"Nearly deserted. The protection spell is still holding, but barely. I'm not sure how much time we have."

Because of the secrecy decree, the black market had become first priority for the Wizard Guard, for her. Magic, especially black magic couldn't spill into the nonmagical world. Annie would have to put the Fraternitatem on the side—at least until the market was officially gone and the shapeshifters returned to their original form.

"I think I should forget about the Fraternitatem for a little while and work on fixing the market." She sighed.

"They've—"

"No, Annie." Milo's booming voice vibrated throughout the lounge. His short strides made him look as though he was hopping rather than walking. He strolled to the fireplace and stared into the dancing flames. The wood popped and cracked. "Absolutely not. You need to find this group, whoever it is. They still don't have their ring, and that means they'll be after you."

That, for Annie, explained why he hadn't let her leave for the prison even as the storm had stopped. "Well, I can't do much in here. And we have a huge problem at the market." It wasn't much of an argument. Milo had the final say. Annie would have to stay the course, pursuing Benaiah's murderers. "When will I leave?"

The front door of the lounge swished open, Shiff and Brite, a Wizard Guard team from the southwest satellite office, joined them, taking a seat in the conversation area. At the same time, a back wall shimmered until a door was formed, and Cham stepped inside, harried and tired.

"Tomorrow morning," Milo finally answered. He bent over and meddled in the fire, adding magic. The flame grew exponentially, and the heat made the room warm and stuffy. "Anything else on the Fraternitatem?" Milo asked, pulling himself up with a grunt and groan.

"Nothing yet," Annie said. "Except I think Arden Blakely might have been one of their agents. Did she say anything to you about that?" Annie asked Cham, who had just walked up.

"No. She was in and out of reality. She might have PTSD. She… well, it was weird. I'm not sure if she's capable of doing much of anything right now."

Though disappointed, Annie understood. After reading what

she had of Arden's diary, it made sense. "I was hoping she might point us to the location of the Cave of Ages. Based on her diary and my dad's corroborating notes, it's somewhere in the Israeli desert, and that's where the Fraternitatem are based. I have a map, but it's not specific. We need a starting point."

"Have Lial work with Mrs. Cuttlebrink, Emerson, if she's not busy with the spell translation," Milo ordered. He bored easily and didn't like to work in the field. Visiting Annie at school was deemed field work. He paced. "Spencer, you have anything on the Aloja?"

Spencer reiterated what everyone else already knew and then shared something new. "They left this note. You're to wait for instructions for a trade. The ring for Zola." He showed Annie the note.

I wouldn't have expected anything less.

"Fine. Spencer, you take Shiff and Brite back to the market—glamor or disguises, I don't care how, but check it out. Gibbs, stay with Annie. We're moving her in the morning. There's no snow in the forecast."

❊

"Thanks, Graham," Annie said into her phone. "I appreciate you taking care of the reporter. At least now I don't have to watch my back." Rebekah Stoner had proved to be a larger problem than Annie could manage on her own. They were dangerously close to be exposed.

"Call earlier next time," Graham admonished with coolness in his voice. Annie had expected that and took it in stride. Everyone had warned her.

"I promise; I won't let it get this bad ever again."

"That's all that I ask, Annie," Graham finally said, resigned to her quirks. "It's my job."

"Thank you."

Finishing with Graham left her plenty of time to continue with

Arden Blakely's journal. Milo had stated it and she knew as well: they had to stop the Fraternitatem.

"Rebekah's done?" Gibbs asked.

"She's forgotten anything related to me and magic." Annie offered a half smile, mostly out of relief she no longer had to worry about the reporter, but partly sad. She couldn't imagine how confusing it would be for her to know something was amiss but to not know what. "Anything more about the djinn or the Fraternitatem?"

"I'm gonna continue on the archaeologist's journal. Maybe there's something new in here." Gibbs handed her a large bag. "Time to pack. We're moving you now."

She sighed and packed away the notes for Tartarus Prison.

CHAPTER 22

ARDEN TOSSED AND turned, leaving both her and Ariana unable to sleep. Anxious and jittery, she craved air and space, both of which Ariana withheld.

She turned to her right side, away from her lover, feigning sleep just long enough for Ariana's muscles to go slack and her breath to slow. Once she was sure Ariana was asleep, Arden slid out of bed and dressed in the bathroom.

Though the apartment was packed full of boxes, artifacts, and furniture, Arden knew her way through the rooms. She had the layout memorized and was very persnickety when Ariana felt the need to straighten and remove her things.

They're mine! Arden would shout, and the items remained, collecting dust and cobwebs.

Her bare feet shivered against the cold floor. She wrapped her arms around herself for warmth.

Switching on the single light above the kitchen sink did little to keep out the dim gray moonlight that enclosed the courtyard behind the apartment and seeped into the house. Arden shivered, feeling lonely and empty as she poured herself a cup of coffee and warmed her hands against the ceramic mug.

Back through the living room, Arden switched on the desk lamp. It threw out dingy yellow light, illuminating the items, papers, and folders strewn across her desk. She lovingly fondled everything that belonged to her, everything she had so carefully collected and studied over the last four decades. Every pile was etched in her memory; every thought she'd ever had on the ring was here in this room.

But her diary.

It's not here.

Her heart pounded, she slumped in her desk chair and closed her eyes. Her diary, her every thought, the recollections of a lifetime—missing. She remembered the culprits, the wizard guards who came and tore apart her life. She glanced at the chair where he sat, where the girl sat. Both of them had touched her belongings. They were so mean, so accusing because she knew who they really were. Arden plunged through the piles.

The spell is gone too!

Those people had absconded with her things. Arden's hands shook as she sipped her coffee. Some spilled to her pants, but she ignored the heat and wet. Instead, she studied the thick file at the top of the pile. The manila folder, forty years old, was marked with food, ink, and years of dust. It hid in plain sight, and its presence tugged at her. Opening the worn cardboard brought Arden back to the market in Morocco, a long-ago trip filled with hope and promise but ending only in despair and anger.

The map of the market sat on top of the pile of scribbled notes. It was hand drawn by a boy who had been so eager to help. There was even a circle around the stall where Arden had naively believed she would at last be united with her ring. The memory caused a headache to form at her temples.

So close to finally understanding.

Shuffling through the notes, maps, names, and places, Arden found the instructions, the translation to the spell that allowed the wearer of the Ring of Solomon to end this nightmare.

Arden's only desire was to repossess the ring, to hold it and prove to the world she was not crazy.

I don't trust them. They'll steal my ring.

Arden touched her temples, which throbbed with the lack of sleep and too much caffeine.

I need to find him.

Her only focus was retrieving her ring, the one she found so many years ago. It would fix everything, even the headache that took control of her brain. She popped the pills and took a sip of her nearly cold coffee.

"They have my ring," Arden said to the room, which was empty except for Solly who lay asleep at her feet.

Returning the cup to the kitchen, Arden opened a large cabinet, above her head. She pulled out a box of corn starch and shoved her hand inside, pulling out a gun and a large vial containing a purplish black liquid. She hid both items inside the large pockets of her cargo pants and sat at the table, waiting until a more respectable hour to pay a visit.

❈

Light streamed into the sunny yet small bedroom. Rebekah rolled over and wrapped herself in her comforter, knowing that she was free for the weekend. When the sunlight hit her face her eyes fluttered open. She shielded them and for a moment turned before sinking back into her blankets.

Images filtered through her brain, pieces of whole pictures running so fast she couldn't place them. Any feelings, thoughts, or smells associated with them seemed to disappear before she could capture their meaning. Her head felt empty and calm. After a few minutes, her eyes opened. She sat up in her completely sunlit room, the first time in weeks that Rebekah had seen her room in full daylight.

The weekend was her time to relax, to recharge. It meant she could take things slowly. She meandered her way through her apartment, past her large armoire in her bedroom, through her living room to her desk where her laptop lay open.

What was I working on yesterday?

Her foot smacked into the chair beside the sofa. She hobbled for a moment and sat down, rubbing her big toe.

When her toe felt moderately better, Rebekah finished her stroll through the apartment into her kitchen, pouring herself a steaming mug of coffee. It was ten thirty in the morning, and she smiled at the thought of the whole day free.

With her computer in her lap and the television on, Rebekah searched the Internet for nothing in particular, checked her Twitter and Facebook feeds, and shared and liked some interesting articles. When she'd had enough of people bragging about their perfect lives, she pulled up her browser news and realized it wasn't actually the weekend.

"What the hell?" She glanced up at the television, turned up the volume and searched for the weekend news. "Crap! Crap! Crap!" Rebekah shouted, realizing it wasn't Saturday. She flew from the sofa and scrambled around the apartment, searching for her phone, thinking she last saw it in her work bag. The bag was where she left it, on the floor by the front door.

Why is it here?

Rebekah shoved her hand in the bag's pockets and searched desperately for the phone. Finding it at the bottom of a pile of notebooks and other essentials, she fumbled for the power button.

What do I have to do today? File a report!

She read her phone and saw messages starting at four in the morning, filling her screen. Calls from her assistant, her producer, the general manager. "Fuck!" she screamed.

What did I miss? Why can't I remember yesterday?

Her last thought from the prior day was putting the keys in her lock when she arrived home. From then on, nothing.

Rebekah ran through her small apartment, searching for clues to her momentary amnesia. But the room was just as she left it, her computer was off and untouched on her desk, the furniture... the chair was out of place.

Did I move it yesterday?

Rebekah ran to her kitchen, noting nothing unusual or out of place. No food had been left out, no dirty dishes in the sink, the coffee maker set to go off at... *3:30 p.m.? It's not the weekend.*

Her phone buzzed against the glass coffee table, and she sprinted back for it. Reading the screen, she saw it was her boss calling again. Her stomach roiled.

"I'm so sorry. I think I'm sick and never heard the alarm." Rebekah could scarcely hold back the tears. They rolled heavy down her cheeks.

"This isn't the first time. You've been distracted for months," he yelled into the phone.

For months? Why? I go to work. I file my reports. After Princess Amelie's murder. all those stories I filed gave me more air time. I've done my job. Why can't I remember what he's telling me?

"I'm so sorry..." Her voice trailed off.

Yesterday I was assigned the story about the school budget crisis. The day before, I bought that new suit. Last week... last week I was assigned the City Hall updates. But yesterday...

"I... I have no excuse. I don't know what happened."

Her boss's voice carried through the phone. She held it away from her ear, perfectly able to capture each word, each nuance as he let the insults fly.

What else have I forgotten, and for how long?

Rebekah fell into her sofa, her head falling forward as her boss continued to berate her. She wrapped herself in the blanket.

"I don't know what you think you're doing. This is the last straw. Your work has suffered. You're fired."

"Yes. I understand," Rebekah mumbled, still holding the phone long after her boss hung up.

CHAPTER 23

WITH A WAVE of Brite's palm, a square, gray rock dematerialized, revealing another passageway, one that Annie had never seen before. They traveled through the walls, keeping their presence secret as they made their way to the forest beyond the school grounds.

Gibbs entered first, scouting for danger.

Overkill!

Annie grimaced as she followed him, prying a shivering Bitherby from her leg. Shiff and Brite followed after, keeping the rear safe—a procedure Gibbs insisted on. Annie's arguing did little to convince him otherwise.

Flashlights lit their way through the tunnel, which hadn't seen use in at least a decade; dust and cobwebs covered candle sconces that hung along the wall.

Their hard-soled boots clinked against the stone, reverberating off the hard surfaces. It was the only sound as they made their way out; they were all concerned with a possible attack.

Yeah, because whoever's pursuing me is gonna look here.

Beyond the beams of light, Annie heard clicking. She turned her light to the right, spying a rat the size of a dog scurrying from one hole to another. It stopped, paralyzed by the bright light. Its glowing eyes stared at Annie, and she jumped. Bitherby squawked and tightened his grip on her hand. The rat squealed and scuttled off through the hole at the base of the wall.

"That makes you jump?" Shiff chuckled. They swerved to the left, following the curved wall.

"Only if they see me first." Annie made no apologies. She would readily admit that many creatures grossed her out.

The school was built in the 1700s. Detailed stone work and carved woodwork were the standard for the building. The doors were no exception. Most in the school were hand carved from thick, strong oak, grand and beautiful—all but the door in front of them, which was plain and slightly damp, possibly covered in mold and mildew. Annie assumed it led outside.

Brite whipped a hand across the lock. When it clicked open, he pulled the door out.

What the hell?

"All that to get to the basement," Annie grumbled. Gibbs agreed with a grunt of his own.

They congregated in the corner as Brite waved his palm again, revealing another hidden door. Once again, it was industrial, made of metal, and serving no other purpose than a utilitarian one.

"Damn, I wish I'd known about this when I was here," Annie said.

"How many did you know about?" Shiff asked.

"We knew about five of them. They all entered fairly busy hallways. This one is cool."

Gibbs opened the door to the outside, beyond the school grounds in the thick trees. Waiting for them was Headmaster Turtledove, who offered a wane, tired smile. Annie glanced one hundred yards from their hiding spot. One of many teachers strolled the perimeter.

That's not suspicious.

"Annie, come back if you need anything." The headmaster hugged her, tight and secure, a little awkward. "I still say we're just as safe."

"I know. I appreciate the protection; it's just that this is the school. There are students here. If these men try anything…"

Headmaster Turtledove kept a hand on Annie's shoulder. His mouth was drawn with worry. "Take care of yourself. If there's anything else, please let me know."

"I will. And thank you. For everything." She pointed to Bitherby. "So, Bitherby, what do you say?"

The small elf, still holding her hand, bowed slightly. "Thank you, sir," he whispered.

Headmaster Turtledove had prepared a separate and hidden teleportation spot for them, nestled inside several thick trees, surrounded by needleweed, and hidden under a thick layer of snow. They jumped across the submerged vines.

Shiff teleported first; his job was to verify they were safely landing outside the prison. He sent word via crystal, a simple greenish glow. Gibbs reached around Annie's waist, teleporting both her and Bitherby to the landing spot.

Spells flew through the prairie; Annie met a rush of air just above her head as a jinx sliced through the air and collided with the tree behind her.

"What the hell?" Gibbs shouted. He grabbed Bitherby and Annie's good hand and ran from the teleportation clearing for the prison.

Shiff sent successive jinxes into the bushes bordering the teleportation location, where a group of wizards lay in wait for Annie to arrive. He covered Annie and Gibbs as they ran for the path to the prison.

Brite teleported into a rain of jinxes.

"Go after Annie!" Shiff ordered his partner.

Fog rolled over the island, blanketing them. It was as thick as pea soup. Annie was barely able to see in front of herself as jinxes and hexes were cast in her direction. A jinx made contact and singed her hair.

"Damn it!" Letting go of Gibbs's hand, she patted down the

cinder caught in her massive curly waves. Brite broke through the fog, found Annie, and pulled on her arm. They ran.

The prison should be in full view by now!

"We're being chased!" Gibbs shouted. Air popped and swished as it was cut by broomsticks. Annie couldn't tell how many flew above them. It didn't matter. They blindly and dangerously threw jinxes down at the ground.

Hex holes sprung out along the lane, Annie's foot landed awkwardly in an irregularly shaped one, and she flew forward. Brite cast a spell freezing her and keeping her from falling to the ground.

"Come on." Brite helped her out of the uncomfortable position and pulled her along the path.

A gust of wind blew over them, rolling across the island and breaking up the fog. The view opened, and for the first time they got a look at their pursuers. Four men Annie had never seen before sailed through the air.

Fraternitatem?

Brite flung a hex; the rider tilted off, rolling to the earth. The unattended stick fell to the ground. Brite summoned the handle, jumped on, and dragged Annie across the stick.

The hum of the protection spell vibrated against her skin and in her ears. Annie braced for impact.

They crashed into the magical protection, Annie tumbled four feet to the ground, landing on her tender shoulder. The shattered broomstick fell around her.

"Crap!" She rolled over. Two large hands the size of plates lifted her up, pulling her through the gate and laid her in the dead grass. Squeals and cries filled the courtyard when Gibbs tossed Bitherby to a giant who caught him midair.

"Let go! Let go!" Bitherby shrieked and kicked short, thick legs. The giant was undeterred.

Annie shivered, cold from the wet snow and from the wind that blew across the lake. Gibbs, Shiff, and Brite lobbed matching hexes and jinxes to their welcome party. Bodies knocked from brooms that were still racing in the air landed with heavy thuds on the hard earth. One man lay unconscious as a giant roughly yanked on his arm, dragging him through prison gates.

Sparks flew, ash dirtied the white snow, and smoke and the stench of burning flesh wafted to Annie. She lay dizzy with pain. The world spun. Annie fell...

❀

Weightless, she floated in the clouds. Angry voices, distant and hazy, wafted to her a million miles away from where she lay.

Where am I?

A groan escaped her lips. It took several minutes, maybe hours, even days before the fog lifted, before the voices grew louder and clearer with anger. The paralyzing grayness lifted, and the clouds shifted and blew away. Annie opened her eyes to the harshness of the room; it spun around her, and her stomach churned.

When Annie shifted, the cot mattress squeaked. Voices stilled. She pulled herself up, but lightheadedness overwhelmed her so she leaned back against the cold wall.

She had been heavily medicated. The aftertaste stuck in her cotton mouth.

"Annie, you're awake." Relieved, Ryan rushed to her, even before Cham had a chance to join her on the cot. Ryan hugged her, patted her hair, and gingerly touched her shoulder.

Though Annie knew Ryan loved her—he had cared for her since her father died—he had never coddled her.

What the hell?

She glanced at Cham through Ryan's stifling hug; his jaw was tight, his Adam's apple bobbed as he swallowed. He looked away.

"Who's gonna tell me what the fight was about?"

They hid from the question, looking away and staring at fixed points in front of them.

They're fighting about me.

Uncomfortable and lightheaded from the medication, Annie crawled under the covers to stop the nausea.

"Annie…" but Cham couldn't answer. Ignoring Ryan, he fluffed the flat pillow, gently placed it under her head, and pulled the blanket to her chin.

"Sorry, sweetheart. You're safe now," Ryan tried to assure Annie. She closed her eyes as if not seeing her friends would make them disappear.

"I was safe at school," she said through gritted teeth. "So don't pretend it didn't happen. What were you arguing about?" When she reopened her eyes, she glowered at them. They each squirmed under her angry stare and exchanged glances before answering her.

"We were discussing who knew you were being moved. Why Gibbs, Shiff, and Brite failed to bring you here safely." Ryan was angry; his glare directed at Cham was cold.

"This isn't their fault, and why you blame Cham makes no sense," Annie murmured.

"Annie, this shouldn't have—"

She held up her good hand. She didn't want to hear it. "How many did they get?" she asked.

"All four. They're in prison now. You need to rest." Cham said. The room spun again, and closing her eyes did little to assuage the movement. She reached for Cham. His warm hand wrapped around hers.

"Ryan, go home and tell Kathy I'm okay." It was an order, but through her slurred speech, it held no weight.

"No. I already called her."

"Then don't interfere."

Cham fidgeted beside her. His leg bounced up and down on the cot and rattled the bed.

Annie unwrapped herself from the blanket, sitting up before swinging her feet to the cold floor. Taking a breath, she stood and fought the fogginess in her head. When she felt steady, she headed to the table across the room.

"Annie, please sit," Ryan pleaded.

"Please stop! Everyone, stop! This is bad. You're fighting, and Zola's missing! Just stop!" Feeling little stronger with each step, Annie inched her way to the table, to the uncomfortable metal chairs that squeaked as she sat. "Where is everyone?"

"They're nearby. But this can wait. You have a concussion," Ryan said.

"It can't wait. Bring them in!" She rested her head in her hands.

"Okay," Ryan whispered.

Feet shuffled, and chairs squeaked. After a few minutes, Shiff and Brite, Milo and Lial, and Spencer and Gibbs entered the room, an icy chill hanging over them.

Did they hear the argument?

"As far as I remember, this is my case," Annie announced once everyone was present. "So this is the problem."

The assembled group waited patiently for Annie. Her pursed lips held back the vomit she thought might come up. She took a deep breath and felt their stares on her as she gathered her thoughts.

"Annie?" Ryan asked.

"Someone knew when I arrived at Windmere, and someone knew when I left." Her brain filtered through her stay at Windmere. There were exactly two people who were there when she arrived, though several teachers knew they were leaving.

The teachers wouldn't have turned me in!

She thought of the man who blamed her for bringing the elf to the school. Her stomach churned for no other reason than that he had called someone at the market and turned her in.

"Annie, who knew you were at Windmere?" Milo asked. Annie knew he already knew the answer.

"Headmaster Turtledove and the stable master, Mr. Jacobi. I saw one teacher protecting the border when we left. I suppose there were more. I have a hard time believing any of them would turn me in."

"Headmaster Turtledove was there both times, Annie. We'll have to bring him in," Shiff advised.

Annie sighed. *Only a student from another school would even suggest that!* Of the group assembled, Shiff, Brite, and Lial hadn't attended Windmere.

"Mr. Jacobi was there too. I don't know him," she argued. "The headmaster didn't do it. He wouldn't." Annie was argumentative; it came with the pain and discomfort, but she believed in her heart that her former headmaster wouldn't turn her in to anyone anywhere, especially the black market. If Mortimer would take a beating before he gave her up, she had no doubt Headmaster Turtledove would too.

"How do you know, Annie?" Lial asked.

"Because I know him. He wouldn't."

Annie rubbed her temple. A headache pounded.

Think. Think.

"What about Archibald Mortimer? He knows me. Do you know what else he said?" she asked. Anything but blaming the headmaster.

"Annie, he's unconscious. We won't be able to ask him. The hospital will call me when he wakes," Gibbs said.

"You'll have to consider the headmaster as well as the stable master," Shiff advised again.

Annie glared. "It's not him!"

Milo listened intently to the argument. When he had enough of the impasse, he pushed his chair away from the table and hoisted himself up with much difficulty. Whatever was ailing him appeared to be getting worse.

Annie expected him to scribble on the whiteboard, but he looked off to a corner of the room as if gathering his thoughts.

"Have we found Zola's location?" he asked Lial.

Lial pulled out a map of the market. "It's changing and shrinking and growing. The aisles are moving, but this here—this is always the same. I've been watching all day. I think this is the dungeon, and I think we start here, if we can get back in."

"What do you mean, if we can get back in?" Milo accused.

Lial and Spencer exchanged glances. "Well, the portals appear to be failing. We need to get in now," Spencer said.

Milo paced. Annie lay on the table and closed her eyes as if that could block it all out.

Zola!

Cham placed his hand on her head. All she could concentrate on was Milo's boots that shuffled and dragged against the floor.

"Talk to the elf about the black market. Get confirmation, find out any secret passages. Just do it. We need to find Zola before we lose the market. Shiff and Brite will go in with Lial when we know for sure how to access the dungeon. Ryan, you go home. Cham and Gibbs I assume are staying here with Annie."

"Uh, where's the elf?" Spencer asked.

Eyes darted around the room. Bitherby was nowhere to be seen. Brite and Shiff headed out to find him.

"While they're searching for the elf, Gibbs, what did the attackers say?" Milo asked.

"Nothing. They won't admit to who sent them or how they knew where Annie would be. I recognize two of them from the market. Realizing that, I'll make the jump; Gladden sent them to finish the job."

Annie lifted her head from the table, and glanced at Gibbs. "Not the Fraternitatem?" she reiterated.

"Annie, they could not have acted more surprised when I questioned them about the group," Gibbs said. "After capturing some magic, we could tell immediately. Their magic is not as sophisticated or precise as the Fraternitatem."

"Humor me—does their magic match the crime scene?" she questioned.

"We did a precursory test for the magic. It's definitely not a match to the clearing at the portal," he replied.

A last-ditch effort for Gladden to save himself. I'm not surprised.

As Annie contemplated the new information, Shiff and Brite entered the bleak, cold conference room—without Bitherby.

"The elf is gone," Shiff announced.

CHAPTER 24

WHEN THE HUMANS fought, Bitherby snuck out. It had been easy to leave the small conference room; the humans were busy...

Busy being mean.

No one knew he had gone.

Bitherby had spent his life in the shadows. It was how the elves survived living in the black market, and it was how he escaped. Putting his head down as he came to the security desk, he waited until the nice lady sitting there rushed to the shouting to see what was happening with the Wizard Guard. Bitherby simply pushed open the exit door and ran outside.

The elf worked toward one goal and nothing, not the Wizard Guard, Miss Annie, or the security at the prison could force him from his mission. He jumped inside the tall grasses that bordered the lane to the teleportation area, hiding himself as he made his escape.

A blustery wind continued to blow, and even the tall grasses couldn't keep the wind from pushing against the small elf. Bitherby ducked his head low as he anxiously stepped into the teleportation area, where he had last witnessed an attack. While he debated his decision to leave, his eyes darted across the grasses and trees looking for trouble. He took a deep breath and hoped the wind wouldn't whisk him away as he teleported to Busse Woods, outside the farthest, most difficult portal in the forest.

The conditions were no better in the forest. Bitherby fought against the heavy wind as he walked onto the nearly nonexistent, overgrown path lined on either side with a thick cluster of thin young trees. The undergrowth was deep and moist with a thin layer of new snow. Bitherby ducked a low-hanging branch, avoiding the sharp branches only to find himself eye level with another branch.

At the patch of needleweed, the elf teleported and precariously landed between an evergreen and the portal with barely any room to maneuver. The cold air washed over the elf, and he shivered as the portal popped and hummed. He glanced around his location ensuring he was alone.

The wood handle of his cursed knife was smooth in his rough hands. He twisted it, getting a good hold of it before plunging the two-inch blade into the entrance. The air spun and sparked. A torrent of wind pushed the elf into the tree behind him. Fighting mightily against the tornado, Bitherby lunged into the portal and landed face first in the silky loose dirt.

The market seemed settled and quiet in the morning, Bitherby expected to see no one in this section and worried he would stick out. After jumping through the portal, he couldn't have imagined the scene.

Rancid smoke hovered over the market, still unable to escape through the protective shield. With so many merchants no longer selling their wares, there was no need to light the candle lamps that lined each side of the aisle. Bitherby no longer worried he'd be discovered.

Bitherby had only gone from the market a few days. He glanced in the direction of the dormitories. Where they should be they weren't, so he searched for the source of the smoke—the incinerators. Finding his trail, he headed to where he knew the dormitories must be.

Bitherby crept behind a long-haired collie. Bothered by the elf, it stopped and sniffed him, licking the greenish skin across his nose.

"Not now. Lead me to the incinerators," the elf squeaked and swatted the dog's snout. The dog growled and turned, Bitherby crouched alongside the beige-and-white dog, following the new outer path to the incinerators.

The pair rounded a curve, coming to what had once been the center of the market. Though its location was now at the south end of the marketplace, little else about the market center had changed. Several dead trees still greeted them at the entrance, and the stage at the far end was still there, though covered in soot and ash.

Birds chirped, and a dog barked. The wild sounds masked the footsteps heading in their direction. Thinking it was a demon—or worse, the master coming after him—Bitherby smacked the dog and ran for it.

His heart pounded in his ears. He could barely take in air as the smoke poured from the incinerator doors in front of him. He ignored the rancid smell and lunged across the threshold, falling to his knees. Crawling beneath the smoke, Bitherby reached the back door to the basement where the elves and trolls lived. Popping open the door, he took a tentative step down the staircase.

The staircase consisted of two by fours supported by more two by fours and held at a precarious angle with elf magic. They swayed as Bitherby took each step. He held on to the railing as he carefully made his way to the hard stone floor of the basement.

The stairs led into a large room with a kitchen to the left. It was nothing more than a fireplace and a large prep table. Four creatures, one troll and three elves, prepared a morning meal of gruel, which boiled in a large pot. The mostly soupy mixture popped against the thick metal of the cauldron.

Hard biscuits baked in the fireplace were nestled in the hot coals. His mouth watered thinking of the bread, of the warm broth. But what waited for him back at the prison was why he had come back here. Rather than making contact with his brethren in the kitchen, Bitherby slunk to the other side of the basement where bunk beds lay end to end.

Hundreds of beds filled the room. Some were metal, others were shaped from wood planks. They created zig-zagging aisles, making travel through the basement challenging at best.

The elves and trolls not working in the market slept. They lay nestled on piles of dirty clothing, rumpled sheets, and worn blankets. Little bodies in deep sleep rose and fell with each breath. Rumbling snores rattled from tiny mouths.

Single light bulbs hung from thin cords every ten feet, providing Bitherby with just enough light to see inches in front of his face. Knowing the room as well as he did, he sidestepped a large hole at the head of the aisle and headed deep in the bowels of the room.

The room croaked and groaned, and snores and squeaks wafted to Bitherby. He shuddered as he walked through the space, which was so well-hidden underground that even the Wizard Guard knew nothing about it. He missed the warmth of the barn he blew apart. Even the prison felt safer, warmer, sweeter than this.

He continued to Huxley's bed, kicking a pile of clothing as he felt the edge of each bed, his fingertips grazing rough, dirty fabric. The two elves had grown up together and found themselves in the precarious circumstances of living and working for the black market. It didn't pay well and offered no opportunities; they lived nearly as slaves. But Huxley and Bitherby worked because that's what they did, and there was little opportunity for them.

He jumped Miss Annie's teleport without much thought after Huxley told him what the wizard guard wanted. He'd been worried sick about his friend ever since and hoped to find him safe. And as he thought of that, he wished to be back at the prison even with the humans there. But first he needed Huxley. Bitherby promised himself to bring Huxley with him when he returned to the prison.

Bitherby's fingers grazed the beds as he passed. He sniffed and recognized the scent that Huxley carried. The elf held his hand over his friend's mouth, startling the sleeping creature. Unable to scream, he bolted upright and heard a soothing "Ssshh," beside him. "Huxley, it's me."

Huxley removed Bitherby's hand. "What are you doing here? They see ya and you're dead." Huxley's eyes darted around the room as if the humans lurked in the shadows.

"I need your help," Bitherby ordered. Huxley's bruised eyes grew wide with fear, his swollen lip trembled, and his green skin turned ashen white and glowed in the darkness.

"You can't be here. They find you and kill you." He quivered in his bed, which vibrated against the stone floor. Bitherby placed a hand on his friend to calm the nervous elf.

"Shhh. You wake everyone. I need help. The wizard guard protects me; she'll protect you too."

"Why you come back?" Huxley asked.

"Her Aloja fairy is in the dungeon," Bitherby whispered angrily.

"You risk your life for her fairy?" Huxley spat.

"Hafta. I need your help. Wizard Guard don't know the market. Will never find her." Bitherby wrung his hands and glanced around at his former mates, expecting them to wake and turn him in. They were all still asleep.

Huxley climbed off the bed so he was eye level with his friend. "You stupid elf."

Bitherby let out the stale air from his lungs. "They still looking for the girl. And you," Huxley protested.

"I gotta," Bitherby said.

"You gotta. You gotta be stupid," Huxley said and led his friend from the basement.

✳

"Cham. You need to come home," Dave Smith commanded. As the roommate of a wizard guard, he was familiar with the crazy schedules and hours. But as he stood in his pajamas at five thirty in the morning, the wizard zoologist wasn't familiar with this particular scenario. He anxiously stared at the woman standing in the hallway outside his shared apartment with his best friend. She was pointing a gun at his chest.

"Wha... the ma... er?" Cham's voice broke up over the phone line. Reception on the island was weak at best. In the early morning, between the thick fog and the overabundance of magic surrounding the prison and the island, most cell signals were blocked or splotchy at best.

"I can't hear you!" Dave yelled into the phone. Panic rose, and bile sat at the base of his throat as he stared down the end of the gun barrel. He could barely tell Cham what was happening.

"Goin'... side?" Cham's voice cracked as he exited the prison.

Dave fiddled with his phone while Arden stared at him through glazed eyes, watery from the biting wind. She patted down her windblown hair. The messenger bag draped across her shoulder slipped and opened, revealing several folders and thick stacks of paper. Again, she waved the gun in the air.

"Okay. Sorry. What's up?" Cham asked.

"Arden Blakely is here to see you," Dave responded. His arm hung down along his side, his palm open and facing the woman.

Arden pointed to the gun and placed an index finger to her lips reminding Dave to not say a word.

"Arden Blakely? What the hell is she doing there?"

"She's very insistent and wants to talk to you." Dave's eyes darted around the room as he planned his escape. Maybe he could teleport out the window—if he could reach it before a bullet pierced his body.

"What does that mean?"

"I'm staring at a very cold metal object. Just get home."

Arden's hand shook as she waved the gun, motioning for Dave to enter his house. He backed into the living space, stumbled against an ottoman, and sat.

"Get out if you can. I'm on my way," Cham ordered.

Arden glanced around the room, from the sofas to the windows to the television and down the hallway, assessing the space. Her eyes stopped on Dave, and her frown grew deeper. She sighed, grabbed her bag, and held it tightly against her chest as she sat across from him. He watched the gun, which was still pointed at his chest.

"Can... can I offer you something?" Dave asked, trying to keep her calm.

"No, dear. I'll just wait here for Mr. Chamsky."

"He's on his way," Dave assured her.

"I'm sure. I heard you talk to him. I'm not stupid, you know." Arden aimed the gun at his head.

"You are a doctor of archaeology. I would never think you were stupid. I do think the gun is unnecessary. I called Cham. He's on his way," Dave reiterated and ran his hand through his hair, his palm facing her.

After Dave's reassuring words, she appeared to relax. She shifted in the seat, lowered the gun, and loosened her grip. He had never summoned a gun—he'd always worried it would backfire if he did—but if he didn't try...

What the hell.

With a simple summoning spell, he called for the weapon. It easily slipped from her grasp and landed in the palm of his hand.

She neither looked upset nor surprised, even with the gun now pointed at her.

❄

Cham still hadn't caught his breath. Worried for Dave, he ran to the conference room where Annie lay sleeping, and he slipped on his shoes.

"Where are you going?" Annie murmured

"Arden Blakely has more information for me. I'll go get it and come back. Go back to sleep."

"Okay," Annie said and rolled over.

Cham arrived home less than ten minutes after his phone call and took the stairs two at a time to his third-story apartment. Not wanting to frighten or upset Arden Blakely, he cautiously opened the door and poked his head around the edge. Dave sat across from Arden, holding the gun and pointing it at her, though his grip was halfhearted.

That's a relief.

Arden was nonreactive, off in her own world, sitting with the messenger bag in her lap and her hands wrapped around the straps so tightly her knuckles turned white.

"Arden, what the hell are you doing here?" Cham asked through shortened breaths. He had done little to ready for the trip back home except throw on his shoes. The laces dragged and flopped against each other.

I'll worry about how she found me later.

Dave handed him the gun and sat back down. Crossing his legs and resting against the back of the chair, he shrugged when Cham looked at him.

"I found the translation. I had it all along." Arden laughed nervously. Her small voice was wracked with pain, confusion.

She seemed childlike in many ways, possibly from PTSD, Cham guessed. Her anxious hands played with the strap on her canvas bag, rattling the lock in a rhythmic pattern. Cham clenched his fists and took a deep breath, observing her carefully.

Arden looked through him, toward the blank back wall.

What is her true motive?

"Why did you really come?" Cham asked.

Arden slowly turned her head, her smile wide and somewhat creepy. Cham shuddered when she said, "You have my ring and I want it back. It's my job to protect the ring."

The Fraternitatem!

Staring at her sixty-year-old face, Cham could see the years of wear and pain. Her eyes were glassy and unfocused, hazy as if she wasn't mentally present and only barely physically here. The woman quivered against the leather sofa.

"Are you a member of the Fraternitatem?" The archaeologist didn't answer. The question seemed to upset her; she took to rocking in her seat.

"It was my job to keep the ring safe." She rocked harder, and the leather squeaked under her weight.

What did they do to her when she was kidnapped?

"I want to go with you to the market. Make sure the spell is used correctly." Her voice wasn't authoritative. It was robotic, as if she were brainwashed and merely relaying a message.

Is she part of some plan?

"Nonmagicals are forbidden in the market. You should know that from your research," Cham advised.

A smile broke across her lips and grew wider, fanatical. Arden held open her bag, showing him all of the contents. "But Robert, I can help. See."

We have the untranslated spell. That can't be the translation. It's too much. Besides the ring, what the hell does she want?

"Listen, Dr. Blakely. I can't just take you to the market. Let me call and ask permission. Give me a sec and I'll be right back."

"Oh. All right, Mr. Chamsky. Go make your call." Arden sighed and closed her bag holding it stiffly on her lap.

"Not until you tell me why you want the ring so badly."

Deep lines grew deeper around her mouth and her eyes, her skin much like leather. She lived much life under the sun.

"I found the ring in 1970. It's mine. I want it back. I've been tracking it since I lost it. You will take me to it."

"Are you a member of the Fraternitatem of Solomon?" Cham asked her again. She smiled and raised her brows while stroking the strap of her bag.

A buzz came from Cham's back pocket. Not taking his eyes from Arden he answered Annie's call.

"Not a good time, Annie."

"I went back through her diary. Arden's a trained assassin."

CHAPTER 25

ANNIE HAD AWOKEN at five thirty in the morning, when Cham left for an unexpected call about Arden Blakely.

Odd.

Awake and shivering, she climbed out of bed, wrapped herself in additional blankets, and sat at the table in the room while the elf taking care of her needs tended to the heater under the window. Annie offered a wane smile to the poor elf, who had been woken too early. Then she picked up her notes from Arden Blakely's diary. There had to be something in there that explained who the archeologist really was.

December 1970

I've been here so long I don't remember what the sun looks like. Nicky stopped looking at me as his boss so long ago. He orders me to work for him. He threatens me with violence. I only needed him to hit me once to realize how mean he really is and to know my safety was only threatened if I don't do what he and the rest of them ask. If I want to get

out of here, I will do what they say. It
will hurt otherwise, if I don't. I wish
I knew where Nicky's hate came from. I
really do.

January 1971

The work is long and tiring. This ring, the
Ring of Solomon that I found at the
dig site, it's magical. If I had only read
this, I wouldn't have believed it. But I
saw it. Saw it with the spell. It worked.
I finally translated the ancient language
and they-the Fraternitatem of Solomon,
magical beings with the power to move
objects or cast spells-they made the
ring work. It was horrible. They turned a
poor man into a shapeshifter. I watched
his nose grow out and hair cover his
entire body until he no longer resembled
a human. I saw the man become a dog,
right before my eyes.

March 1971

They promised they'd let me go. I've
heard it so many times before, I no longer believe it. And yet I still have hope.

They offered me freedom, but it will
come at a price. I must work for them.
The Fraternitatem of Solomon. It's a

funny group, charged with finding and
protecting the ring.

April 1971

I'm near black belt level of karate.
And now they've given me a gun, an
added weapon with which to do my
job. There's power in the steel. In the
smooth steel inside my palm. I practice
every day. I can hit the target in the middle of the forehead. I can hit the target
in the chest.

They've exposed me to so much, to the
magic and the potions. Magic is exhila-
rating, even for an onlooker who lacks
the power. Simply knowing that it exists
gives me a rush.

I started small and killed a goat. It was
easy with the gun.
With weeks of practice, I've become a
good shot.

Because I lack magic, they've taught me
potions-herbs and minerals and other
ingredients and their chemical reactions.
It's much like cooking, I've noticed.

May 1971

They've sped up the training. I've shadowed Benaiah on several occasions. He's
stealthy and quiet. As we came upon the
man, the one with the sword belonging to
the king, I saw how easy it was to take
his life. The potion I created, the death
potion, worked better than I could have
imagined. And as all the ingredients are
natural, though magical, the police will
never know what happened.

I shadowed Benaiah again tonight, and
this time, it led to a hand-to-hand fight.
The punches flew, and since I am so
close to a black belt in karate, I was
able to take the man down fairly easily. Adrenaline flowed. I felt strong, until
Benaiah handed me the gun and I had to
make the choice to shoot. With a shaky
hand and a desire to go home, I pulled
the trigger. It didn't feel as badly as
I thought. And with the man dead, we
took the magical talisman that had once
belonged to the king.

June 1971

To prove myself, I went on a solo mission. It would be easy, they told me.
Ask the man for information. Take care
of him when he did or when he didn't.
I would have to choose. In Tibet, I
heard my ring was here. But it wasn't;

it had already been sold. And the man, a man who's name I forgot, he begged for his life. But he had promised me the ring would be mine. He lied. And now he's dead.

I was welcomed into the Fraternitatem of Solomon for my loyalty to my kidnappers, for finding and giving them my ring. I took the oath as a newly minted member, and in return I will be sent home with the knowledge that should they need me I will appear, regardless of the case or what needed to be done.

Home...

"Crap!" Annie shouted loud enough for Gibbs to fly into her room. She was so shocked by his appearance, by his rather urbane long-sleeved pajama dress, that she nearly forgot what she had read.

Her stare confused him; he blushed. "Annie?"

"Sorry. Sorry. She's an assassin. Arden Blakely was gone for a year, forced to investigate the ring and then..." She showed Gibbs the book.

"I'll be damned."

"Crap! Cham! She's at his house. He just left."

Her fingers fumbled over the buttons as she dialed him.

"Not a good time, Annie," he answered.

"I went back through her diary. Arden's a trained assassin."

He was silent on the other end, and she feared she had found this too late—maybe Dave was dead or injured.

"Makes sense. When Dave called, she had a gun on him, though given her condition he easily summoned it from her."

"Good. I was so worried. Did she tell you why she came?" Annie asked.

"Translation spell. Though there's something more here. I found a strange potion in her bag when I looked at the spell. I'm going to bring her in. It's getting weirder," Cham said.

Annie's heart pounded wildly, but she was relieved he and Dave were fine. "Did you ask her about the Fraternitatem of Solomon?"

"I tried. Her smile just gets creepier."

"She's definitely a member, according to her diary," Annie explained. Her hand shook and rattled the papers.

"Let me finish this, and I'll come soon."

"Be careful," she said before hanging up. She would worry regardless until he arrived with the archaeologist.

Though with magic, he and Dave should be okay. Still...

Milo was twitchy when he arrived at 5:45 a.m. He and Gibbs nodded at each other and poked their heads out of the door, staring into the hallway, verifying they were alone. It was as if they worried someone would be able to break into the prison.

"What? No one can get in or would be stupid enough to try," Annie said.

"Text Cham and have him bring the archaeologist here," Milo grunted.

"Already done." Annie pushed herself up and trudged from her cot to the table where the food had been left. "Have the attackers given their names yet?" Gibbs sat beside her and reached for an apple. He sniffed it before taking a crisp bite.

"Nope, nothing last night. I've recorded their conversations during the night. I'll have the security personnel see if they said anything," Gibbs said and rustled his copy of *The American Sphinx*.

The elf, who had been brought from Wizard Hall to help with Annie's protection and care—as if Annie couldn't care for herself—brought more than enough food to feed the entire department and the satellite offices. Annie started to think they'd soon be joined as she reached for an individual loaf of bread. It was still warm, and the butter melted and ran down her fingers. For a moment she thought of Zola, who made this snack for her all the time. Her heart sank. Even as her stomach growled, she couldn't take another bite.

"You need to eat," Milo admonished as he sat down and helped himself to a Danish, a loaf of bread, and a hard-boiled egg from the bowl.

Annie's stomach lurched with the next bite. It was not prison food and quite good, and yet it roiled in her stomach.

"No word from the elf?" Milo's gruff voice grated on Annie's nerves. She balled her fist in her lap, squeezing tightly.

"No."

Bitherby had left the day before and hadn't returned. Annie hoped that he wasn't stupid enough to go back to the market. She feared that he had gone to fetch his friend and was recaptured and taken to the dungeon.

What if he went after Zola, too? That stupid elf is going to get himself killed.

❋

Huxley quaked beside Bitherby as they ascended the steps from the elf dormitory. Through the door to the incinerators, the smoke had thickened into a congealed state and hung heavy in the air. Holding hands, the elves dropped to their bellies and crawled out of the incinerators to the market.

With the aisle clear, they left the relative safety of the incinerators and scampered into a nearly abandoned market. They dashed underneath the nearest table, which was covered in a thick canvas cloth.

Huxley peered under the dirty canvas. Animal paws scratched

across dirt, and human feet shuffled behind a cart with squeaky wheels. Another merchant was heading out of the market.

"Humans are gone," Huxley said. He wiped away sweat and smoke from his face, exposing a darkened bruise around his eyes. He licked his dry, split lip covered in blood.

"Why they keep you alive?" Bitherby squeaked with horror.

"Don't know." Huxley shrugged. "You a stupid elf, coming back here. Run under tables. That way." He dropped the canvas and sat at the farthest corner, ready to make a run.

Together, they squatted and inched their way to the next table, climbing underneath the battered gray cover. The aisles clear of people and creatures, they continued around the market, from table to table toward the hidden dungeon.

Stopped quickly, a clowder of cats sauntered down the path, preventing the elves from reaching the next table.

"Now what?" Huxley asked. "They're everywhere. Why you help the witch?" He glanced between the flaps of the table covering. The cats sniffed the ground, pawing at the dirt.

"She protect me. The school is clean and warm. Now we need to get her fairy." Determined to reach the Aloja fairy, Bitherby slid from under the table and sidestepped through the cats. His small foot stepped on a long, swishing tail.

The cat hissed and swiped the tail, joining the rest of the clowder through the market. The elves slipped and slid underneath the next table. Bitherby's heart pounded wildly.

"Fine. We go." Huxley tugged on Bitherby's arm, pulled him from the table, and scurried down a path that curved inwards as if they were heading to the market center. They crawled through a pile of garbage and rotten food to avoid being spotted. Bitherby skirted around a pile of dung and into the legs of a short, rotund wizard.

"Watch it, elf!" The wizard glared at the tiny creature and bent low to get a good look at both of them. He examined their dirty clothing and Huxley's battered face. Then he headed in the opposite direction to deal with his personal mess. Terrified, the elves scrambled along the path.

Up ahead, the same German contingent that had been conducting business the entire week finally wrapped up their business in the market, indifferent to the changes that had come in the short time they had been there. The elves ran closely behind the group, hiding alongside their long legs. Busy with their conversation, the Germans never noticed the small creatures at their feet. The humans turned outward, looking for the portals, Bitherby and Huxley continued down the path, coming to the door they wanted.

They ran for the metal door, reaching for the shiny handle and opening it with shaking hands. Lunging inside, they slammed the door shut, plunging into darkness.

The school day started in one hour. In his twenty years as headmaster, Fitzgerald Turtledove had never been away during the school day. He sat in the interrogation room at Tartarus Prison, his hair tied neatly in a holder, his robes pressed and clean. Confident and unfazed, he waited patiently for the interview to begin.

Milo refused to allow anyone else to interview him. Shiff and Brite protested that decision, as they were not emotionally attached to the headmaster and insisted it should be one of them who questioned Turtledove. Milo brushed them off and entered the room, much to their dismay. The wizard guard sat directly across from the headmaster and smiled warmly at the other. They had been friends since their own days at Windmere.

"Fitzgerald. Thanks for coming in." Milo's tone, warm and pleasant, surprised Shiff and Brite, both of whom hid behind the two-way mirror, watching the interview.

"I didn't think I had much of a choice, though anything to help Annie and the Guard." Headmaster Turtledove offered a smile that was not too wide and not weak; perfectly warm and friendly. He placed his hands in front of him, resting them on the table.

"If a student or former student comes to you, are they generally safe at the school?"

Not rattled, Fitzgerald Turtledove looked Milo in the eyes. "Ask what you really want to ask, Milo."

"Fair enough. Who got to you?"

The headmaster was well aware of why he was summoned to Tartarus prison, though the directness of the question caused an eyebrow to raise, only slightly, as if his friend had been forced to ask the question. "I don't scare easily, and this is Annie we're talking about. I did not and would not ever turn her in."

"Anyone else there with you when she arrived?"

Headmaster Turtledove summoned a folder, thick with papers. He pushed the contents to Milo. "Standard background check. Nothing out of the ordinary. So I hired Mr. Jacobi. He was with me at the stables when Annie first arrived."

Milo glanced behind him at the two-way mirror and scowled before returning to the folder and scrawling notes in his personal book. Not working in the field for so long had rendered him slow. He tapped on his notebook as he collected his thoughts.

"So Annie arrived and then what?"

"We left Annie alone with the elf. She came to collect him and I assume bring him here. Mr. Jacobi and I waited outside for a moment. It was snowing heavily by that point. When I had given her enough time to speak with the elf, I came back inside the barn. We were attacked not long after that. I got her out through a hidden door to the basement."

"Did Jacobi come back inside with you?"

The question concerned the headmaster, his eyes crinkled as he thought about that night. His eyes raised in remembrance. "No. Annie and I noticed how quiet it was, and then the jinxes hit the building. I don't know where he ran off to."

"Did Jacobi attend Windmere? Did he know Annie at all?"

"Jacobi didn't go to Windmere and came to work for us within the last year, so I don't expect he'd know Annie from the school. Jacobi was very displeased with the damage the elf caused. The stable was unusable, and he blamed Annie. Just ask her." A small grimace crossed the headmaster's lips, though it didn't remain for long.

Milo glanced again at the papers, shuffling through them at a quick pace and stopping on an arrest report. He slid the document to the headmaster.

"Yes," Turtledove said after skimming the document. "He was arrested last summer at the black market while purchasing an illegal poison to control stoorwood snakes. They aren't native to this country and therefore attack the creatures we use in the advanced creatures class for the zoology program. After his arrest, I gave him a stern warning and accepted his apology. He assured me this wouldn't happen again. I believe in second chances, though a second offense will end in termination."

"Fair enough, though this gives him a connection to someone at the market." Milo tapped his fingers against the table, his thoughts swirling in his head.

"Milo, do you have a thought?" Turtledove asked.

Milo trusted his friend. He believed that Mr. Jacobi had made a contact at the market and used it, whether someone there needed his help to protect themselves from the master or he was threatened for some reason.

Maybe he's just mean.

"Usually the Wizard Guard are not welcome in the black market, but we're generally left alone. I mean, we don't go in with palms blazing or anything. But this time, someone there snitched on Annie and Gibbs. The patrons are more than willing to do so, probably to protect themselves from the djinn that now has control. My guess is that Jacobi has a contact and snitched to someone there who needed the protection, or he was coerced, or maybe he's just mean."

"Jacobi doesn't use modern technology," Headmaster Turtledove put in.

Milo raised an eyebrow. "That's good to know. Easier to find his connection to the market." Without the magic help, Milo understood it would be next to impossible to find out who had alerted the djinn that Annie and Gibbs were there and that Annie was at Windmere. Especially now that the market was nearly empty. Though Milo also knew he might be able to scare that information out of the stable master. "I doubted you'd turn her in."

"I'm very fond of Annie. We spent a lot of time with her after Jason died. Which leads to my lack of a motive. I have absolutely nothing to gain from harming her. I actually want her to come and teach." He offered a smirk as he waited for his friend's reaction.

Milo returned a grin, but unlike Annie's reaction to that proclamation, he didn't laugh. "You'd be lucky to have her. Does she know?"

"She does, and she laughed."

Milo returned the papers to the folder and crossed his hands on top of it. "Good luck to you. Do you think Jacobi would do this?" Milo asked.

With a shrug, the headmaster responded, "I wish I could say he wouldn't. That's not to place blame away from me, it's just that he was angry and has connections at the market."

Putting away his notebook and pen, Milo stared at his old friend. "So if we find something on Jacobi, what would you like us to do?"

"Whatever you have to. And I'll do what I have to."

"Fitzgerald, thanks for coming in." Milo pushed the folder back toward the headmaster.

"Keep it. Give it back when you find or don't find anything."

❋

Shift and Brite watched the headmaster leave the interrogation room, escorted by a giant. Milo followed and handed the folder to Shiff. "Did you catch that?"

"Yes."

"See if Jacobi has any contacts at the market. He should have a communication crystal in his personal things we collected. Find a connection, and I'll handle the interview."

"No problem, Milo."

When the two wizard guards turned out of the hallway, Milo entered the second interrogation room, which held Mr. Jacobi. After thirty minutes alone in the empty, cold room, the suspect fidgeted with his hands in his lap. He glanced at Milo when he entered the room and offered a sustained glare, never taking his eyes from the wizard guard.

Milo ignored the reception and sauntered to the table, sitting across from the stable master. Jacobi's brown eyes darted from side to side as he wrung his thick hands. With each movement, the chair groaned under his weight; it was almost too much for the thin metal chair.

"How long have you worked at Windmere School?" Milo asked finally.

"Why am I here? I didn't do nothing." His stout body looked small in the interrogation room, childlike and afraid.

"We're asking everyone involved in the first attack at the school some questions. That would be Headmaster Turtledove, Annie Pearce, Bitherby the elf, and you, of course. So please relax and just answer the questions. Okay?"

Mr. Jacobi nodded in agreement and continued kneading his hands together; they were rough and scratchy, and his calluses sounded like sandpaper when he rubbed them together. "I started at the school a year ago."

Long after Annie left, Milo noted. He pulled out a report from the employee file, handing it over to Jacobi. "You were punished for interactions at the black market."

Jacobi looked at the report, and his hands shook.

"I'm not here to debate that," Milo went on. "My question is; did you have that contact at the black market before or after you purchased the illegal poison?"

"I know people who work all over. I knew a guy there. Said he'd help me out. Had to get rid of those snakes before my creatures died."

"Of course. Yes, of course. I remember seeing them slither from the forest all the time. Caught one in the bathroom once. Nasty scar across my hand." Milo held up the top side of his left hand. Two circular scars shone brightly in the fluorescent light. "Took several spells to heal it." He smiled, but Jacobi glared. Sweat beaded in his short black-and-white hair and rolled into his dark brown eyes.

"What school did you attend? Was it in the States?"

"What's that got to do with anythin'?"

"Just curious." Milo offered another smile.

"Went to Tennyson in the south. Fine school. Better than Windmere, I've seen."

Milo had worked with enough Wizard Council members to disagree with that, but he moved on. "So you don't much like Windmere. You haven't become loyal to the school or teachers?"

"Nah. Not at all. Love the headmaster. He's good man. Gave me a second chance and all. Students are crazy wherever you go. I like it enough. It's just not as good as Tennyson, that's all." Jacobi attempted a weak smile.

"You were alone just before the attack. Did you call anyone, talk to them about anything in particular?" Milo said, failing to keep the anger out of his voice. Whether it was out of loyalty to Windmere or to Annie or just plain disdain for this crude man, he couldn't help his tone.

"I didn't do nothing! Don't like phones anyway. Too much trouble."

A knock rattled the two-way mirror and flustered Mr. Jacobi.

Milo stood. "Excuse me a moment."

Shiff stood inside the viewing room. "Look at this." He handed Milo a translucent, light-yellow crystal. "Took it from him when he entered." Shiff waved a palm across the stone, lighting it. A video-recorded scene began to unfold in front of him. Milo watched the scene and listened carefully. Very clearly, Mr. Jacobi and a second man were discussing Annie Pearce. Milo smiled.

"Brite's off to fetch the second man. It's Jacobi's brother." Shiff handed Milo the crystal. His phone rang. "Yeah…" He listened as a smile crept across his lips.

"That was fast."

"Not even hidden. Found him at home, he's coming quietly. He already gave up his little brother about the phone call. Though he didn't admit to telling the master," Shiff said.

"Probably told someone who told the master. Anyway, I'll finish here. Let me know when the elder douchebag is here."

Armed with the new information, Milo re-entered. Jacobi glowered once again, his hands crossed against his chest.

"You don't have a cell phone. Do you, Jacobi?"

"Why does that matter?"

"This is your communication crystal, yes?" Milo swiped his hand across the yellow rock, lighting it up. Jacobi's eyes grew wide as inside the crystal, the picture of two men deep in conversation replayed. Like crystals that track magical energy, this particular one was not only used to converse with someone but also was able to collect and save the conversations, storing them deep inside the crystal strands. Milo swiped his hand across the rock, increasing the volume.

"Winn, that girl. She's here!"

"What you talking about?"

"That girl from the market. She's come here to Windmere. The elf's here too!"

"Really? You sure it's the same one."

"Yes! It's them."

"Well, goody. I tell the master; he'll leave me alone. Can get my work done then. Finally you good for nothing, got something right..."

Jacobi shook his head.

"I know he's at the market. I'd recognize that dirt and the crowds anywhere. Who did you talk to?"

"Just my brother. He works at a market. You don't know. It's changed. It's not the place it useta be. Gotta do what you can to stay alive," Jacobi pleaded.

"Did you hear they were being hunted? Did you get paid?"

"Protectin' the family. I didn't do nothing wrong."

"Right. You didn't do nothing wrong. Jackass. By the way, your brother came here willingly, and he's talking. You working for the master, is that it?"

"NO! No, I'm not working for the master." Jacobi's voice squeaked and grew silent.

Milo motioned through the window, and two guards entered the door. Each grabbed hold of Jacobi's arms and assisted him up and out the door. The giants tossed him in a lesser, magically enhanced cell and locked him in.

"You got no right to hold me!" the stable master yelled.

"We've got a conversation that says you turned in two wizard guards. We got ya," Milo said.

"I called m'brother, 'bout the girl and the elf. I did it. But it was my brother's fault!"

"Sure it was," Milo said and walked away, leaving Mr. Jacobi alone in his cell.

CHAPTER 26

THE HIKER PARKED his car in the empty lot, the same lot that had been home to reporters and police vehicles for the better part of two weeks. Though the sky was clear and the sun bright, gusts of wind continued to blow icy air over the forest and through the trees, creating dunes of snow to the left of the clearing. Where the sun reached the earth, shallow snow piles began to melt, leaving many of the trails thick with mud and sand.

Prepared for the early spring conditions, the hiker pulled on thick waterproof boots and tied the long laces twice around his leg, securing them. Stepping onto the parking lot, his boots crunched against the remaining snow and ice as he trekked onto the trail.

The earth, still too frozen from the low temperatures, was a sea of ice and mud. He slipped across a muddy patch, righted himself, and took the trail around the clearing to pick up the southern path. It led him close to the anomaly, where the wind blew in like a wind tunnel, icy and cold. He shivered violently as birds squawked a fearful, panicked tune above him. The sky darkened and shadows grew long and dark in the clearing. Curious, the hiker glanced upwards, where the birds flew against the backdrop of billowing black smoke. It came from somewhere deep in the forest.

A fire?

The hiker sniffed the air, which clean and fresh with the aroma after a spring storm.

Where's the rancid smoky smell?

Animals scurried out of the forest. Three deer—a mother and two small fawns—ran across the path, ignoring the hiker as they escaped the fire. Plumes of smoke stretched through the dense trees and wound around the hibernating trunks, rising higher above Busse Woods, and curling out across Chicagoland.

The man felt a chill unlike anything he ever felt before and glanced in the direction of the cold air, unable to see what caused the dread at the pit of his stomach. Stepping away from the icy spot, from the turbulent air, he took a long look inside the trees.

Where's the fire?

The hiker broke free of the trail and stepped inside the trees, expecting to be overcome with smoke. The air was clear though a little damp from rotted leaves and other foliage. Venturing further inside, he whiffed the scent of dung and matted wet animal fur. He turned around and searched the trees for the animal, but he was alone. Directly above him through the bare branches, the smoke still billowed upwards—and yet the source of the smoke should have been right where he stood.

"What the hell?" he said as he ran out of the trees. Snapping a picture of the fireless smoke, the man called 911, reporting a fire in Busse Woods.

❊

Max White sat at his desk in the communication center located in the basement of the Wizard Hall. After being suspended last year for missing an incoming police call and nearly risking exposure of magic during a double homicide, he'd become the model employee, always arriving before his 8:00 a.m. shift and not using his cell phone for anything except emergencies.

Today was a slow day, and yet he monitored every police scanner and message that came in, looking for hidden meanings or connections. But the calls were all arbitrary acts happening to random people at indiscriminate locations. Bored, Max lovingly touched his phone, longing to fly some birds, but he resisted. Instead, he turned his attention back to the job, listening to the movements of the police, fire, and ambulance calls as they came in.

"Fire at Busse Woods..." the voice on the radio cracked. The hairs on the back of Max's neck pricked.

The black market!

Max dialed Milo right away. His heart palpitated rapidly; he felt nervous to speak with the Wizard Guard department manager after his major mistake.

"Yeah, what?" Milo hadn't forgiven the telecommunications specialist, believing it was his fault that magic was nearly exposed to the entire world. And that was enough for Milo to remain angry.

Milo's tone made Max jump and his palms sweat. "A fire was reported at Busse Woods," Max said, trying to ignore Milo's antagonism.

"When?"

"Just called in now."

"That's not good," Milo groaned.

❄

The genie had tricked him with promises of power and total control of the market. Gladden Worchester, low-level thug, had almost had it all.

It got so out of control.

Gladden knew the minute he made the deal with the genie that it was a bad idea. Genies were always tricksters, and the genie was always the one with the control. And Ezekiel wanted more, including complete control of the shapeshifters. To do that, he needed the ring. He needed and found Benaiah.

Or did Benaiah find him?

The man who claimed to have the Ring of Solomon failed to return, only to be found dead outside the portal.

Who left him there? They ruined the market. It was them who made this happen!

The master had exploded in anger the day Benaiah was found outside the market. Any control that Gladden imagined he had was gone.

Still without the ring and without Annie Pearce or that stupid little elf named Bitherby, he could no longer return to market. Instead, Gladden would run, leaving all that he knew behind him for parts unknown, leaving for a culture a world away.

Entering his dark apartment to pack his meager belongings, he decided that wouldn't miss the grime-covered gray walls and worn carpet. It reminded him of how far he had fallen from grace.

Rather than packing, he immediately met a hex that flew out of the darkness.

He woke to severe pain. It pulled from his shoulders down both sides of his body as if something tore him in two.

Where am I?

Coming to awareness, Gladden twisted toward the sound of moaning beside him. His wrists, bound tightly in iron shackles, rubbed into his skin. He pulled and rattled the chains that were submersed inside thick stone walls.

The dungeon!

His fog lifted, and his eyes grew accustomed to the low light of the dungeon. The smell of death assaulted him.

Gingerly Gladden faced the man beside him. The man must have been thrown in the dungeon weeks ago, but Gladden knew the man was dead. His rotted body still hung from chains, his left hand had slipped from the shackle, and his body dangled and twisted in whatever breeze blew through the stones.

Why was he here?

Beside the dead man, lay the fairy, trapped in the dungeon with iron shackles around her hands and ankles. She sat against the stone wall, her eyes closed and her breathing steady. Her golden hair hung dull and ratted, and her eyes… those eyes were dark pools of pure, black anger—anger that dripped from her voice when she spoke. Gladden had stopped engaging her in conversation when he was still free to leave. She no longer cursed or threatened him. And now she glanced up at him and observed him for a moment with a sneer across her lips. It sent shivers up his spine.

Gladden shrunk against the wall when the steel door at the top of the stairs squeaked open and slammed shut. Small footsteps shook the staircase, and small voices whispered between each other.

They squealed when the dungeon door swung open again, and then they bounded down the stairs, hiding in the darkness.

Gladden stared at the entrance carefully until out of the blackness the master, whom he feared above anyone or anything, appeared in the low light and yanked his chain from the wall. "You come with me and see what you created."

The master dragged a still-shackled Gladden through the dungeon, his boots scraping against the floor. Gladden's shoulders burned as the master forced his arms above his head with one quick jerk of the chains upwards.

The fairy gave him one last look through her still swollen eye and smiled at him, exposing her perfect white teeth. Gladden shuddered as the genie easily pulled him up the stairs. His battered body bounced against the treads.

As they entered the market, Gladden closed his eyes; the bright sunlight blinded him.

The black market he once knew was no longer the same place. The master, determined to keep control of the market, had called forth the shapeshifters. Thousands of them had answered the magical summons, unable to resist the pull of the dark magic. Once the unsuspecting shapeshifters passed through the protection spell their animals forms took control, and they had been unable to revert back to their human bodies or leave the market. For several weeks, these animals—really humans—had roamed the aisles, booths, and stalls, as the djinn had little control of them or their magic without the ring.

For the djinn it was a misguided attempt to scare Gladden into submission; with an army behind him, the djinn could have total control. But Benaiah had never come back with the ring.

When Gladden was finally pulled from the dungeon he shaded his eyes from the sunlight, from the fires that burned in the incinerators; the smoke rose out through the protection spell.

"What did you do?" Gladden asked. His jaw was so tight that he could barely speak through gritted teeth. The master yanked on the chain and dragged him across the dirt. His foot landed through a pile of dung. The smell permeated his nose, and he grimaced.

"I told you they were coming," Ezekiel growled. "And without that ring, they can't be controlled. The market is burning, and it's all your fault."

"I didn't do this! You invited the shapeshifters here. This is your plan! This is all your doing!"

The djinn wrapped the chain around Gladden's neck and yanked, choking the wizard. "You summoned me, and this is your consequence. There is always a price for getting what you want, and this is yours!"

Gladden didn't know what the backfire to the spell was, nor did he care. He could taste the power within his reach.

I lost control so fast.

But he hadn't lost control; it was never his. The djinn had always had control, and Gladden hadn't realized at first because it was subtle, quick. There wasn't a single merchant or patron that didn't fear the djinn.

When Benaiah came with promises of a ring that would control the djinn, Ezekiel had his final piece of the plan. But Benaiah stole the ring from his brethren and paid the ultimate price with his life. As a result, the plan and the market changed. The disintegration of the market was the djinn's backfire for the spell he used.

BANG!

The ground rattled as an incinerator exploded. Gladden turned toward the sound. Black smoke rose high into the air, above the tree lines and out through the magical protection.

The protection spell is dying.

Elves screamed, and trolls grunted. Feet pounded against the dirt as animals stampeded and headed toward them. The master yanked on the chain and pulled Gladden from the aisle as a pack of dogs ran for the portals.

"Be careful what you wish for," Gladden sighed.

"What?" the master roared, but Gladden, defeated and accepting his fate, slumped against the thick table leg that belonged to a wizard no longer selling in the market. The booth was abandoned, and all that remained were scraps of paper and a few potion ingredients that fell to the ground.

Gladden and the master stayed secure inside the booth as animals and wizards ran for the last remaining portals. Many carried what they could in their arms or dragged carts loaded down with cauldrons, magical herbs, and other items obscured from their view. A witch nervously glanced at them, at the master with his hand tightly holding the chain tied around Gladden's neck. She looked away quickly as she struggled with the rope attached to the cart. It was slow moving toward the portal.

"So now you know your consequence," the master sneered.

The fires that raged at the incinerators, spread to the abandoned booths via floating embers that flew through the air.

Gladden spotted the elderly witch several booths down; she lit a pile of her items on fire for warmth and rubbed her hands together. He thought she might be crying. Gladden realized that without the protection spell, the market was no longer a balmy seventy degrees. Instead, it was taking on the temperature of Busse Woods. Gladden saw his breath evaporate in cold air and felt his fingers sting with the frigid air.

He stood and swayed as he gained his bearings. The witch's tent burst into flame, the elderly witch hobbled away, leaving Gladden to grimace at her misfortune.

"The market will be discovered! You idiot!" Gladden shouted. The genie, no longer interested in Gladden, held out his hand and aimed a lightning strike at Gladden's heart.

❇

The master wasn't aware he had followed the elves into the dungeon. They hid behind the dead man still attached to the wall. As they hid, they observed the master drag Gladden from the dank, stone-lined basement.

"Stinks," Bitherby said as the basement door slammed shut above them.

"Too close," Huxley squeaked.

"Shhh." Bitherby smacked his friend on the shoulder and peered around the dead body.

His eyes now acclimated to the light, he saw the Aloja fairy sitting in the dirt. Her once pristine white dress was now gray and dirty; her hair was mussed and fell down her arm. Her crushed wing flopped to the side, unable to move.

The two elves snuck out from behind the body and tentatively strode to the fairy.

"I'm here to rescue you," Bitherby announced.

Zola opened her eyes and glanced at the two elves standing before her—their battered bodies, their tattered clothes, their eager, helpful smiles. The Aloja fairy smiled before breaking out in uncontrollable laughter. Bitherby stared at her incredulously until she stopped. "You? Really?" Zola finally asked.

"And me," said Huxley, annoyance in his voice.

"What about the Wizard Guard?" she asked.

"Couldn't find you. I can," Bitherby said and grabbed the first shackle. He noticed the red, blistered patches of skin around Zola's wrists and ankles where she was bound by iron.

"Don't! Please, it hurts so much," For the first time since being tossed in the dungeon, Zola cried. Tears rolled across her smooth skin and landed in her lap. Bitherby ripped a piece of cloth from his shirt, the hem now in tattered uneven shreds, and wrapped it around the burns on Zola's left wrist where the wounds leaked puss.

"We get you out," Bitherby assured her.

His magic was old and simple but incredible accurate. He held a hand over the fairy's wrist. Glowing, magical light weakened the iron until it popped apart.

Huxley worked on the second wrist shackle; easily it pulled apart, exposing a less burned wrist, though it still irritated Zola. She whimpered as he wrapped the left wrist with dirty fabric.

The ankle restraints were larger, thicker, and took longer for the magic to crack them open. They popped and cracked, exposing many burns and cuts.

Once free of the four restraints Zola gingerly stood and groaned in pain as she moved her ankles with her first step.

"You're not as obnoxious as I made you to be," Zola said and took deep a breath. Holding on to the wall, the fairy waited for her nausea to settle before taking another step.

"The market's changed. I can get us to the portal, but you need to get me home. The iron sapped my strength."

Zola leaned on each elf as she hobbled up the stairs. Her injuries burned and oozed. She moaned with each torturous step.

The top of the stairs couldn't come fast enough for Zola. She slid to the ground when they exited the dungeon door and looked out into the black market, a desolate, burning, dead land.

"What the hell happened?" Zola asked with shortened breaths.

"The master, ma'am. We need to go," Huxley said and helped Zola up. She leaned on both of them.

"Where's the portal? It looks so different," Zola said.

"It's... well..." Bitherby glanced around the new incarnation of the market, following the trail outward. They were only feet from the portal. One of the last portals in the once vibrant market was crowded with the remaining wizards and shapeshifters pushing and pulling their way to the exit.

With both elves holding on, the weakened Aloja Fairy teleported them to the portal and landed roughly in the dirt. Above them, a fight broke out between the elderly witch and a dog baring its teeth.

"Get us through now!" Zola shouted over the din.

"But we can't get through," Bitherby whined.

Standing up and leaning against him, Zola's anger and fear created a whirlpool of air around them. With what little energy she had left, she added magic to the whirlpool and pushed the wizards and witches from the line, away from the exit. The two small elves pulled her through the portal. In the cold of Busse woods, the elves held on, Zola floated as cold air swirled around her. She twisted and twirled, unable to control her body in the teleport. And when she was pulled from the teleport, she crash landed into the wet and icy ground.

The world stopped spinning, and the nausea settled. Zola opened her eyes, safe on the ground, and glanced around at the barren landscape. The prison sprung up at the horizon. "You missed the teleportation area. They're going to come," she said, her voice weary and tired.

"Yes, they come," Bitherby agreed.

CHAPTER 27

"TWO ELVES LANDED along the lane with a small woman," a security guard named Sweeney said, sticking her head into the conference room.

"Bitherby?" Annie asked.

"I'm sorry. I don't know. The giant fetched them," Sweeney added before leaving to greet the visitors.

Voices carried easily with plenty of hard surfaces to bounce off of. As soon as they entered the building, Annie knew Bitherby had returned and brought a friend—she could hear a familiar high-pitched voice she couldn't place.

"Let go. Take me to Miss Annie. I show her. Let go!" Bitherby shouted.

The commotion—harried voices, feet scraping against the stone floors—continued down the hallway.

Annie's heart pounded. Gibbs's demeanor changed immediately; his hard-soled boots clicked against the stone as he ran from the room and down the hallway.

Gibbs's low grunt was met by a soft-spoken female voice.

Zola!

Annie couldn't imagine or believe the elf would have gone back for Zola. It wasn't safe for wizard guards in the market; it couldn't have been easy for the elf either. She stood to meet them. Sure enough, Gibbs returned carrying her Aloja fairy, tired and dirty, into the room.

"Zola!" Annie bounded for them but watched in horror as Gibbs lay her down on the cot. "I thought—"

"I know, Annie dear. I'm okay," Zola whispered. Her eyes fluttered closed.

Attendants rushed in to care for Annie's fairy, bringing balms and lotions with which to heal the burn marks across Zola's wrists and ankles. The prison fairy, a nurse of sorts, placed a poultice across Zola's swollen eye.

She's safe, Annie thought.

"What happened?" She turned toward Bitherby, who had survived his trip to the market. His friend she soon recognized from the incinerators as the creature she had given her card.

He wasn't discovered!

"I brought your fairy," Bitherby said. "Man here say they check the dungeons. Couldn't get there. Bitherby could, Miss Annie. So could Huxley."

Annie watched Huxley, who was standing before her with a sheepish split-lipped grin. "Well, thank you, Bitherby, and thank you, Huxley. It was brave and a little stupid what you did, but she's going to be okay."

Annie squatted until she was eye level with the elves and pulled them into a hug, wishing immediately afterwards that she hadn't. They reeked of being elves and of the market and of fire. Annie could have guessed the market had gotten worse.

She pulled away, offering a smile before returning to Zola, who was resting comfortably on the cot. Annie reached for her once-soft hand, which was now covered in cuts and bruises.

"I was so worried," Annie whispered. Her happy tears rolled down her cheeks.

"I wouldn't ever leave you," Zola said through difficult breaths.

Behind them, Gibbs's voice rose in fear.

"Is someone on the ground?" He paced the small conference

room. "Okay. Thanks." He finished the call. Annie knew from the foreign expression on his face—the downturned lips and the crinkles around the eyes—that something bad happened.

"Annie, the protection spell is open and letting out smoke. There's been a 911 call to the woods," Gibbs said.

"Crap. That's really not good," Annie groaned. Her thoughts wandered through the timeline, starting with the phone call from Jack. It had been so simple, the thought that the John Doe discovered in Busse Woods was a wizard victim of a magical killing.

It wasn't so simple.

Annie dialed her phone, placing a call to Jack Ramsey so she could warn him of what was to come.

❋

"Jack, hey," Annie said into the phone. Through the line, she could hear the sounds of island life playing.

At least he's enjoying himself.

"Hey. Give me a sec," he said. She heard soft voices discussing. "I promise," Jack said multiple times before coming back to the call. "You're calling me back. That can't be good." He sighed into the phone.

"If it was a simple murder, I wouldn't have. I just need to warn you before you come back to Chicago," Annie said. She glanced at her watch.

"What happened?" Jack asked cautiously.

"The quick version: your John Doe was a magical, killed by magic, but the case got complicated. Suffice it to say, the protection spell around the black market is breaking down. The portals to the market are all dead except for one. And what's left of the market is on fire. The smoke is pouring through a hole in the protection spell," Annie summarized.

"Crap, Annie! How in the hell did all this happen?"

Annie sensed Jack's anxiety through the phone line. "Yell at me later. I just thought you should know before you came home."

"Sorry. I'm not yelling. It's just so… you guys have such a handle on these things all the time, right?"

"We screwed up. All the Wizard Guard units throughout the world ignored the subtle signs. We didn't communicate, and now there's a big problem for all of us. I'm sorry to screw up your vacation. And I'm sorry to not answer your question, but I have to go. Lots to do." Annie sighed.

"Tell me what I can do," Jack said.

"Not now, Jack. When you come back, we'll see where to put you. I really have to run," Annie insisted and hung up the phone before Jack could ask again. Glancing at her watch, she noted the time and ran for Zola before the chaos sucked her in.

❊

Zola convalesced; her injuries healed while she slept, though her eyes behind the lids moved rapidly.

"She's okay," Samantha Chamsky said. Though she was relieved, she shook against her younger sister's pant leg as she stood beside her.

"She'll be fine. And I can't stay. Is John going to sit with you?" Annie inquired of her sister. Recently married to Cham's older brother, Samantha had flown from Wizard Hall to be with Zola and had taken several hours before alerting John of her whereabouts.

"Was he mad when he called?" Samantha asked.

Annie reached her arms around Samantha and kissed her cheek. "Worried, not mad."

"You smell like elf," Samantha commented and reached for Zola's hand.

"Thank you. I need to go. Will you be okay here?"

"I'm a big girl. I think I can handle the prison. It's not like I haven't been here before," Samantha said bitterly. She was, after all, a Wizard Council lawyer and had worked cases for prisoners. "Sorry. I'm concerned. You're hurt and shouldn't go back to the market." Samantha focused her attention on the fairy. She pushed Zola's dirty, matted hair away from her face, tucking it behind her ear.

"I have to go. Everyone will be here soon," Annie reiterated.

"Just be careful." Samantha looked at Annie with sadness in her face. Her lips turned downward, and tears welled in her eyes. "I almost lost Zola, I can't lose you too."

It was the same conversation Annie had with her sister with every big case she ever worked. Regardless of how well-trained, confident, and prepared Annie was, Samantha worried. Annie refrained from sighing and pulled away.

"I have help. It'll be fine. Take care of her." Annie touched her sister's hair and squeezed her shoulder as she reluctantly left Zola and Samantha for the larger conference room that overlooked the barren courtyard, where it was snowing again.

❀

"That's possible?" Annie asked into the phone. While she listened to the South American Wizard Guard unit on her cell phone, she watched the storm grow in strength.

"I promise, Annie. We will have to move quickly before it collapses, but yes. We will move the Patagonian portal off the mountain to the flat plane. You can start sending medical personnel and other officials there. We will join you." The voice on the other end of the line belonged to Pedro. When he had finished assuring Annie of their next steps, she turned back to her to-do list and checked off *The Portal.*

"Thank you, Pedro. This will help. How many can you spare?" she asked as she scribbled additional notes, listing the team she had currently available and assigning their groups.

"However many you need, you will have," he said in his accented English.

As they finished their quick conversation, Annie typed *conference room, ten minutes* into her phone and waited to be dropped into chaos.

❁

Dave Smith landed at the base of the mountain trail leading to the portal and stared into the wide open space. This was where they would be building the paddocks and barns to house the shapeshifters until the Wizard Guard could return them to their human forms.

"We should have done this earlier," he commented to his boss, Tad Singer, who was marking up the land and verifying that they had enough space for an animal corral.

"What's done is done. Lead maintenance over there and help them set up the paddock," Tad ordered as he reviewed the map once again.

❁

A large tent was directed upward by busy hands that waved and swished. Canvas sprang forward and landed upright in the spot marked on the map.

"What's this?" Danny Chamsky, Cham's younger brother who was attending with his medical class, asked.

"This will be the main medical tent for less severe injuries. We expect mostly minor wounds of the nonmagical variety. Those who can be transferred will be sent to the hospital. Others will stay here until they can be teleported home," Dr. Christine Anderson instructed as she finished setting the tent. She looked to the medical students who awaited their orders and pointed to what appeared to be a large pile of very small boxes. "Bring in those boxes there. Increase their sizes and start unloading the contents. When we get ten beds set up, I want you in the market looking for victims," she ordered as she pulled open the first bed, waved a hand across it to grow it to its original size, and placed it in the tent.

❋

Annie paced the conference room and glanced at her watch; it was ten minutes before the rest of the team was due to arrive. She stared at the phone; the disembodied voice on the other end belonged to one of seven members of the Executive Council of the larger Wizard Council. She rolled her eyes for Milo and Ryan's benefit.

"Just do it!" the council member ordered.

"Yes, sir. We will find the djinn and trap him in the vessel," Annie repeated back to him.

"We also believe the best course of action is to eviscerate the market. Reduce it to nothing before the protection spell is gone. Get out as many victims as you can, and then do it."

Annie and Milo exchanged glances. Ryan sighed.

"On whose orders? Yours, or is this an international council request?" Milo asked. He glared at Ryan, who shifted uncomfortably in his chair.

"This is our decision. Just make it happen." With the tense phone call finished, the Executive Council disconnected the call.

"You run the Executive Council; why can't you stop them?" Milo shouted at Ryan. As the Grand Marksman, Ryan was in charge and could veto the decision if he chose to.

"I could veto it. I could say no, and we could keep the market intact as it were, or at least until we find every victim. And to what end, Milo? There's nothing left, and once the protection spell is gone, the market—or what's left of the market—will be exposed. Just make it happen," Ryan said with finality.

❋

A whirlwind of activity descended on Annie as the team congregated. She checked her phone, reading several text messages before checking off her list; medical, zoology. In the distance, Milo's booming voice called the meeting to order.

"People. People. Enough!" Milo stood his small, squat frame on a chair as if that would silence the din of voices that echoed off of the stone walls. Everyone here was concerned about the market's demise; theories and plans were discussed amongst the crowd.

Milo stomped his feet on the metal chair; it pinged, and that was enough to quell the noise. All of the wizard guards assembled, quieted, and stared at their boss. "Annie, you ready?" he asked her.

"Yeah. Zoology is on the ground, building barns and a paddock to house the shapeshifters we retrieve from the market or those that we find in Busse Woods. The medical team is building several tents to house any injured victims. Most importantly, we're going to enter the market through the Patagonia portal. We'll teleport into the region from the bottom of the trail. Pedro in South America assures me he can move the portal, as long as the market hasn't crashed yet. We'll enter there."

"They can do that?" Lial asked.

"Yes, and we need to get supplied up and meet them there in an hour. This half of the room"—she pointed to her right—"head to Zoology. They have things for you to take. And this side"—she pointed to her left—"go to the hospital. Same thing: they've got field packs for us to bring with," she said.

"What about those who already died inside?" Brite asked the question that weighed on everyone's mind. Based on reports from the market, several shapeshifters had died while captive in the market.

Annie shuddered. "The hospital will pull out as many victims as they can, identifying bodies."

Milo took a deep breath, an embodiment of the stress they were all feeling. "It's been discussed at the Wizard Council. The market will be eviscerated with all the dead inside, should the portals completely break down and we can't use the remaining one." Sweat beaded along Milo's forehead; he wiped it away. The reality of the black market's demise and the number of people who had lost their lives was inconsolable for the entire Wizard Guard. They hadn't been prepared for this eventuality.

The weight of the problem caused Ryan Connelly to stay in the prison the majority of the day as the plans were hashed out. Once a Wizard Guard and partner of Jason Pearce, he might have offered perspective on the situation. But all he could do was sit and observe.

"That's not right," Emerson said softly through tears. The plan was not optimal, but the magnitude was too large, and they were running out of time. Most of the team remained silent, lost in their own thoughts; anger and sadness sat in their hearts and roiled in their stomachs.

Ryan, now at the mic, offered Emerson a soft glance. As if he was speaking directly to her, he said, "I know this isn't good. This isn't how we'd like to play out this scenario. But the size of the market and the number of people force us to make difficult choices. I'm sorry we have to handle things this way, but the market grew bigger than any of the wizard guard units throughout the world could handle. It's all of us who failed to keep it in check, to notice the changes. And we have to pick ourselves up and deal with what's at hand, no matter how awful.

"As that stands, we move forward. Vampire Attack Unit has been in Busse Woods since the call came. They're keeping the protection spell from disintegrating. They're being assisted by the Scottish and English Wizard Councils. We move in ten minutes. Annie, this is your case—do you have your plan ready?"

Annie had rushed the plan because there hadn't been much time. She had utilized past plans; she knew her team could handle whatever came up. She began to pass out a stack of papers. As they were received, each wizard guard read the bullet points.

"Here's the deal. I'm waiting for word when the portal has been moved. We hope it doesn't collapse as they move it. Like Busse Woods, the portals all over the world have been twitchy, humming, and vibrating."

Annie rummaged through the package. "Once we're through, Cham, Lial, Gibbs, and Spencer sweep the market for the master. His picture is in the packet." Paper fluttered as all guards shuffled through the papers searching for the image. "If you need clarification, the picture is a compilation from Zola, Bitherby, and Huxley."

Annie glanced at Ryan. He shrugged and offered her a wan smile.

"Don't kill the master, djinn, genie, whatever the hell we should call him. Trap him, keep him alive. The Executive Council wants him imprisoned and stored for future use."

"Why? Why would they let him get away with it?" Emerson cried out.

"He has some usefulness," Milo grunted. His disagreement with the Council's order was obvious in his voice.

"Listen, we're not happy with some of these things. We just have to move on," Annie said. "And with that, I'm taking Shiff and Brite. Come with me. We will go to the incinerators with Bitherby and Huxley to make sure the elves get out safely. Make sure you have masks. The smoke by all accounts is thick and difficult to breathe in." Annie took a deep breath in the stuffy conference room air. "For the rest of the team, comb through the market. Any shapeshifter, real animal that broke through the protection spell, any person—witch or wizard—that's stuck or trapped, get them out. Direct them to the Patagonia portal or assist them. If necessary, drag medical personnel in to help. They're on sight and waiting." She stopped when her phone buzzed in her back pocket.

"South America is ready for us," Annie announced after checking the text notification she had just received from Pedro. "Any questions?"

Annie wasn't surprised when no one asked any. They were highly trained, smart, and resourceful. Stick them in the middle of any situation, and they would find a way to succeed.

CHAPTER 28

"**I**'LL BE DAMNED," Annie said as she stared at the new location for the Patagonia portal. It no longer hung between a large boulder and the face of the rock cliff near the summit of the mountain. It now resided on a flat piece of land at the base of the rocky path. Not difficult to access, it was suspended in the vast openness of the Patagonia region of Argentina, exposed for the whole world to see, should someone want to hike in the mountains.

"No worries," Pedro affirmed as she thanked him for his help. "We've set a perimeter around this area. We are safe from any prying eyes," he promised.

Thick puffs of black smoke billowed from the portal. The entrance twirled and shrunk; lightning struck repeatedly, though they hadn't opened the portal yet. It was as if the entrance was protecting itself from use.

I hope we can get back out alive.

Pedro and his partner, Fredrick, plunged a cursed knife into the portal. Rather than opening with a whirling mass of storms, the portal simply stretched wide, and shimmered in the gray day. The two men stepped through; Annie and her team followed them into the market.

They stood in awe of the once bustling black market. It looked as though a bomb had already exploded; most of the tents were destroyed, and those that remained were singed and ripped. For other tents, the internal structure was the only thing still standing. Wizards and witches trapped inside the market roamed aimlessly through the dead remains and piles of trash.

Smoke from the incinerators rose high above them, no longer held in by the protection shield. It billowed upward and out of the market, blanketing Busse Woods in thick, black smoke and ash. Through the hole, tall trees waved in the gusty wind off of Lake Michigan.

Animals scurried across the aisles to escape the smoke and flames, finding the most used portals.

"Why haven't they turned back to human?" Rico Esposito asked. He worked at the Northwest satellite office and had joined them this morning to assist in the market.

"I'm not sure we'll ever know for certain. Maybe the djinn cast a spell on them to keep them in this form," Shiff answered.

"Maybe that's what we need to do with the ring," Annie said. "Just get as many of them out of here."

The rest of the team broke away, scattering through the market. Rico, his partner Georgianna, and another from their office, Eddy Woods, desperately tried to convince a group of terrified shapeshifters to use the Patagonian portal. Even more headed toward the group.

"This is bad," Spencer commented. "We're losing all access to the evil and illegal. The world's a big place, and all these former vendors will have so many places to hide and sell their illegal wares."

As awful as the market could be, at least the Wizard Guard had known where it was and how to get there. Without it, they no longer knew where to find the black magic.

Dogs barked, and soft meows wafted through the mostly silent market. Above them, anxious birds flew. One dive-bombed Annie, entangling its talons in her hair.

"Damn it!" she shouted and swatted at the bird.

As she waved her hands about, Cham impatiently detangled the screeching bird from her curly locks. When freed, it squawked at her before flying away.

"Thanks," Annie said, her cheeks burning red from embarrassment. She watched the bird as it flew away, scared and wobbling until it was higher than where the protection spell should have been, soaring through a hole in the spell.

"Be careful," Cham whispered and kissed her. Ignoring that they were in public, Annie wrapped her arms around his neck.

"I love you," she whispered.

"I love you."

"In and out," he said, his fingers lingered against her cheek. She watched him leave with his assigned team as they made their way to a location where they thought the djinn might be found.

Annie jogged to catch her team, who had started a slow trek to the incinerators. She knew the last time she was here; she had walked in the opposite direction.

It's all turned around.

Animals poked their heads out from behind stalls, garbage, or the dead. Their eyes followed Annie and her team as they side-stepped piles of junk and garbage and left behind wares. She could have stayed here pleasantly happy as she searched for rare treasures. Instead, she knew that by day's end, the market would be nothing more than nothing.

Another squawking, dive-bombing bird attacked Annie, crying out as if complaining.

"Shapeshifters are dogs, cats and snakes, yes?" she asked, swatting the bird away.

He seems so humanlike.

"Yeah," Shiff said. "But this bird seems…"

"Human." Brite finished his partner's sentence. "I guess it's possible."

The bird flew beside Shiff, squealing loudly. "Draw attention to us, and you'll never get back to normal. Come with us if you'd like, but shut up," Shiff ordered. The yellow-and-red bird seemed to understand the command as if there was a human underneath the feathers. It landed on Shiff's shoulder.

"You have a new friend," Brite joked.

"Fabulous." Shiff glanced at the bird, who nestled against his neck and gently pecked his sunburnt skin. "Do you think he's another shapeshifter?" The bird rested his head against Shiff's face.

"We'll worry about it when we leave the market. We need to move quickly," Annie said.

Bitherby quaked with fear at being back in the market, though he had wanted to come, wanted to save his friends from the fires. His short, thick fingers grabbed Annie's hand as they walked farther inside the death and destruction.

Shiff and Brite stopped at a junction between two aisles, the paths still visible under the debris, ash, and smoke burns. Several green bodies slithered through the small crevices, where it was dark and safe.

One last snake with diamonds across its scales curved around Annie's foot. She jumped and bellowed; Bitherby screamed.

"What the hell?" Shiff asked. The snake glided away, joining the rest of the snakes under a large pile of charred wood from what looked like a storage unit that used to sit in market center.

"Snake," Annie said through winded panic, "Around my ankle."

Shiff and Brite chuckled and sent up a flash of light. It hung in the air, marking the spot for the zoology department to find the hiding animals.

"I'll remember: no rats and no snakes," Brite remarked. He led the team around a bend in the passageway.

"Sorry. They just give me the creeps." It was that slithering thing that made her shudder.

A pack of elves huddled in the center of a junction between two aisles and cautiously observed the wizard guards as they neared the group. Recognizing a friend, an elf in a dirty pink dress ran for Bitherby. Her tiny hands gripped his shoulders tightly.

"Go away! The incinerators are burnin' out of control!" she squealed in fear.

Bitherby, unsure of what to say, glanced at Annie, who kneeled beside the pair.

"We're here to help," Annie cooed with a gentle touch the elf's arm. It did little to ease the creature's fear; she had been through a lot, and was covered in dust and soot. Her matted hair was singed, and her distrustful eyes darted back and forth across the barren landscape of the market. "Head to the Patagonia portal. There's help on the other end. Do you understand?" Annie placed her hands firmly on the elf's shoulder. The elf shook her head again.

"Go, Sirina. I promise. There's help. I go with Miss Annie to get the others. Go," Bitherby pleaded. Sirina, wanting to believe Bitherby, nodded slowly before she scampered back to the rest of the elves. Her high, shrill voice explained the situation, and their heads nodded in understanding. Sirina waved to Bitherby, and the group ran toward the last remaining portal in or out of the market.

"They're coming out of hiding," Brite said as a single dog hiding under a fallen tent stuck its head out from under the canvas. Brite squatted beside the creature and lifted the tent. "There's a pack in here. I'm going to lead them to the portal. There are just too many of them," he volunteered.

"Direct them out. Send word to Milo that we need more help. There's just not enough wizard guards here." Annie sighed

"Be careful, and call if you need me," Brite said. He reached for the bird still on Shiff's shoulder. "Come with me. You'll be safer in Patagonia." The bird obeyed and joined the pack as it crawled out from the limp tent and followed Brite down the aisle.

"We're almost here. This way." Bitherby pointed around the final curve, where the incinerator door was off its hinges. The *No Admittance* sign lay on the ground, burnt around the edges. Thick smoke rolled out the door and billowed up through the protection spell.

"I can't even imagine what's going on in Busse Woods," Shiff said.

The ground rumbled beneath them, shaking them. Bitherby grabbed Annie's leg as she fell into Shiff.

"What the hell?" Shiff said.

"The incinerators are going to blow!" Annie shouted above the roaring fires.

"We need to go. Get out as many as we can, and then we leave!" Shiff said. They donned their masks, which were too thin for what they needed to do, and dropped to all fours, just below the smoke. The group trailed Bitherby inside; the smoke already choked them.

Maybe we shouldn't have come.

Through dung and dirt and rancid smoke, they crawled slowly until the door to the dormitory came into view. Along the back wall, the door was open, and smoke billowed out. The fire roared, drowning out any other sound, except...

Are those cries from inside?

"No!" Bitherby ran from Annie and lunged for the entrance.

"Bitherby, no!" She screamed, but he was already enveloped in the smoke and fire.

"Crap, Annie, we have to get him!"

"Tell me something I don't know!" Annie shouted and ran after the tiny elf.

CHAPTER 29

OVER THE COURSE of six months since he made a permanent move to the Wizard Guard headquarters in Chicago, Lial Peng had proven himself to be the most proficient tracker in the department. Today was his biggest challenge: to find a powerful djinn in an ever-changing market—if the demon was even still there.

Hiding in one of the remaining standing tents, Lial unfurled a magically enhanced map of the black market and waited for it to catch up with the many latest changes. The map shimmered and then dematerialized, leaving the paper blank. After a few moments, the new map shimmered and revealed itself to them.

"How often does this update?" Gibbs asked.

"I've had this map linked to the market for years, so it changes as the market changes. It must've just changed," Lial said.

Gibbs grabbed the map and looked outside the tent. When he finished, he tossed the map on the table and shrugged.

"Okay. I've placed us on the map, so it should reflect our location regardless of the layout changes. I also permanently marked the location that from what the elves told me would be Gladden's tent." He pointed to four red dots at their location.

"We're here. And…" He bent over the map. "Oh. His tent is here. We're pretty close."

They followed the map to location where Gladden Worchester's tent should have been. It still stood but had been attacked; embers had burned holes in the roof, and scorch marks stained the walls. A large plank of wood sat overturned in the corner, and papers were scattered across the floor.

"What the hell?" Spencer asked.

They took out their crystals, examining the air for magical trace. Cham stopped and turned on his spot.

"Did you hear that?" he asked.

"Hear what?" Lial stopped searching for magic. There was so much in this tent, it was difficult to distinguish the type of spell, the age of the spell and the owner of the magical trace.

"Shhh."

Cham casually strode to the corner and removed the large plank of wood. Lying in the corner was a beaten and bloodied elf. Cham pushed the wood away. "We need medical attention," he called out.

The elf glanced at Cham through swollen eyes and whispered something unintelligible through a split lip.

Lial stepped outside the tent and sent up red sparks of light into the air, alerting the medical staff that help was required. Spencer checked the elf's pulse. The creature looked at him before turning away.

"Hi. I saw the sparks. How can I help?" asked a gangly man with floppy brown hair. Danny Chamsky pushed it from his face and grimaced when he saw his older brother Cham holding the elf.

"Hey, worm," Cham said with a wary greeting.

"Damn." Danny summoned a stretcher and unfurled the legs. "Put him on."

Securing the creature, he placed an IV into the elf's arm. "I'm good here. You guys finish what you need to. When he's stable I'll teleport him out," Danny said. After so much pain, the pin prick had little effect on the elf.

"You sure? I can stay," Cham offered.

"Go. I can protect myself and the elf. Just readying him for teleport." Danny strapped the protective belts across the small creature's chest, adding one at his feet to ensure he couldn't move during teleportation.

"Call if you need me," Cham said. "Didn't know the medical students were helping."

"It's a madhouse at the mobile hospital in Argentina. Everyone's helping. I'll be in Patagonia soon. Be careful, or mom will get mad at me," Danny added. He unlocked the wheels on the stretcher and pulled the elf from the tent.

The ground vibrated, and the canvas tent shook wildly. Danny lay across the elf as the earth rumbled. Footsteps ran through the aisle, voices screamed, and angry grunts growled across the market.

Gibbs called Milo. The Wizard Guard manager currently patrolled outside the black market, searching for stray animals that didn't belong and overseeing the magical preparations as they took place. "We need more help in here. There's a stampede because of—"

The incinerators exploded. Several consecutive booms thundered across the remains of the market.

"Annie!" Cham shouted.

"The incinerators are blowing apart!" Gibbs shouted through the phone.

"Get the rest of the team and get out! The clearing is a mess! The nonmagicals have taken over. Just get out of there!" Milo yelled back. Gibbs's phone clicked off without a sound.

"Milo wants us out, now. Danny, get the elf out of here. Grab whatever human or creature we find on the way out. Since I won't be able to stop you, Cham, you get Annie and her team out of here!" Gibbs ordered.

While Cham ran in the direction of the billowing smoke, Danny and Spencer teleported the stretcher to the Patagonia portal while Gibbs ran through the market, looking for the last of the stragglers.

✳

A thick layer of smoke gusted from Busse Woods, blanketing the entire Chicagoland area. Though the sun was out, the region was dark as if it were night. Because of the strange anomaly, O'Hare Airport was shut down and currently covered in a thick layer of ash.

"We're lucky we got in," Amanda said. Their plane had been the last allowed into the airport before it was shut down.

Jack glanced out the window with apprehension before disembarking; he had said little on the plane ride home.

I wish I never knew about Annie and magic. Maybe…

"You okay?" Amanda asked him as they waited at baggage claim.

"Yeah. I will be." Jack hadn't told Amanda everything, especially who and what Annie was, just that she was a colleague and the fire had something to do with her case. He dialed her as they waited for their bags, but the call went to voicemail.

"You couldn't reach her?" Amanda asked. She looked stunning—well rested and tan, compared to Jack's worry lines, long face, and tight jaw.

Even after a week in the sun, Jack was still pale. He grimaced and grabbed for the first of their bags. "I should go to the crime scene. I can't reach Annie, and I'm concerned something's happened." The second bag came along the conveyor belt. He pulled it off and handed it to Amanda.

"Are you sure? We still have a few hours of vacation left."

They followed the steady stream of weary travelers to the doors. "I'm sure. You take the taxi, and I'll call you when I know she's safe."

"But Jack, are you sure this is the same case?" asked Amanda, clearly upset. They'd had plans for the night, a little time in bed watching movies before their vacation truly ended.

Jack sighed. "Yeah. I sent her the case. I know it's related to that body dump."

They spoke little as they exited the airport, and Jack waited until their pre-ordered taxi found them. "You go. I'll see you soon." He kissed her, long and soft. He really didn't want to leave. The vacation had been too good to let it end like this.

"Don't stay too late." Amanda offered a concerned look as she climbed into the taxi, waving as her car sped away.

Sighing, Jack jumped into an available taxi. "Busse Woods please."

"There's a fire in the woods. They're not letting anyone in for any reason," the cab driver said.

Jack volunteered his FBI badge for reinforcement.

"Yes sir!" the driver responded and pulled away from the curb and out of the airport.

Thick smoke hung above them in every direction, blocking out the sun and the blue spring sky. It looked as though a storm was directly over them. "What have you heard about the fire?" Jack asked casually.

"It's weird, they say. No one can find the fire, and the fire department has no idea what's causing the smoke. You were lucky you were able to land. Airport's closed," the cabbie advised.

"Yeah. Heard that on the way in."

The driver tapped his fingers against the steering wheel in tune with the music on the radio. "You think this is the same case as that dead body?"

Jack raised his eyebrows. He wasn't the only nonmagical to make the connection, then. That worried him, for Annie, for her team, for magic. "Too much of a coincidence. Don't know for sure, though. That's what I'm trying to find out."

The traffic moved at a snail's pace. This was not completely abnormal for Chicago, but today it barely moved, taking twice as long to get onto the expressway than it normally would. Exiting onto Route 53, the on-ramp was merely a parking lot, housing thousands of angry drivers.

"Is there any other route we can take?" Jack asked after thirty minutes of stop-and-go traffic just to reach the freeway.

"Doing my best, bud. I'll have you there as soon as I can," the driver defended.

Over an hour and a half later, the driver pulled up to the side of the road, letting Jack out.

"Best I can do," he said. "They're not letting anyone into the parking lot."

"No problem. Thanks for your help." Jack paid the cab driver with a large wad of cash and watched him pull away into traffic.

The entire park was closed to the public; the only vehicles in the parking lot belonged to emergency personnel. Ten fire trucks, twelve police cars, and six emergency ambulances were parked haphazardly, ignoring the designated lines. One vehicle was parked across the entrance to keep nonessential personnel from entering.

It didn't stop the hordes of onlookers from parking their cars along the sides of the street and heading into the woods, creating a larger traffic nightmare as a whole lane of traffic on either side of the four-lane road was unusable. Horns blared, and angry shouts rang out.

Jack grimaced and followed the other curiosity seekers through the trees. He trekked through snow and mud, covering his new running shoes with thick, heavy muck.

"I can't wait to see this," said a redhead to a brunette.

"Do you know what this is?" asked the brunette. They turned and smiled at Jack, who managed a wan smile.

"What?" asked the redhead. "You know, don't you?"

"No. I wish I did. I'm just curious like you," Jack offered.

It was the last he heard from the two women as they entered the packed clearing where John Doe had been found the week prior.

Police officers paced up and down the barriers, keeping people from entering the clearing. Their presence did little to keep onlookers from hiking through the trees. Some of the patrols entered the forest, but resources were thin enough that several people trekking to see the anomaly were finding their way to the fireless smoke.

Soot rained down, covering trees and turning the snow into

dirty gray, muddy slush that clung to shoes and clothes. As Jack trudged through the dense undergrowth around the clearing, his eyes darted across the crowd in search of Annie and her team.

The crowd ebbed and flowed; the forest was swollen with people. If Annie and her team were here, Jack figured they'd be inside the portal.

Jack crossed into the clearing, finding a harried police officer ordering a group out of the trees. Jack flashed his badge.

"Special Agent Jack Ramsey," he volunteered to the officer. "What the hell is going on?" He coughed. A heavy breeze was pushing smoke downwards. Jack inhaled the pungent smell of dung mixed with a musty scent of wet dog.

"The smoke is coming from somewhere in there, but we've been through those woods, and there's no fire," the officer replied. "No one knows what's going on. It's odd."

"Sounds it. Mind if I head in?" Jack asked.

"If you think you know what's going on. By all means, please. They're looking for anyone who can figure it out. And send anyone out who doesn't belong," he shouted after Jack.

Jack followed a path that had been beaten down by the hundreds of investigators and onlookers that had combed these woods for the better part of a day. Glancing through bare branches, he followed the billowing smoke until he was standing directly under the location where the smoke mysteriously appeared in thin air.

What the hell?

A strong odor wafted to him. He immediately could tell that it came from another place. It must have floated beyond what should be a protective shield holding the magic inside. Jack closed his eyes, thinking of the black market he had visited, a place where transactions of the legal and illegal variety took place, here and yet not, someplace he couldn't quite imagine.

Smoked puffed out as if from a smoke stack. Jack could see the single column of blackness as it escaped.

There's a hole in the protection spell?

Annie had once told him about the protection spell as not only protection for the market from exposure, but as a deterrent for nonmagicals from hanging too long near the portals. She described the icy air, the sense of dread that was always there in the forest. He closed his eyes and felt for the spell, for the chilly air that would be colder than anywhere else in the forest. He shuddered.

"What are you doing here?"

Jack scrambled around until he spotted Milo behind a tree, covered in soot, his clothes singed.

"I can help," Jack said immediately.

Milo laughed as he pulled himself out of the brush and into the open. His eyes darted across the forest, through the trees.

He's looking for nonmagicals,

"No. I think you've done enough. Good catch though." Milo grimaced.

"Milo. I can help. Give me something to do."

Jack felt naked as Milo regarded him and observed his slightest movements. After a moment, Milo waved him over.

"Fine, follow me." Milo sighed. He led Jack farther into the woods, away from the billowing smoke.

As they walked through the dense underbrush, thick trees, and new growth, Jack found himself alone with the wizard guard behind a large clumping of trees. Here in silence, away from any investigators, animals, or living creatures, Milo gazed into the trees.

"Where is everyone?" Jack asked.

Milo smiled. "They're in the market. Rescuing whoever or whatever is still inside. Look up." Milo pointed to the smoke.

I've already seen this.

But here Jack saw several lines of smoke puffing up through the trees from ten feet above the ground. "The protection spell is weakening. Soon, the entire market will be visible to everyone."

"But where is—"

Twigs snapped and leaves crunched as someone neared them.

Milo pushed Jack against the tree and held him there, motioning for him to not speak.

Duh. Of course I'm going to stay quiet.

Jack held his breath as he waited for Milo to remove his hands. Peering around the tree trunk, Milo let go of Jack after a moment and greeted two men and one woman.

"Graham. How's it going?" Milo asked.

Graham's eyes were dark circles.

"For now, we're safe. Looks like the spells are warding off non-magicals from coming this far in."

Milo pulled Jack out from behind the tree. "Except for this one," Milo said.

"Jack Ramsey. So you're the one we should thank for this. Good catch," Graham said and shook hands with the FBI agent. They had met several months ago when Jack arrested Wolfgange Rathbone.

"I'm here to help," Jack offered.

"Good to have you." Graham glanced up at the blackened sky. Jack noticed that both sleeves on his jacket were singed, and he was covered in ash and soot. "We're going to add more strength to the perimeter spell, to keep others away from here. At least until we obliterate the market. By the way, Jack this is Allen and Sky.

After they shook hands, Milo questioned, "And the Patagonia portal?" Graham sighed. "Still holding for now. The Wizard Guard teams from Europe and Asia have been blocking their portals best they can. Shapeshifters can only escape through Patagonia. It's a madhouse in there." Milo processed the report as he glanced into the forest.

"Maybe Milo, Jack can tour the area, look for stray animals that escaped the portals. Lead them off to the holding area," Graham suggested.

Milo looked at Graham and back to Jack; a smile cracked his drawn face.

"I can do more than that!" Jack argued. In this sealed-off part of the woods, the silence was eerie in its sereneness; Jack's frustrated voice bounced on the wind.

"There's too much work and not enough people. I'll be walking through the forest too, Jack. You can join me. Help me deal with your people if needed. The market, it's not safe for anyone anymore," Milo said.

"Whatever you need." Jack's answer was terse and confused.

Milo pulled the three wizards to the side. Though they were not whispering, Jack had difficulty understanding their conversation. Instead he watched the smoke billow out and swirl in the wind.

"Jack, you'll head with me." Milo's voice pulled Jack from his rambling thoughts of Annie and her team.

"We're looking for shapeshifters." Milo explained. Jack followed him away from the smoke, farther from the crowds and into the thickest, quietest part of the forest.

"What's a shapeshifter?" Jack asked. He had been wrapped up in the magical world, but now he glanced around to ensure they were still out of earshot of anyone who might have gotten past the protection spell that Jack somehow managed to pass through.

"Humans that can turn into an animal at will."

Okay, why am I not surprised?

Jack supposed he had heard of them somewhere before, maybe as part of an old folk tale or story from the past.

"How is that… never mind. Magic."

"Listen. Shapeshifters are rare humans that can change into cats, dogs, or snakes at will and change back again. Hundreds have been summoned to the market, and they're essentially stuck in their animal form. We're not sure why yet," Milo said.

"What happened here?" Jack asked. "This started as a simple murder."

Their footsteps crunched against the ice and snow. Every time a crack or pop occurred, Jack grew anxious, and his eyes darted across the forest, searching for others.

"So who would do this?" Jack asked, still nervously glancing around the trees.

"The short story is, a wizard named Gladden Worchester made a wish to a creature call a djinn, what you might know as a genie. He wanted control of the market. When you make that kind of a wish, there is always payment, and though Gladden wished to control the market, his payment was a partner in this djinn. Beyond that we're not sure what this creature did, but the market's been destroyed."

"And the body dump?" Without additional information, Jack couldn't see the connection.

Maybe Annie could clear it up for me.

"The victim, a man named Benaiah, was involved with this djinn, though we're still hazy about the why." Milo paused for a moment and watched the stacks of smoke rise in the air. Before he could blink, one of the lines disappeared without a trace; he sighed in relief. "The victim was a member of a secret society and was here to sell an artifact called the Ring of Solomon, something his organization was sworn to protect. Hence, why he was selling it. Which gives us motive for his murder," Milo explained.

The Ring of Solomon?

"You mean, THE King Solomon?" Jack asked, trying to control his voice and not alarm Milo with his growing stress.

"Yeah. That's the one."

Jack thought back to his Sunday school days and vaguely remembered the story about the king.

But I don't remember hearing about a ring.

"What does that have to do with the shapeshifters, the fire, and the destruction of the black market?"

Milo watched another smoke stack disappear. He sighed. "The ring was said to control the shapeshifters. We can guess all we want as to why the djinn wanted the ring. We think the djinn wanted to protect himself from Gladden, who wasn't happy with his new partner. We think once the shapeshifters are out of the market and in a controlled environment, the ring should turn them back to human." He stopped for a moment, still staring in the sky as another tower of billowing smoke disappeared. "But the rest, it's guesses. Someone inside the market was trying to fix a whole host of errors, and it just got out of hand. Now we're stuck cleaning up the mess."

After finishing his explanation, Milo looked into the low bushes and crouched behind a downed tree to investigate a set of paw prints in the mud. He pinched a beige hair from the print.

"What is it?" Jack asked. Milo held up his finger, signaling he needed a minute to investigate, and followed the track. A female lion lay on an open patch earth, licking her paw. Jack jumped and backed away. The lioness glanced at them, yawned, and placed her head on top of her paws.

Laughing, Milo said, "This would be a shapeshifter. I'm sure you're aware lions aren't native to Busse Woods."

Jack observed Milo cautiously approach the animal, holding his hand out for it to sniff. The lioness took a breath, gave a lick and lay back down. "I'm sending you off to the Argentina portal. You'll be safe there, honey."

Jack watched in awe as Milo held his palms above the majestic beast; it glistened as it disappeared.

"Why Patagonia? Seems a bit rough."

Leaves rustled above them. Milo glanced up as if he was expecting a flock of birds to descend on them. Bare branches swayed in the wind, scratching against each other.

"It is. But it's also the least-used portal in the world with virtually no nonmagicals within a hundred miles of it."

"Shapeshifters take the form of any animal?" Jack asked as they meandered through the trees.

"Cats, dogs and snakes. Usually they're not big cats or wolves. Domesticated, mostly."

"Why a lion then?" Jack asked, confused.

"We're finding other species in the market that act rather

human. Not sure how or why that is, but it is. We can figure it out later," Milo answered.

Branches cracked. Animated voices shouted, growing closer to their location. Milo pushed Jack behind the fallen tree where they sat in the wet earth.

"It's sooty here. Smell that." Fire rescuers hiked through the trees, bending and searching. Their footsteps grew louder, closer.

Jack felt his heart racing; it rang in his ears. Holding his breath, he watched Milo rise just above the felled tree. The wizard waved his palm, increasing the strength of the protection spell. The boost of magic created a chill, a warning to the rescuers to leave.

"It's not here. There's no fire," shouted a firefighter. The men in their heavy gear backed away and headed in the opposite direction. "Over here, the fire has to be over here." They headed west, away from Milo and Jack.

"Don't know why the shapeshifter took the form of a lion," Milo said again. He sat back in the mud. "We don't know why some things are happening." Sinking lower, he sighed.

"Is this how it always is?" Jack asked.

"It's not normally this bad," Milo answered. "This is the worse exposure risk we've ever had. Not even your princess was as complicated or as close as this is." Milo lay his head against the tree and closed his eyes, waiting for the next group of nonmagicals to sneak inside the forest.

CHAPTER 30

BITHERBY RACED INTO the dormitory as the smoke flowed outward. Annie and Shiff crawled to the door. The smoke overwhelmed them; hot air and the stench of body odor and dung seeped through their masks. Annie coughed and sputtered until Shiff cast a spell upwards, pushing the smoke against the ceiling.

The incinerators rumbled beneath them. Pressure built quickly, and the ground shook and popped; an explosion burst from one of the incinerator tubes. Annie fell forward and held herself steady against the door frame.

"Bitherby!" Annie shouted, but her cries were drowned by the fires, the explosion, the screams wafting to her from below. He was lost in the darkness.

Rock walls vibrated, and chunks of stone crashed against the rickety wooden steps. Hesitating to take her first step Annie turned to Shiff. "We'll teleport if we have to."

"I got ya," he responded and followed her down.

Their flashlights cut through the smoke in the stairwell. The fire and heat rendered the wood brittle. Annie held tightly to the handrail as if that would stop her from slipping and falling. It barely held against the wall.

Sweat beaded down her forehead and dripped to her chin.

Panicked, terror-filled shouts drew her downward, growing louder as her boots moved forward on the earthen floor.

The room swung to the right, where they found themselves in a large room filled with tiny creatures hiding under chairs and tables, behind dirty mattresses, or under oily rags. Some ran in panicked circles across the basement room, screeching.

"Oh, shit! Bitherby, help them upstairs!" Annie screamed through the chaotic shrill of voices. "Take this." Bitherby ran with the flashlight back to the stairs, dragging several other creatures with him.

"Now, this way!" he called out with a deep command in his voice. "Come now, follow the light!" Scared creatures peered over their hiding spots and gingerly stepped into the open, following the light out of the basement.

Without a flashlight, Annie couldn't see the detail of the room; she crashed into an overturned bed, sending shocks of pain through her shin. Losing her view of Shiff, she glanced upwards; shadows, smoke, and fire twirled and twisted toward the center of the room where he guided it away from everyone in the basement. His arms shook as he engaged the spell, holding it steady. Cautiously, Annie followed the firelight, avoiding lumps and piles on the floor, though she missed an outstretched foot and tumbled to the ground. The rest of the body lay under the bed. She slid the creature out and felt for signs of life.

Her hands shook as she lifted the still-breathing elf and ran the creature back to Bitherby at the stairs.

"Miss Annie!" Bitherby looked horrified.

"Take her. She's still alive."

Bitherby whipped his friend over his shoulders and carried her up the staircase.

"Up this way!" Annie shouted, her voice becoming the guidepost out. The exodus of creatures grew thicker. "One at a time, this way." Her fingers grazed shoulders as they passed.

Fifteen made it out, I think.

Amongst the deafening fire, she heard grunts and strained cries.
Shiff!

"Annie, help!"

The smoke and fire whirled above her. As Shiff grew weaker, the smoke dropped closer to the floor, ready to engulf him; he was tiring from the expenditure of magical energy. With a burst of energy, Annie jumped over a broken chair.

"I'll take over." She raised her arms, pushing the spell from the ground. Gratefully, Shiff lowered his shaking rubbery arms, wiping sweat from his forehead and neck.

Even with the smoke away from her face, the stench was pungent; she felt a wave of nausea and dizziness creep in on her.

"Do you have crystals?" she shouted above the roar.

"A few."

"Take them out and summon mine," she ordered. Her arms shook, she clenched her muscles.

"We have seven," Shiff said. Following her train of thought without Annie needing to say it, he waved his palms across the first.

Her legs and core muscles shook.

Depositing the first, he lit a second, adding additional magic, making the crystal's light strong and visible in the smoke and dark. Lighting all seven, he created a trail out of the dormitory.

Her arms and abdomen and legs burned as she fought to hold the magic at the ceiling. Above her the smoke undulated and danced at her command. It grew into a large ball and shrunk again, pulsing like a beating heart.

Fire roared behind her. She glanced over her shoulder; bright colors in shades of orange, yellow, blue, and green intertwined with purple, pink, and red. The fire ate away at the wood supports, they cracked and popped. Another explosion roiled through the incinerators on the other side of the stone wall behind her. The earth shook and rumbled above her head, and the fire hissed, reminding her it was coming for her.

Even with time and resources, this fire couldn't be extinguished. It was a magically enhanced fire. One set by a genie.

He planned to kill them all!

Shiff shouted above the noise. "Everyone follow the light out! Head toward Patagonia and you'll be safe!"

"Careful," Bitherby ordered, pulling a charging elf from the crowd. "One at a time," he admonished.

"Annie!"

She heard her name roaring above the chaotic cries around her. It wasn't Shiff; he was beside her, holding his hands in the air, sharing the spell.

It's coming from the stairs!

"Here!" she shouted through a gravelly voice, tired and rough from the smoke. Her heard jumped at the sight of Cham flying from the staircase.

Why is he here?

Cham's flashlight illuminated the room and found them at the center where Annie and Shiff held the spell keeping the smoke and flames from devouring the room. It was almost time; she couldn't keep her arms upward any longer. Cham lunged forward, his arms up and ready.

"I got this." His spell took over, allowing Annie and Shiff to drop their arms. The sustained magic use had drained them of their energy. Annie could barely stand.

"Are they all out?" Cham yelled.

"I'll take a last sweep." Shiff ran through the corners of the room, leaving Annie and Cham alone. They watched the light of flashlight bounce in the darkness as he rushed around before returning to them. He carried one creature over his shoulder and was followed by five others. "This is it," he shouted. A beam in the ceiling popped and cracked. Embers rained around them. "We need to go!"

"Annie, go!" Cham barked.

"You too."

"I'm good. Go!"

She couldn't leave him, but his face was determined. Shiff grabbed her arm as Cham contained the smoke on his own. She reached down and pulled two of the elves along with her. "Follow me," she said. At the stairs, she tossed them up a few steps.

"We're good—let's go!" she shouted to Cham.

Halfway up the stairs, smoke broke free and poured out of the stairwell. Cham had let the spell go.

As Annie lunged from the stairwell into the incinerator area, the elves she carried ran forward. Annie fell to the ground, sucking in the fresher air.

The incinerators exploded in a massive boom. The earth quaked, and when she looked inside the doorway, the basement wall crumbled down the stairs.

"NO!"

❋

Cold.

Blustery wind whipped across Annie. Canvas rustled, and water droplets melted against her skin.

Where am I?

Her cold hands fumbled as she reached behind her, searching for a covering.

"Cold," she murmured and shivered.

A warm blanket covered her. She rolled to her side, but it burned when she sucked in fresh clean air.

Smoke.

Images flashed in her wary brain.

Where am I?

She reached for the warm blanket, pulling it to her chin.

The basement.

"Cham," she mumbled and reached into the nothingness. A gentle touch wrapped around her hand and squeezed.

"Cham…"

The world materialized before her, and the memories snuck into her consciousness where she didn't want them. The pain—it hurt too much. She coughed; her lungs ached.

The fire.

The dormitory came into focus. She remembered elves and trolls shrieking in terror, the smoke, her hands, her arms—tired and rubbery from holding the spell.

Tired.

She couldn't open her eyes, even as she tried.

"Cham," she muttered softly. A coughing fit flew from her lungs as they desperately expelled bits of debris and smoke that attached inside. Her eyes fluttered open and dumped her into a rapidly twirling world. She couldn't breathe. She didn't want to be here, not this nightmare. She closed her eyes; it was safer there.

"Cham."

"Annie, here." Someone placed a drenched rag on her parched lips. "Drink from this."

Where am I?

"Cham…" He couldn't hear her, not in the din that surrounded her.

Where am I?

Visions and pictures flipped through Annie's head as she strained to remember. The basement, the pungent, dirty smoke that covered her—the images became more real.

The wall of the basement had fallen into the stairwell with Cham still inside.

"No," she cried out, and the tears fell.

"Annie, it's okay, sweetie. Cham's okay." Annie opened her eyes. The inside of the tent was brighter than it had been in the basement. She closed her eyes against the glare. She held her arm across her eyes, acclimating herself to the light.

"Here, sweetie," a soft voice said, and Annie sucked on the wet cloth again.

When she adjusted to the light, Annie glanced around her. Her best friend, Janie Parker, sat on the edge of the cot wearing an anxious smile. A gentle hand grasped hers—her godmother, Kathy. She had been crying.

"Where's Cham?" Annie's mouth tasted like smoke.

"He's being treated in another tent, sweetie," Kathy whispered in her ear. "He's going to be okay."

"Your elf went in and saved him as the dormitory crashed in." Janie was near tears.

To busy herself, Janie placed the cool cloth across Annie's forehead and wiped away the soot. Annie held her wrist, glanced at her friend, and closed her eyes, just for a moment.

When Annie woke again, the tent was dark, except for small lamps placed at each bed.

It's late.

Annie pulled herself up with weak and rubbery arms before falling back against the metal headboard, giving herself a first view of the large tent she was being treated in. It appeared to be currently half empty, but she judged that it could if needed accommodate several hundreds of victims.

I hope everyone got out of the market.

"Hey, you're really awake this time," Janie said to her, smiling with relief. She wrapped another blanket around Annie's shoulders and added a pillow for support. "Here, have this." Annie glanced inside the steaming mug and grimaced at the broth. "It's not that bad. You need help?"

"Why are you here?" Annie's voice was barely a whisper, rough and raw. Janie reached down and assisted her best friend since childhood with the mug.

Janie Parker's specialty and career revolved around the law; she was a magical lawyer and very rarely ventured into the field. Annie didn't care why Janie was here; she was just glad she was.

"When the market crashed, they asked for volunteers. I wanted to help. Help you."

Janie's hands cradled Annie's as she took a sip of the warm broth. It soothed her mouth and throat. When she'd had enough, Janie took the mug and smoothed Annie's dirty hair.

"Where's Cham? I'd like to see him."

Janie glanced away, her eyes meeting Dr. Christine Anderson's gaze. She was Annie's favorite doctor at the hospital, the doctor who saved Annie's life when her Wizard Guard test as a new guard went severely off course. The doctor grimaced and shook her head.

"Not yet, Annie."

"What's wrong with him? I want to see him. Please Dr. Christine." Annie's bellow was nothing more than a rough whisper. She shrunk back against the cot with a glare for her longtime friend and colleague.

Dr. Christine sat beside her. The extra weight pulled the mattress to the floor. The doctor pulled Annie into her arms, and Annie shook against her. "I promise you'll see him later. Right now Cham is unconscious. He took in a lot of smoke."

"Now. Dr. Christine. Please," Annie pleaded as the tears fell uncontrollably, rolling off of her face onto her thin hospital gown.

"You're still weak, Annie."

"Please. I just need to see him. Please?"

Dr. Christine took little time to make a decision, quickly summoning a wheelchair to Annie's bed.

"Annie, I really wish you'd reconsider," Dr. Christine warned as she helped Annie to her feet and then to the chair.

"Please. I need to see him."

They wrapped Annie in extra blankets and wheeled her from the tent into the dark and cold. She shuddered in the night air, as wind blew from the mountain. Annie wrapped the blanket tighter across her body.

"We're still in Patagonia?" Annie asked. Medics hustled between the tents, carrying equipment and transporting patients.

"Yes. Less critical patients are sent home. The rest of you are still here." Dr. Christine directed the wheelchair to the end of the hospital campus where there was less traffic. It was far quieter and more depressing. Annie's stomach lurched as building doors slid open and she wheeled her stubborn patient into the silent building to Cham.

He lay in the cot, an oxygen mask covering his pale face. Distressed, Annie cried out.

Don and Marina Chamsky, Cham's parents sat by his bed. Don, hearing the wheel of her chair squeak, took her hand and offered a tired smile. "I am so glad you're awake," he said. He stood, offering Annie his spot beside his son, and assisted her from the chair.

"Thanks," she whispered and took up Cham's cold hand, warming it in her own. She shuddered and sighed.

For a moment, Annie's eyes met Marina's. Her tearstained face looked away. As Marina hovered over her son, whispering in his ear, Annie rubbed Cham's inner palm like he always did for her.

"Marina. We should leave them alone," Don said.

"No. I'm not leaving him." She glared at her husband and avoided Annie's gaze.

"This isn't Annie's fault. He's a big boy and chose this life. Leave her alone with him."

Marina was short at five feet tall while Don stood over six feet, and yet in that single look Annie could see how that little woman could intimidate him. Annie herself wouldn't want to mess with Marina. Don reached down, took her by the shoulders, and whispered in her ear, before she relented and stood.

Before leaving, Marina came to Annie's side, placed her arms around Annie's shoulders and squeezed. "I am so glad you are alive. I'm just so…" Overcome with emotion, she buried her head in Annie's pungent hair as if it were nothing and kissed her.

Annie watched them leave, watched Marina's now frail and frightened body walk through the tent designated for more severe cases. They stopped in the reception area near the door, where Marina sat and cried for her son.

Guilt invaded Annie as she turned back to Cham, back to his broken body lying in the bed. She reached over, her lips grazing his ear. "I love you. Please wake up." She touched his cheek, his sparse winter freckles. She ran her hand through his curly hair, which was covered in smoke and soot. His fingers curled around hers, and his eyes fluttered open before shutting again.

CHAPTER 31

THE OLDER MR. Jacobi sat across from Gibbs in Interrogation Room Two. His sundried face crinkled in disgust while waiting for Gibbs to speak. The wizard guard perused the file in front of him, leaving the man to sweat under the intense heat of the synthetic light. If the heat affected Gibbs, he didn't let it show as he read through the history of the two men.

"So you work at the market?" Gibbs finally asked.

"What it's to ya?"

Gibbs glared at him, placed his hands on the table, and stood. "You reported me and my colleague to the master. I don't take well to that."

The large merchant sweated profusely in his sweater and wool cap. The smell wafted to Gibbs. He grimaced.

"You shoulda minded yer own business. And look what happened. I don't have my booth. All yer fault." He fiddled with a callous on the palm of his hand.

"No one has a booth anymore, you asshole. Just answer the questions!" Gibbs shouted.

Winn Jacobi jumped and backed up in his chair.

"So you did report us then?" Gibbs asked.

"Already said, that didn't ya?"

Gibbs understood the motivation. Most merchants in the

market, especially those afraid of the master, wouldn't hesitate. The Wizard Guard weren't welcome there.

Gibbs sat back in the chair. "Your brother's the stable master at Windmere School?"

"Yeah. What'd he do now?"

"He called you and told you where the girl was. And that sent a deadly team after her. That's obstruction, and there's a penalty for that."

The man smiled. "I didn't do that."

Gibbs produced a crystal and lay it on the table. With one wave of the hand, he revealed a moving picture of the younger Jacobi as well as the older Jacobi speaking.

"Winn, that girl. She's here!"

"What you talking about?"

"That girl from the market. She's come here to Windmere. The elf's here too!"

"Really? You sure it's the same one."

"Yeah, Winn. It's them."

"Well, goody. I tell the master; he'll leave me alone. Can get my work done then. Finally, you good for nothing, got something right..."

Winn Jacobi shook his head. "That's not what happened. You made that all up." He sneered, revealing deep lines around his mouth. His jaw clenched.

"Sorry, man. We got you. And your brother confessed." Gibbs collected the crystal and the folder, calling in the giant guards.

Two giants grabbed Winn's arms and dragged him down the hallway to his new home, Cell One of Turret One. He skidded across the floor after the burly giants tossed him into the cell. The cell door slammed shut. Gibbs grinned when the man jerked backward before standing in the small enclosure.

"Whaddaya want now?" Jacobi asked.

"You can help yourself and your brother by telling me where the master is."

The man, stared blankly as if he understood nothing of the

question. After mulling it over, he blinked several times, and his eyes brightened as if he was now present. "Don't know that, sir," he finally said.

"Well, if you think where he could be, let me know."

❀

The Jacobis proved to be simple people who talked themselves into a stay at Tartarus Prison. Gibbs sighed as he entered Interrogation Room Three in Turret Two where Dr. Arden Blakely waited.

When he entered, she was sitting in the metal chair, her back ramrod straight, her hands perfectly placed on the table in front of her. She appeared serene and calm, focused on the two-way mirror across from her, far different than Cham's initial conclusions on the archaeologist.

I wonder what set her off.

"Dr. Blakely. I'm John Gibbs. I have a few questions for you, if that's okay." Her eyebrows rose in surprise, then fell with disappointment. She gripped her hands together and held them tight enough to pull the skin across her whitened knuckles.

"Where's Mr. Chamsky? He's very lovely, and I'd rather talk to him right now." Arden's voice wavered.

"Yes, well, Mr. Chamsky would love to be here too, but there's been an accident at the black market. So you have me. Is that okay, ma'am?"

"Who are you?"

"I said, ma'am, I'm John Gibbs. I work with Robert Chamsky as a wizard guard. I need to ask you a few questions."

Her eye tracked him quickly as she examined every inch of his face, shoulders, hands. After observing him, Arden offered a wan smile. "Very well then. What do you want to know?"

"You're nonmagical, is that correct?"

"Yes. I explained that to Mr. Chamsky already," Arden said curtly.

A layer of her even demeanor cracked, thought Gibbs.

"Well. Help me here. You know so much about magic and the ring of Solomon. Fill in the gaps. Where did you learn all of this?"

Gibbs knew she had been kidnapped by her assistant and others. What he didn't know, what none of them understood, was what they had really done to cause so much stress and anxiety in this woman. Whatever it was must have been brutal—so much so that her diary wasn't specific. Gibbs could tell she was trying with some difficulty to keep her emotions in check. And as she did, her lip quivered, and her hands shook. She removed them from the table and bit her lip.

"Magic is everywhere if you know where to look," she finally said. "You should know this…" She glanced down, and when she faced him again, a smile was plastered to her face. "Though you wouldn't know. You're magical."

Gibbs cleared his throat and pulled open the case folder, hiding his frown behind the file, pretending that Arden Blakely wasn't irritating him. Though he would admit to most of his coworkers that nonmagicals were useless, untrustworthy liars, he tried desperately to be what he wasn't and not respond negatively. Putting down the folder he said, "That's really not an answer, Dr. Blakely."

Arden chuckled. For the first time, her facial expression softened as if she wasn't trying to convey a message but was honestly showing what she felt. "You're right. I'm sorry. Can I see the file?"

There wasn't much in the file, just notes from Annie's research into the diary, copies of the spells she had given them, a picture of the ring. Nothing Gibbs knew Arden hadn't seen before. He slid the folder to her. She lovingly touched the beige cover as she opened it; the paper rustled in her hand. Realizing she was shaking, she closed the folder and placed her hands in her lap.

"I was kidnapped. I'm sure you know that. You have my things, my diary." Arden sighed heavily as if the weight of the memories was too much to bear. Tears welled in her eyes. "It wasn't all bad. I worked hard, I researched, gave them all the information they needed to make the ring work. And in return for my slavery, they showed me the magic. The beautiful ability to create things from nothing."

Without thinking of the ironic timing, Gibbs raised a palm and summoned a box of tissue for Arden. It materialized quickly and she laughed lightly grabbing a sheet from inside. "Not quite so beautiful, but necessary. Thank you," she said blowing her nose and wiping her eyes.

"No problem. Can I get you anything else?"

Arden shook her head. "I'd rather just finish up so I can go home."

"Fair enough. Just a few more questions. First of all, do you know who kidnapped you? Names? Are they part of an organization? Anything you can tell us would be helpful."

"Nicky, my assistant, was part of it. I don't know. I don't know much about any organization. I dealt with him mostly. There was Ari, too. But…" She played with the used tissue. "I'm sorry. I can't help you. They kept me in isolation."

Gibbs knew the Fraternitatem had taken Arden to research the ring and had trained her as an assassin. It would help if she would just admit it.

"So you don't know who the Fraternitatem of Solomon is, then?" he asked.

Arden jumped. Her lips quivered, and she could no longer look Gibbs in the eyes. "No. I don't. I'm sorry."

"Just a few more questions. I promise, you'll go home. Why exactly did you go see Mr. Chamsky?"

Arden stared into the two-way mirror. "I already explained. I found the spell to make the magic of the ring work. I thought Robert should have it," she answered tersely.

The spell she referred to had been handed to Mrs. Cuttlebrink in the library. She had spent several hours translating both spells and confirmed that the second spell—the one Arden brought to

Cham—wasn't the spell to control the djinn. It did something else altogether.

"The first spell you offered him at your condo is the correct spell. You are aware of that. Yes?" He didn't wait for a response. "What does this spell do, Dr. Blakely?" He tapped the paper.

"I'm not magical. I don't know what that spell does."

"You just said this spell makes the Ring of Solomon work. What does this spell do, Dr. Blakely?" His voice was no longer soft and calm; rather, it was cold and bitter.

Arden rocked in the chair, which creaked under the motion.

"Dr. Blakely, what does this spell do?"

She stopped and met Gibbs's gaze, a smirk grew across her lips. "It blows everything up."

Gibbs raised his eyebrows. "You gave us a spell that will blow up what, Dr. Blakely?"

They knew that it was a destructive spell. They needed the archaeologist to connect the dots. What would explode? They assumed the ring.

"Blows everything up." Her hand went up in the air illustrating an explosion. She was giddy.

Gibbs ran through the scenario in his head. Arden Blakely desperately wanted to go to the market. They had assumed it was because she wanted the ring.

But is that it?

She had found Cham and given him the spell.

Were they supposed to blow something or someplace up?

"Did you want Robert to blow up the ring?" he asked.

Thoughtfully, she responded, "No one should have that ring. It's dangerous. I've been searching for it for years, and finally that boy comes by and tells me he has it. It's mine!"

"What were you going to do with the ring, Dr. Blakely?"

"Control the djinn, of course." Her hands playfully tapped the table as she spoke. Her voice was no longer distant, just spacey.

"Of course. So you gave the spell to Mr. Chamsky, expecting that he'd blow up *what*, once he had the ring"

"The ring and the market. Robert should have taken me to the market and BOOM! Blown the market up. Sky high!" Dr. Arden Blakely could barely control her excitement.

"You wanted to blow up the market?"

"Yes."

The market had been created a millennium ago. It was set on an alternate plane of existence, hidden from the nonmagical world. No one in a thousand years had been able to destroy the market; quite the opposite. It had grown in all that time to the bustling marketplace.

Why does she think she could destroy the market?

"Okay, Arden. Is it okay that I call you that?" When she nodded, he continued. "Arden, who gave you the spell? Was it the person who kidnapped you? And why did they want to blow up the market?"

Arden, no longer in control of her emotions after the mention of the kidnappers, began to shake. Her eyes glazed over, and she lost focus.

"Yes. They wanted to blow up the market. "

"Who were they?"

Arden quaked, and she reached inside her vest, Gibbs's hands flew up instinctively as she pulled out a bottle. Taking two pills she swallowed them in one gulp. The act alone, calmed the woman and she stared at Gibbs, eye to eye.

"Those artifacts don't belong in this world. Your market has done this before, selling objects belonging King Solomon. Objects that need to be hidden and never see the light of day. The market you're so intent on protecting needs to be destroyed."

"This was his plan all along? Yes? Robert coming to see you was your way in wasn't it?"

Arden nodded. "Yes. After Benaiah died, after the ring was lost, I knew it was only a matter of time before I found it again. I heard the Fraternitatem was here, I knew the Wizard Guard had the ring. I just needed the ring." She cackled. The sound bounced off walls, Gibbs felt it vibrate against the table.

"The Fraternitatem wasn't responsible for the plan to blow up the market?"

She shook her head. "No. Benaiah asked for my help. He was angry that the djinn wanted the ring. He wanted the market gone. He and the Fraternitatem... he and the Fraternitatem no longer agreed on the direction of the order. They fought. And, well, you know what happened."

"The Fraternitatem kidnapped you and trained you as their assassin. Is that correct?"

Arden's only answer was a wide smile.

Chapter 32

June 1970

The Fraternitatem of Solomon. I can't help but wonder what their true intentions are. They-Nicky-took me. They waited for someone to decide to find the ring. Nicky insinuated himself into my dig for the sake of finding the ring. He took me, took my life, and now I find out it's all for this Fraternitatem.

July 1970

They promise me this is for the greater good. The ring is dangerous and needs to be hidden. I work all day, all night to find the spell to turn the ring on. And then what, hide it forever?

Sept 1970

I found the spell. Nicky said it is good and I'll be able to go home. Home. I've missed so much. They tell me I've been here for a year. I met with the Fraternitatem of Solomon today. This group says it is for the greater good, saving the world from the ring. Keeping the ring safely hidden, away from society.

January 1971

I don't trust them. They want to train me. Reward me for my sacrifice. For my skill. I've helped them so much. They think I will be a good fit for the Fraternitatem.

August 1971

I've been home for months. It feels foreign, like I no longer belong to this world. I belong to the Fraternitatem. I can shoot a gun; I can brew potions. I've seen so much that I can't unsee. I belong with them. Not here, cataloguing bones and shards of clay. They promise me more, saying that I will be useful in the future and be able to continue my training.

September 1971

I've been contacted with my first job. The ring is missing. My ring is gone. How they let that happen I will never know, *and I'm mad, angry. That was my hard work. It's all gone.*

October 1971

The Fraternitatem of Solomon paid for my excavation. After learning about my thesis claiming there was another temple of Solomon hidden in the desert, they offered me the money for the dig. It was them all along. They used me, and I can't escape.

I shot my first man. A market in Tibet. We were both chasing the ring. It should have been here but we're too late. The ring is gone again.

"Hi, sweetheart. Look who I've brought." Kathy entered through the fabric walls that surrounded Annie's bed. She dropped the diary in her lap. Annie let Kathy envelope her in her motherly arms. Kathy didn't let go as she smoothed the back of Annie's hair. The scent of strawberries and vanilla, warm and familiar, wafted to Annie. It was the same scent she wore, the gift Kathy had given her when Annie first came to live with her and Ryan after her father died.

It had been a little treat, one of many she gave to help Annie from her darkness. Eight years after her father's death, it was the one gift that still comforted her. Annie took a deep sniff.

"I'm okay now, Kathy. You can stop." Annie said. She rolled her eyes for Ryan's sake; he chuckled behind his wife.

"Sorry. We just saw Don and Marina. Cham's doing well."

"Yeah. He's awake. I thought you were staying away?" Annie

asked Ryan. As the Grand Marksman, he should be at home serving his term, rather than surveying the situation on site.

"I need to be here, for you for all of this," he said.

"Yeah. It is. The market's gone, there's hundreds of shape shifters that can't change back, and I can't get my work done with all these interruptions." She smiled for their benefit, but only Ryan laughed.

"Annie, you need your rest." Kathy said gently.

"Yeah, you do." Samantha ran into the tent and flopped on the bed. Her arms wrapped around Annie. She offered her sister a kiss on the cheek and grimaced at Annie's stench. "You need a bath," she said.

"Go help someone else. I'm fine."

Samantha pulled away, her lips pursed together. "Yeah, yeah. I have been since you've been asleep. Now you're awake. Can't I visit?" She kissed the top of Annie's head and didn't let go.

I must stink!

"As much as I love you being here, I have work to do," Annie said firmly and shifted on the uncomfortable cot, readjusting the pillows.

"You need rest," Kathy reiterated.

"I need to resolve this." Annie was firm, but Kathy and Samantha were unconvinced.

"Two things. Zola's doing great, by the way. And this came for you." Samantha handed her a scroll, sealed with a wax glob with no particular design inside. Annie broke the seal and unrolled the note.

The second spell is meant to blow up the market. Benaiah's idea. Stop the market from selling anymore objects. Gibbs

"That's a new one." She handed the note to Ryan.

After reading it quickly, he asked, "Have you found anything in her diary?"

Annie fumbled with the diary and opened the book to her last read entry. "I think they're a wealthy group. They funded Arden's excavation. My guess based on Gibbs's note is that the Fraternitatem has basically good intentions. They keep King Solomon's artifacts safe and out of dangerous hands. Benaiah wanted to blow up the market to keep items from entering it. He probably stole the ring, and offered it to the djinn once he was in control. Once he had the ring at the market, he could blow it up. In his mind, without the market there's no place to sell the items. A little short sighted."

Ryan grimaced. "Without the big market, little markets will be popping up everywhere. You're right. This wasn't well thought out. Unless Benaiah just wanted to bring down the Fraternitatem and this is how he chose to do it."

"Why would he want that?" Samantha's frown hung low with worry and concern, though Annie thought she often looked like that without cause.

"It can be a host of things, sweetie." Ryan sighed.

"Sam, Dad dealt with them eight years ago. He knew Benaiah. They told him to drop his case, and they took back the Chintamani Stones he was after."

"But that's a long time ago," she whined.

Sometimes I could just smack you.

Annie rolled her eyes instead.

"Not such a long time if your organization is over two thousand years old. Eight years, that's just enough time to remember. The stones get out, Benaiah waits for the right time, waits to find the ring and he moves forward with the plan. And as it turns out, we'll be the ones who make that plan a reality."

"Anything else in the diary?" Ryan paced in the aisle between Annie's row of beds and the others across from her. Elves, trolls, and wizards were being treated for burns and smoke inhalation. Many of them slept, probably resting for the first time in days. An older witch with long, white, straw-like hair observed Ryan carefully.

Annie nodded once, forcing him to close the walls around her bed.

"Nothing yet. Lial and Mrs. Cuttlebrink are looking for the exact location of the Fraternitatem. I think it's time to bring them down. They caused a huge problem for us."

"I'll see where Milo is on that. Rest," he said and kissed her cheek. "I'll come back when I can."

Preoccupied, Ryan hurried from Annie's bed space and headed out the crowded tent.

"I have work to do. You take a nap." Samantha offered Annie a smile.

"There's no time, but I'll see you later." They touched hands before Samantha headed out to care for the elves. Annie sighed and fell back against the pillows.

"I'm so glad you're okay." Janie squeezed Annie's hand. "Ready to see Cham?"

"You have no idea."

Annie let them assist her into the wheelchair. Though she protested she was strong enough to make it on her own, Kathy and Janie walked with her through a less chaotic medical camp.

Even when she entered the tent where Cham convalesced it felt different—lighter, higher energy.

When she saw him, he was sitting up, resting against several pillows, looking much less pale than the previous night. He smiled widely when he saw her and patted the cot beside him.

Annie waved away help and sat on the cot, which sunk several inches with her added weight.

"Hey." Cham didn't let Annie answer before his mouth was on hers, his near death experience weighing heavily on both their minds. She smelled the smoke in his hair and stifled a cough.

"I'm sorry," she said.

He played with the ends of her hair and touched her cheek and her chin where his fingers lingered. "For what?"

"For leaving you down there." That guilt had been sitting in her chest since she regained consciousness. The walls had crumbled around him; she saw it every time she closed her eyes.

I should have waited with him.

"I was saving you." He leaned his chin against her shoulder. His breath rattled as he inhaled and again with an exhale. He wasn't doing as well as she had been told. "Let me do that for you sometimes."

"We could have done it together."

"We both could have died." Cham coughed and leaned back against the pillows. He pulled Annie to him, and she snuggled against his chest, where she could hear the fluid rattling inside. Annie shuddered, fearful he might still be in danger from something she couldn't save him from.

I almost lost you.

"How are you feeling, Anne Elizabeth?" Annie looked up to see Marina, whose voice was motherly, warm, and loving. Marina was clearly tired. The circles under eyes were dark and deep.

"Much better. Thanks."

Marina reached for her hand and held it, rubbing her thumb against Annie's palm, something Cham did for her regularly. The action calmed Annie; maybe it calmed them too.

Though Marina didn't always like the influence Annie had over her son, Annie knew Cham's mother loved her.

Because I can really control what he does.

Annie smiled to herself.

"You okay?" Cham whispered.

"Yeah. I'm better than okay." Her arm lay across his chest. She rubbed his left arm and stared through the open curtains into the larger tent that had added a few patients since the night before.

"Oh, I am so glad you two are both okay. I've never been more worried." Marina wrung her hands together.

Before Annie could assure her they were both fine, Lial entered the semi-private room.

"Hey Annie, Cham. So good to see you guys are okay. Sorry to bother you." He grinned broadly, exposing a gap in his front teeth. Annie sat and noticed Marina's glare as Lial entered the personal space.

"What's up?" Cham asked.

Lial held up the ring; it shone brightly under the artificial light. *All of this trouble caused by that stupid ring.*

"I see you got into my storage unit just fine," Annie remarked.

"No, not really. We figured it out though. Are you sure you're up for this?" Lial asked.

"We have no choice. We have to turn that zoo back to human." She was reluctant to leave Cham behind, wanting to stay here in his arms. "I have to go." Even as he convalesced in bed, his arms were strong around her, protective.

"Do you have to leave? You should rest too," Marina said in a tone more peeved than concerned.

"I will. When this is over. For now, we have to change the shapeshifters back before we can't." She kissed Cham, and the stubble on his chin scratched her cheek. "I'll come back later."

"I thought the ring will destroy the market. How are you doing this?" Kathy asked.

"We have two spells. One to control the djinn. Mrs. Cuttlebrink is sure that's what it does. And the second spell will eviscerate the market. We think," Annie said.

"Can't someone else do it? You're still weak," Marina asked.

"It's so dangerous," Kathy wrung her hands.

"I love you, mama. It'll be okay." Annie gave her a warm hug and sat back in the wheelchair. With a wave goodbye to Marina and Kathy and a hug from Janie, Annie let herself be wheeled to what was now referred to as the zoo.

CHAPTER 33

"AND THAT'S IT, you think?" Exhausted, Jack followed Milo back to the fourth portal in Busse Woods. They had been tracking roaming shapeshifters all day and sending them to Patagonia. Graham Lightner and his team rejoined them after casting another round of spells that kept the protection around the market mostly intact. Another plume of smoke had just disappeared. The black cloud grew smaller, though not by much.

"Yeah. But keep an eye out." Milo ordered. "Graham. What's the word?"

Graham's sallow, pale face was covered in soot, and a five o'clock shadow had begun to grow in. He had been caring for the protection spell for too many hours. He wiped his hands across his brow, leaving behind his handprint, and frowned, creating deep lines in his forehead and around his mouth.

"All that's left is the protection spell," Graham said. "Did you hear about Cham?"

"What happened to Cham?" Jack asked. He'd been with Milo all day and had no idea when he heard whatever he heard.

"I got a text. The incinerators in the market blew, Cham was in the elf dormitory when it caved in. Bitherby saved him. He and Annie are fine in the temporary hospital in Argentina."

"Why the hell didn't you tell me? I've been worried about them for days." Jack paced in the mud and grasses.

"Jack. I'm sorry. We're all under stress. I saw the note and moved on. I can't change what happened, and we all have our jobs to do." Milo said pointing toward the clearing and the nonmagicals that were still loitering inside.

"Then let me help. I can do more than search for shapeshifters."

"We're going to have to say something to the world regarding this. Maybe then we'll have you help us." Graham advised. "Until then we need to make sure that the rest of the shapeshifters are out of the woods and that we're still fanning the protection spell. I think it's cleaned out. We'll be ready to blow it then."

Jack followed Graham's gaze to the sky and back to the wizards in the middle of the forest. "Um, won't that still leave questions? An explosion in the middle of the forest?"

"It's a magical bomb. We'll wipe the market from the plane of existence, so when the protection spell fails, there won't be anything here," Graham explained.

"So while you do that, can I go to Patagonia?" Jack asked Milo. The wizard guard manager surveyed the forest, listening for nonmagical voices that were still trying to get a handle on the phenomenon of the fireless smoke.

"Actually, Jack, you come with me. I can use you in the market," Graham advised.

"I agree. You okay with that, Jack? I can't have you near the ring. Protection and all," Milo explained.

"Sure, whatever. I'll help in the market," Jack said.

Milo waved and teleported before Jack could protest.

"Come on, Jack. Consider yourself lucky. You are one of the only nonmagicals to ever see inside of THE black market." Graham offered a smile and waved Jack forward.

"I'll consider myself lucky," he griped. If Graham heard his tone he ignored it and led Jack toward the clearing, close enough to hear the din of voices of those still observing the smoke. Before hitting the crowd, they walked a narrow path roughly four inches wide.

"Watch the ivy. It's called needleweed, and once it attaches to you it will grow quickly, completely surround you, and strangle you."

"You have the creepiest things in this world," said Jack. As instructed he kept himself to the thin strip of mud and snow, teetering slightly as he tried too hard to not step on the vines.

I wonder if he's exaggerating.

Jack didn't want to find out and sidestepped his way to Graham, who stood in front of an empty space, staring at it as if there was something there.

"It's one of the only remaining portals," Graham said. He reached his hand through out in front of him and held it there before pulling it back. "It's wrong though."

"What's the matter with it?" Jack worried, wringing his hands since he was afraid to start pacing against the needleweed.

"It was designed to work with the protection spell. Anyone nonmagical coming near would feel a chill, an ominous sense of dread."

Jack reached his hand into the air. He felt a buzz and pulled his hand away.

"It's vibrating," Jack said.

Graham chuckled. "It's the remnant of the magic. For many millennia, the portals fought to control this space with the nonmagical world. Just weeks ago, if you came near one of these the cold would chill you to the bone. The magic's dying."

He sounded as though he was sad about the loss of the market and the loss of the magic in this place.

"It sounds like you'll miss the market," Jack commented. He understood on one level, the desire to monitor the market and the difficulty it would be to do that now. But this seemed weird.

"In a way, yeah. Ask Annie and Cham or any of the other wizard guards. There was something about being in the market. It was all about control." Graham twisted his cursed athame in his fingers and stabbed the weakened portal. It sparked to life with a shot of lightning that flew from the portal, hitting a dead branch behind them. A fire took hold of the evergreen. Jack jumped.

Graham waved a palm, putting out the fire before it could spread in the forest for real.

"Does it always do that?" Jack asked.

"Nope. It's all wrong," Graham responded. The two of them watched the portal grow and stretch, not quite to its normal size, but large enough for two men to enter. "Ready?" Graham asked.

Eight months ago, Jack had been dragged into the world of magic quite by accident when the nonmagical Princess Amelie was killed with a hex. The journey had led him through a world he previously had no idea existed. He'd been to Wizard Hall; he'd watched them tamper with evidence for the cause of saving magic. Jack never imagined what he would see when he stepped through the portal.

The amazingly large space stood before him, and though one foot was still in Busse Woods, this market wasn't there.

Jack followed Graham through the portal, which closed unceremoniously, leaving them inside the remains of the market, a desolate, fire-ravaged empty space.

"It looks like a bomb already exploded," Jack said.

"Yeah. You should have seen it before. It would've blown your mind." Graham smirked and led Jack through the aisle covered in a thick layer of ash.

Jack could see by the piles of debris and the burnt canvases that were once tents just how many merchants there must have been in the market. The piles dotted the land.

There must have been thousands!

The market stank. Jack held his arm across his face. Smoke hung above the market, undulating and rolling, bumping against the remaining protection spell.

"Who are these people?" Jack asked as Graham perused a pile of junk stored in a cart. There were bottles filled with liquids of all colors, strange body parts, and books. It was a veritable treasure trove of odd junk.

"Members of the Wizard Guard from the United States, Argentina, Europe, and Asia. We have other departments here from Wizard Hall. There are a lot of dead shapeshifters, and the bodies need to be tagged and returned to their families if we can get them out. The group over there..." Graham pointed to several wizards and witches tending to what Jack thought was an exceptionally large lizard.

A dragon?

"That group is the Zoological Society. They care for, investigate, and observe magical creatures, depending on circumstances. There are several magical creatures left here. They'll clean up the carcasses and transport those still living. Many of them are here illegally, anyway. It's a big mess."

A group of witches collected books, torn pages from other books, magical items in glass containers, and boxes of stuff in general.

"Most of my group is over there. The fires didn't affect that area and there's a lot of dangerous magical items. We're almost done collecting what we can," Graham said.

"What exactly was sold here?" Jack inquired.

"Anything. Potions, crystals, herbs, illegal and legal artifacts, wands, magical animals. It sold everything you could want." Graham's eyes swept the vast expanse of the burning market. "It will be hard to track anything for the time being." His eyes stopped on a group of wizards around one of the few booths that was still standing, even though it had been caught in the fire. Burn marks dotted the roof, and smoke still rolled off the canvas.

Jack matched Graham's strides, treading along a crowded walkway that was filled with elves and trolls assisting with the cleanup, with wizards and witches pulling carts out of the market, carrying intact items that needed to be removed and stored or possibly destroyed. They sidestepped the dead carcass of a dog. It vibrated and shimmered as it slowly returned to its original human form.

Jack jumped and brushed into a wizard. "Sorry." The wizard grunted and continued along the walkway toward the Patagonia portal.

"You okay?"

"It's just that…" Jack pointed to the dead body at his feet. He'd seen hundreds of them in his career, but none that sprung from the body of a dog. The enormity of the situation overwhelmed him.

"It's hard to watch that." Graham waved a hand over, asking a member of Zoology to join them.

"Hey, Graham. What's up?" he asked and glanced at Jack. "I'm Dave Smith." He held out a hand.

"Jack Ramsey," he replied and shook.

"Oh. You're the FBI agent. I'm friends with Annie and Cham. They told me about you." Returning to Graham, he said, "How can I help?"

"He just turned." Graham pointed to the body below him.

"Yeah. It's been like that all day. We're getting them as fast as we can. Sorry you had to see this. The destruction is… awful." Dave called for backup, knelt beside the victim, and checked for identification in the pockets. He found a wallet and pulled it out, checking for any form of ID. "From Germany." He waved a colleague over and began preparing the body for transport.

"Have you talked to Annie and Cham?" Jack asked as Dave and his coworker began placing the body in a black plastic bag.

Dave looked up at the nonmagical. "Yeah, they're good. I talked to Annie's sister. Cham took in a lot of smoke but he's recovering well. Annie's good. I'll let them know you were here and asked."

"Thanks. Send my best wishes." Jack hung around for a minute longer, watching Dave return his attention to the victim. When Graham tugged his sleeve and pointed to the tent, they headed out, leaving Dave Smith to his work.

"Graham. Glad you're here. We need specifics," a man said from behind them.

"Hi, Allen," Graham said with a wary smile. "There's not much to it. We have three hours to clean what we can, find whatever victims there are, remove artifacts. Victims and survivors go to the hospital; artifacts, potions, and books to Wizard Hall. The wizard guards have the ring and the spell. When they're ready, we'll vaporize the market and lower the protection spell."

"Memory modification?" Sky asked.

"We're waiting for permission from the Wizard Council, but yes, that would be the next step. We have to make everyone forget this… anomaly. Last thing: whoever gets tagged by the Wizard Guard for burning down the market, follow them and then head back to Patagonia," Graham ordered.

"Will do," Allen responded and pulled his team together.

After saying goodbye, Jack and Graham headed farther inside the once-bustling market. "Over there." Graham pointed to a brick wall. The two men walked over to a nondescript door on the wall.

"Stand to the side and wear this." Graham summoned a mask and waited for Jack to stand to the right of the door a few feet away.

The door, hot to the touch, was opened with a swift wave of his palm. As the lock popped, Graham stepped beside Jack and summoned the door open. The pressure of the smoke blew outwards.

"What's down there?" Jack asked as he took a breath and coughed.

"This should be the dungeon."

Of course there's a dungeon.

When the smoke stopped rolling in large puffs, Graham summoned a flashlight and stepped in front of the open door. Still filled with smoke, the staircase was dark. "Okay. Follow close."

They entered into the smoky staircase, gingerly heading down the rickety wooden stairs. The stairs wobbled, affected by the heat.

"What happens if this crashes in on us?" Jack worried; the stairs swayed as he took another step downwards.

"Grab hold of my arm."

After descending the bowels of the earth, they entered a rock-lined room. Graham's flashlight illuminated the shackles still attached to the walls, a dead carcass hanging from one, another body on the floor.

Graham rushed to the adult male body and knelt beside him, turning the face toward him, feeling for a pulse. "Gladden Worchester, the wizard that created this mess," he said.

Graham searched Gladden's neck for vampire track marks. Just because he hadn't seen any didn't mean the man hadn't been turned. He summoned a bottle of holy water. Jack grimaced, remembering his own experience with vampires and the holy water. He knew what Graham would be doing. After Graham poured a few drops on the dead man, Jack held his breath and waited for the vampire to spring to life. But Gladden Worchester was dead. Just plain dead, not vampire dead.

"Milo told me about him." Jack said. "Do you mind?" he asked as he searched the body's arms and hands. Gladden's shirt was burnt at the chest, so Jack pulled open the buttons and saw a large scorch mark across his chest. "Looks like John Doe's," Jack remarked.

"That's odd," Graham said as he pulled out his crystal, running it across the mark. After examining the readings, he said, "Not wizard magic. He was probably killed by the djinn. Let's get him out of here."

Graham unfurled a body bag and placed Gladden Worchester inside. Graham zipped him inside and texted a number, typing a short note.

"It didn't work out so well for him then?" Jack said.

"Not so much."

CHAPTER 34

ORCED TO REST until the last possible moment, Annie sat on her hospital cot, with the spell to turn the shapeshifters human lying on her lap. Mrs. Cuttlebrink and Emerson Donaldson sat near her in uncomfortable folding chairs, working on the spell translation. They had been at it for several hours. An exhausted Annie put her head against the head rest and closed her eyes.

"I can't see anything, Annie dear. I think the spell is good to go," the librarian advised.

Annie's eyes fluttered open. "Emerson, do you see anything?"

Emerson was still reviewing the text, ascertaining whether or not there were any hidden consequences to the words as they were written. She read with glassy, glazed-over eyes. She looked up, her gaze matching Annie's.

"Nope. Based on what the spell commands, there's nothing in here that on the surface is bad. I think we'll be good to go."

"Great. Now all we have to do is contain all of the animals."

Annie lay back and pulled the covers up to her chin. The air chilled her battered, tired body. She closed her eyes again to block out the makeshift hospital.

One hundred feet from where she convalesced, animals barked and scratched, corralled into smaller sections as they waited to be returned to their original human forms. The guards in Busse Woods had already sent hundreds through the Patagonia portal.

With the destruction of the market, it was more difficult to contain the magical exposure. And now the stress of performing this spell overwhelmed Annie.

The drapes surrounding Annie's bed fluttered open, and the din outside the tent grew louder as the team filed into her small recovery space.

"Annie, how are you feeling?" Milo asked. He wasn't his normal gruff self; too tired and stressed to keep up appearances.

"I'm good."

But he isn't.

He paced at the end of her bed. His eyes, circled with purple puffiness, darted across the confined space and spied the ring on the bedside table. "And the ring is okay?" he asked.

"Yeah."

Milo summoned the thick metal ring and placed it on his finger. "All this for an ugly ring." He handed her back the ring. "Are you ready?"

"Yeah. My expert spell makers are confident we're ready," Annie assured him.

"Where are we on the Fraternitatem?" Milo turned and addressed Lial.

"Good news. I figured out the Cave of Ages and its location. When you're ready, Annie, we're good to go. Did the archaeologist have anything else on them?" Lial asked Gibbs.

"Nothing. She's a bit bat shit crazy. Not sure she would even know," Gibbs replied.

"And the master? Have we found him?" Milo enquired of Spencer.

"Nothing yet. When the shapeshifters are safe, I'm going to speak with Bitherby and find out how the djinn was summoned in the first place. I can't imagine a genie won't respond to a summoning," Spencer replied.

"Then let's get this done," Milo said.

Annie, stronger than she had thought she was, pushed herself up and slid into the wheelchair beside her bed. Her brain, a little foggy from the smoke, took a moment in the seat as all eyes waited for her to make a move.

"I'm good," she said and sat back as she was wheeled to the animal corral across from the makeshift camp.

The smell of dung, wet fur, and the slimy scent of rough scales, bombarded Annie as she entered the tent. Even though there were humans underneath the fur and scales, they still in most cases acted and smelled very much the animal they currently were, and they were hard to keep in one spot, preferring to slither or slink across the paddock.

The team positioned themselves around the corral, a large circle enclosed with makeshift metal walls containing air holes. A large fan whirled above them, sucking out as much stale air as it could. The stench was still crushing.

Each wizard guard possessed identical crystals, including Annie's, all which had been cut from the larger rock that rested in the center of the paddock.

Ryan, ignoring all orders to stay home placed a hand on Annie's shoulder. "Almost done," he whispered and squeezed lightly for support.

The Ring of Solomon sat on her finger and twirled when she moved her hand. Annie closed her fist and held it out while waiting for the ready signal. As everyone found their position, they raised their hand in the air. When the entire team was in position, Annie pointed the ring at the center of the corral and chanted.

> *"Mighty Wiccan spirits hear my cry.*
> *Turn them back to the other side.*
> *Make them whole once again,*
> *Bring them back to the original form."*

The ring vibrated on her finger and sent its magic to the crystal that glowed a bright, white light. It shimmered in the dimly lit tent; a white light flew from the stone and sped around the perimeter of the corral, searching for the matching crystals.

Each crystal accepted the magic and smoldered in the same beautiful white light; the magic jumped from the crystals in all of the team members' hands and joined together at the center of the corral where a crystal had been laid. White, shimmering light blanketed the animals in magical light.

Growing up in magic and raised by a wizard guard, Annie had seen a lot. And yet, some spells still left her in awe, this being one of them. The transformation was immediate. As the creatures were covered in the spell, the animals shimmered and vibrated, and their features changed. Fur retracted, hair grew, snouts flattened and became human noses, ears sprouted on the side of heads, legs grew, and arms waved. Some bodies shrank, and others grew taller.

A mist shimmered, swirled, and undulated above them; the magic attached to each shapeshifter, their bodies reverting to their original form.

As they returned to their human bodies, it was as if they all woke from a long nap. Confusion appeared across their faces. Some spoke in hushed tones, and others backed away, confused as to why they were trapped with hundreds of others.

"People. People!" Milo shouted as he stood on a chair. A confused din of voices looked awkwardly at the man above them. Slowly, they hushed until silence filled the paddock.

"I don't know how much you know about what happened to you in the last three weeks, but we will help you sort it out. You've been trapped in your shapeshifter body, unable to escape the black market."

Angry and scared voices reacted with shouts and screams. One man fainted. Medical staff rushed in to examine him as he lay in a pile of straw. After the staff had removed the sick man to a medical tent, Milo began again.

"People. I know this is confusing, but we have several wizard guard units from across the world. They are outside. Find your country of origin, and they will lead you to the hospital and help you get home. If you have questions, please ask the guards." Milo finished his speech and watched as they were slowly led out of the paddock and into the chilly air.

CHAPTER 35

"SO ARE WE all set?" Milo asked Graham. The department managers strolled along the remnants of the market. Though they said they were verifying the location of every crystal needed to vaporize the market, they were really just strolling and reminiscing before it was completely gone.

"We're using our own spell and not the one from the Fraternitatem. Just to be safe." Graham knelt down and repositioned one of the crystals, laying it on the former path.

"Benaiah and the archaeologist got what they wanted." Milo surveyed the former black market. Completely empty now, it looked like an isolated desert.

"Too late to worry about it now." Graham stood and followed Milo's gaze throughout the wasteland. "Are you staying?"

Milo smiled. "Yeah. I should be happy, but I have a sense of dread I can't quite explain. I'm staying."

With all the rocks in position the rest of the wizards headed out through the Patagonia portal, the final portal in Busse Woods along with the rest of the two hundred portals that once graced the world but had just been destroyed.

"Ready to go," Graham said to the team. Allen and Sky from the VAU, Spencer, Gibbs and Emerson from the Wizard Guard. Each crossed the threshold of the portal for the last time.

The entrance was weak and dying; it lacked the requisite

lightning and swirling whirlpool of air. Instead, all it managed was a light whistle of air that grazed Milo's hand as he stepped through. Five wizards stood in the cold desert of Patagonia while Gibbs stood with one foot inside the market and one foot in the non-magical desert. With his palms facing the large crystal at the center of the former market, he silently chanted the spell.

The magic left his hand and traveled the distance, hitting the larger stone. Light dashed around the market, finding each of the carefully laid crystals. A burst of light, created by the magical energy, flashed. As Gibbs took his foot from the portal, the market vaporized, and the last portal to the market was gone.

CHAPTER 36

GYM SHOES SQUEAKED against the spotless linoleum in the quiet hospital wing.

Annie, unfamiliar with this wing since it was known to care for patients with a variety of nonmagical issues, read each door plaque for names and injury or illness. To Annie they had all seemed so benign.

Lucky for them!

Had Archibald Mortimer required care from a wayward black magical spell or bad potion, she would have known where he was. That had been her specialty when she was assigned to work at the hospital.

Not seeing his name on any door, she stopped at the nurse's station. As it was a slow day on this floor, they were watching the Witch Cable Network.

A young nurse glanced up and offered a smile. "How can I help you?"

"Archibald Mortimer's room?"

The nurse grimaced sharply.

He must be a pain in the ass.

The nurse offered nothing more except, "Room 19, down there to the right."

Before Annie could thank her, the nurse returned to the television show, a program Annie didn't recognize.

At Room 19, on the right, she spied Archibald Mortimer's name scrawled on the door, with "assault and battery" written below. She didn't like the man, but seeing his ailment, his reason for being here made her cringe. She owed him more than thanks for enduring what he did as he tried not to reveal her name.

There was no answer when she knocked on the door; Annie hesitated before entering.

The shopkeeper lay sleeping. Though his burns were healed, his cuts and contusions were still a dark purplish red, covering his face and jaw. Some injuries, even with magic, took longer to heal. She held her breath and walked to the bed.

Annie summoned the sad-looking bunch of flowers she had purchased in the gift shop. The flowers were the only color in this depressingly beige room. She wrote a quick note to go with them on the off chance Mortimer would care and left them on the table beside his bed. She was perfectly content to leave it for him rather than make small talk with the odious man.

"Whaddaya want?" he whispered as she turned to leave.

He was small and frail in the large bed, and he didn't resemble himself. His watery blue eyes were paler than normal as if some life had been removed from them.

I think he's crying?

"I wanted to say thank you."

Mortimer closed his eyes and did his best to reposition himself, sitting higher against the hospital bed. He groaned in pain. "Why?" he finally asked.

"You don't like me and could've told Gladden who I was right away, saving yourself the trouble. But you didn't. So thank you for trying for a little to protect me."

Opening his eyes, Mortimer tried to glare, but exhaustion had the best of him. His lids remained heavy, nearly shut. He offered a weak smile. "Won't be doin' it again," he said and coughed; the visit was much too exhausting.

Annie poured a glass of water from the pitcher near his bed, helping him take a sip. "I don't expect you to. Just get better."

"The Fraternitatem," he mumbled.

"We're looking for them."

As she helped him back down, resting him against cracker-thin pillows, she waved her hand, plumping up the pillow.

Not sure that helped.

His speech was slurred as he tried to tell her something. Before she could ask what he said, he was asleep with a smile on his face.

❋

Gibbs and Spencer laid a ten-by-ten-foot piece of wood in the center of the Wizard Hall courtyard. Gibbs secured it in the grass with iron spikes before getting on all fours and drawing out a circle with red paint. When he finished and the first layer of paint dried, Spencer followed by painting a simple five-pointed star, creating a pentagram at the center of the plywood.

Trapping a demon wasn't difficult and only required a few simple items that prevented a summoned demon from leaving.

Annie and Cham, still injured and convalescing, helped as best they could, setting candles around the circle and lighting them. A warm light encircled the demon trap.

"What a waste," Annie grumbled as she lit the last candle.

"Blame the Wizard Council for making us trap him instead of killing him," Spencer said. The entire department was disgusted by the council's decision. He stood with his arms crossed against his chest. "What's next?" he asked as Mrs. Cuttlebrink ran to their project, bringing with her the last ingredient: several boxes of simple table salt.

"You sure this is what we need to do?" Spencer asked.

Mrs. Cuttlebrink smiled. "Yes, Spencer dear. It's as simple as this," she said. "I'll be happy to show you in the book."

"Not necessary." Even in the dim candlelight they could see

he was embarrassed; his cheeks were red. Mrs. Cuttlebrink smiled lightly as she, Gibbs, and Spencer poured the salt in a circle around the trap.

"Why didn't we know this before? I'd keep a box with me at all times," Spencer said.

Ignoring him, Mrs. Cuttlebrink returned to a tattered sheet of paper and looked back up assessing the scene before reviewing the instructions again.

"Can you move the altar please? Just over there." The librarian pointed to the center of the west side of the plywood. The heavy stone was four feet tall with a smooth square top. It levitated in the air and was positioned into place by Gibbs.

Annie, as per the instructions, placed a silver bowl on the stone altar and emptied a bag of items.

"Are we ready?" Milo asked. He paced along the east end, impatiently observing the work.

"Almost," Annie announced across from him. She grabbed the urn and placed it just inside the circle, leaving the lid off. "This should hold him."

"We're good to go," Cham advised. Still pale and weak, he wasn't supposed to join them, but he had insisted, wanting to see this case to rest. He sat outside the circle while Spencer and Gibbs cleaned wayward, unneeded items from the center of the trap.

"Damn Wizard Council. We should be burning the djinn's ass," Milo grunted. As always, Annie refrained from rolling her eyes and returned to the altar, laying the variety of herbs into the bowl and the crystals at each of the corners of the altar.

"They can change their minds at a later date," Shiff reminded them. The rest of the team, for no other reason than finishing the case, began teleporting into the courtyard, watching the preparation.

No one believes they'll change their mind.

"Just trap him uncomfortably," Milo groused. Gibbs, Spencer, and Cham took a side of the wood base, their palms faced inward protectively. Per Bitherby, Annie dropped a piece of paper into the bowl, the name Ezekiel scrawled at the center; she lit the contents of the bowl on fire. It sparked and crackled as the fire grew; flames danced in the light breeze, and the smoke billowed into the air.

The genie, an egotistical, self-centered creature, responded to the summoning with quickness and agility, always helpful and willing to grant wishes. And with that, he would collect his price.

Ezekiel responded to the summoning in dramatic fashion with a gust of wind blowing through the courtyard, surrounding them before he materialized at the center of the trap, like Bitherby told them he would. The djinn shimmered in with a large grin on his face, as if he had just scored.

"You summoned me. How can I make all of your dreams come true?" Ezekiel bowed with eyes closed and didn't notice where he landed.

When he rose, his smile was snarky, confident.

Annie said, "Look down."

With a creepy smirk, he glanced at his feet. Suddenly his eyes changed and grew much more fearful. He twirled at the center of the trap and, for the first time, he saw was surrounded by the Wizard Guard.

"What the hell is this?" Ezekiel demanded.

Annie picked up the large urn and held it for him to see. His eyes bugged out of his long, thin face, like a cartoon character, a joke, and a nuisance. "Come on now. What did I ever do to you? Come on," he said with wide arms and a phony smile, as if he could charm the Wizard Guard. He backed away from Annie, but the edge of the trap was magically charged, so he was unable to cross the perimeter of the circle.

"We're the Wizard Guard, asshole," she spat.

Ezekiel recognized what that meant and became a trapped animal, twirling in the small space searching for a way out. His tricky magic was useless as long as he was in the trap.

Angry, he growled, his eyes darkened, his lip curled. She could feel his anger vibrate off of him.

"Djinn redi ad hydriam," Annie chanted. The spell seemed far too easy, so simple that it made her chuckle at first.

Djinn, return to the jar.

The djinn, bound by the ancient magic, had no choice but to honor the magic spell. He shook and sputtered as his body shimmered into a mist-like substance that was sucked into the urn.

I'm now his master!

He rematerialized inside the container, a tiny version of himself only two inches tall. His shouts echoed inside the clay urn.

"You bitch!" a high-pitched, tiny voice screeched at her; his small hands balled tightly as he shook his fists in rage. "I'm going to get you for this!"

"Not likely. Look at the floor," Annie suggested. The floor of the vessel had been painted with the same trap; the outside contained variations of the pentagram. The urn would subdue the genie well until Annie set him free. She placed the lid firmly on the urn, running her palm along the crack between the jar and lid, and sealing the djinn inside.

"Fraternitatem, then?" Gibbs asked.

CHAPTER 37

ANNIE STOOD AT the window of Ryan's office and overlooked the Chicago River. It was dark green and stagnant as it wound through the city.

I'd rather be there than here.

"And the djinn," a voice belonging to a man named Arthur Diaz crackled into the speaker phone. He was one of the seven members of the Executive Wizard Council, the highest rank in the wizard government other than the Grand Marksman.

"He's currently locked in my storage cubicle on the fifth floor," Annie said. She glanced at Ryan and rolled her eyes. He shrugged.

"We think he's better off in the records chambers. The security is better," Arthur replied.

"Listen, Arthur. This is Annie's case and she is technically the djinn's master. I say for now we leave it where it is. It's actually safer in the Wizard Guard department," Ryan advised. Though he was the Grand Marksman, he always had a soft place for the Wizard Guard.

Annie sighed.

"You're still much too attached to that department, Ryan," Arthur joked.

"Be that as it may, this issue is closed," Ryan said with finality, another disagreement between the Grand Marksman and the Executive Council squashed.

"Fine and good. We need to discuss the Fraternitatem of Solomon then," Arthur said. Six additional voices spoke in agreement, moving the meeting along.

"We have discussed this on several occasions this week. We feel that the Fraternitatem of Solomon, because of the nature of their group, should police their members as they see fit. Give them back the ring and drop the case."

Annie looked at Milo and grimaced. He hoisted himself from his chair moving closer to the speaker phone. "That's an injustice to the victim," Milo bellowed.

"They are a secret society. These organizations have their own goals and ways of handling miscreants. We will not go against them." Arthur spoke with finality.

Annie and Milo looked to Ryan who held his hand upwards, cautioning them to stop.

"Arthur, I realize that this is the direction you wish to go with this, but this group is dangerous. They kidnapped a non-magical, killed one of their own over this ring, and you know as well as I do that they most likely ordered the hit on a fellow wizard guard. According to what Annie has already found in Jason's notes, he knew them. We can't just let this go." Ryan said with much agitation.

"We are not purposely tying your hands, Annie and Milo. We realize that they should be punished, but who are we to interfere with this group? They are dangerous, and it could lead to a world-wide wizard war, something none of us wish to start or participate in. Return the ring. Annie, we have every faith in you that you can ensure we will never have to deal with them again."

"It's the wrong decision. I go on the record with that statement," Annie said.

"And we will record that. But this is our final decision. Should Ryan wish to veto that, just remember on this issue we have the full support of the Wizard Council minus the Wizard Guard members.

It will be a long, drawn-out battle should you try and fight it." Arthur Diaz was smug from behind the walls of the Council.

He's right. We'll never get the votes to change his mind.

"Fine then. I will arrange to meet the Middle East Wizard Guard. We will share information and return the ring to the Fraternitatem of Solomon. Is there anything else?" Her voice was terse and angry.

"No, that's all we have," Arthur said before switching off the phone.

❀

"Why are they so intent on tying our hands?" Annie asked Ryan. Though he controlled the Wizard Council, it was a still a democracy, and that was their final decision. Annie paced around the room to burn off energy.

"It's complicated, Annie. You know there are secret societies all over the world. They have their own laws and govern themselves. Unfortunately, this is one of them. Out of respect for their role in the world society, we can't interfere," he said.

I'm not convinced.

"He's right, you are truly a wizard guard." She offered a smile and stopped pacing.

"And the genie?" Milo inquired.

"I don't get that one either." Ryan leaned back in his chair and swirled to view the Chicago River. "It's a beautiful day today."

"You're changing the subject," Annie said.

"When are you leaving for the Middle East Wizard Guard?"

"Tonight. We should arrive in the morning their time. Do you think the Council is hiding something about dad's death, and that's why we can't go after the Fraternitatem?" Her question was blunt. Had she been able to see Ryan through his thick desk chair, she would have seen him jump.

Beyond the window, traffic was heavy at ten in the morning.

Five floors up, they heard engines revving and cars honking. Ryan sighed. "The Fraternitatem killed one of their own to deal with a problem. I think the Wizard Council fears them, regardless of any connection to Jason."

Since Annie was packed and prepared for the trip, the ring was hidden in a difficult-to-access pocket of Annie's cargo pants. It vibrated against her leg.

Tonight and it's gone. Good riddance!

"Be careful when you're with them. I don't trust them. The fact that the Middle East Wizard Guard has virtually no intel on them gives me a lot of concern." Ryan finally turned the chair to face her.

"We know enough about them. About their willingness to kill for the ring. We'll be careful, I promise." She tried to reassure him, but he did not look convinced.

"I think the connection to your dad is deeper than we think. I joined the council after Jason died, but I bet someone on the council knows something about his death."

Annie couldn't hide her surprise. Her eyebrows went up, and her forehead crinkled with deep lines.

I didn't expect that!

"Do you have proof?" Milo asked.

Ryan offered a drawn smile. "It's my guess, and I think the missing file is the key."

"So if I find the file, you're okay with me pursuing it?" Annie asked.

"I want to know too, Annie. I miss Jason every day. And this…" Tears welled in his eyes. "This is the closest we've come to understanding what happened. I need closure too. I'm sure you'll get the support of Milo. Yes?" Ryan twirled around to face them.

"Annie," Milo said, "you find that file and prove the Fraternitatem of Solomon was responsible and I will defy the order to go after them."

❀

The map of the Cave of Ages lay at the center of a large conference table in the Middle East Wizard Guard office, a structure hidden in an abandoned cave system. Annie huddled inside a large sweatshirt, chilled by the cool air as their newly met Wizard Guard colleagues gleefully examined the map.

Arriving in the dry heat of the desert, they walked half a mile through thick sand until they reached the Wizard Hall, or in this case, a cave system that housed all governmental operations. They were directed through a main tunnel that ran the entire length of the cave system with perpendicular branches bisecting the main tunnel, each heading in different directions leading to different caverns.

By the time they reached the conference room, Annie's fingers were frozen. Though she sat huddled in her chair, the design couldn't have been better had the wizard guards created the caves on their own. The main conference room was a large cavern directly at the center with several doors breaking into additional tunnels.

They had done much work to make this cave system habitable with ventilation that expelled stale air and fans that circulated the clean air inside. However, the heating system was less than impressive; Annie sat in her chair blowing on her fingers and hands.

She arrived with Lial, Gibbs, Spencer, and Milo, and they were welcomed hospitably by the Wizard Guard department manager, named Avraham. So grateful to be assisted by the American Wizard Guard, he proudly gave a tour of the offices and introduced them to the rest of his wizard guards. And now they sat in the chilly conference room joined by Sari, Michael, and Steven.

"This is amazing!" Avraham stated. The jovial man smiled broadly, thrilled with the existence of the map. His large, brown eyes examined the paper intently, and he pushed his floppy brown hair from his eyes as he tried to figure out the map's true location.

His fingers grazed the landmarks, and yet he couldn't place the location. "We've had eyes on the Fraternitatem for fifty years and never got this close to them. How did you find this?" he asked.

"My dad had a run-in with them about eight years ago while chasing Chintamani Stones that had found their way into the black market. From what I can tell, he was summoned to the Cave of Ages and drew the map from memory, hiding it in our Book of Shadows. I just happened upon it in the course of this investigation," Annie explained.

Avraham's eyes grew wide. "He was there? With them?"

"Yeah. He met them in a market in Morocco. I'm not sure why he was at the cave. But he was. What he didn't give us was the starting point—the exact location for the cave. Without the names or the coordinates, we weren't sure where to start."

"Yes, of course. I think I recognize these landmarks. It looks like it's the southwest corner of Israel. But you're right: this map isn't to scale, and we wouldn't know where to begin," said Avraham.

"But you know now, don't you?" inquired Steve. It was his turn to review the map. A smile crossed his lips. "I agree; it looks like the southwest portion of the state."

"Yeah. Several pots of coffee and a night in the library. We finally found the key," Lial said.

He had worked with Mrs. Cuttlebrink in the library, figuring out the true location of the Cave of Ages. And in the early morning hours, they had found the clue they needed. When he called at 5 a.m., Annie had been wide awake, anxiously waiting.

Taking control of the map, Lial pointed to a small circle, hidden within a landmark. It contained a five-pointed star at the center. "Here. This is the key right here."

While they all took a turn to note the symbol, Lial opened an atlas to a page reserved by a sticky note. The map was expertly folded, so thin that it appeared to be a single sheet of paper.

Magic.

He unfolded the many layers, revealing a large map of Israel with another sticky note pointing to something. "Okay. Here is the symbol. We knew we were correct, but the problem is the maps are drawn in different scales. And then this." He shrunk the map that

Jason Pearce had drawn until it matched the scale of the map in the book. He overlaid it on top of the larger map, lining up the two symbols. "And here is the Cave of Ages," he said with a smile.

❄

Wizard Guard training was difficult and incorporated years of book study, daily physical training, and more than one survival training camping trip in the heat, cold, and rain. The training was designed that way for a reason, on the off chance that the wizard guards might hike through a southern desert in the Middle East at four o'clock in the morning during a particularly warm spring day.

Knowing the Fraternitatem would have means to detect their presence, they teleported three miles from their destination. And though they were in a low valley, below the Fraternitatem's location high in the mountains, they were far enough away to avoid detection.

They trekked through the sand without the help of lights, making the walk difficult at best. To avoid detection, they refrained from speaking. The only sound that followed them through the desert was the sound of the boots scratching through the rough sand.

At the base of the mountain trail, they stopped to gather themselves. Annie took a long drag of water, grabbing a little to eat. Beside her, Lial anxiously glanced at the map. The low light glowing from his crystal was barely discernible. The crystal shook in his hand.

"You okay?" Annie asked.

"It's one thing to find the cave, another thing to lead us to our deaths," he hissed.

"We have the best bargaining chip. You're doing fine," Annie reminded him with a forceful whisper. His hands still trembled as he folded the map and shoved it in his pocket.

"It doesn't hurt to be prepared," he said defensively, above a whisper. Annie touched his arm and placed her finger at her lips.

"You did well, and we're going to be fine." She was up against him with a firm grip on his arms. There was just enough moonlight for him to see her with the most serious expression she could muster. His face cracked into a smile. "Better? We'll be fine," she said.

Annie could feel his heavy sigh against her cheek. "Easy for you to say," he muttered. "You're not leading us into danger."

"Really? Like I've never done that before." She handed Lial a thermos of water.

"Thanks." He took a swig, patted her arm. She passed the motion back through the line, alerting everyone they were heading up the mountain on a narrow trail only three feet wide.

Annie's fingers grazed the mountain face as she balanced herself away from the swift edge that dropped downward.

As much as she tried to retain her focus on the trek upwards and away from potential death, she couldn't help but replay their ultimate goal, as determined by the Wizard Council. They were only to return the ring to the Fraternitatem and leave. Regardless of the reason why Benaiah stole the ring to sell, regardless of knowing who killed him, he deserved a certain amount of justice.

It won't come.

Annie most often followed her gut and made decisions on the fly when necessary, with the goal always to put justice first. But as a potion master, she had become a member of the Wizard Council and made an oath as a wizard guard to follow the directives of the majority.

They haven't convinced me this is the right way.

Voices whispered excitedly. The Middle East Wizard Council had never been so close to the Fraternitatem. As a result, they were jumpy and twitchy, like the ring stored in Annie's hidden pocket, which continued to hum and vibrate against her leg. They all felt the magic.

Their footsteps, heavy against the hard rock revealed their presence. Annie pulled on Lial's sleeve and held her hand out behind her, signaling the group to stop.

"What's the matter?" Milo grunted.

"We're loud," she whispered.

"Ugh." Milo waved a palm from Lial to himself in the back of the line. "Try this, girl," he suggested.

The muffling spell he cast did a fair job, lowering the sound decibel as they continued up the trail.

Jason Pearce had described the Cave of Ages as a large cavern build in side the rock with walls that radiated a blue, shimmering light; the haze could be seen for miles in the desert after dark. Annie glanced up and saw that the blue light was indeed brilliant.

What is that made from?

Annie wiped her brow and took a sip from her thermos before putting it back in her field pack. The air was warming quickly, even as they ascended the mountain.

Lial stopped them against the wall, seemingly out of the line of sight from the cave.

"There's someone up there," he whispered to Annie as a jinx landed above their heads and slammed into the rock. Bits of mountain broke apart, cascading around them. Feverishly, the group whipped the rocks, tossing them off the side of the trail and down the cliff. Rocks tumbled and clinked, breaking the silence of the desert.

They waited against the wall, barely breathing as another jinx collided with the cliff. More earth slid down. Everyone's arms flayed as they pushed the falling debris away, which was rough and difficult to do in the darkness.

After a minute, Gibbs cried out, "Fuck! Been hit!"

The jinxes stopped for a moment.

"They're trying to frighten us," Annie said and looked up.

"Everyone mostly okay?" Milo asked.

"Bleeding," Gibbs grumbled. As Annie carefully trekked down the line, Gibbs moved his palm deftly against the cut, cleaning up and restoring his flesh. Even in the minimal light, Annie could see his spell hadn't worked.

"You need stitches."

Never one for nonmagical options, Gibbs grumbled loudly.

"I'll give you stitches later. Okay for now?" she asked.

"Just head up."

As Annie cautiously maneuvered back to her location in line, a third jinx hit above them. It was not as strong, so less rock tumbled down and dusted them.

"I have your ring. Keep attacking, and I'll teleport it to where you'll never see it again!" Annie's voice carried, and bounced across the hard stone. She had no doubt they had heard her.

Harsh whispers wafted down the mountain, though they couldn't make out the conversation.

The ring.

"Prove you have the ring," demanded a disembodied voice. It was deep and calm as if it could assert authority over them.

"You killed Benaiah. One of your own. You either let us pass safely, or we leave and you never see your precious ring again."

"Hard-ass," Gibbs grumbled. He shuddered and leaned against the wall. Blood soaked through his sleeve, more blood loss than Annie had expected.

"You okay?" she asked.

"Fine, girl."

"I'll stay with him. You head upwards," Spencer volunteered and flashed a light on Gibbs's arm.

Harried whispering from the cave carried in the wind.

They've never had anyone pressing up against them, threatening them, or ordering them. They've lived in the cave too long.

"You may pass. Alone," the voice ordered.

Annie chuckled. They thought they could scare her, that they had all the power.

I can teleport whenever I need to.

"No! I'm bringing my team. And if you harm any of us, the Wizard Guard in these parts will come after you."

Again, angry voices discussed her demands—or maybe it was fear in those short, terse discussions.

"Pass," the voice agreed.

Lial led Milo and Annie up the mountain, followed closely by Avraham and Sari, leaving Steven and Michael to back them up should the Fraternitatem reverse this tentative agreement.

They stopped at a bend in the trail and peered around the rock face. The iridescent light from the cave was unreal and mesmerizing.

"Unbelievable," Avraham whispered.

They stepped into the open and approached the cave entrance, positioning themselves in full view. Avraham gulped and Sari chirped; the view inside the cave was awesome, brilliant, beautiful.

The floor and walls appeared to be coated in a layer of water or maybe oil. They shone. Annie couldn't help but touch the edge of the rock. They weren't wet, just hard, cold, and smooth.

They glow! What makes them glow like this?

"Amazing." Milo was just as impressed as Annie by the magic.

Beyond the blue walls, the room was sparsely furnished with only a heavy, wooden throne against the back wall. Modestly built, it contained only one cushion that in the low light might be sewn of simple cotton.

"Where's the ring?" a voice accused.

It belonged to a man who materialized near the back of the cavern. Annie hadn't been sure what to expect from the Fraternitatem, but he wasn't it.

"Where's the ring?" the man demanded. He was dressed in ancient robes of multicolored stripes that in the blue haze looked more like varying degrees of gray. She hadn't expected a costume or his long, white straw-like beard. She had expected a group more like their own.

The man stood perfectly still, allowing her a chance to take in his full regalia with the Solomon's knot at the center of his smock—the symbol of the Fraternitatem. It was the same design

Benaiah had worn and gave Annie confirmation that they were in the correct place.

She summoned the ring and slipped it on her finger. The three remaining rocks shimmered in the light as if they were meant to be there. She held her hand above her head as she faced the man. Light sparkled across the cavern, and he stroked a very long beard.

"Give it to me," he commanded with his hand open wide. Reluctantly, Annie stepped inside.

Dad may have been the last non-member to have been here.

"Why did you kill Benaiah?" she asked. Fabric rustled behind her when Milo and Lial raised their palms in a protective stance.

"We handled a situation amongst ourselves as we've done for many millennia. Now please give me my ring."

"Not until I have your word we will have safe passage from the Cave of Ages. No spells, hexes, jinxes. Just a safe journey down the mountain," Annie ordered.

The man smiled at her. It was neither warm, nor welcoming. She found it more of a sneer. She closed her fist and shoved her hand in her pocket.

"You are a tough negotiator. I will honor you, and you will have safe travels."

Annie held her hand out as if to shake his; she'd prefer a magically binding contract.

I don't think I trust this man at all.

"I'm Anne Pearce," she offered.

His eyes widen in surprise before he could gather his reserve. "Melichi," he volunteered. His handshake was limp, only offering his fingertips. Annie grabbed his whole hand.

"You're Jason Pearce's daughter, yes?"

"He met you eight years ago. You ordered him to stop searching and collecting the Chintamani Stones," she said in an accusatory tone. In her heart, Annie knew they had ordered the hit on her father. It was all that Annie could do to keep her hands from shaking.

"Your dad was a good man," he stated.

Annie gazed at him suspiciously, arching her eyebrows. "I never want to see the Fraternitatem on U.S. soil again. For any reason. Do I make myself clear?"

With their hands still in handshake, with magic swirling around them, Melichi had no choice but to make the deal as stated.

He'd better not add to the deal.

"Yes. The Fraternitatem will not go to the U.S. for any reason. I apologize for the murder of Benaiah outside your black market portal. We should have dealt with the body in a much more discreet manner."

"But you didn't, and you've caused many difficulties. It isn't easy to do a memory modification for the entire population of the earth," Annie accused.

The magic that bound their agreement snaked around each of their hands as a golden light shimmered and sparkled, binding them together. When the magic completed its task, it dissipated in the cave air.

Still with their hands connected Melichi said, "Again, I do apologize for that inconvenience. We had every intention of leaving with Benaiah's body, but we would have been discovered. Better you found him than us exposing magic.

He released his hand from hers. She slipped the ring from her finger and handed it to him.

He sneered at her briefly after putting the ring on his finger. "I didn't order Rathbone to kill your father. Rathbone took it upon himself to handle an unfortunate situation. I actually tried to recruit your father to join us," Melichi said.

Annie couldn't hide her surprise and didn't know how to respond to that revelation.

Dad never would have.

Annie didn't trust Melichi. In her gut, she believed her father had died because of this case, regardless of whose idea it was or who had carried out the plan. The tears began to well in her eyes; she didn't want Melichi to see her weakness.

Without another word, Annie turned and left the cave, teleporting from the entrance to collect Gibbs and Spencer and head home.

PROLOGUE

REBEKAH STONER WAS fired from her job as a television journalist. She was confused as to why she couldn't remember any of the events that led to her dismissal. It was as if those memories had been completely removed from her brain.

Whatever caused her firing mattered little anymore; she had spent the last several days at home preparing resumes and DVDs highlighting her experience. It could only be done in small shifts, since she was far too distracted to sit still. She took to walking around the neighborhood. Every day for a week, Rebekah's walks grew in distance, and she stayed away from home longer. Still, her excursions offered her no answers for the hell her life had descended into.

On a lovely day in early spring, Rebekah walked herself to Millennium Park along Lake Michigan. It hadn't been a plan, and if someone had asked, she wouldn't have had an answer as to why she was aimlessly walking past The Bean. She sat herself on one of the open benches and watched people walk by.

Tourists shopped across the street or ate at the many restaurants in the area. As they flitted about, they seemed light and free of stress as though none of them understood the weight that Rebekah felt in her chest.

This place, this bench felt familiar and comforting, and yet

Rebekah didn't know why. She hadn't been to this park since she first moved to Chicago five years ago. And yet…

The first nice day in many months was drawing visitors to the park; it was crowded. Benches were packed except for hers, so Rebekah wasn't surprised when a woman she didn't recognize, older than her with cropped salt-and-pepper hair, asked if she could sit on the bench beside her.

"Sure. It's public property," Rebekah said and moved a newspaper that had been left behind.

"It's a beautiful day," the woman said.

"Yeah, it is. I'm Rebekah by the way." She held out her hand.

"Arden Blakely." They shook hands lightly and rested them in their laps. It was quiet between them for a moment as they continued to observe the crowds pass by. A family near them took pictures of each other and the city skyline. The harried mother worked diligently to keep her children from wandering off.

"You look familiar," Arden said. "Don't you work for Channel 5 news?"

Rebekah shrunk away. "I used to."

"Sorry. I liked your stories. Why did you quit?"

"I don't know. I don't know." Rebekah couldn't shake the melancholy and wiped a tear from her eye.

"I feel the same. I keep wandering. I just can't get focused."

Arden glanced at the newspaper and then back to the family that had been taking pictures; the smallest child was running off, leaving her mother to drop a diaper bag and run after her. "It's a beautiful day."

"Yes, it is," Rebekah answered.

❀

The minute Annie returned home from the Cave of Ages, she went on medical leave. Being injured twice in a week was just enough to claim compensation time and she gladly stayed in bed past eight in the morning when the sun burst through the curtains, blinding her.

Once she was awake, her mind raced to the missing file that her father had probably stored in the house, if he really had hidden it. Leaving Cham to a few more minutes of sleep, Annie climbed out of bed.

There was only one place in the house Annie hadn't bothered searching for the file, and that was the basement.

Still unfinished, the room was cold and damp, so Annie zipped up her warm hoodie and stood at the center of the crowded space, surveying any possible locations to hide a file. Maybe in the walls or under the floor or maybe in the air vents. Annie only ever used this space for storage and laundry.

She started with the laundry room, going through the door in the back wall. Thumping on the walls, she assessed the sound, searching for a possible void in the wall. When she found nothing, she checked behind the water heater, thinking her father may have shoved it back there. With no sign of a file, Annie turned and saw the remnants of Zola's ordeal. She had been held in this room prior to being taken to the dungeon. Remains of the iron shackles lay on the floor.

Annie picked up the iron and carried them to the next room, thinking of what to do with the hard metal.

Stepping back inside the larger basement, Annie scanned the walls and floors with a quick look.

The crawl space!

There was an open space beneath the staircase that headed to the second floor. Annie had never seen what was stored underneath, if anything was there at all.

She sat on the cold floor and pushed on the panel, but it wouldn't slide open, either manually or with magic. The door wouldn't budge. With a summoned crystal, Annie held the rock over the opening, moving it from top to bottom; the rock glowed brightly.

She captured the magic and stared into the crystal. The magic was old, very possibly eight years old.

"Hey," Cham said, walking over to her as he rubbed sleep from his eyes. "Whatcha doing?"

"I think I found a hiding spot." She handed him her crystal so he could read the magic.

"Ah… that's a really simple spell," he noted.

I thought the same thing.

It surprised her how simple her father had made the spell.

Maybe Dad assumed no one would ever look here.

"You really think it's as easy as that?" Annie asked, mostly because she was still shocked how basic of a spell her father had used.

"Yeah. I do." The doorbell rang. "I'll get it. You open," he offered and headed back upstairs.

Annie waved her palm across the crawl space door, sending a reversal spell into the panel; the door slid open as if it there was nothing to it. "Really, Dad?" Annie murmured. She summoned a flashlight and peered inside the space that filled with cobwebs, dirt, and what Annie thought was a nest. After shuddering, she spotted a box in the far corner. Maybe he had thought the bugs, dead mice, and spider webs would keep someone away.

Like me?

Or maybe Annie could just summon the box, which floated easily to her.

"You got an unmarked package," Cham said, handing her an envelope addressed to her with no return address.

"Odd. But look," she announced proudly and showed him the box.

"So Jason did hide the file. You okay to look inside?"

Am I okay?

Ryan had given Annie his full support to investigate her father's case. She lifted the box and floated it beside her as she walked up the stairs with her unmarked package.

"I don't recognize the handwriting," Annie said. She ran her crystal over the package; it didn't glow.

Feeling a thick paper inside, Annie ripped open the seal and peered inside. It was not what she expected. She slipped the contents on the table.

"It's… what the hell, this is a French newspaper."

The paper was folded with purpose; a picture attached to an article was clearly visible. And at the center of the picture, a red circle was drawn around a face. Annie summon a magnifying glass and examined the picture as Cham looked on from behind.

"Oh crap," she exclaimed as she held the glass and stared into the picture.

"That can't be."

They stared at a picture of Princess Amelie, alive and walking among a crowd.

The End

AUTHOR'S NOTE

IT TOOK ME several years to find the right story for the second book in the Annie Loves Cham series. After publishing what was supposed to be Book Two, called *She Wulf*, I received some horribly bad reviews on the book, and for a week, I couldn't form words. It hurt too much, and all I could do was cry.

Within a few months after releasing *She Wulf*, I promised myself I would pick myself up and dust myself off and start the third book and move on with the series. I had several ideas, and even started writing a few, but I found myself in a position where nothing worked. None of the plots propelled the story of Annie and Cham forward in a meaningful way.

It was nearly a two-year struggle. After trying to write two different stories, I almost gave up. If it weren't for several people, I just might have, but in the end, I couldn't give up on a dream I've had since I was seven years old.

So I did something radical, something most authors don't take on. Before I had a chance to fully think through my decision, I saved the last draft of *The Day of First Sun* as something like draft number 114, and I started a new rewrite.

It was as though I was looking at the story through a new set of eyes. There were plot points that I had never resolved, other scenes that I felt were unnecessary to the story, and an editor told me that out of all of the relationships in the book, none of them were new—they were all already established. Some of them, this editor advised, might be better served as if they were written as new contacts.

And she was right. As I rewrote the entire book, I saw new aspects of the story pop out. I made changes, and the story became fuller, with more action and more trouble. My characters no longer solved the crimes easily. I added purpose.

The decision to rewrite Book One affected the course of my life for two years. And in the end, after three more edits, a new book cover, and a completely restructured series, I couldn't be happier with the end result. While waiting between my final edits, I finally found the story for Book Two that propelled the story further, that allowed my characters to grow and change and allow the series to be more complete and interconnected, like never before.

It was a long journey in which I learned how to effectively edit a story, how to tie up loose ends, when to put characters in compromising positions, how to add color to an otherwise fun plot. While finishing the final edits to *The Day of First Sun*, I was able to finally create Book Two, the story that you now know as *Black Market*. It was the right story in which to continue to build the series, a good vehicle to observe Annie Pearce and Cham Chamsky as they grow and change. It is the right story for the series, for Annie and Cham and their team of friends.

The rest of the series has a structure and a life. The first draft of book three is complete, and the fourth book is waiting for a rewrite. I can't wait to finish the stories and share them with you. I hope you enjoyed the second installment in the series.

I thank my children and my family and friends for their support, for reading the book and offering suggestions, or for selling with me at a local book fair. And I thank the fans who have reached out to me and let me know how much they've enjoyed the story.

www.ingramcontent.com/pod-product-compliance
Lightning Source LLC
Chambersburg PA
CBHW071648260626
47170CB00001B/277